"The memory is buried deep."

Without warning, Master Jaks reached back with his right hand and slipped a Thebin blade from a sheath at the back of his neck. He threw, his aim perfect and centered on Llesho's heart. Instinctively, Llesho adjusted his stance, and when the knife approached, he had turned his side to it and stepped out of its way. In the same motion, he plucked the knife out of the air and sent it spinning back at the thrower. Jaks was prepared for the move, but still the blade nicked him midway up his bicep before embedding itself in a wooden beam in the wall. If Jaks had not moved when he had, the knife would have pierced his heart, the same target he had aimed at himself.

Master Jaks clenched the fingers of his left hand over the wound in his right arm. "Den's been working with him," he said, "But he came to us with that and other equally deadly moves for close work in his bag of tricks. As far as I can tell, with a knife he knows *only* how to kill."

Also by
CURT BENJAMIN

THE LORDS OF GRASS AND THUNDER

Seven Brothers
THE PRINCE OF SHADOW
THE PRINCE OF DREAMS
THE GATES OF HEAVEN

THE PRINCE OF SHADOW

VOLUME ONE OF Seven Brothers

Curt Benjamin

DAW BOOKS, INC.
DONALD A. WOLLHEIM, FOUNDER
375 Hudson Street, New York, NY 10014
ELIZABETH R. WOLLHEIM
SHEILA E. GILBERT
PUBLISHERS
www.dawbooks.com

Cover art by Royo.

DAW Book Collectors No. 1195.

DAW Books are distributed by Penguin Putnam Inc.

Book designed by Stanley S. Drate/Folio Graphics, Inc.

First paperback printing, September 2002
6 7 8 9

Many thanks to the gang—
Barbara Wright, Tom and Cathy Ward, and
Leroy Dubeck, for the roving restaurant
brainstorming sessions. Llesho lives because of you.

PART ONE

PEARL ISLAND

Chapter One

"LLESHO! Has anyone seen Llesho!"

The healer Kwan-ti stuck her head out of the thatch-and-bamboo longhouse and scanned the slave compound. Waves of pale gold sand lapped the shed where the pearl washers worked to the pounded rhythm of their feet on the wood floor and some chantey song of lovers and pearls, but Llesho's voice was not among them. At the edge of the sandy clearing where the camp was raised, pearl sorters crouched under the broad fronds of palm trees, shaking their baskets in a steady circular motion, but Llesho did not sit among them. He was not abed in the longhouse, nor did she see him in line for his lunch with the cooks and their cauldrons.

No Llesho. Old Lleck lay dying on his pallet in the longhouse, calling for the boy in his fever, and Llesho was nowhere to be found. She rested her strained eyes on the distant but ever present cloud bank where sky met the bay, but the murky slate of the rain-drenched horizon offered no solutions. Lord Chin-shi didn't bother to shackle his slaves, which made him a better master than many, but sometimes she would have made an exception for Llesho, who could disappear faster than a magician when the rent was due.

Still, the boy couldn't have gone far. Pearl Island was not much more than a handful of palm trees and scrub that covered the gentle hill of crumbling coral at its center, but no slave had ever escaped it. The sea, dark and cruel, brooded just beyond the bay that cradled the wealth from which Pearl Island took its name. An arm of that great sea separated the island from the mainland to the West, the vast, unreachable sweep of the empire nothing more than a thin line of darker gray on the horizon at the farthest limit of a sailor's eye. Even a Thebin like Llesho would drown before he reached that shore. Kwan-ti knew that some desperate souls sought rest in the jaws of the great sea dragon, but Llesho, for all his difficult arrogance, would never choose the dark path of death and rebirth this early in his life. He had seen only fifteen summers, and cruelty still had the power to surprise him.

Figuring where Llesho was *not* didn't help find him, however, so Kwan-ti tucked a lock of faded hair back into its knot and stepped out into the drizzle. "Have you seen him, Tsu-tan?" she asked the man squatting under the protective shelter of a coconut palm with a pearl basket in front of him.

"He's tending the beds, old woman." Tsu-tan didn't bother to look up from the flat basket in which he was sorting pearls by size. "You won't see Llesho on dry land until his quarter-shift is done."

"That will be too late." Kwan-ti smoothed her tapa-printed skirts with worried hands. Although the pearl beds lay well beyond sight, Kwan-ti stared in their direction as if she could conjure them—and the boy, Llesho. Which perhaps she could, if she wanted to take a swim with an anvil chained to her neck. Chin-shi, the Lord of Pearl Island, frowned on conjuration, however, so no one knew for certain whether Kwan-ti had such powers or simply followed her mother's recipes for medicines like a good Islander.

"Always too late," she muttered under her breath.

Tsu-tan, shaking his basket in gentle circles, paid close attention to Kwan-ti's muttering even though he pretended otherwise. He did not know what she meant, what other time Llesho had been too late, or if the old woman thought that she had come too late to call the boy, or to cure the old man's fever. Still, it was one more clue. He hid it away with the others in the puzzle box of his mind he reserved for witch-finding, which was his true calling.

Returning to the longhouse that served as slave quarters for the pearl fisheries, Kwan-ti made her way to the low pallet she had set up in the corner for the old man. The boy would be too late, of course. Already the old man's skin had grown ashen and powdery with the dry heat that burned him up inside. He picked fretfully at his blanket and his eyes, long glazed over with the hard white shells of cataracts, wandered in his head as if they could find the boy and see him one more time before he exchanged this life for his next on the wheel.

"Llesho?" Lleck's voice rattled in his throat. He gasped for breath, exhausted by the effort it took him to call for the boy. As soon as he was able, he called again, "Llesho! You must find them!"

"Who, Lleck?" Kwan-ti asked him softly. "Tell me who I must find." Llesho's voice had not fully deepened yet; she hoped that the old man might mistake her own voice for the boy he called so piteously.

"Your brothers." Lleck grasped her hand and pushed it away again, seeking the longer fingers and callused fingertips of the boy. "You must find your brothers."

"I will, old friend." Kwan-ti took his hand in a firm clasp and stilled its seeking, stroked the forehead burning with dry heat. "Rest easy. I will find them."

"Goddess go with you." With a last whispered breath, the old one cast aside the shell of his worn-out body, leaving Kwan-ti to wonder, what brothers had the boy Llesho, and what mischief might she unwittingly set in motion if she gave the boy his mentor's message?

The two had not arrived in the camp together. Thebin, high in the mountains of the mainland, bred a short, sturdy people accustomed to the thin cold air of the heights. The children, if carefully trained in the richer atmosphere near the sea, had the breath to remain underwater for up to half an hour without surfacing to refill their lungs. To the ignorant, the skill was a sign that the children had magical powers born of a sea that the gods had raised higher than the mountains of Shan to make the door to heaven. Pearlers knew the Thebins to be as human as any man, but with a skill for breathing that made them efficient at scooping pearl oysters out of the bay.

Llesho had come to Pearl Island in a shipment of Thebin children bought from Harn slave traders for training as divers. The boy had been seven summers in age then, with a dazed expression that soon marked him as soft in the head. He never spoke, and though he followed directions well enough, he could not even feed himself without being told to lift his spoon, and again, lift his spoon. From the start he walked the bay without fear, however, so Foreman Shen-shu considered him worth the effort to train.

Gradually, awareness of his surroundings had returned to Llesho's eyes. Then, one day he laughed at one of Lling's jokes, and his recovery from whatever had stunned his brain seemed complete. If he held his head at too arrogant a tilt or his eyes sometimes glittered with a light too hard and bleak for his youth, a joke or a curse would remind him of his place. Over time he passed out of notice, just another Thebin slave child with salt water in his hair and sand between his toes.

When Llesho reached the age of ten, Lleck appeared. Chin-shi had purchased the aging Thebin for his claims to understand the special ailments of the pearl divers. Lleck quickly made himself useful about the camp, tending to the needs not only of the Thebins, but of those Pearl Islanders willing to accept the advice of one who, it was whispered, had trained in the secret knowledge of eternal life to be found in the far mountains. From his first day in the camp, Lleck had taken a special interest in the boy Llesho, teaching him to read and write using a stick in the damp sand, and showing him the way of herbs in Thebin healing. Some felt that Llesho must pay for this attention with his body, but the longhouse offered no privacy, and pairings of every kind were both visible and audible to whoever had a bed nearby. No one had ever seen Lleck visit the boy Llesho in the dark, nor had Llesho ever been seen to make nighttime visits to Lleck.

The women, for the most part, felt that Lleck must be the boy's true father. Lleck, they reasoned, had followed his son into slavery to protect and raise the boy even at the cost of his own freedom. They admired such devotion of father and son, and while some grew jealous of the two, for the most part the connection between them remained hidden, one of the small conspiracies that all slave compounds nurture in defiance of their masters. And now, Lleck was dead. Kwan-ti remembered the arrogance and the bitterness that lay dormant at the heart of young Llesho, and a shudder of foreboding rippled through her. "Find your brothers." What was the old man unleashing with his message? How could the boy, tied for life to the pearl beds and the island, obey his mentor's strange command?

At that very moment, Llesho had finished his half

hour of rest in the pearl harvesting boat, and was returning to the bay for his next half hour in the water. Naked, as were all the pearl-divers, he sat on the red-painted deck of the harvest boat and snapped the iron shackles around his ankles. The collar chain that tethered him to the boat never came off during his quarter-shift, but the shackles around his ankles were his own choice. The extra weight helped to steady him when he walked the floor of the bay. At the end of his half-hour shift underwater, when he had not enough air in his lungs to swim to the surface under his own power, he would run the chain through the shackles and let the winch draw him up by his feet. On his first day in the bay Llesho had scorned the shackles, but he'd only needed to be dragged onto the boat by his neck once to realize the wisdom of using the ankle chain.

With the shackles in place, he stood at the edge of the boat and waited for the foreman to hand him the tool he would use this shift. A bag would mean he was collecting the oysters most likely to hide pearls, but this time Shen-shu handed him a muck rake. With the implement in his hand, he took one, two, three deep breaths, and stepped off the side of the boat. When his feet touched water, he raised his arms over his head, the rake held close to his side, and plunged like an arrow to the bottom of the bay. Lling was already there, staking out their piece of the oyster beds and protecting it from the encroaching teams that worked about them. She raked up the muck so that the nutrients filled the water with a roiling cloud. Hmishi followed after, landing almost on top of Lling's shoulders. Soon Llesho's two companions had turned the chore into a game of tridents, clashing their rakes together in mock battle while Llesho watched from just enough distance to set him apart from the game. Early in his training his watchful, quiet nature had earned him the fear and suspicion of his fellow slaves.

But he spoke to the foreman and guards no more than he did to his fellow divers, and eventually they accepted the distance he kept as part of his personality. Better that than question the dark shadows in his eyes that occasionally blotted out the here and now. The growing acceptance of his fellow captives seemed to creep into Llesho's bones and make him over as a part of them.

The mock contest of trident-rakes stirred up as much of a silty cloud as if the combatants had applied themselves to their task with all the seriousness they showed when the foreman Shen-shu dove into the bay to check on them. Today, however, Shen-shu had worn a fresh white robe and shoes on his feet, a sure sign that the workers in the water below would have no surprise inspections on this quarter-shift. That left the Thebin slaves to their contest, and to the more difficult task of making Llesho laugh.

Hmishi had taken the offensive and tangled the teeth of his rake in those of the tool Lling flung about as a weapon. Lling lost control of her rake and waved her hand in submission for this round. Her eyes burned with the curses bursting to explode from her lips. Llesho winked, giving her the advantage in the second contest: he wanted to laugh, but fought the impulse for the same reasons Lling fought her desire to swear—they needed to conserve air, and Hmishi would not have heard them anyway through the bubbles they would release in the attempt.

Still struggling against the urge to laugh, Llesho turned away from the antics of his friends. He was shocked to see an old man drifting toward him over the low mounds of pearl oysters. The old man wore many layers of robes and gowns that floated about him like a school of multicolored fish. He had dark hair and clear blue eyes that reminded Llesho of a distant sky, as unlike the sky over Pearl Island as those blue eyes were unlike the hard white marbles of

Lleck's cataracts. That he was Lleck, or some transformed apparition of Lleck, was certain, however, and Llesho gasped in horror.

The sudden breath should have killed him, since both he and the ghost were floating underwater. Instead of the terrifying pain of drowning, however, Llesho felt only crisp, clean air. Thinner than he had grown accustomed to at sea level, the breath that invigorated him reminded him of home—the mountains, the snow, the overwhelming cold. The spirit in the water drew closer, and Llesho shook his head, refusing to believe the truth this apparition forced upon him: Lleck was dead.

"Forgive me for leaving you, my prince." The youthful spirit addressed him in Lleck's voice, using the title Llesho had not heard since the Harn had invaded Thebin and sold the princeling child into slavery. Llesho heard the words clearly, as if he stood on Thebin's high plateau, taking his lessons in the queen's garden and not among the sea creatures of the bay. He wondered if he, too, had passed into the kingdom of the dead.

"I had hoped to live to see you grown, to know that you had been returned to your rightful place. But age and fever have no respect for an old man's wishes." Did the spirits of the dead feel remorse? It sounded as if the king's minister might, but Lleck was smiling at him, a wry acknowledgment that life and all its hopes and concerns were behind him now.

"I have no rightful place," Llesho answered bitterly, his words as clear as the spirit's, and he felt no lack of air to argue further. "I am the last of an old and broken house, destined to die at the bottom of the bay."

"Not the last," Lleck told him. "Your father they killed, yes. But your brothers still live, carried into distant provinces and sold into slavery, each told the others had been slain."

Since that described Llesho's own fate, he found his mentor's words difficult to deny. A new feeling kindled in his breast, so alien to his experience that Llesho did not recognize it for hope.

"My sister?" He could not look the spirit of the minister in the eye, for fear of what he would see there. As a small and spoiled prince he had hated Ping, the infant who had taken his place in his mother's lap. When Llesho was five, he had created an uproar in the court by stealing out of the Palace of the Sun with the intent, he informed the gatekeeper, of setting the newborn princess on the mountainside as a gift for the gods. When the guard had advised him that tigers were more common than gods on the mountain, Llesho had informed him that a tiger would do. Ping had been two years old when the invasion had come, of little use to the Harn as a slave or a hostage. With the wisdom that comes of being fifteen, however, Llesho would have given his life to keep her safe.

Lleck-the-spirit shook his head. "Beaten, and thrown on the rubbish heap is what I heard," he said, "I do not find her spirit in the kingdom of the dead, but I know not in what shape or country she has been reborn."

It was an old grief, but Llesho found it could still hurt, and the more because he had in that same moment learned to hope. "My mother?"

Again Lleck-the-spirit shook his head, but his brow creased in some question. "Your mother, the queen, is not among the spirits of the dead," he said. "She was taken in the raid that killed your father, but no report of her came to me after. They say that she ascended into heaven as a living being to beg the mercy of the gods on her country, but that her beauty so entranced the heavenly creatures that they would not let her depart again.

"I think this is good storytelling, but bad history. If

she has not crossed into a new life, she must be a prisoner still."

Llesho said nothing. He was far too old to cry about his dead, had never given his enemies that satisfaction even as a small child.

"Find your brothers, Llesho," the spirit pleaded with him. "Save Thebin. The land itself is dying, and the few of her people who remain are dying with her." Sorrow ran from Lleck's dead eyes, salt tears returning to the salty bay. "I would have stood at your side if I could. Now, I have only this to offer—" The spirit held out to him a pearl as big as a walnut and as black as Foreman Shen-shu's eyes. "The pearl has magical properties of long life and various protections. Keep it with you, but use it only at most dire need."

At this, Llesho wondered if the spirit in front of him was not Lleck after all, but an imp sent to trick him into witchcraft. "A good trick," he taunted the spirit, "but Lleck would know that I can't possibly carry a pearl out of the bay—I have no place to hide it." He gestured to his own naked body. "And Foreman Shen-shu will search the cavities of our bodies for stolen treasure with as much vigilance today as he does after every quarter shift in the pearl beds. As for swallowing a pearl that big, if it were possible to do so without choking to death, even Lord Chin-shi's guards would notice a slave from the pearl bay searching through the privy trench!"

"Have some trust, young prince."

The reminder of his former state from the lips of his teacher's spirit raised tears that stung the corners of Llesho's eyes, but he refused to shed them. He found little to trust in a world that had taken this last and only comfort from him. "How can I trust what you say, old man?" In the pain of his heartache, Llesho knew only to attack its source. "You said you would stay with me, and protect me. Now you are dead, and if we are truly having this conversation at all, I must be dying as well!"

Lling and Hmishi had long since tugged on their chains and returned to the surface. Llesho knew he could have no air left in his lungs, could not breathe or speak underwater, and yet he did have air, was both breathing and speaking. Surely, he must be dead, or in that stage of drowning when the mind plays tricks on the body.

"Trust," the old man said, with tears glittering in his eyes. He put one ghostly hand on Llesho's neck and with the other hand he held up the black pearl. Using thumb and forefinger, he squeezed the pearl until it was no larger than a tooth.

"Open," he instructed, and when Llesho opened his mouth, Lleck popped the pearl into the empty socket where Llesho had lost a back tooth. "You should have that seen to one of these days," he said, and then he disappeared, like a cloud dispersing in the water.

Watching the cloud spin away in eddies of disturbed currents, Llesho's mouth was suddenly filled with all the things he wanted to say to the old man, all the words of gratitude and love that he had taken for granted all the years of their captivity together.

"Come back," he cried, but only bubbles formed in the water around him, and he realized that his lungs were ready to burst, and that his fingers had gotten clumsy. Somewhere he had dropped his rake, but he could not see it in the swirling muck. He struggled against panic and his own awkwardness to link the neck chain to his ankles, and tugged, hard, to alert the slave at the winch to pull him up. He would have given a sigh of relief when he felt the slack tighten and his body turn upside down, but to vent his emotion now would invite death at the very moment of his rescue. Then he was out of the water, hanging naked and upside down above the boat, coughing and choking, sneezing to clear the water from his nose.

"Where's your rake?" Shen-shu, the foreman, asked. Llesho pointed below him, to the bay. He saw the pinched, anguished expressions on the faces of his shift-mates, and then the winch was lowering him again.

"Find it. You are wasting time," Shen-shu warned him, and then he was plunging headfirst into the bay almost before he could grab a breath, dropping, dropping. There it was. He had the rake in his hands, but he was exhausted, and hanging upside down, and he could not reach up to take hold of the chain above his feet, nor had he slack to tug on. Llesho wondered how long the foreman would leave him in the bay, and if he would survive. Black specks filled his vision, and the laughter of spirits in the kingdom of the dead filled his ears.

Then Lling was beside him, and Hmishi, and they held his shoulders, trying to lift him. Hmishi pried the rake from his numb fingers and swam for the surface, and the winch grabbed his chain. Llesho was rising. Lling, at his side, breathed air from her mouth into his own, until finally they broke the surface.

"Don't fling him about!" Lling shouted as she clambered over the side of the boat. She and Hmishi took his shoulders again, as the winch released his chain. He fell, feetfirst, to the deck.

"What did you see down there?" Lling whispered, but Llesho could only gasp like a landed fish. Rolling to his stomach, he vomited salt water over the side of the boat, and hung there, draped across the gunwales, gathering his strength with each choked breath and trying to see his future in the gentle ripples of the bay. He was so exhausted that he hardly noticed when the foreman searched his body, probing in his mouth for hidden pearls after he had done the same to the other cavities for the pleasure of a minor cruelty. "Rotten teeth!" he grunted, and Llesho realized that yes, the black pearl was real, and that perhaps the spirit had told the truth after all. His brothers were alive somewhere on the mainland. But how was he to find them?

Chapter Two

"WAKE up. You need to get off the boat." Lling shook him by the shoulder, rousing Llesho from the questions going around in his head.

"I'm coming." He bestirred himself, but found he could not control his arms or legs. The boat rocking gently beneath him seemed distant, his body not quite real except for the tight buzzing in his head.

Hmishi offered a hand, and pulled him to his feet, but Llesho's legs seemed to have turned to water. He stumbled, grateful for the shoulder propping him up while he made his wobbling way to the shore. Familiar hands reached for him and hauled him into the slat-sided wagon for the ride back to the slave compound. Llesho found an empty corner on the flat bottom of the wagon and curled in on himself. Lling followed, and then Hmishi, each taking up their post to either side of him. Secure in their protection, he let his eyelids fall, lulled into a shallow sleep where the afternoon puzzled itself out in his drifting mind.

Sometimes, he knew, divers who had suffered enchantment of the deep and survived to tell of it described vivid waking dreams that came to them as consciousness fled. Llesho had not felt like he was losing consciousness while he talked to the spirit under the bay, but his mind must have been starved to convince him Lleck had appeared to him and that he had spoken with the spirit of his old mentor. His heart told him otherwise.

Desperately he wanted to confide in someone, to ask if any of it could be true, but he knew better than to take such a risk, even with Lling or Hmishi. The Harn hadn't always needed to steal Thebin children for the slave trade. The Thebin pearl divers on his quarter-shift all came from small-claim farms scratching out a marginal living on the fringes of the Thebin landhold. Harn raiding parties had robbed their homes and burned their crops, leaving them with nothing but their children and an agonizing decision. They needed the money that selling their children would bring just to feed the younger ones until they, too, were old enough to send to market. He once asked Lleck why the king did nothing to help his people. "In some ages, the gods favor their people, and in others they turn their backs." The minister had wept softly after that. Llesho hadn't understood, but he'd started a list right there of questions he would ask when he met the gods.

For the children trained to dive for pearls, however, slavery was little worse than the devastation they left behind them in the mountains. They knew nothing of kings or princes or palaces laid waste in that last great and terrible invasion. How could they understand his need to rescue his brothers when they could not imagine any rescue for themselves, or any reason to expect one? If they did not believe Llesho mad, they would believe him a danger. It surprised him to realize that he could not bear to lose the only companions he had left in the world.

"Kwan-ti will know how to help you." Lling touched his arm, for comfort and for strength. The jokes and challenges that usually marked the trip home from the bay were silenced today, the pearl fishers watching him somberly. Llesho remembered the first time he had seen a drowning, when Zetch, a diver well past the age at which most had fed the pigs, had stayed below for almost an hour. When they brought him up, his sack was full of pearls, but so were his mouth, his nostrils, his ears, and he had jabbed mother-of-pearl shells into his eyes. Gone mad, the foreman had announced, but the Thebins knew better. The pearls in Zetch's body would pay his rent in the kingdom of the dead, and buy him a new body—a free body—for his next turn on the wheel.

"I had a dream," Llesho said, but gave no description of his conversation with the spirit. Lord Chin-shi, it was said, feared witches, and dreamers could sometimes fall within the web of his superstition. For his part, Llesho wondered if he must be a witch, to have the dead visit him in waking dreams, but he dared not ask. The question alone would be enough to send him to the flames. So he only said, "I didn't mean to frighten you. I must have let my mind wander."

"We'll talk about it later," Lling answered. "Kwan-ti will know what to do."

Llesho knew her to mean that he should say nothing more in the crowded wagon. Good advice, and easy to follow. He leaned his head against her shoulder and closed his eyes.

"Be careful with him. We could lose him yet."

Kwan-ti, that was, and with a tone of command she only assumed when real trouble threatened. For a moment, Llesho wondered what had happened. As his companions jostled him awake, however, he realized that he must be the emergency.

"I'm all right," he protested, struggling to disentangle the hands that reached to gather him up.

"No, you are not," Lling contradicted in tones almost as commanding as those of Kwan-ti. "His mind drifted down below, during quarter-shift," Lling explained to the healer, her voice shrill with her anger. "Then, because he'd dropped his rake when he was fading, Shen-shu lowered him back into the bay to find it. If I had not breathed into his mouth, he would have died with his head stuck in the mire."

"Lleck would have saved me," Llesho objected.

Lling took this as a sign of his condition. "See," she said, "He thought he saw his father below." Like many of the women in the camp, Lling believed that Lleck was the true father of the slave Llesho. And what would be more natural than that the son, dying, should see a vision of his father come to save him?

But Kwan-ti had gone very still; Llesho could feel her tension, like the fizz of lightning about to strike. "When did this happen?" she asked.

"On second quarter-shift," Hmishi gave the answer. "The second hour of the quarter.

"I see." Something of the tension faded, but Llesho felt, though he could not explain why, that Kwan-ti still listened for something the rest of them could not hear. "Bring him inside," she finally said, and Llesho found himself tumbled out of the wagon into the arms of his Thebin shift-mates.

"I can walk," he said, and squirmed out of their grasp. He nearly sank to his knees when his legs would not quite bear his weight.

Kwan-ti raised him by the elbow. "I see you can," she said tartly, and then turned to his companions. "I'll take care of him. You may come by to see him after you have dressed and had dinner."

Hmishi took her at her word, and turned toward his own bed and the clothes basket at its foot, but Lling was not so easy to convince.

"Are you sure?" She touched his arm again, the question in her eyes for Llesho and not for the healer.

"About the clothes? I'm sure." Llesho tried to

lighten the worry in her eyes. "It's hard to forget you are a girl when we are on dry land."

"Hard seems to be the operative word," Lling admitted with a teasing glance at places on his body girls were not supposed to look. "I suppose you will live after all."

"Reassure his shift-mates in that regard. Unless he decides not to follow orders, of course." Kwan-ti smiled to take the sting out of the mock threat.

Lling turned to do as she was bid, but swayed her naked hips like an invitation when she walked. After a few choice paces she looked back at Llesho with a little laugh before running to find her clothes.

When Kwan-ti was sure that the girl had turned her attention elsewhere, she sighed heavily. "Come on, boy. We have to talk."

Llesho allowed her to lead him to the corner of the longhouse where she isolated the sick, but he would wait no longer for news. "Lleck is dead, isn't he?"

"Yes." Kwan-ti pushed him down onto a fresh bed just a short distance from the one where Lleck had died. "He wanted to see you very badly before he died, but I don't have the authority to interrupt a work shift, unless a diver is at risk. Now I wish I had tried anyway. I might at least have spared you from drowning."

The healer covered him in his bed with a light cloth. "You're shivering," she said, and added a blanket.

Llesho realized that it was true, but he seemed less to feel it than to observe it from a distance.

"Rest," she ordered. "You can explain it all to me after you've had some sleep; you're too tired to make sense now."

Llesho stopped her before she could leave him alone. "He left a message for me, didn't he?"

"Yes." She said nothing else, and hesitated even before saying that much.

Kwan-ti had always made Llesho nervous, though not as an enemy might. She had a way of going completely still and looking at him with eyes as sharp as a hawk's that made him think she was reading his soul. In some ways Kwan-ti reminded him of the way his mother had looked at him when he was six and he had sworn he hadn't broken the vase in the great hall. It had comforted him, as a child, to feel in her gaze that his mother could see everything, and love him in spite of his crime. Kwan-ti did not love him, however. He closed his eyes to hide his soul, afraid that it was too late, but with no strength to do more.

"Your secrets are safe with me, Llesho," she whispered. "You don't have to be afraid."

Fear had kept his mouth shut and his identity hidden all the years of his slavery. Lleck had made it clear that only his secrecy kept him alive. But he wanted to believe the healer, and he wondered, as he drifted into sleep, if it could hurt him, just this once, to trust someone.

That night Lling and Hmishi did come to visit, with others from their shift, but Llesho was sleeping, so they went away again with a promise to return. In the morning Llesho still slept, and Kwan-ti sent word to Foreman Shen-shu that her charge had suffered enchantment of the deep, that state in which a diver forgot the difference between air and water, and became a danger to himself and his shift-mates. Foreman Shen-shu sent a message back that Lord Chin-shi had no use for a pearl fisher who could no longer walk the oyster beds, but Kwan-ti ignored the threat, for now at least. With his dying words, Lleck had convinced her that the young Llesho had more pressing business to attend than plucking pearls from their homes in the mouths of shellfish.

When Llesho finally awoke, it was to sunlight breaking through the clouds high overhead. He could count on one hand the days when full sunshine parted the clouds over Pearl Island. What this portended, he did not want to consider, but he knew it was time to talk with Kwan-ti.

"May I have my clothes, please?"

"Of course." Kwan-ti handed him a set of bleached and faded trousers and shirt, and politely turned away while he pulled them on. Llesho piled into his clothes as fast as he could.

"You can turn around now," Llesho called, and Kwan-ti rejoined him, taking a seat on the bed next to his.

"You said he left a message. . . ." When Llesho thought of Lleck, so many conflicting emotions filled him—anger and sadness and wonder that his throat tightened on the name. But of course, Kwan-ti knew what he meant.

"Your father loved you very much," she began, but Llesho stopped her with a gesture. "My father is dead."

"Yes—"

"No," he contradicted her. "My father was dead before Chin-shi's men ever brought me here." She had to know that his father would not have permitted a single day to pass with his sons in slavery if he'd lived.

"Lleck was a family servant. I loved him, but he was not my father." He'd said too much and now he tried to keep the panic off his face. She would know that Thebin hardscrabble farmers didn't have servants.

"And he loved you," Kwan-ti said slowly, seeming to ignore the second part of his statement. She looked into his eyes with that hawklike gaze. Then, as if the sun had touched her, she seemed to open up in front of him, her eyes wide with sudden insight, a tiny sigh escaping her lips before she clamped them closed again, lest she say something out loud that should not be spoken at all.

"I have to find my brothers," Llesho said tentatively.

Kwan-ti nodded. "So he said to me on his death-bed."

"So he said to me in a dream beneath the bay," he agreed.

"You cannot go back to the oyster beds now."

"What am I to do?" he asked; this conversation with the healer felt more like a dream than the one he had with the spirit under the bay. Something about Kwan-ti's eyes, the gentle touch of her fingers on the back of his hand, slowed time to a walk.

"For the present, you must consider what you *can* do that will not kill your soul in the doing," she answered, and the spell was broken. She rose and spoke to someone behind Llesho in the longhouse. "Are you feeling ill, Tsu-tan?"

"Not at all." The hopeful witch-finder bowed his head over the pearl basket he carried. "I just came to see how the young diver was faring. Shen-shu will want him back on the boat tomorrow."

"Then Shen-shu can speak to me tomorrow. Now, we must permit young Llesho to rest."

"Of course, of course," Tsu-tan bowed and scraped his way out of the longhouse. He returned to his place beneath the coconut palm and took up again the pearl sorting basket never long out of his hands. He could see all the comings and goings of the longhouse from there, Kwan-ti knew, as she also knew he was watching her for evidence of witchcraft. She feared that Tsu-tan would now turn his attention on the young Llesho as well.

For himself, Llesho felt no inclination to rest. He had not regained his full strength, but he felt well enough to take a walk on the shore and watch for the red harvest boats to come in from the bay. So he left the longhouse while Kwan-ti was occupied in bandaging the cut foot of the cook's assistant, and wandered out past the cookhouse, onto the road.

Few slaves traveled the road at midday, but those he passed had heard about Llesho's double tragedy, the loss of Lleck and his own near drowning, and did not interrupt his brooding with idle conversation. Llesho had not quite told the truth about Lleck who, as minister of arts and education, was more a servant of the Thebin people than to the family of the king. Lleck had found him in captivity and joined him there, had taught the young prince not only reading and writing, but the arts of strategy that had come too late to save a king. As he walked, Llesho made good use of those lessons, setting evidence against probability, and examining methods to reach his goal.

If the apparition had been a dream concocted by his own starved mind, how had he known the minister had died? And if it was a dream, how could he explain the same message delivered to Kwan-ti? It must be true then: his brothers still lived, in servitude as he did himself. Llesho had to rescue them and together the brothers must free Thebin from the killing grasp of the Harn. If their mother still lived, languishing in the dungeons of her own palace—The thought stuttered out. Llesho could not imagine his beautiful mother reduced to squalor and filth, but the image of his battered sister bleeding into the refuse heap struck him to the heart. He hadn't wanted her dead, not really, he'd just wanted his mother back. By the time Ping had turned two, however, the little princess had adored him. He couldn't help but love her back. Couldn't—wouldn't—imagine her dead.

Since he had arrived on Pearl Island, he had been no farther from the slave compound than the oyster beds. There were no days off for good behavior, no visits to market or the city for a play or pageant. Once he had hated the duties that lined him up, smallest of seven brothers, to wave, nod, and bow at the side of his mother and father. He had longed for the day he was old enough to follow his brothers into the city for stolen pleasure in the night. That had all ended before Llesho even knew what pleasures his brothers found in the city. So why had Lleck come looking for the youngest and weakest, who was stuck on an island nobody ever got off of? Why hadn't he found one of Llesho's older brothers, who could actually *do* something about his deathbed revelation?

Trying to figure out Lleck's reasons wasn't helping him decide what to do. Llesho had walked all the way to the docks without even seeing the road he trod upon, but had only confirmed the impossibility of ever completing the spirit's quest. Who left the island, ever? Lord Chin-shi, of course, and his wife and daughters. Lord Chin-shi's son had not been seen on the island since before Llesho had arrived. The foremen, Kon of first quarter and Shen-shu of second quarter, sometimes accompanied their master to the slave markets to acquire new pearl fishers. But Shen-shu was the older of the two, and he was scarcely thirty. Neither was likely to give up their privileged position any time soon.

Pearl fishers never left the island, not living or dead. If they died of disease, they were cremated immediately to curtail the spread of infection. Rumor had it they did not always wait for death before feeding the fire with the struggling remains. When they drowned, or grew too old to work at all, they were fed to the pigs.

Kwan-ti had been right, though, he could not go back to the oyster beds. His lungs were fine, he could survive underwater as long as he ever could. But if he were visited by a vision again, he would surely drown while he argued with the demon who accosted him. He needed a second skill, one that would keep him out of the pig trough and get him off the island.

While he sat on the dock, thinking, the sun had dropped low, and he heard the taunting challenges of the pearl fishers returning home from the quarter-shift. He looked up, vaguely embarrassed to be wearing clothes when Lling and Hmishi and all of his fellow pearl divers were naked from work. He forgot all about the incoming divers, however, when he recognized the device on the prow of the harvest boat: tridents crossed over a round shield. Of course! Lord Chin-shi made his fortune on the pearl fisheries, but he *spent* his fortune in the arena. Renowned even in the longhouse for their prowess, Chin-shi's gladiators competed in arenas almost as far away as Thebin itself. And gladiators were given a cut of the purses they won. If a gladiator was good, and survived his battles, he might pay his way free before age and injury cut him down.

Llesho elbowed and apologized his way past his companions who were swarming off the boat, mocking him for his clothing and asking after his health. When he reached Foreman Shen-shu at the prow of the boat, Llesho fell to his knees and knocked his forehead on the dock in the formal style of a petition. "Honorable Foreman, sir, I respectfully request that you take my petition to your master, Lord Chin-shi of Pearl Island." He carefully referred to the master as that of Shen-shu alone, accepting by implication that Shen-shu held that position over himself. He'd learned long ago not to show the anger that flared every time he had to kowtow to the foreman: strategy, Lleck had taught him, sometimes meant sacrificing today's pride for tomorrow's victory.

"The witch forbids you to go back to the beds, doesn't she, pig food?" Shen-shu answered.

Llesho lifted his head from the dock and sat back on his heels, his palms resting on his knees. "I know of no witch, Master Shen-shu," he said, ignoring the more pertinent part of the foreman's statement for that which he could truthfully refute. "I come to you with a petition to Lord Chin-shi that I may train as a gladiator for the ring."

For a moment the entire dock went quiet, as Foreman Shen-shu stared at him in amazement. Then the foreman began to laugh. "A gladiator, pig food? A short contest with the pigs, perhaps." In the silence, Shen-shu's words rang sharply. "You pearl fishers are so skinny, Lord Chin-shi's gladiators will use you to pick their teeth."

Llesho reddened to the roots of his black, wavy hair. Beneath his clothes, he knew himself to be as skinny as his companions, whose bones he could plainly see pressing against the thinly stretched flesh that covered them. He imagined the gladiators to be huge men, taller than mountains with muscles like carved rocks, and knew he could not compete against such specimens of manhood. But, he reasoned, even gladiators must once have been boys. They could not have been born with all that muscle and sinew, and they didn't have a Thebin's natural endurance. If they could become great fighters, so could he.

"If I am so skinny," Llesho argued, "the pigs won't miss me, and the gladiators will have some fun breaking me into pieces."

"That they will, boy, and feed you to the house dogs when they are done." Shen-shu, who almost never displayed any sign of good humor, slapped his knee and laughed in agreement with Llesho's assessment of his chances.

"Forget about the old witch and her threats and warnings," he chided with more of that good humor so alien to his nature. "Your shift-mates miss you, and it makes them inefficient."

"They must learn to do without me," Llesho countered, "because I am determined to be a gladiator."

"You are a fool, do you know that, boy?" Shen-shu was no longer laughing.

Although at a disadvantage, being still on his knees, Llesho looked up at the foreman and held his gaze steadily. A good strategist knew when to hold his ground. "Then I am a fool," he accepted. "But I am a fool who will die as a gladiator, not as a pearl fisher. Nor as food for the pigs."

"We'll see." Foreman Shen-shu would say no more. With his authority over the pearl divers came the responsibility to mediate their rare petitions. Those he could not negotiate to a standstill must be referred to the Lord Chin-shi. And the boy Llesho was clearly not going to negotiate.

"Your humble slave gives thanks for your beneficence, in taking this petition to your master," Llesho answered, completing the formal petition ceremony.

His shift-mates, who listened silently while he argued his case with the foreman, stood apart from him with confusion and even fear on their faces. Llesho looked from one to the other, but found no understanding or support, not even from Lling, who turned away from him when he tried to catch her gaze. For the first time in his life as a slave, Llesho found himself embarrassed to see his Thebin shift-mates naked.

I am your prince, he thought, *you owe me more than this.* But they didn't know, and he couldn't tell them, nor did he expect that they would thank him if he did. He turned his eyes to the ground and walked away, ignoring the wagon that silently filled with the divers going home.

Chapter Three

WEEKS passed for Llesho in an agony of suspense. Kwan-ti did not approve of his decision, but she could not declare him fit to work in the pearl beds either. They both knew that left little but the pig troughs for a growing boy with no useful skills. Kwan-ti said nothing, but went about her work with her lips pressed together and her eyebrows drawn down in a frown.

Llesho's strength returned quickly, and with it the need for movement. He missed work, realized that the danger of the pearl beds had kept his mind sharp and his attention focused. And he discovered, to his surprise, that he missed his shift-mates. He had never thought of them as friends when they spent each quarter-shift together in the bay. In the days since he had seen the spirit of Lleck and nearly drowned, however, the pearl divers had begun to distance themselves from Llesho. The experience had set him apart as his secretive reserve had not. The usual quarter-rest banter that bound the group with petty griefs and shared workaday mishaps could not absorb so great a challenge, could not take in this new shape of him and make it ordinary. Llesho recognized the sudden emptiness where Lling's smile used to be, and the absence at his back that Hmishi used to fill. It seemed that he had been wrong on all counts. Not friendless and, according to Lleck's spirit, not without a family either. And not aware of any of it until he found himself well and truly alone. Well, damn.

To fill the hours, he ran. Not fast at first, but as he recovered, his runs grew longer: around the island once, twice, before he stopped, gasping. Even Thebins needed to catch their breath eventually. Some days he had heard the measured tramp of feet falling in unison to a deep voice rumbling out the time—now faster, now slower, while the feet of running men kept the beat. Llesho had kept ahead of them easily, and soon enough they changed direction, moved off on a path Llesho never took, up the hill to the training compound at its height.

Mostly, the running kept him focused on the moment: on the smooth, pale sand shifting underfoot and the fronds of dense foliage grown too close to the path that brushed against him as he passed, marking his skin with the scent of rain and mold and the broken promise of sunlight. The chitter of birds deep in the forest paced his own heart, but couldn't take the place of absent friends. Alone in his weary orbit of the island, he wondered how long he would be left adrift between lives.

In the third week after Llesho presented Foreman Shen-shu with his formal petition, a messenger came to summon the healer Kwan-ti to the main house. Lord Chin-shi had never summoned the peasant healer before. He had his own doctors, and the house servants took care of their own. Sometimes, when the wounds of Lord Chin-shi's gladiators healed over on the outside but festered inside, Kwan-ti would receive a call to treat them. But she had always stayed in the longhouse before, listening to the description of the wounded gladiator's condition, and sending the messenger back with instructions and a potion or packet of herbs. This time, Kwan-ti herself had gone with the messenger, leaving her bag of herbs and healer's pouch behind. Her quick glance, resting lightly on Llesho in passing, told him that he was the object of the summons. Lord Chin-shi, or his trainer, would want to judge her answer for himself when he asked what chance a half-drowned Thebin boy had to survive the rigors of gladiatorial training. She would need no tools of her trade for that.

Wondering what she would say just made him sick in the pit of his belly, so Llesho ran, as fast as he could manage this time. When he reached the landward side of the island, he plunged into the sea. He swam until his legs felt too heavy to propel him forward and he could not lift his arms to pull himself through the water. Alone and at the limit of his strength, he rolled over on his back and let the sea carry him, cradled in its warmth. So far from land, the sounds of Pearl Island did not reach him and Llesho allowed his mind to float with the current, wrapped in the quiet and at peace. He could stay here forever, he thought, with the salty breeze for company and the blood-warm water for comfort. The cry of a bird overhead seemed to come from a different world, calling to him though a bamboo screen set with bright silk streamers. It was another memory from his childhood before the Harn came, shaking itself loose when he let his thoughts wander. In summertime that screen had shaded the window in his mother's sitting room, its ribbons in the colors of the goddess fluttering in the breeze. Llesho wanted to hold onto that memory, to pass into that world of his past that called to him with the cry of birds like the sound of laughter. But somewhere in the back of his mind he felt the presence of his old mentor looking on with disapproval. He had things to do: brothers to rescue, a nation to free from the clutches of invaders and tyrants. No time for rest, eternal or otherwise.

The water seemed to take Lleck's side of the debate. The current pulled him away from the mainland that had grown no more distinct for all his efforts to reach it. After a while, Llesho executed a neat roll and began kicking strongly again, cutting through the water toward Pearl Island.

Too late, he realized that he'd swum out too far. The island was too far away and his legs were leaden, his arms numb. Llesho should have been afraid, but dying didn't frighten him anymore. He'd long ago come to terms with the gray depths as an enemy to his freedom; now he embraced the gentle side of the sea's strength, another friend he was leaving behind.

Something nudged his side, and the bumpy, grinning face of a water dragon broke the surface in front of him. Spume ran off her sides as her green-and-gold-scaled back rolled past him, never more than a tiny fraction of her length visible above the sea. She wrapped a loose coil around his waist. Her delicate forked tongue flicked out, touched his face, his hand; Llesho wondered if she planned to eat him for lunch. He thought he read laughter in her slitted eyes, however; she butted him gently with her tiny curled horns and disappeared, the soft, scaleless skin of her belly sliding effortlessly across his body. Even the water dragon had been company, once he figured out she didn't plan to eat him. But then, just ahead of him, the dragon's head rose out of the sea, coils glistening like gold and emeralds in the sun and the water. She dove, vanishing again into the sea, and he felt himself lifted on her strong back, and carried toward Pearl Island.

"I'm going," he told her, "I get the point."

The dragon seemed to understand. She gave her back a wriggle, and laughed at him between sharp curved teeth. The human sound of that laughter, feminine and musical, should have surprised him more, except that Llesho had grown to expect the impossible from the sea. So he laughed in turn, ran a hand down the gleaming flank of his companion, and nudged her gently with his knees, the way he had directed his pony forward when he was a child in Thebin. When they grew too near the shore for her great size, the dragon dipped her head beneath the waves, and Llesho released his hold. He was close enough now to make the shore under his own power, and he struck out with strong strokes, leaving almost no wake from his smooth kicks. He soon reached the shore, and sat panting and looking out over the water he had just crossed, but the water dragon was gone.

When he returned to the longhouse, spent but at peace, Kwan-ti was already there, tucking stray tendrils of wet hair into her glistening bun. She said nothing to him of her day's errand, nor did she question him about the lateness of the hour. For his part, Llesho made no mention of his attempted escape or the way the sea itself had comforted him and turned him back to face his future on Pearl Island. In the days that followed he still ran, but the urgency had gone out of his pounding feet. Tomorrow or the next day, the future would come for him. Fate was like that.

On the third day after Lord Chin-shi had summoned Kwan-ti, a boy not much older than Llesho himself, but a head taller and with pale gold skin, presented himself at the longhouse with the message that Llesho should gather up his possessions and follow. Since Llesho owned only the clothes on his back and the basket he had kept them in while at work in the pearl beds, he used his few moments to say good-bye to the healer, and to leave a parting message for Lling and one for Hmishi. He would miss them, and for a moment the thought of entering the gladiators' compound, where he would see no Thebin faces, daunted him more than any fear of the danger his new trade might hold. But Lleck had taught him that all of life was a circle. You couldn't go forward for long without meeting your past. Llesho had always hated that saying because he could think of little in his past that he wished to revisit. It surprised him to discover he took comfort in it now.

The messenger was eyeing him doubtfully when Llesho joined him. "I wouldn't want to be you for all the pearls in old Chin-shi's bay," was all he said, though, and the two boys climbed the rise at the center of the island with only the crying of the birds for commentary.

Llesho had seen the gladiators' training compound from a distance, but he had never been within the stout wooden palisade. Up close, Llesho could see the wall as individual tree trunks set upright, side by side, and snaggled at their tops like a hag's teeth. Such precautions seemed unnecessary—if a Thebin trained to the bay could not escape Pearl Island, no soft servant or overmuscled gladiator would do better—but he figured that gladiators must, by trade, be violent men. And they might even be able to handle a boat. For whatever reason, it was as difficult to get inside the compound as it seemed to get out. At the postern gate, the boy who accompanied him spoke to a guard with an empty tunic sleeve tied up in a knot, who opened the gate with his one arm and herded them into a passageway so narrow that the shoulders of a larger man would brush each side as he passed through. Llesho clung to the rough palisade that made up the outer wall of the passageway. The inner wall was also constructed of tree trunks set upright in the ground, but peeled of their bark and smoothed of knots and other irregularities so that they fit snugly one against another. A broad polished band showed that most of the men who passed through these gates brushed against the smooth inner wall. But the sounds of grunts and curses and the clashing of weapons beyond that burnished palisade unnerved him, and Llesho pressed against the scratch and grab of the undressed outer logs for even the few inches of additional safety it afforded him from the sounds of battle within. Combat was part of his life now, but he shied away from the overwhelming reality of his decision as he followed his guide down the passage.

Llesho figured they had traveled halfway around the compound before they came upon a second guard, apparently whole, at an inner bar to their entrance. This man seemed to know Llesho's escort and wordlessly opened his gate. He raised an eyebrow over a twisted smile when he thought Llesho didn't see, but quickly turned back to his work with awl and leather and whipcord when Llesho answered with a puzzled frown. The man didn't look like a fighter, but then, neither did the golden boy at his side.

Before Llesho could give this more than a passing thought, however, his companion had pushed him through the gate and he stumbled on the unfamiliar surface of sawdust under his feet. The smells of blood and sweat, and the sawdust itself, confused him, as did the flash of weapons and the deadly anger that seemed to crackle in the air around the fighting men. Llesho thrust one foot ahead of him, trying to regain his balance, and tripped over a piece of broken metal with bits of flesh clinging to it. With a squeal of surprise he fell face first into the training yard.

"Pick up your feet, fool!"

The words came from somewhere above a pair of darkly tanned sandaled feet that had planted themselves inches from Llesho's nose. He needed to pick up more than his feet, and he didn't want to guess what had made the wet splat soaking into his shirt. Llesho closed his eyes, wishing he could disappear, but his escort wouldn't let him.

"It's the new chicken," the golden boy commented over Llesho's fallen body.

"Master's pet?" the unknown voice asked doubtfully while Llesho dragged himself to his knees and finally to his feet, a better angle to follow the conversation. The boy who had brought him shrugged. "Don't know," he said, and "didn't ask," in a tone that clearly indicated Llesho was not his problem and he would just as soon keep it that way.

"Go back to work, then, unless Master Markko wants you to bring him in yourself."

"Didn't say so." The boy was already heading away from his charge, and Llesho realized he still didn't know the other boy's name. Not a good time to ask, he figured, and tried to look regal for the man standing in front of him, while muck dripped off his tunic. The stuff stank with a pungent tang at the back of his throat, and Llesho crinkled up his nose, trying to identify the mess without sneezing.

"Paint and straw this time," the stranger offered, and Llesho finally noticed the straw man lashed to a post, with bolts jutting from the place his chest used to be and bits of him scattered in a circle of sawdust.

The last time Llesho had seen a crossbow bolt, he'd been seven, and the bolt had been sticking out of his father's throat. He closed his eyes, but that made it worse, not better. Regal just wasn't working for him today. Hadn't, actually, for the past nine summers, but he still drew on old lessons in distress.

"Better vegetable than animal, but don't count on that for next time." The stranger was watching him with sharp features set in a stern, forbidding frown below eyes that were judging Llesho to the soles of his feet. "What are you, boy, and what the hell are you doing here?"

"I'm a Thebin," he answered, though the quirk of a smile, quickly suppressed, suggested that the stranger hadn't meant for him to answer the question. "My name is Llesho. I was sent for. To be a gladiator." He hoped. It was that or pig food, and if he'd been summoned for the trough, he wasn't going to remind anyone.

"Llesho." The stranger paused and seemed to be trying to remember something that escaped him before he could catch hold of it. "I'm Jaks, but you will learn all you need to know about me soon enough." The stranger was taller than Llesho, but not as tall as the boy who had brought him here. His skin was brown and smooth, and he had broad shoulders and powerful arms with the line of each muscle carved sharply in the flesh. The left arm had six tattooed bands, the simplest ones faded with age and more recent ones in increasingly complex designs. Jaks wore a leather tunic with the history of old battles written in the bloodstains that marked it, and a belt with a sheath for a knife at the waist. Metal guards covered his wrists and forearms. He was obviously dangerous, but for some reason which Llesho couldn't quite grasp, Jaks did not terrify him as he thought the man should, given the situation and a grain of common sense.

But common sense couldn't explain why the tension drained out of Llesho at the sight of the gladiator, or why his head came up at a more confident angle. A memory returned to him then, forgotten like so many things about home. His father had hired men like this at court to protect his family. Those men had died, pressed step by step into the heart of the palace, loyal to the last. The man who had guarded Llesho from his birth had looked very much like this Jaks, until he lay dead at the feet of the terrified child. The memory sent a shudder through him, which the gladiator must have taken for fear of his new life.

"I don't know what he was thinking," Jaks muttered under his breath, and Llesho figured he was talking about his petition to train as a gladiator, and didn't like the way the man dismissed him out of hand. But one problem at a time. The gladiator rubbed his neck with a mindless gesture that spoke of old injuries, or—

Llesho's father had done that when faced with a particularly thorny problem. "Right now," the gladiator said, "you need to change your shirt and check in with the overseer, Master Markko."

"Change my shirt?" At first, Llesho thought Jaks meant with magic, and he almost asked what he should change his shirt into. Not that he could do anything of the sort, of course, but he could try, if magic was required of gladiators—he didn't want to begin by showing any more ignorance than he already had. Then he realized, not change the shirt, change himself, by putting a clean shirt on. In Thebin he'd had a clean shirt for every day of the week, and special shirts made of yellow silk embroidered with bright colors for holidays and feast days, for banquets and for public days. Since he'd been a slave, though, he'd had one shirt and one pair of pants, nothing to go under them, and one day a week to wash them in, after which, for modesty, he would wear them wet until they dried. But he didn't think Jaks wanted to know about the domestic arrangements of pearl divers.

"I don't have another," he said, and waited while the gladiator blew out another gust of annoyance like a belch.

"Stupid to even think it," Jaks muttered. Llesho held his tongue with an effort rewarded when Jaks finished, "Of course, Markko doesn't know what he is doing. Not a single freaking clue."

Llesho waited out the storm as it broke harmlessly in another direction.

"You can't see the overseer like that," Jaks pointed out as if it should be obvious. "We'll have to find something for you to wear."

The gladiator led him across the practice yard to a low building made of coral blocks. A covered porch ran along its length to keep out the sun and provide a cool place to rest after a day of practice in the yard. It was more solid than the longhouse of the pearl divers, but obviously meant for the same purpose, which Jaks soon confirmed.

"This is the barracks," Jaks told him, "Master Markko will decide where you will sleep, but you'll need to be able to find the laundry wherever he puts you."

The laundry was actually several rooms clustered at the end of the barracks, each devoted to a particular task in the process of keeping the competitors dressed and supplied with protective coverings. They passed through the leatherwork shop but did not stop, though the strange scents drew Llesho like an old dream. Not fighters, but horses. He remembered horses, and the image in his mind when he thought of that word made him want to weep. But Jaks was leading him through an open courtyard cluttered with vats of soapy water and ladders of vines with clothes and long stretches of plain white cloth pinned to them. The steam pulled the heat up into his face and he felt the slick of sweat on his temples, dripping down his nose and over his lip.

A man with more rolls of fat than Llesho had ever seen sat on the edge of a bubbling vat. Naked to the waist, he reached in to his elbow and drew out bits of clothes, some that Llesho recognized and some that he didn't. The water smelled clean, and the bubbles released their own sharp scent when they burst, tickling Llesho's nose. Curious, Llesho trailed a hand into a vat for himself and pulled it out again, shaking the burned fingers.

"Where did the midge come from?" the fat man asked, and Jaks answered, "Thebin, originally. The pearl beds more recently, and without a stitch to wear."

Jaks was laughing at him with this strange man, who gave a clipped bark of his own laughter. "Madness," the stranger gave his opinion with a little shake of the head, then gave Llesho one of those long, measuring looks that made him squirm. This man seemed to have no status, but Jaks treated him like a confidant, and the man himself looked at Llesho as if he were something discovered on the bottom of his sandal.

"Thebin, eh? Well, he won't be easily winded. That's one thing in his favor." The washerman scratched thoughtfully at his backside. "As far as I can tell, that's the only thing."

Regal was easier in front of an obvious servant, and Llesho's jaw came out, his head tilted just so, his shoulders straight and at ease.

Both men stopped laughing. "It can't be," the washerman whispered.

"Madness," Jaks agreed softly, and added, for Llesho, "Pull it in, boy, if you want to stay alive."

Danger. Llesho remembered the precise timbre of a warning rippling through time at him, and in reflex his eyes darted, looking for a place to hide.

"Dear Gods," the fat man muttered, expression broken in shards of fear and denial. "Have you been on Pearl Island all along?" he asked.

Llesho did not answer. He figured the men must know that, and he wanted to understand what they were up to before he said anything in their presence. He had a feeling they'd know his whole life story if he opened his mouth at all.

"Does Markko know, do you think?" the fat man asked Jaks, as if Llesho were not in the room. "What do you suppose he wants with the boy?"

"Get him a shirt, Den," was all Jaks said, but his voice had gone completely blank. "Not a new one. Old, patched." So the washerman had a name.

"Pathetic," Den muttered, but Llesho did not quite understand who or what was pathetic, so he decided to keep his mouth shut.

Den stood up, wearing nothing but a cloth wrapped between legs as thick as the logs in the outer palisade and covered with their own forest of coarse hair. "Off with it, then," he said, and wiggled his fingers until Llesho had stripped off his shirt and handed it to him.

"We don't have anything in his size." The mountainous launderer wandered ponderously between the ranks of hanging cloth. "But this should do until I can get the stitchers on it."

Llesho had lost track of the washerman somewhere behind him when the scuffling footsteps faded out of his hearing, and so he jumped when a thick arm reached over his shoulder and handed him a shirt. Not ponderous unless he wanted to be, then. Llesho stored that away for future reference while he pulled the clean shirt over his head and smoothed it into place. It came almost to his knees, and his hands were lost in the long sleeves. He made a face, but Jaks ignored it.

"That will do," he agreed. A look passed between the two men that Llesho had the good sense to worry about, but Jaks took him by the shoulder and backtracked them through the laundry. When they were outside again, the central practice yard had emptied of men, leaving only the broken tools of combat behind. Jaks crossed the space without a glance or a word, and opened a door into a small stone house that sat a little apart from the sleeping barracks and equipment rooms.

"The pearl diver has arrived," he told the man who sat at a desk in the elaborately decorated room. "What do you want me to do with him?"

"Leave him here. You may go."

Jaks did so at once, and again Llesho found himself facing a stranger who looked at him with cool, incurious eyes. This must be the overseer, Master Markko, he figured, since that was the name the boy had given, and the same that Jaks had mentioned to Den in the laundry. From the way people had spoken of him, Llesho had expected someone huge and powerful, or grim and forbidding at least. In fact, Llesho could find nothing of distinction about the man at all. He had the golden skin and the dark hair of the boy who had come to fetch him, but Llesho could see no family resemblance beyond the most common ties to a place and a people. Master Markko seemed to be about as tall as the boy with no name, but with his full height, while the messenger had overlarge hands and feet, like a puppy who would be a much larger dog. The man, Markko, wore several layers of plain robes that marked him as a minor official in the lord's household.

He seemed to be ascetically slim beneath the robes, but his face showed no feature of remark, nor could Llesho find any sign about his person that he was or had been a gladiator, or had ever fought in any way.

Markko looked up briefly from the work that lay scattered on his desk. "We've already had an offer for you, from Lord Yueh's trainer," he said. "Do you suppose you are worth such a lordly sum?"

"I don't imagine so, sir," he answered. He didn't know how much Lord Yueh had offered, or what it meant in the scheme of the buying and selling of gladiators. However, Llesho didn't want to go anywhere they knew enough to offer for him when he had no obvious skills or value.

"I suspect you are right," the overseer said. "His lordship has declined the offer, which means you will be under my direction."

"Yes, sir." Llesho couldn't think of anything else to say, so he hung his head as submissively as possible, and hoped that the overseer would soon tire of him.

After another penetrating look through eyes like chips of flint, Markko returned his attention to the paper on his desk.

"The mop is in the corner," he said. "You can fill the bucket at the laundry, and begin with this room. Then the barracks floors need washing. When you are done, you may report to the cookhouse for dinner before you return here."

"There must be some mistake," Llesho suggested, hoping it was true. "I don't know anything about washing floors."

"How difficult can it be?" Markko asked him reasonably, "Mop, bucket, water, floor. In that order." He turned back to his desk, but looked up when Llesho did not move.

"But I thought I was here to become a gladiator."

Markko looked him over with a critical eye, as if he were buying fish in the market. "Do you like to bed men, boy? Large, hungry men with the bloodlust still running in their veins?"

"That would not be my choice, sir."

"It is, however, the only choice I have to offer you," Markko explained to him reasonably. He had not changed his tone of voice, but Llesho realized suddenly that the mildness was a mask, that Master Markko already knew too much about him, and that this was one person he did not want to challenge. He ducked his head and looked as pitiful as possible in his patched and oversized shirt until Markko dismissed him with a wave of his free hand. Then Llesho picked up the bucket and the mop and crept out of the room, unwilling to turn his back on the man who had stared at him with no feeling in his eyes. That, Llesho decided, was what made this man dangerous. He had no feelings at all.

Chapter Four

LLESHO spent his first day as a gladiator in training learning how to scrub barracks. He hadn't been exactly surprised when he found himself on mop duty. A long time ago, it seemed, he'd been the new pearl diver in his quarter-shift. For weeks he'd cleared out dead oysters with empty shells while his shift-matcs gathered the pearls that should have filled his sack. Shen-shu had beaten him after each shift from which he returned empty-handed, but that too seemed a kind of initiation with no real anger behind the blows. After a period of testing, the divers had accepted him as one of their own. Llesho had expected no less from the gladiators, and had braced himself for much worse than a mop when he followed the messenger up the hill.

Still, he was exhausted when he returned from cleaning the floor of the latrine, just in time to see the golden boy leaving the stone cottage. The overseer sat at his desk as if he hadn't moved all day, but set his pen down when Llesho bent his head and stood in a proper submissive silence at the center of the room.

"Lord Chin-shi has requested my presence," Markko told him, and rose from the desk with majestic grace. "I will be at Lord Chin-shi's house for much of the evening. You will doubtless wish to sleep before I return, but as you can see, I am ill-equipped for housing boys here. You will have to make do with a corner of the workroom in the back—" Markko gestured at a closed door shrouded in shadows under the stairs. "Don't touch anything, and don't go upstairs."

"Yes, sir." Llesho did not look up until he heard the door open and close again behind the overseer. With a careful, darted glance to make sure Master Markko had actually departed, he raised his head and reached for the timbered ceiling in a great stretch to unkink his back. He looked at his hands ruefully. He had worked hard in the pearl beds, but his new duties with mop and pail left him with peeling blisters butting up against old calluses. His feet hurt, his back hurt, and his arms hurt, but none of that was going to keep him awake past his exhaustion. Not even his excitement that he seemed to be one step closer to escaping Pearl Island could do that.

After another careful stretch, he looked around him, wondering why he was supposed to stay clear of upstairs. Curiosity was one of Llesho's greatest weaknesses, but the looming shadows painted on the still and dusty air dampened any interest in exploring the upper region of the cottage. He did not want to know what cast those shadows, and so he ducked under the stairs and opened the door.

The workroom was the same size as the office. An L-shaped worktable ran the length of two walls. Above the long side of the worktable, a window with its shutter propped open let in the damp evening air. Shelves ranged above the short side of the table and from floor to ceiling on both sides of the doorway were packed with tools and pots and jars and strange mechanical devices and scrolls and codices. Everything seemed to be neatly in its assigned place, but the workroom felt cluttered. Over everything hung the faint scent of purgatives and something more ominous.

That sensation of clinging corruption deepened as the night darkened around him. The weights and balances, mortar and pestle, compounding beakers, all seemed to blossom like mushrooms in the shadows, growing heads with horns on them, and leering grins. Sleep. Llesho remembered sleep, something one did with the rustle of palm thatching overhead and the muttered dreaming of fellow divers in the longhouse. If gladiators were supposed to be able to sleep in a place like Markko's workroom, Llesho figured he'd already failed his first test.

But the muscles in his legs trembled and burned their determined message: they'd had enough for the day. So he found himself an empty corner and curled up like a badger with his back pressed into the wall. Moonlight streamed through the window, casting shadows that loomed over him in his corner and crept across the floor. Llesho curled himself a little more tightly and slitted his eyes to keep guard against the night.

When the moon had set, Llesho still lay awake, tensed to repel whatever oppressive thing waited for him in the dark. Toward dawn he fell asleep at last, only to be wakened by faint scratches at the door. *Ghosts,* he thought, and shivered, refusing to close his eyes again in case the thing came for him in his sleep. So he was partly awake when a sandaled foot came into view at nose-level. This, at least, was growing tiresome.

"Time to rise, rodent." So was that voice. The golden boy, the messenger. "Master Markko has already gone out. He charged me to get you to morning prayer forms and breakfast. Said you could start in with the mop again. He will summon you if he needs you." The boy seemed to study him for a minute, his face twisted in a sneer of contempt. "I wouldn't hold my breath. Oh, I forgot. That's all you *can* do."

Llesho wondered what he'd done to win the boy's anger. A pearl diver would take his asking as a direct challenge, and the glare that greeted his blurry nod promised a foot in his ribs as the only answer he was likely to get in this new place. Llesho bit his tongue to keep his questions backed up behind his teeth. He understood breakfast, though, and he decided he'd find out what prayer forms were soon enough, and with a lot less pain, if he waited until they presented themselves and figured it out then. Golden Boy wasn't staying for questions anyway. He was already on the threshhold when Llesho stopped him with the one question he really needed an answer to right away.

"Privy?" He was hoping the answer didn't send him across the practice yard and behind the barracks where he'd found—and scrubbed—the latrines yesterday.

The boy pointed out the back. Better than a long trek through the entire compound, but he'd have to go past Golden Boy to reach it. And he was getting sick of thinking about the messenger by his job and his face.

"Do you have a name?" he asked, trying to sound cool and in control as he squeezed passed in the doorway.

"It's Bixei." The boy stuck out a foot to stop him, nose to nose. "Are you the Grand Inquisitor now?"

"I can call you asswipe if you'd prefer," Llesho answered evenly. He would rather not have a full bladder in a confrontation with the bigger and better trained boy, but he knew he had a choice. He could stand up to the bully from the first, or he could learn to like eating mud, because he'd be spending most of his days facedown in it with Bixei's foot in his back. So he held his ground and waited for Bixei to take up the challenge.

"Bixei, rodent, and don't you forget it."

Which was pretty weak as a comeback, but beat a punch in the nose. Llesho shrugged as he passed the boy. Bixei stopped him with a reminder, "Prayer forms start in thirty seconds. And Master Den hates laggards. Enjoy your piss."

The messenger swaggered out, and Llesho followed as far as the front door, turning to complete his own errand around the back. Whatever prayer forms were, he decided, they wouldn't be hard to find. It looked like the entire compound was shaping itself into ragged rows in the practice court.

He arrived a minute late, enough to draw a sharp frown from the washerman who stood in his breechcloth at the front of the rows of gladiators.

"The Gods are waiting," Den gave him a meaningful frown. Llesho had the distinct impression that he meant the words exactly and literally, as if he had one of the Seven at his back, tapping a naked foot impatiently in the sawdust. Llesho quickly took a place at the end of one line, only to discover, too late, that Bixei stood at his right hand. Great.

Once Llesho had drawn himself to attention, matching his stance to the men in front of him, Den made his formal bow and began to mark off the forms, each with a name to describe the action. The name and the action together formed a focus of contemplation, and the form itself became a prayer. At least it did when practiced correctly.

"Flowing river," Den said, and though he seemed to show no particular grace, still his large body made the form look simple, like pulling shirts from the washing vats. Llesho tried to copy the motion, summoning the image of a stream, and overbalanced. He flailed his arms to catch himself, and fell backward into the sawdust. With trained instincts, the men ranked behind him took one step to the side, neither catching him nor jostled out of the form by his crashing fall.

Den halted the company to frown down at him, but said only, "Watch the shirt, boy, it's almost new." Mention of the patched and ill-fitting shirt flamed Llesho's cheeks with embarrassment. The laughter of his fellows seemed good-natured enough, however, and the man in the line in front of him helped him up with a slap on the back.

"You'll learn, chicken," he said with a grin, and turned back to complete the form "Willow bends in the wind," which Llesho had missed completely. Bixei gave a scornful sniff, and ignored him for the remainder of the exercise.

Llesho struggled with the next form and the next, caught one foot around the other and wrenched his ankle in "Twining branches," then tried to lift both feet at once for "Butterfly," and fell flat on his face. But gradually he began to feel a rhythm in the passage from one pose to another, movement gliding from foot to ankle, ankle to knee to hip, up through his spine to be contained between his outstretched hands. When he imagined performing the complex patterns underwater, in the bay, his movements became slower, more precise, more fluid. He visualized the sea at his back, and did not fall. By the time the exercise had ended, he was earning nervous glances from his fellows. Only Den, and Llesho himself, were breathing easily.

Den bowed to the assembled company, freeing them to their morning meal. As the company broke up, he sought out Llesho for a slight nod of acknowledgment. "You are agile enough, and you learn quickly," he said, too quietly for the departing men to hear. "Just be careful not to learn too quickly. All useful skills are acquired with effort."

"Yes, sir," Llesho agreed. He had to be more careful here among strangers, who may have heard stories of Thebin but who had never actually met someone from the high mountain country. Lowlanders often mistook for magic the simple facts of a body constructed to survive the airless peaks. He knew that, but he needed time to discover what weaknesses he must pretend so that no one suspected him of supernatural gifts. And he'd have to figure out what strengths he could develop to compensate for his small stature.

"The gods never call us without giving us the means to succeed," Den said, and Llesho wondered what he'd shown on his face: not the Seven, perhaps, but a cranky old minister who wouldn't stop giving him orders even after he was dead.

"Give it time," Den said, and patted him on the back before moving off toward the laundry.

Time indeed. His plans had taken him this far; now Llesho had to figure out how to survive the training and earn a place at the competitions on the mainland. His stomach growled, and he sighed. Among Lleck's Thebin proverbs, "Listen to your belly" was the simplest, and came down to the lesson, "Don't try to think when you are hungry; all your answers will be food." So he followed the retreating backs toward the cookhouse and the smell of boiled grain and fish. The man who had picked him up after his first humiliating fall that morning caught sight of him and gestured for Llesho to take a place in front of him. The line snaked toward a long table laden with vats of food still in their cooking pots. Llesho hesitated, but the waiting men sorted themselves out to leave a space for him. So he went, grateful when someone pushed a plate and a spoon into his hands.

"I'm Stipes," the gladiator said. "Short sword and net, trident if that is the only contest on offer."

"Llesho." He followed the lead of the other men, filling his plate with boiled grain mush and a double dip of fish heads steamed with palm leaves in the pot for flavor. And in the spirit of the other man's introduction, "I am pretty good with a muck rake, and I can hold my breath underwater."

Stipes laughed at that and led him to a bench where two empty places waited for them. All but one were strangers to Llesho, but Bixei stopped him with a look that would have killed if he had the knack of it.

"Thanks." Llesho gestured with his plate to show his meaning, and turned to find another bench, but Stipes pulled him down, nearly dumping the plate of food on Bixei's lap.

"Not so fast. I thought, if you wanted to come to the barracks tonight, you might share my bunk."

It wasn't the first such offer Llesho had received in his life. In the longhouse new boys or girls his age were called "fresh fish" until they made their own preferences clear. Among the gladiators, the young trainees were apparently called "chickens," but a polite offer deserved a polite answer in both places. Bixei's poisonous glare wasn't the first of its kind he'd seen either, but it put things in perspective. He didn't know what they called it here, but he had no intention of treading Bixei's waters even if he were inclined to accept the offer. Which he wasn't. Made virtue easier that way.

"Thank you," he sat, and Bixei's knuckles whitened around the handle of his spoon. "But I have promised myself to a woman, a pearl diver. She's Thebin, like me. We've known each other since we were seven." He smiled. The memory of Lling, slick as a seal under the bay, lightened his heart. He could imagine her expression if she heard his declaration, the way she would raise one eyebrow and pucker her lips like she'd eaten something sour. She'd punch him, no doubt, for the outrageous lie, and neither of them would ever admit how close to the truth he swam. Laughter sparkled in his gut, and he set it free. "We've been workmates half our lives."

Stipes shrugged good-naturedly. "Then you're best off staying where you are," he advised. "His Honor won't ask, and some in the barracks would make their offer with a fist in your belly. Best to have some friends about you and a bit of a name in the ranks before you take on those offers."

Llesho knew good advice when he saw it, so he gave a little nod of agreement and dug his spoon into the mess on his plate. The fish was passable, the mushed grain tasteless, but he watched Stipes mix the two and found that, when taken together, the food wasn't bad at all.

Llesho noticed that Bixei's knuckles had returned to a more natural color since he'd rejected Stipes' offer, but the other boy hadn't said anything for most of the meal. When Llesho had almost finished, though, Bixei asked a question, tinged with contempt. "You work with women?"

Llesho almost answered with his own challenge, but he saw the gladiators lean closer over the bench and realized that Bixei asked for them all, and that the disdain covered a real curiosity. He relaxed, then, like he'd fitted a puzzle piece into place, and smiled. "Every quarter-shift. Lling saved my life. I had run out of breath and would have drowned." The memory of hanging upside down from Shen-shu's chain, his strength gone with the last of his breath, shivered through him with the terror he'd been past feeling when it happened. "Lling breathed into me, and brought me to the surface. Without her I'd be dead."

Fighting men, it seemed, could understand living or dying by how loyal a man could count his friends, but they still looked doubtful that a woman could share something as complex as honor. Stipes asked the next, and most obvious question. "But isn't it . . . distracting?"

Llesho shook his head ruefully. "Not after the first black eye," he said, and the laugh that earned him seemed directed not at his own defeat in the field of romance, but at Stipes himself, and Bixei, both of whom received nudges in the ribs and a few waggled eyebrows along with the hoots of derision. Bixei flamed red in the face, but raised his chin to defy them all. "And don't forget it, either, Stipes," he said, confirming Llesho's suspicions and giving Stipes a new warning as well.

"Not likely to, am I, boy?" As an apology the words might seem lacking, but they were said with enough fervor to earn Stipes a nod of acceptance.

Llesho had finished his breakfast and waited only for a pause in the brief conversation to make his excuses. Bixei was the next to stand as the rest of the bench also began to clear. He seemed less hostile, but said nothing more to Llesho and left quickly.

"You'll do, boy." Stipes gave Llesho a slap on the back, and followed as Bixei cut through the throng for the exit.

"Sure, I will," Llesho muttered under his breath, though he doubted every word of it. He wished Lling were here now, and Hmishi. Together they might take on the world, but alone he didn't know how he would make it as a gladiator. He wasn't even a good mop boy. But he'd learn. He always did. And there was a mop with his name on it waiting for him at Markko's—His Honor to the fighters, apparently—cottage.

When Llesho returned to the cottage, the overseer was sitting behind the desk folding a sheet of paper. Bixei had arrived ahead of him, and was standing at Markko's right hand with a message pouch hanging from a strap that crossed from his left shoulder to his right hip.

"I won't be needing you for the rest of the morning," Markko said without looking up. He gestured at a tray with a teapot and plate of broken biscuits on the corner of his desk. "Take these things with you, I've finished with them. And, after you have mopped the barracks to Master Jaks' satisfaction, come back here. I may have something for you to do then."

Bixei looked down on him with haughty disdain while Llesho collected the overseer's breakfast things, but something in the look and the posture made Llesho wonder what he was so afraid of losing. If Bixei wanted to be Markko's servant, he was welcome to the job. The least of Thebins made poor ones of it—they were a proud people, but mostly proud of their independence, which they had nurtured and protected for generations on their mountaintops. Until the Harn had come. Unfortunately, Thebins also made poor soldiers. Llesho was going to change that, but not as a servant to a second-rate official in the employ of Chinshi, Lord of Pearls.

Something of what he was thinking must have communicated itself to the golden boy, because the haughty pride slipped a bit. But Markko had a rolled-up paper to go into the pouch, and Llesho ducked away without attracting further notice.

Chapter Five

TWO weeks after he made the trek from the pearl beds to the gladiator's compound, Llesho took his place in the barracks with a bachelor group who showed no interest in him for conversation or anything else. He had grown skilled in the use of the mop and bucket and the prayer forms were coming more easily to him.

As Llesho began to understand the forms, his respect for his teacher grew as well. Built like a mountain, with the warmth of the summer sun in his eyes, the humble washerman was the very image of the Laughing God, who had not walked the earth, it was said, for many human generations. Nor would he return while the Harn held the gates of heaven.

Den's attention seemed everywhere, while his body and soul centered into the action: sinking his weight into the ground for the earth forms, and flowing through the water forms. In the air forms, he seemed almost to take flight, which should have looked absurd on his large body, but didn't. When he demonstrated the water forms, Llesho caught glimpses, like double vision, of Kwan-ti at her workbench. She mixed elixirs and shaped little pills in his mind's eye as Den moved from position to position. Llesho knew to trust the almost-visions that left impressions, like intuition, in their wake. Experience had taught him to keep the flashes to himself, but he determined to watch the teacher carefully, and found comfort in the memory overlaid upon the washerman's movements.

He had realized on that first embarrassing day that the prayer forms demanded freedom of him. His body could not soar with heart and soul tied to the slave block and his chains. To succeed, he must free that part of him the gods owned. So each morning as the students lined up with the least experienced in the front, he found his place quickly. Closing his eyes, he took a moment to imagine himself at home among the mountains that rose above Kungol, the capital city where he was born. His brother, Adar, had kept a clinic in those mountains. Llesho remembered the cold, thin air that forced a human being to move cautiously so close to heaven, and the measured, gentle movements of the healer. He imagined Adar at his back, guiding him through the motions of the prayers; soon he was passing effortlessly through the exercises, wrapped in the warmth of Adar's smile.

At the end of his first month at the compound, and just as Llesho was beginning to think that he would remain a slave to the mop forever, Den pulled him aside after prayer forms.

"You are doing well," he said, and Llesho gave him a little bow, receiving the compliment with humility.

"Are you settling into the barracks well?"

"Yes, sir, Master Den." Llesho had learned the proper form of address for his teacher, and he used it now, waiting for the master to reveal his purpose. He knew that he showed too much of his relief to be out from under the overseer's eye, and perhaps too much of his impatience as well, because Master Den chuckled at him.

"And I suppose you are wondering how prayer forms and mops will make you a gladiator."

"Yes, Master Den." He met his teacher's eyes with a dare in his own.

"Shut that down right now, boy, unless you want to spend the rest of your days in Markko's clutches." Master Den managed to frown at him without ever changing expression, which Llesho didn't understand, except that he dropped his own eyes, and scuffed his feet in the sawdust with all of the confusion he really felt.

The washerman studied him for a moment before releasing a sigh. "Very well," he said, answering the silent demand. "After your work detail, you may join the novices at hand-to-hand combat training. Ask Bixei the way."

Master Den knew that Bixei hated the newcomer, and he challenged Llesho with a crinkle of humor in his eye. "Be nice to your enemy, this time," that look seemed to say, "or stay a slave to the mop forever."

Llesho asked. Bixei wasn't happy, and Llesho wondered if it was another trick when the golden boy led him away from the large central practice yard where the experienced gladiators went about their training. He was more certain of it than ever when they entered the laundry, but Bixei kept going, out the back and through the drying yards to a corner where the other novices waited for them.

Radimus, a member of Llesho's bachelor group, nodded a greeting. "Pei," he said by way of introducing the fourth novice, "Used to be a drover, till his master saw him fight in a barracks match."

Up close, Pei was terrifying, almost as big as Master Den, but with a harder, scarred body. Llesho had never seen a barracks match—the pearl divers settled their arguments in other ways, and Master Markko would skin a man who took a gladiator out of competition for a personal argument. He'd heard the gossip, though, and knew that some lords wagered on the death matches of their own slaves. The former drover returned his curious wonder with a baleful glance that gave neither threat nor quarter—Llesho figured that was all the "hello" he was going to get.

Though new to gladiatorial combat, Radimus and Pei were both fully grown and Master Den paired them for practice, which left Bixei to spar with Llesho. As he picked himself up from the dirt for what seemed like the thousandth time that afternoon, Llesho gave a prayer of gratitude that no one but his small band of beginners could see his clumsiness or his repeated defeats at the hands of his rival.

Den never scolded him for his ungainly efforts, but repeated his instructions patiently. He taught efficiency over drama, elegance in simplicity, took Llesho's hand and positioned it just so, nudged his knee into the proper stance, and nodded approval when he had it right. Then he demonstrated how the clean, deadly moves could be decorated to impress the arena crowds while inflicting little damage to his opponent. Llesho quickly realized that, while Bixei seemed to grasp the underlying deadly purpose of the training, the point of not doing damage to his opponent never seemed to penetrate his skull. As long as his opponent's skill remained superior to his own, Llesho figured he'd be spending his afternoons with his face in the dirt and his arms twisted in knots at his back.

Things didn't much improve until prayer forms one morning at the end of Llesho's first week of hand-to-hand combat training. His body passed through the forms under Den's watchful eye until, halfway through the Flowing Water form, he stumbled. His body was trying to perform two completely different moves at that point in the exercise and the realization stopped him dead in the middle of the form.

Den saw; the muscles in his face relaxed into a smile that never showed itself upon his lips, and Llesho knew he was right. Prayer forms and hand-to-hand were one, each growing out of the same body, the same nature, but leading to different conclusions: peace, or war. The move that he had stumbled on made sense then: he had reached the place in the form where a man must choose one path or the other, and when he had come to that place, Llesho had not known which path to take. But he did now. He completed the morning prayers with no further mishaps, and in the afternoon, in the shade of the drying yard, landed Bixei on his back for the first time. As a warning, he brought the blade of his hand perilously close to the throat of his enemy, then shifted into the more decorated style that would do no harm. The next morning, as he was putting away his mop and pail, Bixei came to him with a summons from Jaks to the weapons room. He was going to be a real gladiator at last!

He knew the way, but Bixei insisted that he'd been told to bring him, which he did. "Good luck," he muttered at the door, and then he was gone, walking away as fast as he could without seeming to run, and in the direction of the barracks. To spread the tale, Llesho figured, and he opened the door and entered alone.

The weapons room was long and narrow, with a beaten dirt floor and a single table running the length of it. Brackets set into all four walls held long-shafted weapons: pikes and staves and tridents, slim spears with gleaming heads as long as his hand and thicker ones hooked at the end of the blade. On the table, all manner of swords and knives and hammers and axes lay waiting next to nets and chain whips. Master Jaks stood rigidly straight, to the right of a door which led into the smith and repair shops ringing with the clangor of hammer on bronze and iron. Llesho hadn't seen him since his first day in the compound, but he looked more terrifying and bleak than Llesho remembered, though only the occasional flex of the tattooed bands on his upper arms showed any of his tension. When Llesho had made his bow, Jaks turned to the door and rapped two sharp taps upon it.

Den came through the door first and settled himself to the left of the jamb. A woman followed him. She wore the plain clothes of a servant covered by a coat with wide sleeves that fell away at her elbows. Llesho figured that for a disguise. She carried herself with haughty assurance, demanding a degree of deference his teachers would not owe a woman of her apparent youth in the lower ranks. Den's mobile features, set in a frozen mask, told Llesho that the woman's presence deeply disturbed him. It disturbed Llesho as well.

"Are you a goddess?" he asked, and wondered if he could be any stupider, to draw her attention with a question that marked him as an uneducated fool, or as a Thebin raised at the center of a religious culture. A slave boy should have no knowledge of the gates of heaven, or the gods and goddesses who passed through them when they visited the living earth.

"He is impertinent," she said to Master Den, but turned the dark, thoughtful pools of her eyes on Llesho and, he saw in them not age but history, and deep, deep, timeless knowledge.

The woman turned to Jaks and touched a finger to the most elaborate band of tattooing on his arm, as if she was reminding him of a secret. "Test him," she said, and withdrew her hand into her voluminous sleeve. Jaks uttered no word that might identify the woman, but bowed deeply and stepped forward. He smiled to allay Llesho's nervousness.

"Don't worry, boy. Nobody is going to hurt you. In weapons combat it helps to start with a natural inclination, if you have one. We are here to find out what that might be for you."

"Yes, sir," Llesho said, as firmly as he could to show that he did understand and that he wasn't afraid, though neither was true. The concept made sense, of course, but the woman's presence suggested that more was going on than a simple aptitude test.

Jaks gave a single curt nod to accept the answer, though the glint in his eyes told Llesho he saw more of those doubts than he let on. "We will start with long weapons," Jaks said, and gestured at the walls around them. "Take your time. Pick up whatever attracts you. Give it a chance, but if it doesn't feel comfortable in your hand, put it back."

Den interrupted then, with as much explanation as he was going to get. "Don't watch us to find your answer, boy. The right answer for Jaks or me is bound to be the wrong answer for you."

Llesho nodded and began to mark the perimeter of the room. At first he kept his hands clasped behind his back, but he quickly forgot his reticence as he handled the weapons. The pikes annoyed him. He tried several lengths of shaft, but the heads felt overbalanced and clumsy. Staves he handled well enough, but he quickly lost interest in them. The trident went to his hand with the easy fit of long practice. After a few awkward passes he centered himself, thought of water, and made a few smooth thrusts and feints, twirled the weapon in a wide circle around one hand and flung it to bury its teeth deep in the dirt at Jaks' feet.

Jaks wrenched the trident out of the dirt with a wry smile. "No surprise there, I guess. Anything else?"

Llesho shrugged, and continued his circuit of the room. He approached the spears with curiosity, but one with a shorter shaft than the others drew him with a fascination so strong he glanced about him to be certain no one in the room had cast a spell on him. That was foolish. No one in Lord Chin-shi's realm would dare to practice magic in the open like this. But the intent expressions on his three testers made him wonder how open this occasion really was. He reached out to it, and the room itself seemed to hold its breath. The weapon felt old, and Llesho could almost hear the high, thin wind of Thebin whistling in his ears when he touched it.

It felt . . . right. Not familiar, like the trident, which reminded him of the rake he used to play at battles with in the bay. When his fingers closed around the shaft of the spear, he felt the "click" of a soul finding its completion, hand meeting matching hand. Mine. He knew he had never held such a weapon before, just as he knew he would not willingly give it up now that he had found it. Not even if he died. Memories far older than the body he wore stirred in the back of his mind, roiling in the muck of time and terror. That part of him that was here and now, a slave with fifteen summers, could not shake the sick feeling in the pit of his stomach; the spear was poisoned, old memory whispered. He threw it away from him, shuddering in disgust even as a longing he did not understand urged him to snatch it up again.

Compelled by that terrifying desire, Llesho crouched to retrieve the spear. Poised, but certain now that the test was, indeed, a trap, and it had just closed on his neck, he tightened his hand into a fist, grasping only air. Master Den watched him out of deep sorrowful eyes, but Jaks picked up the spear where Llesho had let it fall and pointed to the table with it. "Trident, but we'll hold off on the short spear," he said in his most efficient voice, passing the spear to the woman, who slipped it into her sleeve. "Now try the close-in weapons."

The woman watched Llesho with the hypnotic

fascination of a cobra, and with about as much emotion. Llesho gave Den a pleading glance, but his teacher's blank mask did not change.

"No one is going to hurt you," Jaks urged him. "We just want to know how to train you that most ensures your success."

That was only half the truth. Llesho didn't know where the other half lay, but he knew he couldn't see his way to it through the secrets clouding the air between them. He followed the direction Jaks indicated with the tilt of his head, and considered the weapons spread out on the table. A knife rested there, older than the others, with a haft that seemed alien among the scattered blades. He reached for it, felt the weight settle in his hand, flipped it to an overhand grasp, and held it above his head, shifting through an exercise that reminded him of the prayer forms Den led in the morning. Knife and hand were one, flowing into his arm, and he stepped though the form with slow grace, then snapped through it with lightning speed that surprised even himself. When he had come to rest again, Jaks took the knife out of his hand and set it down. "No knifework," he said with finality, "What else suits you?"

But Llesho would not let it go this time. That knife was a part of him, and he wanted, needed to know how. "What is it?" he asked Jaks, seizing the knife from its place on the table and holding it up in confusion. "I know this knife! But I don't remember—"

The woman reached across the table and touched his wrist with the same stroking fingertips that had brushed the tattoo on Jaks' arm. "You will," she said, with something like hunger in her voice. She wrapped her fingers around the blade of the knife and tugged it from his hand. Llesho released it quickly, shrinking from the cold, white fingers that did not bleed though the knife should have cut them deeply. When the blade had disappeared after the spear into her sleeve, Jaks took him by the shoulder and turned him back to the table.

"Try something else."

Llesho glared at him. He wanted answers he could understand, but the hand on his shoulder triggered one of those flashes of almost-vision, confused images like memories of things he'd never seen. This one showed him Jaks' arm, but clean of the marks that banded it. Somehow, the vision related to the woman and the knife.

"Your arm," he nodded at the tattoos on the arm that held his shoulder. "What do the tattoos mean?" He couldn't believe he'd asked, but the visions drove him with their own need, and he gritted his teeth and waited for the next flash, or for his teacher to knock him into the dirt for his impertinence.

Jaks refused to answer, but his expression turned to stone.

"They are his kills." The mysterious woman answered his question and he shivered, wishing she had ignored him as well. "Each stands for a death."

"In the arena?" Llesho turned to face Jaks, wanting explanations from his teacher, not the cold threat in the voice of the stranger. And he wanted the answer to be yes, clean kills, in equal combat.

The woman shook her head, once, slowly, her cobra eyes devouring him with their cold stare. "Assassinations," she said. "The simple bands for lower ranked targets, the more complex bands for targets of a higher rank." She smiled. "Jaks excels at his profession."

Llesho trembled. He was out of his depth, way out of his depth, and had been since Lleck's spirit had appeared to him in the waters of the bay.

"What do you want of me?" he asked, though he dreaded the answer. He'd been on the wrong end of an assassination attempt when he was seven, and he couldn't imagine doing that to someone else's child. He would die first, even if it did sink Minister Lleck's plans for him.

The woman smiled, and something eased in her eyes, which did not come alive, but ceased, at least, to suck him into the black darkness of her soul. "Survival," she said, though he couldn't tell whose, or why. "Shall we continue?"

Jaks turned to the table of weapons and held up two short swords. "Try this."

None of the other weapons triggered a response like the knife or the short spear, but Llesho found himself generally at ease with the blade weapons, and awkward with the hammers and axes, more inclined to trip over his own net than trap an opponent, and for no reason he could set to words, just a feeling that set his external organs clawing their way up inside him that he would not, could not, touch the chain whip. He passed over it three times, and thankfully, Jaks did not pressure him to pick it up. When they were done, the woman took him by the chin and smiled. "We have before us a pearl of great value, Masters. Let us take care that he does not wind up food for the swine."

Llesho's entire body froze beneath her hand. Did she know about the treasure Lleck had given him, that sometimes pulsed in his mouth like a sore tooth? Or had the comment landed like a stray bolt from a crossbow shot into the air? He doubted that the lady ever spoke without thought. She released him without another word, however, and gave a bow to the masters before slipping out the way she had come.

Jaks visibly relaxed when she had departed. He took a deep breath and let it out slowly. "Tomorrow, after breakfast, report for arms practice with the novice class." he said to Llesho, and added, "Ask Bixei—he will show you."

Den frowned from his place by the door, but said

nothing, which was just as well. Llesho didn't need a warning to keep the woman's presence secret. He wanted an explanation if his teachers expected his silence for very long, but at the moment, he felt unready for any answers they might give him. Better to pretend the afternoon hadn't happened. Something of this must have shown on Llesho's face, because Den's frown smoothed into his more usual bland nonexpression. He didn't look happy, though, which Llesho found more reassuring than not. And then he was gone, through the door into the smithy and back to his laundry, and Jaks was staring down at the table covered with small arms as if it held the secrets of the universe.

Llesho gave a perfunctory bow, although Jaks wasn't looking, and went out into the practice yard. The heat danced in waves off the sawdust, but the stir at the corner of his eye was more than an illusion of hot air. The figure disappearing around the corner of the barracks looked like the guard who had greeted Bixei at the inner entrance to the compound on Llesho's first day, but what the man would be doing skulking around the weapons room at rest time he could not figure, except that he didn't trust the man, and hadn't from his first sight of him.

The tense session in the weapons room had set his nerves on edge; Llesho knew the man could be completely innocent of everything but an unpleasant disposition, but it couldn't hurt to keep a watchful eye on him. Some plot was moving in the camp. The woman was one clue. The guard could be her creature or set to spy on her by an enemy. Where one faction stirred, however, he knew that another was surely nearby.

Whatever that meant to the plotters, Llesho figured none of it was good for him. The awareness that he was unskilled and vulnerable, surrounded by professional killers, prickled his skin. The sooner he became one of them, the better for his survival. The word, crossing his mind, reminded him again of the woman's answer to his question, "What do you want of me?" As a means to an end, he believed she meant him to survive. Safer, he knew, to go unnoticed, but if factions were forming in the camp, he was glad to know that he had allies—formidable ones, if his teachers' reactions were anything to go by—whatever his side turned out to be. And whatever interests of their own motivated them to care.

Powerful or not, however, he would have traded the mysterious woman for Lling at his side any day. At least he understood Lling's motives, could anticipate her. Didn't worry that she'd decide he was not as valuable as she'd thought and send an assassin to dispose of him in his sleep.

He didn't realize how much time had passed in the weapons room until the smell of dinner wafting on the late afternoon breeze reminded him that he was hungry. Resting on the long porch that fronted the barracks, Stipes waved a cheerful arm for him to join them, which Bixei accepted with just a fleeting glint of resentment in his eyes. Llesho dropped onto a bench and tried to let neither his uneasiness at the strange afternoon nor his excitement at finally becoming a gladiator show. "Jaks is starting me on weapons tomorrow."

A hungry gleam settled in Bixei's expression then. "That will be fun." He smiled a shark's grin full of teeth and promise. Llesho hoped that Jaks would not let the other boy kill him—at least not on the first day.

Chapter Six

WEAPONS instruction for the four novices—Llesho and Bixei, and the older Radimus and Pei—took place at the center of the practice yard. Around them, the more experienced gladiators clashed in pairs, sword against spear, pike against trident and net, stave against sword. In front of them, a table laden with small arms settled into the sawdust. Long weapons leaning against the table's side bounced sunlight into Llesho's eyes, blurring his mind as well as his body with the heat.

The novices themselves stood weaponless and at formal attention while the sun beat down on their bare heads. Sweat beaded under Llesho's hair and ran down his face to fall unceremoniously from the tip of his nose. Like his companions, however, he did not move until Master Jaks had joined them with a ceremonial bow. They returned the bow, and Master Jaks began his instruction. "Long sword." He lifted the sword, turned it so the sun ran down the curve of blade like liquid gold, and demonstrated a slash-and-thrust move before putting it down in favor of two shorter, fatter blades with a dull gleam on their rough surfaces. "Paired swords," he said, and the blades twirled in his hands, faster than Llesho could see, while Master Jaks moved forward, then leaned back so far that his head brushed the sawdust on the practice yard. Leaping up off the ground, he executed a turn in the air and landed again without breaking the rhythm of the crossing blades. Llesho made a mental note to learn that trick.

"Pike." Master Jaks set the swords down on the table and took up the long-shafted weapon set with a curved hook at its head. He made several lunges and turns with it, spun it overhead, and brought it down again. "Trident." He replaced one weapon and took up the other, and Llesho saw how foolish he must have seemed with his companions, playing at tridents with their muckrakes in the bay. The pearl divers had bashed gracelessly at each other: Master Jaks did a precise dance of death. In fact, Llesho concluded, work with the long weapons compared closely with dance, while short weapons, like hand-to-hand, evoked the prayer forms.

After his demonstration, Master Jaks took the measure of his students, leveling a piercing stare on each in turn. He let that burning gaze rest on Bixei as he explained, "Part of weapons work is knowing how to kill; the greater part is knowing how to control one's own impulses, by the use of superior technique to control both weapon and opponent without doing harm."

Bixei would have spoken out in his own defense, but Master Jaks put up a hand to forestall him. He left them briefly to pass through the ranks of fighting men, tapping a shoulder here, whispering a word in an ear there. He returned with four hardened gladiators, Stipes among them, and took his place again in front of his class.

"Show me what you can do. Bixei?" Master Jaks stood aside while Bixei chose his weapons, paired swords, with one of his shark's grins, which disappeared when Master Jaks added, "Your practice partner today will be Stipes."

The grin disappeared. Stipes quirked an ironic eyebrow at his companion, inviting him to accept what everyone in the camp would know. Bixei would have no opportunity to practice deadly arts on Llesho until he had learned the skill and the control on which Master Jaks insisted. Stipes carried a stave, and took his stance while Bixei changed weapons for a stave himself. But Master Jaks stopped him, with a shake of the head. "First choice always," he said. Llesho saw the panic bloom in Bixei's eyes, but neither his partner nor his teacher acknowledged that the first hit had gone to Master Jaks. Bixei returned the stave and took up the lethal blades. Pei grabbed a long sword, and Radimus took up a pike. Both were quickly paired with experienced fighters.

Llesho stared at the last unpaired training partner with dismay. He was a stranger, fully head and shoulders taller than Llesho, and heavily muscled. "I am going to die," Llesho thought, and reached instinctively for the knife, but Master Jaks forestalled him.

"Never use a short weapon against an opponent with a longer reach," he said, and handed Llesho the trident. Instead of pairing him with the stranger, however, Master Jaks explained, "As youngest novice, you arc stuck with your master. Madon will oversee the practice." With a nod to the gladiator, Master Jaks took his stance with a long sword and jabbed at Llesho, who knocked aside the blow with his trident.

Master Jaks was circling him, forcing Llesho to follow his movements by turning in a tight spin. Llesho thought quickly: if they were competing short weapon against short weapon, he could have devised a defense based on the prayer forms. If both used long weapons, he could protect himself by making his moves like dance. But the defense that might come out of the weapon dance would not suit the forms of the sword which, coming at him again, broke his concentration and brought him back to the moment. He was getting dizzy. If he didn't come up with something soon, he would win by disgusting his opponent when he vomited.

His clothes were damp on his back, scratchy, and the sweat blurred his eyes. Even the sawdust underfoot burned through the soles of his sandals, and the light flashing off Master Jaks' blade was making him squint and flinch with every step—deliberately. Master Jaks was using the sword to intimidate, the glare to blind his opponent. Llesho had to do something, right now. So he decided: he would act as his weapon dictated, and pretend the man in front of him also carried a long weapon that just happened to be . . . short. He would make the rules of the battle, force Master Jaks to take the defensive.

Action followed thought on the instant; Llesho committed to the form of his weapon, felt his body shift into the position of a dancer. He leaped and tumbled with the trident held close to his body for protection and control. With the sun at his back, he planted the shaft of his trident in the sawdust and, clutching it like a pivot with both hands, he swung his body high over the weapon of his opponent. When he landed, he flipped the trident around, cracking the shaft down hard on Master Jaks' sword arm and turned the weapon again, like lightning, to force the gladiator back with the knifelike tines of the trident pressing against his throat.

The wrist guards Master Jaks wore protected him from the blow, but he could not match the reach of the trident with his sword, nor could he angle out of danger without risking death. He dropped his sword with a smile. "Good," he said. When Llesho continued to hold him at bay with the trident, he added a little reminder, "You won. You can rest your weapon now."

"I won?" Llesho looked around in confusion as the practice yard came back into focus, and he realized that he was breathing heavily, the residual effect of adrenaline and fear. For a moment, in the heat of the competition, he had lost himself in a terrifying past, when men with swords had come for him and carried him away to slavery. He had been seven, frightened and alone among his dead. His hands tensed around the shaft of the trident: even now he wanted to kill the man in front of him, to prove to himself that he was helpless no longer.

"Llesho." Master Jukt stood perfectly still, except that he moved his left hand slowly over his right, slipped out of the wrist guards and dropped them to the ground next to the sword.

The seconds beat in the pulse at Llesho's temple; the sound of the blood rushing through his body drowned out the trumpeting glare of the sunlight. No other sound existed. The gladiators practicing in the yard had fallen still, as if a spell had paralyzed them all. Then a voice reached out to him, pitched to catch the attention of a small boy. Llesho wondered how he had let the enemy draw so close.

"Let it go, child." Not an enemy. Master Den, the washerman. Suddenly the trident burned in his hands, and he dropped it, horrified at what he had almost done. But Master Den was there, with a hand on his shoulder and he turned into the warm comfort waiting for him, and cried against the broad fleshy shoulder as he had not cried in all the years of his captivity.

When the tears had exhausted themselves, he let out an exhausted sigh. Couldn't keep his face buried in Master Den's shoulder forever. He had to face the camp. He would never—not ever—live this down. But when he pulled away, the practice yard was empty.

"Master Jaks is in the weapons room," Master Den said softly, with a reassuring pat. "Find him and apologize. Then go to dinner."

Llesho bowed his head in submission to his teacher's wishes. As he turned to go, Den added, "I think you've had enough of mops. Tomorrow, you will start in the laundry. I'll clear it with Markko."

Numb, Llesho nodded with none of the enthusiasm he would have shown before weapons practice. Then, he would have jumped at any chance to get out of mop duty. He was still grateful, but now he yearned only for the peace that seemed a part of the washerman. In the laundry he could hide from the derision of his companions, and from their fear of the "mad" student.

"Go on. Master Jaks will be expecting you." Den sent him on his way still heavy of heart, but with hope and no little terror. He had to face Master Jaks and explain, somehow, why a lowly student and former pearl diver had nearly killed him in weapons practice, after the competition had been ceded. And without revealing his past, or what there was of it that his owners might not already know.

Taking a deep breath, Llesho entered the weapons room so quietly that Master Jaks, sitting with his head bent over a sword he worked with a polishing cloth, did not hear him come in. "Master," he whispered, and Master Jaks looked up at him, his face empty of all expression.

"I am sorry, Master." What was he supposed to say next, he wondered, that would make it better? "I am sorry I tried to murder you" seemed somehow inadequate, and "I don't know why I tried to skewer you during practice" would confirm that he was mad.

Master Jaks put down his sword and folded the polishing cloth carefully before addressing his student. "Sometimes the enthusiasm of the battle overtakes us, even in friendly practice," Master Jaks said. "That is why the master always takes the newest student for his partner. If anyone deserves to die of a student's enthusiasm, it is the teacher who inspired him." A smile twitched at his lips, and Llesho wondered if perhaps he was not the first student to best his teacher by surprise. Llesho doubted those other students had held their instructor at trident point long after the bout had ended, however.

While he could not trust his story to anyone, Llesho owed this man he'd almost killed much more than he had given. He bowed deeply, abjectly, and felt the tears form again. Not now. He couldn't cry in front of the weapons master. Not again. Too mad for the pearl beds, and now too mad for the arena: they would feed him to the pigs for sure.

"I did not mean to hurt you, Master," he blurted. "For a moment I was elsewhere, but it won't happen again, I promise."

Master Jaks had come around the table to stand face-to-face with his student. He was shaking his head, and Llesho stopped breathing. His apology was not accepted. He was lost. But then Master Jaks took his chin in his hand and tilted his head up. With the thumb of his free hand he wiped the tears from the hollows beneath Llesho's eyes. "I know where you were," he said. "And I am the one who is sorry. You reacted exactly as Den told me you would, and even warned, I was not ready." He released Llesho with a sigh. "Den was right. We can't afford many mistakes with you."

For Llesho, the world stopped turning with his teacher's words. What did Master Jaks know? What did he intend to do about it? His gaze fell on the knives on the table, lingered there.

"Are you going to sell me to the Harn?"

"I don't buy or sell anybody, boy. I train fighters for the arena." Master Jaks' voice took on a hard edge. "And the Harn are unlikely to care overmuch about a peasant turned pearl diver, poorly trained into the semblance of a gladiator, now are they?"

"No, Master," Llesho agreed. Perhaps he had misunderstood everything that had happened to him in the past two days, or perhaps Master Jaks was telling him that he had allies in the camp. He figured he was safe at the moment, anyway—from the Harn *and* the pigs—and obeyed with alacrity when Master Jaks sent him off to his supper.

His apologies had taken him into the dinner hour, and the gladiators and novices had all made their way to the cookhouse when Llesho left the weapons room. He felt peaceful, in the way the sea was calm after a storm. He knew he had to face the ridicule of Bixei and the others, but lingered in the practice yard to hold onto that precious sense of peace as long as he could. So he was alone when he saw a man creep into the stone house of the overseer. He would have thought nothing of it—messengers for the overseer came and went at all hours of the day—except that he was sure he recognized the man. But what business could Tsu-tan, the pearl sorter, have with the overseer of the gladiators? The question was on his lips when he joined his bench mates at dinner.

"That is not the frown of a man being sent to market," Stipes noted. "What's up, Llesho?"

"I just saw someone I thought I knew, from the pearl beds."

Deep inside, Llesho felt that the puzzle of Tsu-tan was more important than his own embarrassment on the practice field, though he could not have said how he knew. Bixei seemed on the verge of drawing the conversation to Llesho's lapse in weapons' practice, but Stipes jabbed him in the ribs, and he shrugged with a sullen glare, then turned to the question at hand. "Maybe another pearl fisher has figured out that a fighting life would at least keep him dry."

"Tsu-tan isn't a pearl diver, he's too old, and not

Thebin to begin with. He's a pearl sorter." He didn't say what he'd long thought: that Tsu-tan was a worm of a man with an evil eye who almost never left his pearl basket, but sat under the palm tree that faced the longhouse like a scruffy spider at the center of a dusty web.

"Tsu-tan." Stipes frowned. "A creature with the look of a weasel and an eye that would shrivel a man in his britches?"

"That's him." Llesho almost laughed at the description, so much like his own impression.

"He's the overseer's witch-finder," Stipes said, "and sly as they come; I've heard it said that he is no man at all, but a demon who lives on the screams of Markko's victims. If he's here tonight, you can be sure there will be a burning before the week is out."

Kwan-ti. In his mind's eye, Llesho could see the evil man sitting with his back against his tree, his eyes following the healer with avid fascination. He had to warn her. But in his months of training, he had not once received permission to leave the compound. There had to be a way. He considered his companions at the table, but could not ask them for help. He already owed too many explanations, and he couldn't expect men who depended on Markko for their well-being to risk the overseer's wrath by helping Llesho warn his prey. There had to be a way, but dinner ended and he still hadn't figured out what to do.

He followed his bench mates to the long covered porch that fronted the barracks, where the gladiators rested in the cool breeze of the evening. Radimus was there, tossing bones in a gambling game for favor-chips; Bixei joined him, but Llesho moved on to investigate a noisy group that had formed a knot at the far end of the porch. Pei sat on a solid chair at the center of the laughing and hand-clapping circle, thumping his broad foot in a steady rhythm on the floorboards. Joining the circle, Llesho picked up the rhythm with his clapping hands, encouraging the champions to begin a song contest. Madon finally stepped forward with a bow.

Placing his hand over his heart, Madon recited his challenge in time to the beat of the clapping hands and tapping feet:

"The Seven watch over the fighter,
who swings his sword in their praise
who sleeps with his sword like a lover
And carries his sword to his grave."

The circle of fighters cheered wildly. Madon signaled his victory with a wave of his fist in the air and bowed an invitation for his opponent to begin. A stranger stood away from the railing on which he had rested and set a hand to his breast like Madon had done before him. As Pei picked up the beat again, the challenger intoned his response:

"The Seven watch over the fighter
who vanquishes foe in their name
who conquers with net and with trident
And lives beyond death in their fame."

The stranger's side of the circle exploded in cheers to support their combatant, but the contest went to Madon, whose lines were closer to the classic rhyme pattern of the ancients than his opponent's effort. Grumbling, the challenger vowed retaliation in a limerick that made outrageous claims about the parentage of the victor, and promised retribution in fair competition, which any could see had not happened here. No one took offense at the classic challenge, but many returned the insults in less poetic form.

Llesho laughed along, but he soon abandoned the group, slipping away to find his own bunk. Grateful as he was that no one had reminded him of his blunder on the practice field, he could not shake the sense of disaster that had hung over his head since he had seen Tsu-tan enter the overseer's cottage. He had plans to lay if he hoped to warn Kwan-ti in time. But the day had been long, and too fraught with emotion for Llesho to think about strategy. He soon fell asleep, where evil dreams pursued him, of Kwan-ti burning and Tsu-tan leering at the fire. Sometimes, Llesho was at the center of the dream fire, and Markko stood in the doorway of the stone cottage with a beaker of poison in one hand and a leash in the other, a hell-hound with Tsu-tan's face lying at his feet. Llesho rested little, and woke with a start at dawn.

After prayer forms and breakfast, Llesho made his way to the laundry where Den greeted him with a sour pucker of his lips.

"I don't suppose anyone ever taught you how to wash shirts?" he asked.

Llesho shrugged. "I've washed my own shirt every rest-day since I was seven," he said, "But the water came from what I could save out of my drinking ration over the week. I don't suppose that was what you had in mind."

"Not exactly." Den introduced him to the pump handle and showed how, when he worked it up and down, hot water from an underground spring gushed out of a curved spout, bubbling and steaming as it filled the vat. Mesmerized by the waves that lapped away from the point where the water fell, Llesho's thoughts drifted back to the pearl beds and the long-house. The hiss and roar of the tide as it rose and fell with the crossing of the moons had underscored his every move, every thought since coming to Pearl Island. Now the sound, in small, reminded him of Kwan-ti, and the death of Minister Lleck.

Lleck had trusted Kwan-ti, had known the healer would protect his secrets and the boy in his care. He wondered if he could do the same. Could he trust

Master Den with this secret, that he knew who Tsu-tan, the witch-finder, sought? When he realized that he was hesitating not out of concern for Kwan-ti, but for fear that he would draw Markko's attention to himself, Llesho knew what he had to do.

As if reading his mind, Master Den dropped a heavy hand on Llesho's shoulder. "I have broad shoulders, if you need help with that burden," Den said, and Llesho understood that the washerman did not refer to the sacks of laundry waiting to be tumbled into the washing vats.

"I have to get outside the palisade." Llesho sat on the edge of the washing vat, his brow drawn down in a worried crease. "I have to warn—someone—that they are in danger."

"From the witch-finder?" Den asked. He sat heavily next to Llesho and nodded for emphasis. "Tsu-tan has been creeping around again; I wondered if you had seen him, or knew what he was about."

"I have to warn her," Llesho insisted, "I owe a debt of trust."

"Have you considered, Llesho, that the charge against your friend may be true?" Den seemed to be looking for more than he said in the question, but Llesho had enough of puzzles and secrets of his own.

"She is no witch," he said. "I have known her for all my seasons on Pearl Island."

The washerman did not remind him that his seasons measured very few in the schemes of witches and spirit demons, but pointed out what must be obvious to a pearl diver:

"Think, Llesho. If she is guilty of witchcraft, her magic puts her beyond the power of the likes of Tsu-tan and Master Markko. But if she is innocent, she is trapped already: there is no way off Pearl Island without Lord Chin-shi's blessing—or his boats."

It hurt to realize Den was right. He would risk everything—his life, even his kingdom—in a pointless display of misplaced chivalry that could have no good outcome. It hurt even more to know he was going to do it, or die trying, anyway. Master Den saw the decision harden the expression in Llesho's eyes, and seemed himself to come to a decision.

"I have a message for the healer, Kwan-ti," Den said, and pulled himself upright. He left the washroom for a moment and returned with a small parchment, tightly rolled and tied with a ribbon and seal. "Show the seal at the gates, it will give you safe passage. But come back as soon as the message is delivered. No dawdling."

"Thank you, Master Den." Llesho bowed low in gratitude, and Den sighed.

"In the long run, it may comfort you to know that you did your best to help your friend. But learn this lesson well: only a warrior who suffers failure with fortitude can accept the accolades of success with grace and humility."

"Yes, Master." Llesho bowed again, but in his heart he admitted no possibility of failure. Then he turned and ran, through the laundry and the leather works, across the practice yard, and to the first gate, where the guard looked at him with suspicion and inspected the rolled parchment from every angle to assure himself that the seal was authentic and had not been tampered with.

The outer gate was easier. Madon was on duty, and waved Llesho through with a cursory glance at the seal. Madon was no fool, and if he had any suspicions about the message, he kept them to himself. He merely pointed to a less worn path leading away from the compound, suggesting, "You could take the long run, but this is a shortcut to the bay."

The shortcut required greater concentration, since it was less well tended and air roots and trailing vines frequently snaked across the path to trip up the unwary. Llesho had to make a few incautious leaps to avoid a twisted ankle, but he reached the longhouse in short order, and unseen. To his dismay, however, he could not find Kwan-ti. His own quarter-shift mates were at work in the bay, but he asked the divers on quarter-rest, and the old men who fished and the old women who gathered fruits and vegetables to flavor the grain food Lord Chin-shi supplied for the cookhouse. No one had seen Kwan-ti since the night before. All the boats were accounted for, so she could not have left the island, but still, no one could find her.

Finally, taking his courage in his hands, Llesho approached the witch-finder, who curled in a brooding huddle beneath his palm tree.

"I have a message from Master Den for the healer," he said, pretending not to know of Tsu-tan's nocturnal visits to Master Markko. "Did you see where she went?"

"I did not," Tsu-tan snapped. "And if you don't want to roast on a spit yourself, you will mind your own business, pig food."

Llesho thought the witch-finder's voice shook a little. If Tsu-tan was afraid, so much the better. But Llesho refused to believe what he heard whispered in the longhouse: the witch had gone, called a dragon from the sea to take her away from the Island and the witch-finder and his virtuous Lord, Chin-shi. Once, a water dragon had rescued Llesho, convincing him without words to cling to life and to his faith. The creature had laughed her joy with him, a human sound, with the voice of the healer. He could believe no evil of Kwan-ti, but he could not deny that she was gone, and by her own power, not spirited away to await death at the hands of the witch-finder and his employers. How or why, he refused to think, for fear of where his own evidence would take him.

Still carrying Master Den's message, Llesho returned to the compound. Madon still guarded the gate and waved him in with a smile. A new man sat at the inner turnstile, however, someone he knew by sight, who delivered a message of his own.

"Overseer Markko wants to see you as soon as you return."

Llesho nodded to acknowledge the order, but his heart froze. What did the overseer know of his errand, and what would he do about it?

"I have done nothing wrong," Llesho reminded himself, "I only acted as a messenger, as befits my station, to deliver Den's message—" He would be lying to himself as well as the overseer, he realized: was this what Den had meant about suffering failure? He knocked on the door to the stone cottage, determined to answer truthfully any question the overseer asked of him.

Master Markko was at his desk, as usual, with Bixei standing at attention while the overseer sprinkled sand on his writing and tapped it clean. He rolled and sealed it, and handed it to Bixei, who left them with a last cold glare at Llesho. Llesho ignored the animosity of the other boy; Markko was looking up at him with false concern oiling his frown.

"Let me see it, boy." Markko held out his hand. "You had a message from Master Den for the witch. I want to see it."

In a cold sweat, Llesho wondered if he could withhold the parchment roll. Kwan-ti was lost to him, but perhaps he could save Master Den from the stake if he took responsibility for his actions. "It was my fault," he said, "I wanted to see Kwan-ti. Master Den tried to persuade me not to go, but I persisted, and so he made it possible for me to visit the longhouse."

"And did you see the witch?"

"I have never seen a witch," Llesho answered with precise honesty. No one had ever identified themselves to him as a witch. If required, he might have guessed the woman who had watched him that first afternoon in the weapons room practiced the evil arts. He would have offered his own life, however, as surety that Kwan-ti had no evil in her.

"I see." Master Markko considered him thoughtfully. "But I would still like to see the message Master Den gave you for the woman."

"Yes, Master." Shivering, though the day was warm, Llesho held out the parchment. He paled when Markko took a small knife and carefully lifted the seal. Unrolled, the parchment revealed only a request for a simple poultice. Markko frowned at it, then he lit the candle on his desk and held the parchment over it. The edges began to curl and smoke, but still no words appeared on the parchment. Flicking the false message at Llesho, he asked, "What do you make of this?"

"I don't understand." Which was true, except that Llesho thought he might be figuring it out, though he wished he had Lleck at his side to guide him through the twists of what began to take on the outlines of a game of Go played by masters. He knew he wasn't up to the mettle of the players, but he suspected it would prove no easier to be a stone.

The overseer carefully brushed the burned edges off the parchment and rolled it again. Markko picked up the seal, which he had lifted whole with his knife, and held it over the candle.

"If you feel ill again, come to me," Markko said as he watched the wax of the seal soften. "You are too valuable to our lord—as a gladiator in training, you understand?—to rely on superstitious old women for your care."

A scent like illness, but with more of death in it, clung to the air in the overseer's cottage. It tickled a warning at the back of his nose, and Llesho determined he would have to remain very healthy from now on. He nodded, willing to agree to anything if it would get him out of the cottage.

"Just so we understand each other." The overseer pressed the seal back into place over the ribbon on the roll of parchment and handed it back to Llesho. "You never stopped here," he instructed, "and I never saw this."

Shaking, Llesho took the scroll. "But, honored sir, Bixei has seen me. Won't he tell the others?"

"You needn't worry about Bixei. At least," Markko added with a sly smile, "in the matter of my secrets." Dismissed, Llesho bowed and made his escape to the practice yard. With a deep breath to settle the trembling that had started in his whole body, he tried to set his mind to the promise he had made to the ghost of Thebin's minister, Lleck.

As the youngest prince of Thebin, Llesho knew he'd been born a stone in a game whose board spanned whole kingdoms. He'd been swept from the board once already, and he didn't relish the idea that he'd been put into play again without knowing if he was cast as the white or the black. He wished, badly, to rest his fears and questions and promises on those broad shoulders Master Den had offered. Even a stone in a game he does not understand wishes to survive, he figured, but the people Llesho trusted were disappearing at a rate that did not bode well for any new advisers he might adopt. For now he would keep what secrets he possessed.

When he put the scroll into Den's hands, therefore, he told him only that no one had seen Kwan-ti, and did not mention his audience with Overseer Markko. Master Den did not speak of his errand, or what the healer's absence must mean. He returned the scroll to its place among the clean shirts without looking at it, and picked up a rake that looked very much like the muck rake that Llesho had used in the pearl beds. This one had smoother, rounded ends to the tines. "You use this to agitate the water and stir up the shirts," Master Den explained. "Not too energetically, or you will tear the fabric, but enough to keep the cloth moving, so the dirt doesn't settle back again."

The technique was easy to pick up after seasons in the oyster beds, and gradually, Llesho relaxed into the work. Almost, he could believe that the interview with the overseer had not happened. Almost, he could believe that Kwan-ti the healer was not a witch.

Chapter Seven

LLESHO discovered that he actually enjoyed laundry duty. Den taught him the simple tasks of washing and hanging and darning and sizing with a wellspring of patience that reminded him of Adar, who had been much thinner, but who shared the love of humble work. "If a digger of ditches receives a pittance for his service to the land, how much more must a king serve his people to merit the honors they bestow on him?" Adar had asked. When Llesho was six, spending a chill afternoon in the mountain clinic, the answer had included a broom.

Master Den had lessons for him as well, which he taught through the stories he told as they worked: stories with a moral Llesho was supposed to understand but usually didn't. Neither of them minded much, since the stories were interesting anyway. When the time came that he needed the lessons, they both knew Llesho would figure it out, like he'd learned the mopping and the laundering, and the prayer forms before breakfast.

Den himself was a puzzle. Everyone in the training compound bowed to the washerman and called him master. He led prayer forms every morning, and the most skilled among the fighters came to Master Den for instruction. None of his stories touched on the master's own history, although the names of many famous gladiators wandered through the tales. Master Den told his tales with an air of authority, as one who had seen the events and knew their actors, which Llesho supposed he must have done. After all, when the compound emptied for the competitions on the mainland each month, Master Den disappeared with the fighters. He wasn't doing laundry at the games; that came back in stinking bales to be cleaned and mended on Pearl Island.

Llesho could not imagine anyone of Master Den's girth fighting in the arenas, but he'd never seen the man bested at hand-to-hand either. When Llesho asked about his master's place in the stories, however, the launderer would shake his head and insist, "They are only tall tales, boy," as if Llesho had let the famous names distract him from the purpose of the story. Which, he eventually figured out, he had.

For all his skill, Den worked at one of the lowliest jobs. So had Adar, of course, cleaning up the slops of his patients with his own hands. And Shokar, eldest of the princes, had worked the land as a farmer when their father had not needed him for statecraft. That Master Den was involved in Pearl Island's own narrow struggles of statecraft seemed clear. Before the old minister, Lleck, had died, he had taught his young prince enough of strategy to understand that Overseer Markko played some game of power and nerves with the humble teacher, but why or with what stakes he could not guess.

In a lot of ways, Master Den reminded Llesho of Lleck, though the old minister, like most Thebins, was short and slight with a round bronze face and Master Den was tall and pale as the belly of a whale, with a shape like a mountain. Like the minister, though, Master Den spoke most softly when his words were most valuable and taught using stories that meant more than they appeared on the surface to be. Over the months he spent in the laundry, Llesho came to believe that, like the minister in the longhouse, Master Den hid a whole life and identity beyond the washing vats and drying lines. When he asked the older gladiators questions about the master, however, he discovered that no one knew anything about his past. Den had always been a part of Lord Chin-shi's stable of fighting men, according to the oldest of the active gladiators. Master Jaks might know more of the washerman's history, but when Llesho considered asking the weaponmaster, he decided that his answers might cost him more than he could pay for them.

In spite of his unsatisfied curiosity, Llesho found that he actually enjoyed the three months he spent in the laundry. His lessons in combat kept his mind as well as his body sharp, and during their time in the steaming washroom, Master Den was starting to fill the great gaping hole in Llesho's defenses where Minister Lleck used to stand. Llesho didn't fool himself that his teacher felt the same devotion to Thebin and its prince that old Lleck had. If it hadn't been for hand-to-hand practice, Llesho would have believed Master Den liked him.

Standing in the shade of a billowing length of cloth on the drying lines with Bixei and the other novices, however, Llesho concluded that the teacher must surely hate him, and simply hid it well during laundry duty. If he could have figured out the problem Master Den had with him, Llesho would have changed it. But the harder he tried, and the better his skills became, the more he met with the sharp side of Den's tongue.

"Don't think, boy! Move! A decent opponent will have you on your arse before you decide to hit him at all." A shift of his weight, a flip of one wrist, and Master Den had demonstrated the fault by dropping Llesho to his knees. Then he moved on to Bixei, and his tone softened; Master Den played out the same move, but slowed many times so that the students could see how the wrist twisted and how a nudge with the side of one foot brought the man down. "Good," Den said, and slapped Bixei on the back while Llesho seethed.

He had thought that his swift improvement would win him the praise of his teacher, but in fact Master Den ignored him much of the time, except to correct him for imperceptible flaws in his technique, while calling upon Bixei to partner him when the master wished to demonstrate a new combination. Llesho had stopped trying to impress his teacher weeks ago, and found that the forms came even more easily now, when he *didn't* think. If Master Den had shown some appreciation of his skill, the students might have shaped their attitude toward him around their teacher's good opinion. But as Master Den became more disapproving, his classmates became more distant. Llesho could have ignored the others, except for Bixei.

Bixei had two things which Llesho did not: Stipes, and his work assignment as Markko's messenger and servant. He protected both against the newcomer, and Llesho could not convince him, no matter what he said or did, that he wanted neither Stipes' attentions nor the favorable eye of the overseer. The laundry suited him just fine, and he preferred girls.

His move to the laundry had come to him with deceptive casualness, just a word at the end of a practice session as if nothing important had happened at all. Llesho was therefore unprepared for the way his whole life seemed to shudder and tilt on its axis when Bixei arrived late for instruction with the announcement, "His Honor the overseer wishes to summon the novice Llesho to serve him for the coming cycle,"

Expressionlessly, Den bowed to acknowledge the command, which Llesho himself heard with dread. Llesho would take Bixei's position with the overseer, while Bixei himself would rotate to weapons. With one announcement, Llesho made two enemies: Bixei, who had already passed through weapons repair, resented his loss of position. And Radimus, who should have rotated to the overseer's office, likewise resented his return to mop duty.

"I am content to work in the laundry," Llesho said with a humble bow, his eyes downcast to hide his very real fear at the change. Since his first days in the compound he had avoided the overseer's cottage, which had terrified him from the start with its vague sense of watchful evil. Since he had seen the witch-finder skulking around it, he'd put a face and a reason to his dread. And it was Bixei's task assignment, or had been. The other boy was not pleased.

However much of this Master Den understood, he said nothing, but pointed out with an arched eyebrow, "Lord Chin-shi is not in the habit of giving slaves their choice of assignments. One does, however, have the option of taking up one's task with a beating or without one."

"Without, Master. I apologize for my pride." Llesho fell to his knees and knocked his head into the sawdust of the practice area. Master Den accepted the apology with a small bow and broke the class into partners to practice the most recent lesson, Llesho found himself alone and staring into the face of the golden boy, Bixei, who glared back with a cold glitter in his eye. It was worse even than Llesho had guessed.

"Are you going to strike me down with your witchcraft, pearl diver, or will you pretend to use the arts Master Den teaches?" Bixei asked, his arms folded across his chest. So much for the overseer's opinion of him.

"I am no witch," Llesho stood up to face his accuser.

"Witch," Bixei repeated. "Everyone knows you consorted with a witch who now stands accused, and that you use the magical powers she taught you to conquer your opponents rather than fight fairly." Bixei meant more than the training exercises: he was furious to have lost his position in the overseer's office. Llesho thought he might even believe the charge, which frightened him more than his opponent's jealous fury.

Witchcraft had an evil reputation in the camp. Llesho had attempted to warn a hunted witch and had spoken to spirits. But his own present danger meant nothing: Llesho reacted to the taunt with all the rage and the pain of a lifetime of losses knotting his hands into fists. His home was gone, his brothers scattered, his sister murdered. And Lleck was dead, nothing left of him but his demanding spirit. Kwan-ti was gone, disappeared just ahead of the witch-finder, though only the gods knew how she had escaped. Without realizing it, Llesho had reached out to Master Den for the kindness he had lost, but his teacher watched him as if he was one of Master Markko's experiments, and said nothing in his defense.

"Lord Chin-shi has put a bounty on her head, and you will be next. You will burn in her place."

"No!"

Technique fled in the face of Bixei's shattering denouncement. Looking into the eyes of his opponent, Llesho felt in his blood that it had come to a killing moment between them. He reached for his accuser with his fists, not to knock Bixei down or control him or even kill him with one clean blow. He wanted to tear the golden boy apart with tooth and claw, to stomp his flesh into a pulpy stew in the sawdust and rip the pieces into shreds when he was done. But his rage made him clumsy; Bixei deflected his blows, though he had to struggle to match the insane speed with which Llesho attacked.

"She's not a witch," he growled, and landed a blow that knocked the wind out of his opponent.

Bixei had been waiting for the moment, luring him

in, and even while Llesho was glorying in the feel of his fist impacting on the body of his foe, Bixei grabbed the extended hand and twisted his arm, flipping him on his back with an elbow in his throat.

Llesho thrashed on the ground, ignoring the pressure on his throat and trying to get a purchase on his enemy.

"What is she, then—your lover?" Bixei taunted while the students, and Master Den himself, looked on. Llesho shook his head, though the motion ground sawdust into his hair and brought Bixei's elbow closer to strangling him. "Teacher," he gasped, and Bixei smiled as though his teeth were a trap that was about to close on its prey. "Are you her sorcerer's apprentice, then?"

"She was good," Llesho insisted. He knew Bixei would consider him a fool if he said any more, and probably the other boy would be right, but he had to try and make him understand. More important, he had to make Master Den understand. "She taught me that goodness could still exist in a world I thought the gods had abandoned." He looked into Bixei's eyes when he said it, willing the other to understand something he didn't quite understand himself.

"It's a shame she didn't teach you how to fight." Bixei pressed his elbow tighter against Llesho's throat, so that he stopped his opponent's breathing altogether. Then, having won his point, he released Llesho and offered him a hand up. "She tricked you. Evil rules the world now, and she is part of it."

It was hard not to believe, with Thebin under the power of the Harn and everyone he had ever loved dead or lost to him. But the spirit of his mentor had given him hope. So he took the hand Bixei offered, and kept hold of it when he was on his feet again.

"First we take the world back," he said, "and then we see who helps us and who tries to stop us." It felt like a pledge, and Bixei met his level gaze uneasily.

But he offered his other hand, and they clasped, their wrists crossed in the age-old symbol of allegiance. Neither knew exactly where it would take them, nor how soon the unspoken pact would be tested. They both knew in their hearts, however, that this was something slaves did not do. Llesho expected Master Den to stop them with a lecture on humility, but their teacher watched them with the look of a merchant toting up a trade in his eyes.

Where success had earned him fear and envy, Llesho's failed attack on Bixei had created a wedge of sympathy that Llesho was quick enough to foster with occasional well-timed lapses in his performance. Master Den no longer watched him with faint disapproval, and even pulled him out of the class on occasion to demonstrate a new move or an improvement on an old one for his classmates. Llesho hated his new assignment in the overseer's service, but even that worked to his advantage. If Bixei was still jealous, at least he didn't blame Llesho for his lost status. They might never be friends, but Bixei seemed to have abandoned the feud he'd waged since Llesho arrived at the compound. He could imagine their uneasy alliance more easily in moments like this, however, when Bixei was not present.

Llesho was sitting on the covered porch with Radimus and Stipes and others from his bachelor group and dinner bench. His chair was tilted on two legs so that the narrow, slatted back rested against the coral blocks of the barracks wall. Bixei was still at work in the weapons room, so Llesho had relaxed more than usual, listening to the others trade stories when Radimus, who leaned against the railing to watch him, asked, "Why a trident? That's a tall man's weapon, like the pike." Radimus, who preferred the pike, pulled himself away from the railing and straightened to his full height as a demonstration.

He'd let his guard down too soon, Llesho realized, setting his chair down on its four legs with a thump. He knew, without being told, that the story of his choice of arms in the weapons room must remain secret. Llesho had never again seen the woman who watched him there, nor, since that day, had he seen a knife like the one she had slipped up her sleeve. But he remembered the tension that had clenched in his stomach, and it was doing a return appearance under the curious eyes of his companions. Better to offer a lesser truth, he decided.

"The food the pearls like best tends to settle to the bottom. You use a long-handled rake to stir it up." He twitched a shoulder to acknowledge that they would surely find his story foolish.

"My quarter-shift mates and I would imagine our rakes were tridents, and would wage mock battles in the water. We stirred up the bottom enough with our scrabbling feet, and had more fun than applying the rake head to the muck. When Master Jaks told me to choose my weapon, I felt awkward with a sword, but the weight of the trident isn't much different from a muck rake, and it didn't feel all that different to my hand, after I got used to being on dry land."

"I'm sure Master Jaks can find you a muck rake if you really want one," Stipcs suggested.

The gladiators laughed companionably at the story and Llesho wondered if they each had an equally harmless tale to tell—a sword that reminded one of a cooking knife, or a stave that felt to the hand like a drover's prod. Llesho's explanation quickly turned into the story of how his friends saved his life, though he didn't mention the spirit of his old mentor—

"And I came out of the water dangling from my ankles like a pig on its way to slaughter. Foreman Shen-shu took one look at me and said, 'Where's your rake, boy?' and down I went again, sputtering with water up my nose to look for the damned rake."

"I'd think after that you would avoid the trident like it had a pox on it," Stipes remarked.

Radimus laughed. "Master Jaks probably assigned him the trident because he knew it was the one weapon that Llesho wouldn't ever lose."

Llesho expected the joke when he told the story, but this was close enough to the truth that Llesho flushed when he heard it—not because the rake was the reason he chose the trident, but because Jaks had directed him to the weapon and away from the knife that went to his hand like an extension of his body. He laughed quickly enough that his companions took the blush for embarrassment, except for Stipes, whose sharp gaze seemed to be looking for a chink in the face Llesho wore. He wouldn't find one, Llesho determined. The trick to keeping secrets, he had learned from Master Den himself, was in not appearing to have secrets at all. So Llesho smiled blandly at the gladiator and greeted Bixei when he joined them on the porch.

" 'Lo, Bixei," he said. "You just missed the story of my heroic rescue from the briny deep."

Stipes kicked a chair over to where his partner stood, but Bixei rejected the offer, while giving Llesho a warning about his tale: "Don't tell Master Den, or he will start having practice in the bay," he said, rubbing at a bruise the size of a coconut on his backside. Finding a support post to lean on, he grumbled his complaint, "That would make as much sense as hand-to-hand combat practice."

Madon, who still worked with the novices at weapons exercises, heard the complaint as he passed on his way to a group of senior gladiators spending their rest time with similar stories on the other side of the porch. "We can all see that you have a deep-seated aversion to unarmed combat, Bixei," he drawled. "Something

Master Den really should get to the bottom of, before it interferes with your training."

Llesho tried to keep a straight face, but even Stipes was snickering, and Bixei's face turned so red it seemed to glow of its own light.

"I don't mind taking an injury in practice if it teaches me something useful," he complained heatedly, and Llesho wondered which injury angered Bixei more: the one to his fundament, or the one to his pride. Since he was the only person on the porch who was smaller in build than Bixei, and had also been present when Master Den dumped Bixei in the dust, he decided not to ask. Bixei wasn't giving anyone a chance to interrupt him, however.

"Weapons practice makes sense, even equipment I don't plan to compete with. A gladiator has to understand his opposition and use that experience to devise a counterattack. If a fighter should lose his own weapon during a battle, he has to be able to pick up his enemy's and take the day with it. But an unarmed man cannot compete against a trident or a pike, or a sword. So why does he waste our time with something that will never serve us in the arena?"

"You think you cannot save your life with your own hands?" Madon rolled up the right sleeve of his shirt to reveal a jagged scar that tore across his biceps. "The shaft of my pike had a flaw in the wood and broke with the first thrust of my opponent's sword. His second thrust did this."

"See—" Bixei tried to interrupt, but Madon silenced him with a look.

"I lured him inside my guard, and when he was committed to the strike, I did this—" with his left hand Madon lashed out in the "striking snake" move, stopping with the curved knuckles a whisper of air away from Bixei's throat—"I suffered a wound, but the swordsman died."

Llesho stared at the man in wonder. Madon *looked*

like a hero out of legend, so he didn't know why it surprised him to discover that the gladiator was a hero in fact. Bixei, however,had turned deathly pale in contrast to the recent angry blush.

"Of course, that was pure luck." Madon relaxed his striking hand and examined his knuckles as a warrior checks his weapons for nicks or damage from the damp. "Master Den teaches hand-to-hand as an exercise in concentration and control; I wouldn't depend on it to save my life against a trident. Unless, of course—" he gave the younger group a sly smirk—"Llesho here was holding the trident!" Laughing, he left them to return to his own bench where more laughter soon rippled out from the senior warriors.

Bixei was seething, but Llesho gave him a smug grin. "We'll get him," he said. "Just give it time."

Bixei didn't want to listen, but with Stipes to tease him out of his brooding, he soon entered into the outrageous plans for taking down the hero. Mud featured in many of their plans, as did pig slop. The night ended in laughter. Llesho would not hear that sound again for a very long time.

Chapter Eight

THE new assignment worried Llesho. Bixei had run errands to Lord Chin-shi's house, fetched and carried about the compound, and he'd even been sent to bring Llesho himself from the pearl fishery, all tasks for someone who had earned Master Markko's trust. In the first week of his new service, the overseer hadn't said anything about Kwan-ti, or witchcraft, but he hadn't sent Llesho out of the compound with messages either. Instead, Llesho swept out the workroom and the front office, then, up the narrow staircase, he scrubbed the loft room under the steeply sloping roof where Master Markko slept.

The sleeping chamber held a single bed and two chests. The larger held the robes and breeches that Llesho was forbidden to touch; a servant came daily to tend Master Markko's personal needs, and disappeared again to whence he came before the minor sun had joined its fellow in the sky. The second, smaller chest, was covered in a thick layer of grime and stuffed in a dark corner under the slanted eaves, as if forgotten. But when Llesho had tried to explore it, he found the chest bound with straps and locked with a complex mechanism he had never seen before and could not open.

Llesho brought his master breakfast and a midday meal from the cookhouse, and sat in a corner when he wasn't needed, trying to fight the boredom that pulled at his eyelids. With an occasional bland smile that didn't help at all to hide the calculation in his eyes, Master Markko watched for Llesho to slip up and reveal himself as a witch. Since he knew nothing of magic, he couldn't very well slip up there, which was almost a relief after his trial in the weapons room. So he wasn't prepared for the day when everything changed.

The overseer was not in his office when Llesho arrived, so he called out, "Master Markko, sir?" as humbly as he could.

"In here, boy."

Llesho followed the answering summons to the back room, where he found Master Markko setting tightly lidded jars on a shelf over the worktable, marking each one off on a list in front of him. Llesho recognized some of the herbs hanging in bunches from the beamed ceiling, but others were foreign to him. He remembered Kwan-ti's warning about touching the unknown plants in her healer's pouch—the cure for one person might prove to be a poison to another—so he kept his hands clasped behind his back.

"You have finally honored us with your presence," Markko said, his voice dripping sarcasm.

They spent the day mixing compounds that Llesho did not recognize. While Master Markko had his midday meal, Llesho cleaned the noxious herbs and powders from the worktable with a basin of pure water and a soft cloth. After weapons practice, Llesho took instruction from Master Markko in the storing of the various potions they had prepared that day, and then learned how to bury the cloths they had used in a patch of dead weeds behind the privy. Poisons, then, and likely no use for healing any sickness but that of life itself. When he had carefully cleaned his hands, Llesho returned to the workroom and presented himself to the overseer, his head bent in due humility.

"I am finished, Master, if there is nothing more?" He sincerely hoped the overseer would find no late tasks for him to do before he left for his dinner and a well earned bed. On this day, however, Master Markko measured Llesho from top to toe with his cold, cold eyes.

"Your predecessor in the post was born of slaves, and knows nothing but Pearl Island," Markko said. "And, of course, he does not consort with witches. He valued the small freedoms his work with me afforded, and his gratitude made us friends as well as slave and master."

The overseer gestured at the shelves crowded with jars full of potions and herbs. "I had hoped that if I revealed to you our mutual interest, we would likewise become friends. But that hasn't happened, has it?"

Llesho said nothing, but he had begun to tremble, fine tremors that shook him from his heart to his fingertips. He knew the identity of Lord Chin-shi's witch now: Master Markko could kill him for that knowledge at any time.

"I *am* sorry, but if you are going to be of any use to my real work, I will have to be more cautious with you." As he said this, Markko set an iron collar around Llesho's neck, and clipped a chain to a link at the throat. Then he took the other end of the chain and snapped it into a ring newly set into the floor in the corner of his workroom.

"I have informed Master Jaks that I will need more of your time than I found necessary when Bixei worked for me. I did not accuse you of malingering at your tasks, of course. But it must be understood that one so new to my needs would not work as quickly or as efficiently as another more experienced in the ways of this compound. You will, therefore, make your bed here."

Llesho felt the protest well up in his throat, but he clamped his jaw and refused to let the words escape. He was, after all, in the power of a master poisoner and a witch. And so he waited to see what Master Markko had in store for him.

"Good." The overseer noted the wary question in his eyes and smiled. "You are learning already.

"I have sent word to the washerman that you have withdrawn from unarmed combat training to spend more time learning your duties." He sneered when he mentioned Master Den. "You may, of course, continue weapons training for the arena, provided you keep silent about all that passes in this house. If you say a single word that does not relate to the weapon in your hand, however, you will remain here, tethered like a dog the day and night together, until you have given me what I want from you."

Llesho didn't have what Markko wanted—the whereabouts of Kwan-ti and the secrets of her witchcraft—but he could die of Markko's efforts to extract them, and he had truths of his own he could not share with this man. So he obediently dropped his gaze, letting none of his terror show. The overseer gave him a cold, cold smile, and abandoned him to his chains and the darkness that would become his whole existence.

As days passed into weeks, Llesho's silence deepened. When Markko grew tired of his stubborn refusal to speak, he would beat Llesho with the chains that bound him to the workroom. The beatings grew less insistent as he learned to perform each task to the overseer's satisfaction, however, and Llesho began to hope that Markko was tiring of him. Then he woke drenched in sweat from a terrifying dream he could not remember, his muscles in knots and his guts heaving.

"How does that feel?" Markko crouched down beside him, tapping with a stylus a muscle in his thigh that lifted in a rigid band at the touch. Llesho could not answer, could not breathe, could not catalog the ways and places that he hurt.

"Good." Markko tapped the stylus on Llesho's belly, triggering a spasm that twisted the body beneath it in wrenching knots of agony. "We'll just see how this goes."

He sent word to the practice yard that Llesho had fallen too ill for prayer forms or weapons practice. When the worst of the pain had subsided, he ordered delicate food from the cookhouse which he fed to Llesho by hand, all the while asking, "Was it undetectable, boy? Did you taste the bitterness in the brew?"

His voice a rusty whisper, Llesho broke his silence to confirm what he already suspected: "What did you do to me?"

Master Markko shrugged a mock apology. "You were never in danger. I gave you a small dose, so that I might judge the efficacy of the intended measure. On the whole, I think our client will be well pleased with our work."

No less than he had imagined, the overseer worked a side business as a poisoner. It made no sense to Llesho that a man who feared a simple healer, as Lord Chin-shi seemed to do, would keep a man of Master Markko's trade in his service. He suspected that as a poisoner's test subject, he would not live long enough to puzzle out an answer to the question.

Markko let him recover before trying out any new compounds on him, but Llesho grew wary of eating any food from the overseer's hand. He weakened, but feared murder if he told anyone the dark secrets of the overseer's back room. Weapons practice might have tested his resolve, but the apprentices now worked with the general population. Llesho often found himself matched with men he did not know, who were not inclined to talk if he had wanted to.

Most of his day he spent bound to the workroom, tending to his master while he mixed the potions for which strangers called at the back window after the suns had fallen. When the day's work was done, Llesho lay in silence, waiting to discover if another poison from Markko's bench had found its way into his food. Exhaustion warred with fear of the vaporous creatures of twisted evil that had come to inhabit his dreams, but his body could not long endure the strain, and he slept despite his fervent desire to remain on guard for his own sleepless rest.

The dream began with the memory of white light: the sun rising through the gates of heaven, pierced the eye of the needle atop the Temple of the Moon and shed its light on the gleaming mud walls of the Palace of the Sun. Along the path of light walked the goddess with the face of his mother, her smile as warm as the sunbeams she trod upon. Llesho reached for her, and fell into a garden rich with fruits and flowers.

"What are you doing on your bum, little brother?" Shokar strode between rows of plum trees, a rake over one shoulder, and stopped to lend him a hand to rise.

"I thought you were dead," Llesho told him.

The dream Shokar dropped his shaggy head so that his chin almost rested on his broad chest. "I thought the same of you."

"The rest of our brothers—are they here with you?"

"Where is here?" Shokar's voice remained, but his thick farmer's body faded like a mist, and behind him Adar and Balar, Lluka and Ghrisz, and Menar, who was a poet, stood together, straining their eyes, as if they were searching, but couldn't see him.

"Adar!" he called out in his sleep; and, "Menar! I'm here!" But his brothers broke into a mist and tangled milky strands among the plum trees.

"Adar!" He woke with a start, tugging on the chain that ran from the collar around his neck to the ring in the floor. His brothers were gone, and Llesho was alone again with the terrors of the night and the worse nightmare of the waking world.

Llesho's body shook all the time now, and waking to another day in Master Markko's clutches, he wished that he had died beneath the bay, following old Lleck to a new life in the great cycles of creation. When he thought of the spirit that had come to him in the bay, the black pearl in Llesho's mouth throbbed like an aching tooth. Lleck and his gift both had been real, though neither offered much in the way of comfort. Llesho might buy his way free with that pearl, but Markko would doubtless take it from him if he knew about it. If he reported Llesho for theft, Lord Chin-shi would have Llesho's hands cut off. Or the overseer might use it for proof of witchcraft; Llesho would find himself burning on the pyre the overseer had planned for Kwan-ti.

It seemed that, with the pearl, Lleck had given him one more torment and Llesho wondered how much he was supposed to endure. He did not want to imagine a greater need from which the pearl was sent to rescue him, when the overseer was killing him hourly and by inches. Surrounded by Markko's poisons and the tools of his loathsome trade, he knew only that he could not reach any one of them to end his misery.

Markko had seen to that and Lleck, in his own way, had bound Llesho to this wretched life with the hope of an impossible quest. He wasn't alone in the world. He would find his brothers, if Markko didn't kill him first. Llesho wept until the tears had wrung out his heart, and when he slept again, the monsters came and pulled him down with them into the darkness.

* * *

Morning began like all the others since he had come to Markko's service. The overseer rattled his chain as he unlocked the collar. "Go," Markko said, the only word they shared before noon, and Llesho bowed deeply as he had been taught. When the overseer left the workroom, Llesho slipped into his shirt and pants to fetch his master's breakfast, a few dry rolls and a pot of green tea, which he placed on the desk where Markko was working.

Prayer forms had been his one comfort, leaving his mind blank and his body free among men he had come to count as friends and under the bright sun. As he weakened, however, his technique faltered. Llesho stumbled on the simple Flowing water form; in the weeks he had served the overseer his forms had become increasingly clumsy, as if the burden on his soul tripped him up at each move. Frustration brought him close to tears again, but no one laughed now. Radimus pulled him up from where he had fallen and brushed the sawdust off his back with reassuring pressure, but said nothing as his eyes slid away from the iron collar around Llesho's throat. Bixei, who had resented his own rotation out of the overseer's service, watched him with confusion, and even guilt in his eyes.

Llesho turned away; almost, he would rather remain chained in Markko's workroom than suffer the public exhibition of his humiliation. But Lleck was counting on him to find his brothers and win back his country from its conquerors, so he struggled to regain his sense of balance, and pushed through to the end, grateful when Master Den let his arms drift to his side in completion of the final form.

"Llesho—" Master Den called as Llesho turned toward the overseer's cottage. Llesho stopped, but did not turn around, and finally, with a deep sigh, Master Den released him, "Go, boy. Don't let me keep you."

"I wish I could," Llesho thought to himself. He risked a deep breath, thick with the smells of sawdust and sweat and sunshine, and a tension that grew more pungent each day, like monsoon weather crackling in the air. Bad times were coming for all of them, he figured, and he longed for the storm when everything would be overturned. For him at least, any change had to be better than what he had.

With a last gaze into the sky soft with morning haze, he ducked back into the stone cottage. Markko awaited him in the workroom, where he crushed some noxious element that released a sickening smell of rot into the air.

"I have to go out," he said, never stopping his slow, patient grinding. "But I will return before weapons practice is over, and I will want to speak to you."

A tremor passed through Llesho's body at that—more questions he could not answer, more threats. Markko would beat him, as he had in the past. But Llesho would tell him nothing.

Markko cocked an eyebrow at him. "You think you won't talk now, but you will." With a brush prepared for the purpose, he scraped the yellow powder into a shallow cup that rested on a tripod over a brazier filled with hot coals. Then he stirred the mixture gently with a silver wand for a moment before putting a lid on the cup. "Pour for me," he said, and Llesho picked up the pitcher of clear water and poured it over Markko's hands. The water ran into a basin that discolored in pinpricks of corrosion as the few stray grains of powder sank to the bottom. As Markko dried his hands carefully on a clean white cloth, Llesho noticed that the skin had mottled patches where the powder had found it, but the overseer ignored the tainted spots. "Dispose of these in the dead garden," he said, tossing the cloth over Llesho's arm.

Llesho cringed away from the cloth. The dead garden. Only the most perilous of Markko's elixirs went to the dead garden. Llesho took a second cloth and carefully wiped off the mortar and pestle that Markko had used to grind his ingredients, and set them aside to purify. He took both cloths and the bowl into a patch of garden where even the rankest weeds wilted in deathlike colors. A short-handled shovel set with its point in the ground marked the most recent burial place. Llesho took the shovel in hand and moved two paces, and then he dug a deep hole. First the cloths went in, and then the water. Then he scrubbed out the bowl using the freshly turned earth to absorb the corrosives that pitted the glazed surface already. When all of the poisoned materials had disappeared into the hole, Llesho rubbed his hands thoroughly with the dirt before shoveling it back into the hole again. When he was finished, he stamped on the ground to level it.

His work in the dead garden meant that Llesho was running late. He had a choice—food or weapons practice—that he'd had to make too often since Markko had called him into his service. As usual, he chose practice. Llesho ran as fast as he could and reached the weapons room just as the last group of gladiators filed through to select their weapons. Llesho knew them all. It surprised him a bit until Stipes passed him a small loaf of bread instead of his trident. No words passed between them; they might not know why, but his fellows had come to understand that Llesho's safety depended upon his terrible silence. Stipes' anger was clear, however, and tears that Llesho feared to shed choked him as he tried to swallow the bread.

Jaks watched him with eyes of stone, but a decision had been made; the master looked down at the small arms table, and Llesho followed the glance. For the first time since that day when the masters had tested him in the presence of the mysterious woman, Llesho saw the strangely shaped knife lying among the swords. He picked it up, feeling his body settle around the weapon, become a part of the weapon. Jaks nodded with a satisfaction so grim that Llesho shuddered.

Bixei looked at him with surprise. "You should have picked the knife before," he said, but Stipes put a hand on his partner's shoulder, his eyes wide with a question turning to certainty.

"You never saw the knife," Stipes told him. "Come on, Madon will be waiting. I'll spar with you today."

"Madon?" Bixei started to ask the question, but stopped, frowning, when Stipes increased the pressure on his shoulder. "Everybody else knows what is going on. Why not me?" he grumbled.

Llesho sighed, letting some of the tension go with the breath. "Not everybody," he said. "I don't understand it either."

Bixei seemed to accept that for the moment. He shook his head and muttered something halfhearted about favorites that brought a blush to his face when he looked at Llesho. Then he took up his own weapon and followed Stipes into the practice yard.

"Sit down." Jaks pushed a three-legged stool toward him, and Llesho absently tucked the knife into the cloth belt that tied his shirt. The belt split and fell at his feet along with the knife.

"Sorry." He flopped down on the stool and put his free hand over his eyes. "I can't believe I did that."

"I can." Jaks didn't smile. "A long time ago, you carried a knife like that in a scabbard at your belt."

"I did?" Llesho took a bite of his bread and chewed without thinking about it, giving his teacher his full attention. When he had swallowed, he asked, "So why don't I remember it?"

"I don't know." Jaks kicked another stool over and sat so that he faced Llesho, locking gazes with the youth. "It might hurt too much to remember."

Llesho gave him the snort that deserved. He remembered the Harn soldiers coming for him, his bodyguard dying, the weeping of women in the corridors as his captor carried him out of the palace. He remembered his father, dead with a crossbow bolt in his throat. How could the knowledge that he once carried a knife hurt more than that?

"You were very young when you were taken to the slave markets, weren't you?" Jaks asked him.

"Seven summers." He'd used the Thebin measure—trading seasons rather than the cycles of the lesser sun. Master Jaks seemed to understand anyway.

"And yet, you wore a knife—not just any knife but the ceremonial knife of Thebin. Someone trained you well in its use, too."

That scared Llesho more than Markko had managed to do. He wouldn't ask the question that terrified him—do you know who, *what,* I am?—but he thought maybe Jaks knew the answer to that better than he did himself.

"I think someone hid the knowledge from you, to protect you," Jaks said. "When it is time, you will probably remember it."

"Do *you* know what it is I've forgotten?" It took more courage to ask than he'd ever summoned in his too eventful life, but he held his teacher's gaze, implying the question: "Am I safe with this knowledge in your hands?"

As answer, Jaks took a sword from the weapons table and knelt on one knee before Llesho. He bowed his head, and when he looked into Llesho's eyes, his own burned with a fire of regret that stunned the young prince.

"We will not fail again," he said. He started to reach out, then withdrew his hand, veiling with downcast lashes something fierce and personal in his declaration.

"You were there," Llesho whispered, but when Jaks spoke again, he had set the question aside.

"Master Den has missed you. Let him take a look

at you, get a new belt, and come back here when he is done with you."

Llesho blinked, trying to catch up to the shifting conversation, but Jaks was speaking again, warning him, "Don't tell anyone what you know, or what you suspect. And watch yourself around Markko."

Llesho didn't need Jaks to tell him that. But Jaks was gone, into the practice yard where he snapped an order for Bixei to pick up his pike, and not to treat the weapon like a plow.

Llesho found Master Den in the laundry. The washerman took one look at the shirt hanging from his shoulders like the clothes on a scarecrow and sighed. "Eat your bread," he said, and pulled a band of cloth from a cubby. "Then wrap this around your waist." When he had done as he was told, Llesho followed Master Den into the private area where Den had taught unarmed combat to the novices. A wide sword rested against the fence; Master Den picked it up and took an attack stance.

"I'm taller than you are, and my weapon's got reach on you—what do you do?"

"Run?" Llesho suggested.

"Try it."

Llesho turned to escape, but before he could take a step, the flat of Master Den's sword came down on his shoulder. Den wouldn't hurt him. Llesho knew that instinctively. But the touch of the sword on his shoulder snapped him into the past, swords flashing, blood spurting. Llesho wanted to curl into a screaming ball, but a memory moved within him and he snarled, slipped under the sword and inside its guard, brought the knife up. He came to himself with the sword on the ground and Master Den's hand tight around his wrist.

"A longer reach is only useful when the opponent

stays outside of it." Den gestured approvingly to where Llesho's knife rested just below his own sternum, pointing upward. "To counter, move inside the reach."

A killing stroke. When Llesho realized what he had almost done, he dropped the knife into the sawdust and drew his arms tight against his chest. His face crumpled, but he'd learned not to weep in the daylight, so he waited with his eyes grown huge and glittering with shock.

"It's all right, child." Master Den wrapped him in a huge hug that soaked the trembling out of him like a warm blanket.

"No damage done," Den whispered. "We had to find out how much you had learned before you came to us." He pulled Llesho away just far enough so that he could look into his student's eyes. "Trust me. I won't let you hurt anyone by accident."

That last was said with an ironic twist of a smile, and Llesho wondered who the teacher expected him to hurt on purpose. But he'd leave that for another day. He was simply too exhausted to think about it now. Den read the droop of Llesho's shoulders, and tousled his hair.

"Clean the knife," he said, "and we'll have a little visit." Den did not seem to mind that Llesho said nothing; the teacher had enough stories, and when he finally heaved himself back onto his feet with the announcement, "Weapons practice is over; you'd best get back before you are missed," Llesho returned to the overseer's cottage with a lightened heart.

His mood sank almost immediately. Markko stood behind a thin, narrow-eyed man in the robes of a noble who had taken the overseer's place behind the desk. In an elaborate chair that Llesho had never seen before sat a woman, much older but with robes as elaborate as the man's. Had they come to expose him?

Llesho wondered. Markko smirked, fawning over the seated noble, but said nothing about his suspicions.

"Lord Chin-shi and his consort have come to ask you some questions of their own about the witch, boy."

"No one is going to hurt you, boy." Lord Chin-shi sat forward with his forearms crossed in front of him on the desk and his hands tucked into his wide sleeves. "Can you tell us your name?"

Behind their lord, Master Markko nodded his head, signaling his permission for Llesho to speak. Briefly, Llesho wondered if Lord Chin-shi would recognize him by his name, or if he knew it and was waiting only to trap him in an untruth. But Markko knew already, so lying wouldn't help.

"Llesho, of Thebin, my lord," he answered and bowed low, first to the lord behind the desk, and then to his lady in her chair.

His lordship nodded encouragingly. "That didn't hurt, did it?" he asked with a thin smile. "Did you know that Thebin is infamous for its witches, Llesho?"

"It is not so in Thebin, my lord. Or was not when I was taken away." Llesho looked at him curiously. "Perhaps it is the Harn witches who give Thebin its reputation?"

Lady Chin-shi frowned at him. "Don't be impertinent, boy. You can still be hanged for treason."

"I am sorry, my lady." Llesho bowed deeply again, "But I don't see how I can be of any help. I know nothing of witches or witchcraft." And he would have sooner believed that Master Markko was a witch than Kwan-ti.

Markko himself made a bow, and spread his hands as if to demonstrate a point. "I beg your indulgence, my lady, but I did mention that the boy was soft in the head. He is small, but physically quick, and Thebins are known for their endurance, which will make him an asset in the arena. But Llesho had a mishap in the pearl beds, and it addled his brain. He can answer simple, direct questions, but he has little subtlety of wit."

"If you can do better with the boy, please do so." Lady Chin-shi waved a hand impatiently. "I plan to watch unarmed combat practice this afternoon, and wish this matter disposed of."

"I presume that means I will be spending the evening alone?" Lord Chin-shi asked her, and Llesho ducked his head, trying to pretend he wasn't there. But Markko walked over to him and lifted his chin. "The boy is quite innocent," he commented over his shoulder. "It comes of a simple mind. Perhaps his lordship would like to question him at his convenience—alone?"

"A good idea." Lord Chin-shi rose from his chair, and beckoned with long fingers. "Come with me. We will leave my good wife to her shopping."

Chapter Nine

OUTSIDE the palisade a sumptuous sedan chair and its six bearers waited for Lord Chin-shi. The bearers stood in rigid silence until their lord had entered the chair and arranged its brocaded curtains to keep out the dust. Then, in one smooth motion, they lifted him to their shoulders and carried him up the hill. Llesho followed: through the last of the dense wild vegetation on the hillside, across the wide lawn smooth as a knotted silk carpet, to the gracious house of three levels that rose above the island on the hilltop. The procession stopped at an entrance overhung by elaborately curled eaves and flanked by two guards of stony countenance and ready weapon. A house servant ran forward to open the curtains of the sedan chair, and Lord Chin-shi alighted.

Llesho followed his master into a hall decorated in mother-of-pearl and pale-veined jadeite, with characters painted on the elaborately carved ceiling. The palace at Kungol had looked very different, but the sense of quiet power was much the same. So were the guards. He could have warned Lord Chin-shi how fragile such peace could be, that his guards would serve little purpose if he found his palace overrun by the Harn. His experiences since the slave market had shown him that no one listened to a child and a slave, however, and that he was safe as long as they didn't notice him.

A servant dressed as elegantly as a duke came forward and bowed low. "My lord," he murmured softly.

"I will show our guest the way myself," Lord Chin-shi said, "We will be in my apartments—send someone with a tray, and then make certain I'm not disturbed." He dismissed the servant, who bowed low over a smirk that made Llesho squirm.

Up a broad flight of stairs, down a corridor, and up again, this time they climbed a more modest staircase, each level flanked by its set of matching guards. Lord Chin-shi finally stopped at a room with a bed that looked big enough to sleep the entire barracks in the gladiators' compound. Llesho dug in his heels. He knew how little choice a slave had in matters of his personal disposal, but if he made himself inconvenient—

Lord Chin-shi did not stop at the bed, but went through the room to a door in a corner. "Come along," he said, and slid the inner door open before motioning Llesho forward with a distracted wave of his hand. Llesho obeyed, and found himself in a workroom like Markko's but brighter, and with a fresher scent that reminded him of Kwan-ti. He smiled without realizing that he had done it.

"Sit." Lord Chin-shi pointed to a chair in the corner, by an open window with wildflowers drying in the breeze. Llesho studied the floor, but found no iron rings for chaining slaves, so he sat, and found himself relaxing into the pleasure of the sun on his face, and the soft wind carrying the fragrance of the drying flowers on the air. Lord Chin-shi himself pulled up a three-legged stool and sat, his elbows propped on his knees and his chin resting on the arch made by his clasped hands. He studied Llesho with a thoughtful, but not threatening, frown. It reminded him of Master Jaks, and their conversation in the weapons room. Llesho suspected that it would be too easy to forget that he was a slave and in danger if his identity were known to this man. He tried blinking stupidly, but Lord Chin-shi just laughed softly.

"Who are you?" he muttered to himself, not waiting for an answer he would not receive. "A slave from the pearl beds who sits as comfortably in a nobleman's laboratory as he does on a gladiators' bench. A boy smart enough to know that playing the idiot is better protection than the wisdom of the sages."

"I don't play at the idiot." He felt the need to defend himself on that one, even if it did mean he was talking. "People who ask stupid questions should not blame others if the answers they receive are stupid as well."

"Fair enough." Lord Chin-shi stood up and wandered over to a clean table on which a beaker full of a red liquid stood. "I shall try not to ask any stupid questions."

Llesho blushed with embarrassment, and no little fear. He hadn't meant to insult Lord Chin-shi, but knew his lordship might easily have taken it that way. The lord laughed, softly again, as if at a private joke, however. It seemed strange that the lord of the island should need to dissemble in front of his own slave, which Markko was as surely as Llesho or Master Den. Before he could set to serious work on the question, however, Lord Chin-shi had returned, carrying the beaker, and all humor was gone.

"Do you know what this is?" He handed Llesho the beaker with deadly seriousness.

"Blood?" Llesho waved a hand over the beaker to waft a safe measure of the fumes under his nose. "Not blood," he corrected himself. "It smells like seaweed."

"Not stupid," Lord Chin-shi commented. "It is called the Blood Tide in the *Chronicles*." He took the beaker into his own hands then, and stared at it with the grim fascination that Llesho reserved for the soldiers of his enemies. "It invades the living sea like a goiter and smothers everything that lives there. Already, the pearl beds are dying. Strange creatures of the deep wash onto the bloody shore and gasp their dying breath out on the land."

Lord Chin-shi's voice dropped, thick with sorrow. Llesho remembered the water dragon that had saved his life, and imagined her lying dead upon the beach. He bowed his head, sharing a new grief with his master. So the lord's next words slipped under his guard like a knife:

"Master Markko swears that the Blood Tide is the curse of the witch, Kwan-ti. He says we must find her, and burn her, to restore the balance of heaven and earth. Only then will the sea flourish again."

"If you are looking for curses," Llesho snapped, "I suggest you seek closer to home and leave your healers to their work."

"Master Markko also says that you disappeared from the compound on the day the witch vanished, and that you know where she has gone."

Lord Chin-shi's fingers had gone white where they wrapped around the beaker of red death. Llesho winced, and the lord frowned in concentration, carefully easing his grip on the beaker and setting it on the floor between them. "Tell me where she has gone, boy."

Llesho grew dizzy with sudden fear. He had forgotten his position; lured by his master's calm, and a sense of well-being that rested lightly in the sunny room, he had forgotten how dangerous the man in front of him was. Lord Chin-shi could have him put to death with a word, and no one would deny his right to do so. But the pain for the dying sea in the man's eyes was real. Llesho reached for that fact: Lord Chin-shi loved the sea, and it was dying, and Lord Markko had told him that Llesho could make it stop. The only problem was, he couldn't.

"I don't know where she is," he said. "I did try to warn her, that's true, but she was gone before I left the compound. No one saw her escape, or would tell me anything about it." He sat up straighter in his chair as he had seen his father do countless times in the palace at Kungol, though he scarcely remembered that now, and willed his lord to listen and believe him. "Kwan-ti is no more a witch than you are, and she would no more hurt the sea."

Lord Chin-shi gave a guilty start at that and Llesho followed his glance to the beaker on the floor. He did not comment on the similarities he saw, but added, "Kwan-ti is a healer. And you need a living healer a lot more than you need a dead witch."

"It seems, however, that I shall have neither." Lord Chin-shi picked up the beaker and rose from his footstool. He led Llesho to the bedroom, where a tray waited on a carved and lacquered table. "You must be hungry—take what you want. For your personal safety, you will spend the night in these apartments and return to the compound in the morning. Rest—no one will disturb you. Do you read?" Llesho nodded, though he realized afterward that he had given too much away with that admission. Lord Chin-shi did not seem to notice Llesho's sudden unease, but pointed to a third door in the bedroom. "There is a library through that door if you are bored." With that the lord took a small plate of fruit from the tray and returned to his workroom. Llesho found himself alone with the food-laden table and the big, big bed.

He succumbed first to the lure of the food: thin pancakes filled with scallions and herbs, cold dumplings and hot ones, rice and millet and pig flesh in half a dozen different sauces, fruits that grew wild on the island, and fruits carried down the long trade roads from far inland. Tea, and a liquor that burned and made him cough and his nose run.

With his stomach full, he wandered around the bedroom for a while, examining the country scenes lacquered into the doors of the wardrobes and running fingers lightly over the carved figures of jade and crystal and ivory scattered on fragile tables about the room. He avoided the big bed in his explorations, turning to the library when he had exhausted all the other niches and alcoves in the master's chamber.

He had resisted the pull of the library, because the memory of books always brought with it the image of his mother, and he did not want Lord Chin-shi to find him weeping over some philosophical text. But it was still early in the night, and only the one door remained. He slid it open along its groaning track, and stepped inside while an invisible hand seemed to wrap cold fingers around his throat. A desk filled the center of the room, with a low bench behind it and a soft, thick carpet in front. Beneath the room's single window, shaded with an oiled parchment screen, a low, cushioned divan sat next to a table with an oil lamp on it. Shelves covered the walls from floor to ceiling of a narrow gallery that wrapped the room and continued the shelves right up to the roof, where a square of tiles had been removed for a wide glass pane. A stout wooden pole propped open a trapdoor that would cover the sky window to protect the contents of the library during storms.

The shelves on the floor of the library were divided into wedges and stuffed with scrolls of parchment and rolled bamboo and heavy silk. A room in his mother's library had likewise been fitted for rolled documents. Thebin stood at the top of the world, where heaven and hell touched on the heights of the mountains that held the capital city of Kungol. Through its mountain passes all the trade of the living world traveled, most especially that of learning. His mother had loved knowledge. To the king's mock astonishment, she had asked only gifts of writing from the many travelers who stopped in the capital city to rest on their journeys to foreign lands. Like his mother, Llesho had prized the books and scrolls and rolls that came to them from distant lands. He'd loved to touch them, despite the many attendants who shooed him away while they polished and dusted.

Someday, his mother had promised, he would learn to read them all, as Adar and Menar had done. A healer and a poet, those brothers had teased that he must be the mathematician, since their mother was the priest, to make the set of scholars complete. Time had seemed limitless then, of course, and he had looked forward to many years of study with his mother and his brothers. Then the Harn came.

Llesho took down a rolled bamboo and spread it out on the desk. Lord Chin-shi's library, he decided, had too much dust, too much light. Perhaps he would warn his master of the damage the elements could do to fragile materials: already, the images were fading. In the upper right-hand corner, in pale shades of blue and green, the artist had depicted a mountain waterfall, with a deity sitting cross-legged at its foot. A small tripod stood in front of the deity. In one hand, he held a short wand over the tripod and in the other hand he held a vial of pills. Ancient characters filled the scroll beneath the image, as beautifully painted as the work of art. Unconsciously he curled his fingers away from the surface, however. He could not read the text, but he recognized the symbols of an alchemist in the painted decoration, and took it for a warning. No one was what they seemed, Lord Chin-shi least of all. With a wistful sigh he rolled the bamboo up again and replaced it in its place on the shelf. Had the Lord of Pearl Island read every one, he wondered, or merely hoarded them like a dragon on a heap of bones?

Up an open wooden stair he found the gallery ranged with codices: books with wooden covers or leather ones, with long sheets of paper folded between them like a fan. Llesho took one down, then another, but the letters ran together, foreign and impenetrable. Another, another. A low shelf in the far corner of the gallery held some dusty books and Llesho went to them with a noise of disgust in his throat for their shabby treatment. When he reached to take one in his hands, his fingers tingled, and when he lifted it from the shelf, he saw the dust clung only to the parts that one could see from the ground. In all other respects, it appeared that someone had treated the codex with great care, oiling the leather-covered boards and cleaning its pages.

Its pages. Opening the codex, Llesho wept. The writing was Thebin. At first, he could not read it at all, for he had forgotten what he had learned before the raid, and the letters looked different on paper than they did scratched into wet sand on a beach. But gradually, the shapes came into focus on a prayer his mother had taught him when he was a baby, and had recited over him every night before he left her side for bed, until the day his world had ended.

Mother Goddess watch this child
Protect his eyes from cruelty
His fingers from mischief
His heart from sorrow.

Let him grow in courage
Search with wisdom
Find his destiny.

The book had many prayers, which he read with his fingers as well as his eyes, touching each page with reverence and love. A few he knew, most he did not, for they concerned matters of an adult nature unsuited for the child who had lived that life of temple and palace. Prayers for a lover, a dying parent, to bring children or the thaw. As he read each one, he heard his mother's voice, softly just for his ears, or ringing to fill the Temple of the Moon, where the goddess dwelt. And he remembered her in her robes and glory, looking out across the city square to the Palace of the Sun where her husband waited for her to come to him in darkness.

It hurt too much to remember, but he could not bring himself to return the book to its shelf. Curled over it, his fingers caressing the prayers he found there, he fell asleep. Sometime in the night, he felt hands lift him and arms carry him down the wooden stairs. When he was settled on the thick mattress, those hands covered him in blankets of silk, and went away again. The comfort seemed to leech the last bit of strength from his bones, and he let himself sink back into nothingness. For the first time since Markko had dragged him out of the barracks to spend his nights on the workroom floor, Llesho slept long and deeply, without nightmares.

When he awoke, the sun was shining in his face and he felt more at peace than he had since the Harn raid. Then he realized that he was no longer alone. Lord Chin-shi slept like the dead on the far side of the bed. More to the point, however, the lord's consort stood with her face inches from his own. Startled, Llesho jumped to a crouch in the middle of the bed, cursing himself silently for letting his guard down. From that position he could see that Madon, his face completely blank of expression, stood in the center of the room, while Radimus lingered in the hall with a smirk on his face and a small but weighty money pouch swinging from his outstretched fingers.

The disturbance must have awakened Lord Chin-shi,

who rolled over, muzzy-lidded and bumped into Llesho, who leaped again, this time for the foot of the bed and escape.

"Don't let him send you back without your tip, Llesho." Radimus gestured with the swinging purse, and Lady Chin-shi followed this advice with a cackling laugh that set Llesho's teeth on edge. He looked to Madon for an explanation, but the gladiator turned his head and pretended not to see.

"Fighting and dying you do for nothing, because they own you," Radimus explained. "Anything else, they pay for. It's tradition."

A system that paid a slave for eating and sleeping, but not for the hard work he did every day seemed strange to Llesho, but Lord Chin-shi reached over and picked something up from the floor next to the bed.

"Don't ask questions," he said. "Just take it and go." And he thrust four silver coins into Llesho's palm.

Llesho scrambled from the bed, grateful for the permission to leave more than he appreciated the coins. Even as he was heading for the outer hall, however, he yearned to turn and enter the workroom behind the far door instead. Madon was watching him carefully, but said only, "You haven't had breakfast."

Before Llesho could speak, Lord Chin-shi's voice interrupted from the bed. "Take whatever you want."

Madon bowed. "Thank you, my lord," he said, and filled his hands with pieces of fruit and bread, which he passed to Llesho as they walked. When they were halfway down the hillside, and well away from anyone who might overhear, Madon asked him, "Are you all right?"

Llesho thought for several minutes before he answered. Finally, he had to admit, "I don't know. I wish Kwan-ti was here."

"The witch?" Radimus asked him, and Llesho shook his head. "Not a witch—" and he was getting tired of saying it—"but she may be the only one who can help us."

"Don't say that around Master Markko, unless you want to take the witch's place at the stake," Madon warned, and gave him a sharp smack on the back of his head for emphasis.

"I know," Llesho answered. But he still wished for the healer. He was not so blinded by Lord Chin-shi's kind manner that he put his owner's interests in the dying pearl beds ahead of his own survival, but he knew that the healer would not allow the sea to die if she knew about it. He kept his mouth shut around the news of the Blood Tide, however, adding it to the well of secrets he carried about with him.

In the afternoon, as Llesho joined the gladiators in armed contest, training with the trident, word came down from Lady Chin-shi. The school would travel to Farshore on the mainland for the next competition. And at Farshore, the school must be broken up, its competitors and students sold to pay his lordship's debts. The pearl beds, men whispered to one another, had given up no pearls since the witch, Kwan-ti, had set her curse upon them before disappearing into the wind.

Llesho was going to the mainland. He would win his freedom there, and find his brothers, and free Thebin, as Minister Lleck had bid him. He did not know how he would do all this, nor how he would reach Thebin, at the end of the thousand-li road, but here, today, he had silver in his pocket, and he took his first step.

PART TWO

FARSHORE

Chapter Ten

LLESHO watched the shoreline grow closer as Lord Chin-shi's yacht cut through the Blood Tide. When he began his training, he had thought only of what would come after, reaching the mainland and searching for his brothers as a lowly freelance. He hadn't known how terrified and proud he would be to don his own first set of leathers: tunic and leg wraps and cuffs to protect his wrists. This was his first step on the road to freedom and to the salvation of his people and his country. And all he had to do was kill other men, slaves like himself, for the pleasure of their masters.

Someday soon it would come to that, he knew; he would kill or die for the money in his purse. As a novice with but the rudiments of his training, however, Llesho would not fight in this, his first competition, but would participate in a demonstration of armed combat forms with the trident. But he knew he was saying good-bye to the only life he had known since his seventh summer, when the Harn had sold him in the marketplace. Until he had come under Overseer Markko's scrutiny, he'd had a hard life, but not a bad one. He'd had friends, and work, and the security of a guiding hand, first in Minister Lleck and Kwan-ti the healer, and later in Master Den, and even Master Jaks.

Now all of that was changing. Lleck was dead, Kwan-ti vanished. The pearl fishers had gone to market weeks before, unable to earn their keep in the dying oyster beds. He could smell the rot rising from the dead fish and the bodies of larger creatures floating on the surface of the sea, and he prayed the Flowing Water form in memory of the water dragon that had saved his life so long ago it seemed, though it had been less than a full turn of the seasons.

Alone on the polished aft deck, he moved into the prayer forms that evoked the earth to calm him. Today, Lord Chin-shi would offer his gladiators for sale in the arena. They would compete, and Lord Chin-shi would take home purses or lose them on the contests, but he would return to Pearl Island without his gladiators. Some of the men he thought of as friends would die today, and others would find themselves traded far away. Llesho wondered who would waste their money on an untrained boy with no prospects of height or weight ahead of him. He remembered the lady in servant's clothing, who had watched while he revealed too much of himself with the short spear and the knife, and shivered. Whatever her interest in him, he hoped it did not include his performance in the arena.

"You will do fine, you know." Master Jaks wandered up from belowdecks and braced himself with both hands on the guardrail. Looking out toward the land, so that Llesho didn't have to meet his eyes, he added. "Lord Chin-shi will make sure of that."

"I don't understand him," Llesho acknowledged. "He did not bed with me, although he wanted the others to think it."

He stole a glance at Master Jaks, who did not look surprised at this revelation.

"He was kind to me." Which had confused him, after weeks as the overseer's prisoner.

Master Jaks nodded sagely, but did not turn his head to look at Llesho. "As kind as a man can be who would burn a witch, and who sets his slaves to fight and die in the arena for his pleasure."

"I thought that was Lady Chin-shi's doing," Llesho admitted. The Lord of Pearl Island had fed him gentle foods, and put him to bed when he had fallen asleep on the floor among the books. His workroom had none of the smell of death that soaked into the very walls of the overseer's cottage. He could not reconcile in his head the man who had shown him such mercy with the buyer and seller of children in the marketplace.

But Jaks shook his head. "Lady Chin-shi certainly takes an interest in the gladiators," he said, "but she is less interested in the arena of combat. Lord Chin-shi would not, perhaps, wish to see his people come to harm, but like many good men he has a weakness for the display of martial skill, and too much liking for a wager."

"Is he really afraid of witches?" Llesho wondered what had drawn the lord's attention to him, he who had little skill as a warrior and none at all for magic.

Jaks's answer didn't help. "I think his lordship knows that there are wicked practitioners of the dark arts in the world, and would protect his home and lands from them. But if you mean, did he believe Kwan-ti to be a witch, I think not."

"Then why did he summon me?" Llesho knew why Lady Chin-shi had wanted Madon and Radimus delivered to her quarters, and he figured most of the servants in the lord's house thought his lordship had the same kind of interest in him. Except he hadn't—he'd asked some questions, and then left Llesho to his own devices while he worked.

Master Jaks turned away from the sea to study Llesho's puzzled features. "I don't know," he said. "Perhaps he has learned that you are more than you appear. But if that is so, I don't know why he didn't sell you to your enemies, or kill you for the threat you pose."

Llesho said nothing. He knew what lay in wait for him if the enemies of Thebin knew he was alive and planning to take back his homeland. If Lord Chin-shi meant him harm, or even wished to squeeze the greatest profit out of him, there were simpler ways than putting him in the arena. Jaks might be able to tell him, but in all the summers since the Harn had invaded Thebin, he had never spoken aloud his identity. Whatever his masters knew or guessed of his origins, he could not relax the habits of caution to confide in them. So he looked out across the water, where his future drew nearer with each surge of tide and wind. A hundred questions bubbled up behind his tongue: How did you come here? What do you know about me, about Thebin? What am I to you, and to the lady who watched too closely in the weapons room? And who is she, and what is she to me? But he could not ask. With no choice that he could see, he kept his silence and waited for a moment when the questions might be taken out and examined in safety.

"The city is called Farshore," Jaks told him, accepting that their personal conversation had ended. "Shan, the capital province of the Shan Empire, is almost as far inland as Thebin. Generations ago, when the first emperor reached out across the land, his grasp ended here, at the place they called Farshore. It was thought then that the world ended at the sea, which must go on forever, since no eyes could see a farther shore. The sight so terrified the emperor's armies that the generals had to stand behind them with spears and swords, and cut down their own men who tried to flee. Later, of course, the empire learned to build boats that could dare the ocean crossings. But the city still carries the legacy of those old times in its name.

"How far is it to Thebin from Farshore?" Llesho asked him, and Jaks gave him a warning glower.

"Too far. Don't even think of escaping."

Llesho didn't tell him that he thought of nothing else, and had since the ghost of Minister Lleck had appeared to him in the pearl beds. Everything since that day seemed to conspire to move Llesho farther along the path to Lleck's goal. He had no doubt that he would go home, and felt the presence of the gods at his back, like the wind in the ship's sails, with each step toward his objective. But he still wondered how long the journey would be.

"It's like a dream," he noted, looking out toward the many-tiered city. The sharply steeped roofs and elaborately curled eaves grew more solid as they approached.

"Shan is bigger," Jaks said, and Llesho wondered if he realized that he was revealing himself in his words. "The palace there is one of the great wonders of the world. But Farshore has the courage of its contradictions. The tallest buildings you can see are its temples—see the roofs, rising like umbrellas over the city to protect it from the might of the sea, while to the west, the city huddles beneath the walls that protect it from the invasions that invaders always fear. In all the years of the empire, Farshore has never relaxed its vigilant watch on the West."

Thebin lay to the south while Shan, the jewel at the heart of the empire, lay to the north. Both were west of the easternmost city of the imperial expansion, and between them lay the Harn. Llesho wondered if the Farshore walls were meant to beat back an invasion from the Harn, or were a reminder to the conquerors who had come out of the north. Who did Farshore fear most?

The yacht nudged its way into its berth at the bustling

docks, and Llesho found himself suddenly surrounded by the gladiators come above decks to watch the boat reach shore. Jaks was nowhere to be seen, but Master Den moved among the gladiators, dressed, for a change, in loose breeches that came to his calves and an equally loose white shirt crossed over his ample stomach and held in place by a wide cloth belt woven in the colors of Lord Chin-shi's house. Master Markko, in the long robes of his rank, commanded the forward deck to sort out his gladiators and begin the procession to the arena, setting the cymbal players and the drummers at the front, and ranking the fighters from foremost to least, where Llesho found himself paired with Bixei.

"Good luck," Llesho said as they stepped onto dry land. Bixei nodded his acknowledgment, but said nothing.

He, too, was wearing his first set of leathers, but today Bixei would participate in his first true fight in the arena, an equal match, and specified to first blood rather than to the death. Both boys knew that accidents happened in the heat of battle, and sometimes not accidents but old scores found themselves settled on the bodies of the fighters. Llesho did not speak anymore, busy trying to maintain the stern features and fierce demeanor that the marching gladiators affected to draw the poorer audience to the upper decks. As they paraded, they left the warehouses and docks behind them, and wound their way through narrow streets with ramshackle houses pressing over them, lined with cheering and jeering mainlanders. Finally, they came to a wide thoroughfare that crossed the city like an arrow, smooth and straight, and lined with trees laden with fragrant blossoms. Bixei jabbed him in the ribs when his eyes grew too wide, but Llesho could not tear his gaze from the riches spread out before them on the thoroughfare. On each side, set back as if the road were not worthy to touch the hem of the rich garments on either side, tall iron gates barred high walls. Inside the private barricades, the wealthy of Farshore waited out the heat of the day and defended themselves from their own poor at night.

At the city limits farthest from the sea, the thoroughfare ended at the arena, an open area of sand and sawdust, with tiers of benches rising on both sides, and boxes for the owners and wealthy patrons ranked at each end. The Governor's box, and the Mayor's box, at the center of the long north axis were covered with bunting of red and yellow and the whole was ranked around with banners on poles like soldiers standing at attention. Jaks led the procession of Lord Chin-shi's house to the eastern rank of benches, where a wooden door both tall and wide lay open to admit them. Under the seats, Llesho discovered, were benches for the fighters, and barrels of water, and heaps of bandages. Against the wall next to the open door rested a stack of leather slings stretched on long poles, to carry the wounded and the dead of their house off the field. Llesho's stomach clenched at these reminders that the arena was a game only to the spectators: to the men who fought, it meant life or death.

Once they had stowed their small bits of personal gear under the benches, Master Den led them out onto the field where the contests would be held later in the afternoon. Lifting his arms in an offering to heaven, he began the prayer forms, and the gladiators fell into their ranks and followed through the cycle of prayers to water and air and earth and fire, to sun and moon and rain and falling snow, to the growing millet and the rice floating in paddies of water, to the lotus rising out of the muck, and the snail on its belly and the butterfly, sacred among gladiators who likewise grew in secret to burst forth in glory for one day, and die.

When they were done, and Master Den had dismissed

them with a low bow, Master Jaks broke them up into pairs and teams to practice weapons forms. Llesho went through the exercises with his trident, leaping and stabbing, twirling somersaults over the axis of the staff of his weapon. After the workout, Master Jaks gathered the gladiators together for the blessing of the warriors, and then he led them under the stands again, where a trestle table had been set up and laden with the most blessed foods to sustain a man in combat. Llesho had no appetite. His terror at all that was strange and new around him clenched his stomach tight, but he filled his plate anyway, like the others, so that no one would know that he was afraid.

Bixei sat alone, looking out onto the playing field with grim determination setting his jaw. Llesho would have shared his own plate with his sometime enemy, but Stipes already carried an extra for his partner. So he followed, and took a seat on Bixei's left, leaving the right side for Stipes while putting himself at a distance from the object of Bixei's jealousy.

"You'll be fine, Bixei. The cooks say that we will compete against the house of Lord Yueh today." Stipes ate for a moment. "Lord Yueh lost many of his best men to disease last season. He wishes to make a number of purchases from Lord Chin-shi, and has wagered each match to the first blood only, as he does not want the merchandise too badly damaged." He noted Bixei's glum face and added, "Of course, as a novice, the rules of your own competition already demanded blood only. But it means I don't have to win my own bout to keep my head."

Bixei nibbled on his bread, but finally threw it down in disgust. "Lord Yueh is not the only buyer in attendance, and he needs experienced fighters to rebuild his ranks, not a novice fresh from his first fight." He sighed deeply. "I knew, even before Lord Chin-shi lost his fortune, that one or the other of us might be sold or that in some future bout one of us might have to watch the other die. But Master Jaks sets all of his lordship's bouts, and he never sets old partners against each other in the arena. Lord Yueh is known to do so to increase his sport."

"I won't ever kill you in the arena, boy." Stipes cupped a hand around the back of Bixei's neck and gave it a companionable shake. "And you'll never be good enough to take me, so we are safe as can be."

Bixei didn't snap at the bait offered in that taunt, but abandoned his plate to stand by the open door and watch the audience filing in. Llesho watched him go, so intent on the tension screaming from every muscle that he forgot Stipes until he dropped a hand on Llesho's shoulder. "It will be all right," he said, but Llesho could tell from the pensive frown that the gladiator didn't believe his own words. Overhead, the sound of eager feet and the settling of benches marked the presence of the growing crowd.

"Lord Yueh wants to buy Master Jaks," Stipes said. "He must believe that Lord Chin-shi's trainers are better than his own. We must prove to him that they are."

With that last word of encouragement, he dropped his half empty plate on the trestle table and went to join Bixei at the open door. They argued for a moment, and then wandered away together into the shadows. Llesho watched them go, then he put his own plate back and strolled outside to watch the crowd pour in. Soon, the riser in front of each bench was filled with stamping feet as the crowd clapped and shouted for the games to begin.

Suddenly, a hush fell, and a dozen trumpeters at the entrance to the arena heralded the coming of the governor. Master Markko called to Llesho to take his place in the grand march around the arena, the crowd's last chance to view the competitors before betting closed. He responded in a daze. Thebin did not have such games, and Llesho had not, in his entire life, seen so many people gathered together in one place for anything. Soon he would be a part of it. He took his place at the end of a line. At a tone that Master Markko had been waiting to hear, the gladiators of Lord Chin-shi's house strode out into the sunlight and the sawdust.

A shout went up from the crowd, and colorful banners waved at them. At Master Markko's command, the gladiators all raised their right hands over their heads and shook their fists in the air as they circled the arena. The competing houses of Farshore's lords did likewise, some marching in the same direction and some parading counter to them. The two lines met at the center of the arena, and spread out to face each other. A fanfare sounded again, and the gladiators dropped to the ground and kowtowed deeply, with their forelocks in the dust, forming a living promenade of backs offered to the master's lash. As he passed, the governor flicked the ceremonial willow switch above the fighters with words like "courageous," and "valiant," and "dauntless" to exhort them in their battles. In this manner the governor made his way to the official box, with his consort following.

By tradition, the youngest gladiator to be blooded on that day would receive the favor of the governor's consort. Accordingly, the lady lifted Bixei to his feet; with a smile, she set her ribbon upon his right-hand sword and a kiss upon his lips. "Win for me, today," she said.

Llesho recognized that voice, and when he looked up from his ceremonial kowtow, a woman with a cool face and eyes much older than her years was offering a smile of the mouth only to Bixei, who blushed red under the attention. It was the woman who had tested Llesho with the spear and the knife in the weapons room on Pearl Island. She showed no recognition of Llesho, but returned to the side of her husband, who invited the audience to rise and meet their new hero,

Bixei of the house of Lord Chin-shi. The governor bowed graciously to the young champion of his lady, who held out her hand to him. Bixei touched his forehead to her fingers in the ceremonial pledge, to fight valiantly in defense of her favor. The couple bowed to the mayor and his guests, and ascended the carpeted risers to the official box. Together the governor and his lady took their places beneath a silk umbrella with many tiers in recognition of their rank.

The trumpeters again blew their fanfare, and the directors of the bout met between the two mock armies to assign each man to his predetermined foe. Llesho had only a moment to see Bixei drawn away to face a boy much the same age and build, but carrying a pike. "Fight inside his reach," Llesho thought to himself, but then he was called to attend to his own demonstration. He would go through the motions of a bout, while his opponent would do the same. Because of their youth and limited training, however, they would not engage each other with their weapons, but perform the exercises that would display their skill level at a distance of a few paces from each other.

His opponent carried her knife and sword far differently than Llesho did in his own training, but he quickly picked up the rhythm of it, and moved to counter and attack with his trident. She was good, and Llesho wondered again why Lord Chin-shi trained no women fighters. She came at him, a little close on the next pass, and he could see that she knew his attention had wandered, and that it annoyed her. "Like dance," he thought, and picked up the tempo of his action, meeting her next slash with the move of his own devising he had practiced to smoothness—using the staff of his trident to support his vault, he leaped high over the sword and landed lightly behind her swing. Her right side was exposed to the blades of the trident he brought to bear with lightning swiftness.

A ripple of applause followed the move and Llesho

looked around, to see who of the more experienced fighters had landed the admired blow, but his opponent was bowing respect to his strike, before taking her stance again. This time, she moved inside his reach, and rested her knife lightly against his gullet. "Not so pretty a move," she conceded, "But you would be dead, and not merely blooded, if I chose to press my advantage." She did put a little more pressure behind the knife, and Llesho froze, immobilized by the surprise, and his fear that she would truly slit his throat if he should move.

But her arm seemed to sag a little, and so he knocked her hand aside, feeling the burn as the point of the knife scratched its way across his throat, and when he felt the metal clear of his body, he brought the trident up, set to skewer her on its three sharp blades. When he stepped back to clear her reach, she followed him in; she twisted and ducked under his weapon and swept one foot in a low circle in front of her, taking Llesho off his feet. He bounced back again before she could immobilize him with her sword, grateful for Master Den's lessons in unarmed combat. The hand-to-hand forms worked just as well, he realized, in combination with his weapons training.

Their bout came to a halt when a monitor blew the whistle. Llesho analyzed his bout as he had been taught. His opponent sucked in air harshly, in broken gasps, while Llesho still breathed normally, if perhaps a little faster than he would at rest. Clearly, if the monitor hadn't stopped the bout, he would have won it, thanks to his Thebin capacity to control his breathing. But in a true bout, the results would have been less certain. He would have had first blood when he caught her by surprise with his trident leap, but she would have taken the prize in a fight to the death.

He thought that, as he had tricked her with a move she had never seen, she had also tricked him with her sex. He didn't expect a woman to be able to fight, and had not guessed that her fight would be different from a man's, going for the quick kill rather than a wearing down and wounding over the course of an extended bout. Her strategy made sense, but he knew he would have to work hard at making up for his lack if he wanted to survive in competition to the death. And his plans called for staying alive long enough to win his freedom.

He bowed respect for his opponent's skill, as she bowed to his. Then she shocked him to the core of his being when she turned to the monitor and said, "I'll take him. Lord Chin-shi may have his price; have him cleaned up and delivered before the victory banquet tonight."

The monitor bowed low and she departed, not toward the staging area under the benches, but up the carpeted risers to the governor's box, where she took a seat behind the governor and his consort. Llesho could see that she was still breathing heavily, and she wiped her arm across her brow to clear the sweat streaking it, but the governor made no comment, just raised a sardonic eyebrow at her and leaned over the balustrade to examine her purchase. Llesho stared up at them, dumbly, until the monitor of his bout took him by the arm.

"Come on, boy, you are in the way here," he said, and nudged Llesho in the direction of the door that would take him into the staging area below the eastern benches. "Wait with your own house; someone will be down to fetch you soon enough."

The smell of blood under the benches almost covered the smell of sweat and the body's fighting humors discharging in vapors off the skin of the gladiators. Bixei lay on the trestle table. A bandage already wrapped his forehead, with an extra thickness over his right eye and a piece of leather clenched tightly in his teeth. He grimaced as Master Den cheerfully bound up a wound on his thigh. "That pretty face of yours will heal clean," Master Den commented as he wrapped the thigh with bandages, "But your new master will enjoy playing 'find the scar' with this one. And I hear that he tips very well."

Stipes, with no sign of injury on him, was glaring at Master Den, but before the bandaging was done, a guard poked his head through the open doorway to announce the arrival of Lord Chin-shi with Lord Yueh. Lord Yueh entered with the boastful swagger of a man who judges his own courage and skill by the success of his gladiators, and who has thus proved himself victor. Lord Chin-shi followed with the desperate look of a man who has lost everything on the toss of a coin, and now asks himself how he could have been so foolish as to gamble against a crooked house.

Their two very different consorts followed behind: Lady Chin-shi boldly examined the gladiators in their various states of nakedness and coverings of bandages, while the much younger Lady Yueh trembled in the wake of the party, her sad eyes downcast and her cheeks red with embarrassment. She looked, Llesho thought, like a slave newly brought to market, shamed by her newfound station in life and unsure what that station would bring. Her husband was pointing among Lord Chin-shi's gladiators. Master Markko took his place at the side of his lord to record the sales.

"Madon, of course." Lord Yueh pointed to the gladiator, who sat resting his weight on the table. The wound on his chest had not yet been tended; it leaked a red trail down his naked torso, but he did not seem to notice it. "He is mine by the rules of the contest," Lord Yueh added with a smirk. He seemed to enjoy Lord Chin-shi's discomfiture.

Madon stared at his new owner with predatory aggression stamped upon his jaw, the reek of battle and blood stinking on his damaged muscles, and Llesho permitted himself a tiny shudder. The rules of gladiatorial combat were clear. If, in a fight to the blood only, a competitor should kill his opponent, his own person was forfeited to the offended lord, whose property had been taken from him in the unfair contest. In such cases, the primary owner had the right to punish his slave for the damage he did to the honor of his house, and for the cost to his house of the gladiator's flesh and skill. It was not unusual for the offending gladiator to die of his chastisement, with his dead body presented to the holder in payment of the blood debt.

It made no sense. Madon, rumor had it, had refused all deadly combat since a lord with too many gambling debts had shifted the order of his own gladiators to give Madon a battle to the death with his old lover. They were both good, and his lover had not died quickly of her wounds. After days had passed, when Madon had realized that she could not recover, he had sneaked into his opponent's encampment at the outskirts of the city and had slit her throat while she thrashed in the fever nightmares that boiled her brain. Madon had returned half mad, the barracks story was whispered, and had recovered slowly. He had made a vow that he would not kill again, and it was said that Lord Chin-shi had honored his vow. As little as he knew Madon, Llesho was sure that he had not broken his vow deliberately. Lord Yueh, it seemed, had found a way to break it. And now Madon belonged to Lord Yueh.

His lordship, however, had passed on from an examination of his prize. "That one," he said, pointing at Stipes. He skipped over Pei and Bixei, seemed not to notice Llesho at first, and gestured at Radimus. He sorted out the rest of the stable in a manner that seemed unthought but left him with the most experienced of Lord Chin-shi's stable, and Radimus, whom he chose with a thoughtful gleam in his eye. Of his selections, only Madon had a wound.

Lord Chin-shi examined the list, and nodded his

head in agreement. "Radimus will need further training before he is ready for a fight to the death," he said. "He is full grown, but new to the arena. Madon should do well as a teacher, he has studied with Master Jaks and Master Den for many years, and knows their techniques well. And in terms of skill, he is the equal of Jaks, and inferior only to Master Den in hand-to-hand."

"I intend to fight Madon in the arena for at least another year or two, if he survives," Lord Yueh said with a twisted leer. He clearly expected Lord Chin-shi to kill the man who may have ruined his chances at financial recovery with the deathblow in the arena. "I had hoped to purchase the teacher, Master Jaks, to replace the trainer I lost to the fever."

"You should have spoken sooner," Lord Chin-shi bowed apologetically. "Another bidder made an offer, and the contract has already been signed."

"Am I come at an inopportune time, honored sirs?" A stranger dressed in the sumptuous layers of a lord, but with a thin gold chain around his throat that marked him as the personal slave of some great house, joined the lords at their negotiations."

"Not at all," Lord Chin-shi gave the stranger a thin smile. "I was just explaining to Lord Yueh why Master Jaks is not available for his purchase."

Lord Yueh bowed deeply to the newcomer, and his face when he straightened had grown very pale. "I understand completely, my lord."

"Still and all," the stranger said with a pointed glance in Madon's direction, "you seem to have done well enough for yourself today, Yueh."

"Yes, my lord." To Llesho's astonishment, Yueh bowed again, almost groveling at the feet of the wealthy house slave.

"Who is he?" Llesho whispered to Stipes, who answered, "With luck, you will never find out."

If luck were involved, Llesho thought, he was in trouble. Lord Yueh, who had ignored him in his first hunt through the ranks, had returned to face Llesho. He was now looking at him with the hungry eyes of a wolf. "Throw the boy in and we will call all debts canceled," he said. "Not worth the value of the debt, of course, but he appeals to me."

The stranger cast a careless glance at Llesho in his corner. "I think he's mine as well," he said, and with a last look around caught sight of Bixei with his wounds newly dressed on the table. "And I'll take this one on his excellency's authority. We can arrange the fee at your convenience."

Bixei started to rise, but Master Den pushed him back down again. "The boys are much in need of further training before they will be of use to you," Den said.

The stranger gave him a soft smile. "And they don't like each other much, do they?" he asked.

"Not really."

"Time will change that." The stranger bowed to Master Den, but gave only the slightest tilt of his head to the lords, who returned the gesture of respect.

Lord Yueh hesitated, as if he was hoping the other man would leave first, but the stranger waited patiently. Finally, Lord Yueh made another bow.

"Send my property along before nightfall," he said of his purchases. With a last furtive glance at Llesho, he darted out from under the benches and made his way to his box, leaving his consort to follow as best she could.

Lord Chin-shi's competitions were over, his house crashed about his head, but other houses remained, offering higher stakes. Lord Yueh was well known for betting death matches.

When Yueh had gone, Madon leaned heavily on the table for a moment before pushing off and presenting himself to his lord. He fell to his knees, his eyes round as copper coins with the shock, and bowed his head, waiting for his fate.

"His man was drugged to induce madness, you know." The stranger addressed Madon, who made no move to rise or answer the stranger.

"On balance," the stranger continued, "his excellency decided that the lives of two men could not stand in the way of peace in the provinces."

Lord Chin-shi set his hand on Madon's shoulder, but addressed the stranger: "The Blood Tide?" Llesho recognized that soft tone, saw the wheels within wheels in Lord Chin-shi's eyes and the ironic half-smile that accompanied the stranger's shrug.

"The source of that plague, like the source of fever in Yueh's compound, remains hidden to us."

"It was none of my doing," Lord Chin-shi assured him, and the stranger shook his head. "I thought not. Had it been so, of course, the peace would have been broken, and we would be at war, and not sharing entertainments together." He spoke ironically, his eyes fixed on the back of Madon's head, but his false smile held a warning. The governor had weighed the life of an honorable gladiator and the fortunes of one lord against the threat of war in the province, and he had decided. He put out his hand, and into it Lord Chin-shi placed the strangling rope.

"Relax," the stranger said, and tipped Madon's head back to rest upon his leg. Then with a movement Llesho could hardly follow, the cord was around Madon's throat, and the harsh "snap" of bone cracking cut the air like an ax. "I'm sorry," the stranger said, and when he released the cord, Madon fell dead at his feet. "Have him delivered to Lord Yueh with my regards."

He strode to the open doorway without looking at the body on the ground, but turned to Master Jaks almost as an afterthought.

"Bring the boys," he said, and for a moment he was nothing but an absence in the light of the doorway. Then he was gone.

"Who *is* he?" Llesho whispered to Stipes in the frozen silence that followed, but it was Master Jaks who answered the question. "His name is Habiba. He is the governor's witch."

Lord Chin-shi shivered in his heavy robes. In the corner, his consort wept silently, her arms around Radimus' neck. "We are ruined," she moaned into the sweaty leather that covered his chest, "Ruined. And that Yueh is to blame."

"Not Yueh," Lord Chin-shi corrected her carefully, his attention fixed on the body at his feet. "But fate. What man can wage war against his fate?"

"A true man," his wife taunted him. She let her arms slip from Radimus' neck, trailed questing fingers down his arm until she could catch his hand in hers, and led the gladiator deeper into the shadows.

Lord Chin-shi did not look away from Madon's body. "You'd better go," he said, with a vague gesture at Master Jaks. The teacher bowed, though his lordship did not see him or anything beyond the inward vision of his eyes as he walked away, into the sunlight of the arena.

"Damn," Stipes muttered. He helped Bixei to stand and supported him to the door, where Master Jaks commanded a leather sling and two servants to carry him. Llesho followed through a silence that had grown thick in the air, like a coming storm.

As he moved from under the benches and into the sun, he saw a splash of brightly colored silk crumpled in a scarlet pool that was quickly soaking into the dust. Lord Chin-shi lay dead, his own knife buried in his heart. Master Jaks did not stop, or even slow his small procession, but stepped past his former lord without looking down. Llesho swallowed hard, and tightened his hands into fists, but followed the lead of his teacher. Bixei gritted his teeth, but the tears leaked from his eyes anyway. Llesho didn't know if he cried for Stipes, gone from his life forever, or for his lord, now dead at his own hand, or for the fate that awaited them in the wake of the governor's witch.

Llesho almost felt guilty that he still had Master Jaks, his teacher, while Bixei had nothing. But Minister Lleck had taught him to plot his course and then take one step toward it at a time, focused on that one step completely until the next. He was a gladiator, more or less, and off Pearl Island—steps one and two on his path—but an empire's reach from Thebin. Before he could decide his next move, he had to figure out where this last one had taken him. With Lord Chin-shi dead, there was certainly no way back.

Chapter Eleven

THE stranger, Habiba, led them to a door in the thick wall that circled the arena. He handed Llesho a torch and, with a snap of his fingers, set the fuel-soaked end of it on fire. The bearers carrying Bixei followed, then Master Jaks, who closed the door before lighting his own torch at Llesho's flame. They were in a long tunnel that sloped gently until Llesho was sure they were no longer inside the wall, but were under the arena itself. The roar of the crowd was muted here, though the pounding of so many feet thundered over their heads and shook dirt into their hair. Llesho wondered if the roof of the tunnel would hold, but neither Habiba nor Jaks seemed concerned, so he turned his attention to figuring out where they were going. Away from the main entrance, that was clear. Since he hadn't seen anything beyond the arena at the outskirts of the city, he couldn't tell much other than that they were heading away from the direction in which they had come.

They passed other tunnels feeding into the one they followed. One, with a heavy door barring their entrance, Llesho thought must lead from the official boxes of the governor and mayor of Farshore province and city. Just as he had started to wonder if the whole trip would be taken underground, the floor of the tunnel began to rise again, until they faced a closed door and nowhere else to go. The door had no handle. Llesho pushed, but the door didn't budge.

"Locked," he said, and Habiba moved past him with a tight little smile.

"Aren't we lucky we have the key?" he asked, though he carried nothing but a lit torch.

Habiba waved his hand over the door and muttered a phrase that Llesho couldn't hear. Then he gave the door a light tap. It opened inward and Llesho jumped back, crashing into Bixei's litter in his effort to avoid being hit by the door.

"Get off me!" Panic edged Bixei's sharp voice, and he gave Llesho a shove that overbalanced the already precarious bearers and propelled Llesho out into the gloomy light of the minor sun. He was standing alone in a wood of low, gnarled ginkgo trees that stank of fallen fruit in the quickening breeze of nightfall. A moment later, Jaks exited the tunnel, followed by Bixei on his litter. Habiba came last; when they had all assembled outside the secret passage, he turned to secure the door with another wave of his hand. Again he accompanied the flourish with a muttered charm, but Llesho wondered if it wasn't really the tap on the door itself, at the center of a coiled dragon carved into its surface, that sealed the tunnel.

Jaks seemed to know the way; he led their little band no more than a quarter li to a lane canopied by the twisted branches of ancient trees on each side. The lane's deep, sinuous curves snaking through the forest hid them from anyone coming up from behind, but likewise hid from their sight anything waiting for them ahead. At first, when Llesho could see no houses or temples, he thought they must be leaving the city. Then the stranger rounded a bend and disappeared between two ordinary looking trees at the side of the road. Master Jaks followed, with the sling carrying Bixei right behind him, and Llesho took a deep breath and slipped between the same trees.

He found himself on a carefully manicured path set with flagstones of varying sizes that artfully mimicked the meandering flow of a stream. The flagstone walk led them to a series of low-roofed structures. A network of ponds and waterways separated the buildings from each other while a series of gracefully arched bridges connected them again. The dim light of the minor sun wrapped the whole in a soft green slumber. Dumbfounded, Llesho stared back the way he had come and saw behind him a stone wall rising higher than his head. From the lane that wall had been invisible. Not just out of sight, he realized, but *invisible,* hidden by some spell that buried the quiet garden in deeper privacy than even the high stone wall. Bixei had likewise looked back, and he met Llesho's astonishment with an attempt to look worldly, but missed.

"What have we got into?" Bixei asked him with a look, and Llesho's answering glance said, "Trouble."

That Master Jaks showed no surprise at all only made matters worse, as far as Llesho was concerned. The governor's witch: Llesho wanted to know what his teacher knew about witches and witchcraft, and why he had let Llesho suffer through months of Overseer Markko's torment in search of answers Master Jaks could have given him for the asking. But they were crossing one of those fragile looking bridges, over a pond on which pink-and-white lotus flowers rose on stems above the water, swaying in the slight breeze.

On the other side, they passed under the roof of a gatehouse that led them into a private garden where a pale, cold woman waited to greet them. Llesho recognized her. She had tested him with the short spear and the knife in the weapons rooms on Pearl Island,

and she had accompanied the governor when he greeted the gladiators in the arena. Master Jaks bowed with bland courtesy, as if to a stranger, so Llesho did the same. He trusted Jaks, though he was beginning to wonder why, as he worried about what plot not of his choosing he had unwittingly fallen into.

The woman opened her arms to greet them with a calculated smile that warred with something darker in her eyes. "The governor of Farshore Province welcomes you to his service," she said. "You will need rest, of course—especially the young one with the wounds. Habiba will take care of your papers and show you to your quarters. And he will answer your questions."

The governor's lady gave a slight nod of dismissal, then she turned and entered one of the low wooden houses that surrounded the garden. When the door slid into place behind her, Llesho could not tell where it had been.

The stranger, Habiba, bowed to Master Jaks and smiled at the boys. "This way," he said, and gestured toward another bridge, leading deeper into the complex of houses and waterways. Over the bridge, down a path between two slightly larger buildings with two tiers of curled roofs they followed him, to a small house with fragile, greased parchment screens for walls. Habiba slid a screen aside, and they entered the office of an overseer. The bearers of Bixei's litter set him down and departed, leaving the novices alone with their teacher and the governor's witch.

Habiba went to the elegantly fragile desk and pulled out a sheaf of papers, turning first to Master Jaks. "Do you have your prize-book?"

Jaks reached into his leather tunic and pulled out a worked leather case that hung by a cord around his neck. From the case he pulled a small book, which he handed to the overseer.

Habiba opened Jaks' prize-book and studied it for

a moment. "You were close to winning your freedom when Lord Chin-shi put an end to your aspirations, Master Jaks."

"Lord Chin-shi pulled me from the arena before I had earned my price," he confirmed. "His lordship valued my skill as a teacher, and did not wish to lose my services to death or manumission." Master Jaks recited his history in a flat voice, but Llesho saw the muscles in his teacher's throat tighten with restraint. Manumission: the freeing of a slave. What emotions the master hid, Llesho could not see, but he imagined them much as his own at his captivity: a helpless rage more suited to a child than the powerful man-at-arms.

"Some day you must tell the tale of how a hero with the bands of an assassin on his arm landed himself in the arena at all," Habiba commented, "and how it was that your kin allowed the slight to remain on their honor for so long."

"I have no clan," Master Jaks answered with a voice like stone falling on stone. "My family all lie dead."

Llesho remembered the bodyguard who had died to keep him safe. *Was he your brother?* he wanted to ask. *Your family, did they all die fighting at Kungol, too few against the invading horde?* But he could say nothing in front of Bixei or the governor's witch, who flitted an expressionless glance over Llesho before returning his attention to Master Jaks in front of him.

"So I have heard." Habiba reached for a chop and an inkstone, as if the conversation had revealed the likelihood of rain, not the destruction of a clan of mercenaries and assassins.

"Her ladyship's family rules, in the emperor's grace, at Thousand Lakes Province, where slavery is outlawed," Habiba explained, his voice soft but commanding, and terrible in its quiet anger. There was no comfort in his voice—a warrior would acknowledge no need of comfort—but Llesho felt the softness of his words tame some hurt he felt in his own breast.

Master Jaks inclined his head, an acceptance of comradeship if not peace.

"According to her marriage contract with his grace, the governor of Farshore Province, her ladyship's household shall always be a mirror in which she may see the Thousand Lakes reflected. No one serves here as a slave."

He stamped Master Jaks' prize-book with the governor's chop and returned it solemnly. "The gift to his lady of your freedom has cost his excellency very little."

Habiba then held out the contract with its blue seal. "Your manumission papers," he said, and added, "her ladyship would like to hire you, Freeman Jaks, to train the warriors for her house. The contract is here," he offered a second folded packet. "If you need someone to read it to you, a scribe will be supplied for you."

"I can read," Jaks informed him.

Habiba nodded. "In that case," he said, "shall I offer you rest in the guards' quarters, or in the guest quarters?"

"In the guest quarters, until I have read the contract."

Habiba gave them the blank smile of officials everywhere. "If you choose to accept the contract," he said, "this will be yours." He handed Master Jaks a slim gold chain like the one he wore around his own neck. "It marks one as being in his excellency the governor's service, and should be worn at official functions and when representing the household in a formal capacity." The overseer's smile seemed more genuine when he added, "Her ladyship does ask that you leave it at home if you decide to go pleasure-seeking in the city, so that no scandal may fall upon his lordship. At any other time, you may wear it as you choose for the protection this house may afford you."

Master Jaks took the gold chain and slipped it into the leather case where his prize-book had rested. "I will keep that in mind," he said, and bowed his thanks for the papers he now held in his hand.

So the gold chain had not marked Habiba as a slave in this household, as Llesho had believed. He wondered how much difference there truly was between a free man who acted the slave, and the slave he pretended to be, but Habiba did not look like he invited the question.

"As for the boys," Habiba continued, "her ladyship faces a dilemma and must, for a time, bow her head to the decree of the land. His divinity, the Celestial Emperor, has foreseen the possibility that the unwanted infants of slaves may be cast upon the mercy of the empire for their upkeep. The empire has enough prostitutes and thieves already, and further has no wish to act as nursemaid to the castoffs of its lords and nobles. The law therefore requires that children born or bought into slavery must remain the property of the slaveholder, with all the responsibilities that entail to property ownership, until the youthful slave has developed the skills to sustain his or her own life at no expense to the empire."

"I don't understand," Llesho said, though it terrified him to speak up in front of the governor's witch. "What does all of that mean?"

The witch, Habiba, leveled the full power of his gaze on Llesho, and Llesho quaked on the inside but held his ground. He had a destiny, and had better start acting like it or he'd spend the rest of his life hiding like a rabbit.

"It means, Llesho, that in the eyes of the law, you and your friend will remain the private property of her ladyship until you pass your seventeenth summer. During that time you will each choose a trade according to your talents and needs, and at the end of that time, when you have proved to the governor, in accordance with the laws of the empire, that you can provide for your own needs, you will receive these—"

he lifted from his desk two packets sealed with blue ribbons. Manumission papers. Freedom. And already signed, or they would not have the governor's seal on them.

"What do you want to do with your life, Llesho?"

Llesho met the witch's gaze. The man would think him a fool if he told him the truth, or he would think him a spy and a traitor. By law, the entrails of a spy were torn out in the public square, their place in the spy's body filled with hot coals, and the flesh sewn together around the coals with whipcord. The coals cauterized the wounds while they burned the hidden flesh; it took a long time to die. Llesho had already seen the witch's idea of mercy—Madon was dead—so he said nothing about his quest.

"I only wish to serve," he said.

Habiba studied his face for a long moment. He must have seen the color disappear, the life fading behind the stone of Llesho's eyes, because he sighed and broke the contact to glance over to Bixei, including him in the questions to follow.

"Can you read and write?" he asked, and Llesho answered, "Yes," while Bixei shook his head.

"Sums?"

"A little bit," Llesho said, and Bixei shook his head again. No one trained slaves destined for the arena in the arts of the nobility, and Llesho little knew how much he had given away about himself with his simple assertions of truth.

But Master Jaks did understand. "An educated slave, a prisoner taken in battle from the same land as Llesho, took an interest in the boy when he worked in the oyster beds. He taught the boy a little of reading and arithmetic."

Which gave scant credit to Llesho's palace tutors, and shied the truth a bit about Lleck's captivity—not a battle, but an invasion, the few left alive dragged into captivity behind the horses of the conquerors.

Llesho kept his mouth shut about that, too. He liked his guts exactly where they were, thank you. Liked his head in its current position, too, though beheading as an enemy of the state was preferable to the end of a spy.

Habiba accepted Master Jaks' explanation with a wry twist of his mouth around the sour taste of doubt.

"Can you fight?" he asked. Bixei, from his litter on the floor, answered "Yes!" while Llesho shrugged his shoulders and said, "A little."

"Spells? Incantations?"

"NO!" both boys answered in unison. Bixei responded with the usual horror of the unknown, but Llesho could not hide the shuddering dread of the months he had spent chained in Markko's workroom. Suddenly, it was too much for him, and his traitorous legs betrayed him. He sank to the floor in front of the governor's witch, and covered his face to hide his shame. "I don't know anything," he cried. "Nothing!"

Cringing at the humiliation, he did not at first feel the gentle hand on his shoulder, the man reaching to draw his palms away from his eyes. Habiba, the governor's witch, knelt before him, all the irony and formal distance fled from his eyes, which were warm, and sorrowful, and full of understanding that ran deeper than Llesho understood himself.

"It's all right," Habiba said. "Mistakes were made with you, but no one will hurt you here."

When the witch rose to his feet, he seemed more tired, older than he had just moments ago, and when he shook his head, Master Jaks looked stricken and guilty, though why, Llesho didn't know.

"Maybe later, when we gain his trust," Habiba said. "We'll see what Kaydu can work with him, but he may never realize his potential."

"Her ladyship will be disappointed," Master Jaks pointed out, and Habiba sighed again.

"Before we make any decisions, let's see what

Kaydu can accomplish. Have you thought enough about her ladyship's offer of employment?"

"I haven't read the contract yet," Master Jaks replied, with a bitter laugh. He gave Llesho a long, thoughtful look. "But, yes, I agree to her terms. Whatever they are." He drew out the packet and opened it, took the pen Habiba offered, and quickly sketched the characters of his name.

Habiba smiled, gracious in victory. "I'll have the servants put you in guards' quarters after all. As your first duty, you will work with Kaydu on training."

Master Jaks nodded. "I suppose I'll have to keep her chain, now."

"In time, you will find that it weighs lightly at the throat," Habiba replied. "It is the chains you cannot see that bind you.

"For the boys, silver." He held out a chain to Bixei, who set it around his neck as if it had been a gift, and not a symbol of his servitude. He did not offer the chain to Llesho's hand, but settled it himself around the neck of the boy. And something in his eyes told Llesho that the last words to Master Jaks had been meant for him as well. Not the chains he could see, but the ones he couldn't. Still, the one he could see was coming off just as soon as he was out of the overseer's office.

"Bixei," the overseer asked, "does the life of a warrior suit you?" and Bixei answered, "Yes, sir," with speed and a bit of arrogance considering that he could not, at that moment, stand under his own power. "I am a fighter by trade, sir."

"Perhaps not yet," the overseer commented, "But with time. I think you have, indeed, found your calling. Take him to the infirmary," he said to Master Jaks. "When he is healed of his wounds, we will decide where to put him."

"Yes, sir." Master Jaks managed to make his bow

ironic. Llesho wished he could do that, and decided that he was in enough trouble as it was.

"As for you." He studied Llesho's closed face with a serious frown. "I have been led to believe that you will be pleased with your accommodations. You can train with the guards, and then come here for scribal training with the clerks. Once you settle in, we'll see."

Llesho didn't like the sound of that "We'll see." Habiba had said nothing about sending him off to decorate his lordship's bed or chaining him with the poisons in an alchemist's workroom, which meant he was already ahead of where he'd been. With an effort, therefore, he subdued his panic, determined to wait and see where this next step would take him. In the meantime, he would learn all he could. But he seriously wondered how this put him any closer to his goal.

Chapter Twelve

HABIBA summoned the litter bearers and instructed them to take Bixei to the infirmary. As they left the overseer's office with their burden of objecting gladiator-in-training, a young woman with dirt streaking her nose and sweat beading at her temples squeezed past them in the doorway and bowed carelessly. Then she wrapped her arms around Habiba's neck for a quick hug. Presently she released his neck, but held onto his arm while she gave Llesho a swift glance that inventoried him down to his toes

"So you found him," she said, and grinned.

Llesho stared at her like she'd sprouted a second head, while the color rose in his face.

"Let me introduce my daughter," Habiba said, "Kaydu, Master Jaks. I believe you have already met our young friend."

"Yes, indeed," she said. "I'd put my money on his skill in a blooding fight, but in a fight to the death, I would bet on his opponent even if it was my great aunt Silla."

As a slave, Llesho realized he shouldn't have been surprised that what seemed to be a courtesy introduction quickly turned into an analysis of his potential in the ring, but it rankled. He straightened his spine with a bit of the regal tilt to his chin he reserved for humiliating situations. Master Jaks shot him a warning glance, though, and he lowered his eyes, chastised. Until he decided for himself whether he was among friends or foes, he knew it wasn't safe to give the sharp-eyed witch and his daughter any more to study about him than they already had. But Master Jaks rolled his eyes with a slight shake of the head. Too late, then. Habiba had already seen, and had already drawn his own silent conclusions behind sharp, hooded eyes.

"You think he won't kill?" the witch asked his daughter, as if Llesho weren't even in the room.

"I can hear, and speak," Llesho reminded them. "If you want to know something, ask me."

"Llesho—" Jaks began with a stern frown. Habiba raised a hand to stop the teacher, and turned the blazing intensity of his scrutiny upon Llesho for a moment before the naked calculation disappeared behind a blandly polite facade. He tsked a reprimand, but did ask, "Have you ever killed a man, Llesho?"

"No, but—"

"Then you don't know how you will react when the time comes."

"Neither does she—"

At Habiba's silent command Master Jaks had stood a little apart from the verbal skirmish, his arms crossed over his chest as if to hold in check his own worried response to the questioning, but he spoke up now. "Kaydu is right, of course. At least, he would not kill in the games—I am sure of it."

"We don't train gladiators here, as you well know, Jaks. We need to know if he could kill in battle, or to save his life, or the life of his charge against assassins."

Llesho would have objected again that they were still talking about him as if he weren't there, but Habiba's words robbed him of anything to say. Assassins?

"I don't think he would kill at all, for any reason, now," Kaydu continued her assessment. "Certainly not to save his own life—he's been taught he's worthless for more than half of it. Maybe, though, to save someone else, but it might destroy him if he had to do it."

"You haven't seen him work with a knife," Jaks said. "He only knows one way to handle the traditional Thebin blade; I suspect he was lethal even at seven. And I'm not sure he hasn't killed before, though he certainly hasn't since he came to Pearl Island."

"If he has, the memory is buried deep," Kaydu said. "I saw no evidence of the knowledge of death by his hand when we fought."

Without warning, Master Jaks reached back with his right hand and slipped a Thebin blade from a sheath at the back of his neck. He threw, his aim perfect and centered on Llesho's heart. Instinctively, Llesho adjusted his stance, and when the knife approached, he had turned his side to it and stepped out of its way. In the same motion, he plucked the knife out of the air and sent it spinning back at the thrower. Jaks was prepared for the move, but still the blade nicked him midway up his bicep before embedding itself in a wooden beam in the wall. If Jaks had not moved when he had, the knife would have pierced his heart, the same target he had aimed at himself.

He clenched the fingers of his left hand over the wound in his right arm. "Den's been working with him," he said, "But he came to us with that and other equally deadly moves for close work in his bag of tricks. As far as I can tell, with a knife he knows *only* how to kill."

Aghast, Llesho stared at the blood dripping from his teacher's arm. Never, in all the weeks of Den's instructions, had he ever drawn blood with the blade. He had become so secure in practice that he had stopped thinking of it as weapons training at all; he had worked the knife as a pure form, like prayer, to be perfected for its own sake. Killing was the part of being a gladiator that he hadn't taken into consideration when he'd decided to follow this course to freedom. And Master Jaks could have paid with his life for the oversight. Llesho's mind rejected the nagging insistence that Master Jaks' thrown blade might have killed him instead. The teacher had known what would happen, and still, he had put his life in Llesho's hands. And Llesho had almost taken it from him.

"I'm sorry," he stammered, and clamped his hand over his mouth. "I am going to be sick."

"Don't!" Kaydu took his arm and ran with him out of the overseer's office, to a corner of the house crowded with green growing things. "Now, you can go ahead—no one will see you, and you won't be the first to honor these bushes. You don't ever defile his house, though. It would take weeks to purify it again, and the time could cost us dearly."

She spoke to him more as an equal now, and he wondered if he'd somehow won her respect under false pretenses. He hadn't killed, and even the thought of doing so left him squatting in the bushes bringing up his tonsils like a baby. But she crouched beside him and shook his arm to get his attention.

"It's nothing to be ashamed about," she gestured with a shift of her shoulder at the bushes he had poured his graces out on, "I won't fight with a man who could come that close to killing a friend and remain unmoved."

Llesho supposed that she meant to comfort him, but her words had the opposite effect. He had come within inches of killing Master Jaks; only the fact that the teacher *knew* he would react with a deadly counterattack had kept Jaks alive. Llesho started to shake. His teeth clicked with the spasmodic clenching of his jaw that caught his tongue and bit to the quick.

"No," he said, rocking himself to ease the trembling while his arms wrapped his belly, which threatened to turn itself inside out again. "No, no, no, no, no."

"Shock," Kaydu informed him, and dragged him to his feet. He managed to follow her, putting one foot in front of the other even though he couldn't feel his arms or legs anymore. She led him to the door of the overseer's office again, but did not go in.

"He needs something hot to drink, and about ten hours of sleep," she informed the two men inside.

"Take him, by all means, and get him settled," Habiba said. "I'll explain his absence from the formal audience with the governor somehow."

Master Jaks said nothing, but he lowered his eyes when Llesho caught his glance. Before he'd hidden his feelings Llesho caught regret but not apology in the teacher's eyes. From somewhere in the terrified fragments of his past, a Thebin teaching surfaced in his mind. "You can't force self-knowledge. You can only make an opportunity for the seeker to find himself." Was that what Master Jaks had been doing with that little trick? Making an opportunity for Llesho to know himself as a killer, trained to be so from the cradle—the murderer of a friend? He did not want this knowledge, refused to embrace it as part of himself. He did not, would not, kill. Kaydu had said it, and Habiba had agreed with his daughter. Only his teacher marked him as a taker of life. Only the man who had trained him, and watched him, and knew him.

If the pond beneath the bridge they crossed had been deep enough, he would have thrown himself in and drowned. The water was shallow and reed-clogged, however; he would only succeed in humiliating himself and ruining the only clothing he had. So he followed Kaydu to a low house on short stilts with a green curled roof and paper windows propped open to the fading light. The house had one room and little furnishing: four narrow beds, four chairs, a small cooking hearth gone cold in the afternoon, and an assortment of hanging baskets with the various linens and supplies of the household.

Two of the chairs were occupied when Llesho came in. Their occupants looked up from what appeared to be a cheerful argument over mending, and let out twin squeals of surprise and joy. "Llesho!"

Lling was the first to jump up and come to him, giving him a hug before wrinkling her nose. "You need a bath."

Hmishi followed her to crowd around him. "They said in the cookhouse today that you bested Kaydu with the trident!" he said, and Kaydu cuffed him in the head. "Because I let him," she answered back with a laugh.

"No, she didn't." Llesho managed a smile. "I taught her a thing or two of my own devising, and we called it a draw."

"Actually, he won," Kaydu contradicted, "But a little thing like victory shouldn't impress you. It was a lucky break."

Llesho knew she was teasing, that she meant his friends to know that he had conducted himself well in the arena, but he was too tired to trade banter, and the part of his mind that was processing the afternoon in the overseer's office was demanding greater and greater amounts of his attention.

"I have to lie down," he said. "Which beds are taken?"

"You are to have that one," Kaydu said, and pointed to the bed farthest from the door and set away from the wall.

He nodded and shambled over to it, unbuckled his belt, and pulled his leather tunic over his head. Since he didn't know where to stow his gear yet, he dropped it on the foot of the bed and followed after it, pitching into a darkness thicker than tree sap.

When he awoke again, the light had a sweeter taste to it. Morning filtered through the fall of weeping willow branches swaying in the breeze outside the window and painted dappled shadows on the walls. Even the air smelled of renewal. And soap. Someone had washed him while he slept, and covered him with a soft blanket. Off in the center of the room he heard the shuffle of sandaled feet, and the clink of crockery, the sound of water pouring, and then the pungent vapors of tea rising on the sunlight. When he pushed himself up on his elbows, Lling was squatting next to his bed with a worried frown crinkling her brow.

"He's awake," she called to her companion, and when Llesho croaked, "Tea, please," she smiled and amended her news to, "and alive."

"We wondered if you were ever going to wake up." Hmishi handed him a steaming cup of tea, then steadied it with a supporting hand when it trembled in Llesho's fingers. He waited until Llesho had drunk, then answered the curious frown with a relieved smile. "You've slept the day around, and another night. You didn't even wake up when Habiba washed you. He's the healer around here, as well as the overseer. He told us to let you sleep, that you needed to heal, though neither Lling nor I could see anything wrong with you on the outside."

"I figured it must be something like enchantment of the deep," Lling said. "It takes a healer to see it because the wound is so deep that it's hidden on the inside. Habiba's been in to check on you a dozen times at least, and Kaydu, his daughter, almost as often." Lling's voice seemed to etch the name of her rival in acid on the air.

Hmishi interrupted her then with a warning glance, and Llesho wondered if they had been told not to trouble the patient. "A man who said his name was Jaks spent a long time watching you from the corner of the room. He didn't move much or say anything once he'd introduced himself, but he waited through most of the day, and a good part of the night before he finally left."

"I don't think he would have left at all," Lling added, "except that we made it clear we were watching him as long as he watched you. When the moon had nearly set, he gave a funny little sigh—"

"He laughed at us!" Hmishi interrupted, remembering the indignity.

"—and he told us to get some sleep. Then he left." Lling finished on a yawn.

"I expect he won't be gone long," Hmishi added. "If you want to get dressed, visit the outhouse before he gets here—"

"Tell us who he is—"

"I'll help you up—"

Llesho realized that he was naked, and flinched when Hmishi reached to lift his blanket. "Lling, perhaps I could eat a fresh bun from the cookhouse." He gave her a wan smile, and she was up, bouncing on the balls of her feet, almost before the words were out.

"I'll leave you two to make Llesho decent," she agreed, and Llesho knew he'd hidden none of his embarrassment from her. "But first, I want to know if we have a problem with that man Jaks."

"He's my teacher."

Lling accepted that, though only Llesho knew how little that explanation answered her question. Jaks had his own agenda for Llesho, as, apparently, did the governor's lady and his witch. How closely that tied into Llesho's own task set for him by the ghost of his father's minister, he did not yet know.

"First, clothes." Hmishi brought his mind back to the present, holding out a pair of loose trousers. "We each have an extra set here. These are mine, but you can borrow them until they've fitted you out. The shirt is Lling's; we thought it would fit, but your shoulders are bigger than they used to be. It looks like you'll have to settle for the trousers."

Llesho took them from his friend's hand and slipped into them. "Outhouse?" he asked, and Hmishi pointed the way. When he returned, Master Jaks was waiting for him, and so was Habiba.

"You are looking better." Habiba smiled at him, and Llesho wondered what he looked better than. He hadn't been wounded, or sick. But he realized that the tight knots between his shoulder blades were gone, and that the tension had smoothed away from his forehead. He did feel better, though he could couldn't quite figure out how the unclenching of muscles all through his body had been accomplished, or why the mere fact of it made him feel so much freer when he still wore the governor's silver chain around his neck.

"Yesterday was rest-day," Habiba continued, "But you missed it. Her ladyship wishes me to inform you that she grants this one day of celebration for your safe delivery. Use it well." He smiled then. "And give her ladyship's announcement to your companion, Lling, when she comes in." He left then, with a little bow in Llesho's direction that drew a warning frown from Jaks and sent a pained look across his face. Hmishi turned to him in amazement. "I don't get it," he said. Llesho shrugged, unwilling to trust his secrets to voice and air.

Master Jaks watched the healer leave and then came forward himself. "Here in her ladyship's gardens, you are as safe as you can be in Farshore Province," he said. "But soon it won't be safe anywhere. Learn what you can in the time you have, but if it comes to a choice, choose to heal."

"Tell that to Kaydu," Hmishi interrupted.

Kaydu picked that moment to enter the low house with Lling in tow and a white-faced monkey with soft brown fur on her shoulder. The monkey wore a practice shirt tied with a warrior's knot and a tiny wizard's hat upon his head. The monkey's hands wrapped around Kaydu's chin, and his long, supple tail curled over her opposite shoulder.

"He doesn't have to tell me," she said, "Habiba already has."

The monkey shrieked and jumped up and down on Kaydu's shoulder. Master Jaks gave her a pained expression, but ignored the monkey. "Will that stop you?" he asked her, and she laughed.

"Nope. I'll push him until he cries uncle or until he pushes back. That's my job.

"Oh, and by the way, I caught a spy." Kaydu reached behind her and dragged Lling into the room, causing the monkey to screech again and lunge for Lling's hair.

"I'm not a spy!" Lling twisted her arm out of Kaydu's grip with a glare of special loathing for the monkey. "I was keeping watch. And you didn't catch me; that horrible creature did."

"No better a guard than a spy, to let Little Brother find you out!" Kaydu taunted.

"If you'd meant Llesho harm, I'd have killed you with my bare hands, and your stupid monkey, too."

The monkey seemed to understand, because he screamed at her again and jumped up and down on Kaydu's shoulder in a flurry of agitation. Llesho figured Little Brother still wasn't safe from Lling's wrath.

Kaydu studied her intently, then smiled. "This one will kill."

"Kill?" Hmishi whispered.

Kaydu raised a scornful eyebrow. "His excellency wasted his money on that one, should have left him to Yueh."

"Not if you want anything out of me," Lling warned, and moved to stand at Hmishi's left shoulder.

Llesho didn't understand the argument, but he knew where he stood on it. "Nor me," he said, and took up his position at Hmishi's right. "We are a team."

Exasperated, Kaydu looked to Master Jaks for support, but he shrugged. "As familiars go, a pearl diver is at least one step up from a monkey." A smile tried to escape his tightly pursed lips, and he didn't work very hard to suppress it. With a last nod to Llesho's companions, he ducked out of the house, leaving Kaydu and her monkey to level matching glares at Hmishi.

"If you screw up," she said, "I will feed you to Lord Yueh's men on a platter." The monkey screeched his own disdain before leaping from Kaydu's shoulder and scuttling away through the open window. Secure in having had the last word, Kaydu followed Master Jaks out the door.

To Llesho's surprise, Hmishi was the first to collect his wits about him. "What have you got us into, Llesho?"

They were both looking at him now. Llesho considered telling them the truth: who he was, what Master Jaks thought he had done, and even the vow he had made to Lleck's ghost in that terrifying hour in Pearl Bay. But he still hadn't figured out why he was here, or how much any of those who wove their plots around him actually knew. So he threw himself on the bed, sat cross-legged with his elbows on his knees and his chin in his hands, and shrugged. "I don't have the slightest idea."

"Well, that's just great." Hmishi sat beside him, his own hands clapped to his forehead. Lling joined them, so they were like three monkeys sitting in a row. "But if you need anyone killed, it seems I am your girl."

The two boys grunted their indignation. But none of them could think of anything else to say.

Chapter Thirteen

WHEN the three friends were alone again with the promise of a day off, Hmishi turned to Llesho with a crooked smile. "Time for the grand tour," he said. "Lling can protect us both if we come across any assassins in the cookhouse."

Lling cocked her head at a superior angle, but followed Hmishi out of the wooden house. They wandered along a flagstone path that snaked between ferns and clumps of bamboo, winding beside one of the narrow canals that threaded the compound. First they took Llesho to the cookhouse. A lean tyrant with a stick in his hand ordered his undercooks with the precision of a military review while the Thebin friends raided his pantry for cinnamon buns. They found no assassins, though Llesho wondered about the cook.

Juggling the hot buns from hand to hand between bites, Hmishi and Lling showed their companion the practice yard, a small island cut off from the rest of the compound by dreamy pools of dark water adrift with water lilies and lotus blossoms. Two small footbridges gave access to the island, where a cadre of the governor's guard were drilling spear exercises. Llesho recognized the forms, and his muscles jumped in sympathetic flexure to the grunts and curses of the fighters.

"Jaks taught us to do that one a little differently," Llesho commented, watching the guards go through their passes, "though I work better with the trident than with the spear."

Hmishi snorted around a mouthful of sticky bun. "Kaydu says I'd be better off with a rake and a hoe, but she's trying to teach me trident and spear. Lling is the one you have to watch out for. She fights like a demon."

"Only compared to you," she parried with a sniff of derision. Then she asked Llesho, "What was it like to actually fight in the arena?"

"You'll find out soon enough." Llesho tried to sound more superior than he felt about his demonstration bout.

"No, we won't," Lling corrected him. "Only slaves fight in the arena. Since the governor's house keeps no slaves, it fields no stable of gladiators."

"I fought Kaydu in the ring myself," Llesho reminded them, licking the last of the sticky cinnamon from his fingers.

Hmishi shrugged. "That was a demonstration bout. At some point she tests us all. I don't think it is just a fighting test, though, or I wouldn't be here. She's a witch, like her father."

Llesho hadn't needed anyone to tell him that. But he wasn't convinced about Her Ladyship's good intentions. He lifted the silver chain he wore at his throat. "What about this?"

Hmishi shrugged. He didn't need more explanation of Llesho's question—he had a similar chain around his own neck, as did Lling. "Something to do with the law, and that we need a legal guardian or owner until we are of an age of independence."

"There was a big argument when they first brought us here," Lling added, her attention bent on catching a raisin that had leaped from her bun when she bit into it. "Her ladyship wanted an adoption contract or a guardianship for another couple of summers. The governor wouldn't hear of it, of course. He made a few pointed remarks about dragging every pig farmer and dirt scrabbler from Thebin over his threshold to stain the honor of his house. Habiba was on the governor's side for that one, and her ladyship seems to take his advice more often than not."

"He's the governor's witch," Llesho stated, referring to Habiba, who hadn't seemed that frightening except in the power he wielded. "Even the governor's lady must be afraid he'll put a spell on her if she opposes him." But he didn't believe that for some reason. Nothing about the lady testing him in the weapons room led him to believe she would back down from anyone, not even a witch. Lling seemed to read his mind.

"I think maybe he's her ladyship's witch, actually," Lling said. "She's not afraid of him, that's clear."

She thought about the question for a moment before she gave a further explanation. "It is more like she understands that bringing her father's position against slavery to Farshore is a political weakness that leaves her husband vulnerable. Habiba doesn't like slavery either, but he doesn't let that cloud his judgment. There is more going on than philosophy between them—get your mind out of the outhouse, I don't mean that."

Hmishi gave her a less than chastened nod. They hadn't spent months in Markko's back room, or a night in Lord Chin-shi's bed while the lord struggled with the Blood Tide destroying Pearl Island, however. They hadn't taken weapons testing under her ladyship's cold eye, or watched Habiba kill a good man with sorrow in his eyes but no hesitation in his hands.

"Her ladyship is playing a deeper game than we know, I think," he advised his companions, uncertain whether he helped or hurt them with the knowledge. "I suspect that Farshore doesn't matter much in her plans at all. So I wonder why we *do* matter, and why we remain slaves if our freedom was important enough to bring three fairly useless pearl divers into the governor's house guard."

"Slaves in name only," Hmishi objected. "His excellency showed us the papers, already signed, but dated for our seventeenth summers."

He could have argued that the governor could tear up those papers as if they had never existed. When He thought about it, though, he had to admit that whatever plots her ladyship wove with her witch, she was still alive, and so was Llesho, which was more than he expected.

Markko would have burned Kwan-ti to death in the training compound at Pearl Island, and Lord Chin-shi would have let him. Now Lord Chin-shi was dead and Kwan-ti was gone, vanished like a god from the roadside. If Llesho had to choose, he'd take the witch over the poisoner. It still left them with the governor's silver chains around their necks, however, and the governor's lady laying her plots around them.

"Whatever we will become at seventeen, we are slaves now," Llesho argued. "They can use us, or throw us away in the arena any time they want."

"Not the arena," Lling insisted. "Kaydu is training us to be soldiers. I heard her talking to her father when they brought you in; the governor bought the freedom of the man you call Master Jaks because he wants to hire him on contract to train us. Kaydu doesn't have the time to train novices; she is needed to run the standing guard through its paces."

She didn't volunteer how she had heard this, and Llesho carefully didn't ask, but let her distract him with a finger pointed at the fighters now divided into pairs and thrashing at each other with swords. Some of them, Llesho noticed, were women, though all were older than he and his companions. Their swords were curved differently than the one Llesho was used to, and they worked with a buckler on the weaker arm rather than a knife in hand, but the stances and motions seemed familiar, if combined strangely.

Curious, he rose from his place beside his friends and slipped over the narrow footbridge, sliding around the perimeter of the combat area, until he came to the thing he was looking for, a rack of swords and bucklers, and a smaller collection of knives. He picked up a knife and a sword, and danced them through their paces. He became so lost in the motion and the weapons in his hands that he did not notice the experienced house guards falling still around him. Finally, no sound could be heard in the practice yard except for the frenzied dance of thrust and parry and underhand, overhand, sidewise slashing strokes of Llesho's knife.

He ended his exercise up on the ball of his right foot, his left poised like a crane about to take flight, the sword held high over his head for a downward penetrating strike while the knife flicked at the end of a curved sweep that protected his belly. Going still at the apex of his thrust, he blinked as the silence filtered into his consciousness. Six months ago, this sudden awareness of the rapt audience would have sent him scurrying in embarrassment for anonymity at the back of the crowd. Or, he would have pulled about him the dignity of his father, the tilt of his chin and the cold stare he had perfected by seven. Six months of training with Masters Den and Jaks had set new instincts into his muscles, however; he looked about him with the flinty challenge of a warrior in his eyes.

At first, it appeared that he had no takers, and he began to relax his stance. But then, Kaydu herself came forward, armed as he was with knife and sword and the same look in her eyes. She threw down the sword like a dare and he did likewise, shifting his stance, curving his spine to draw his gut as far from the reach of her arm as possible, his knife held in a horizontal line like a fence between himself and his foe. Then his wrist turned and his body shifted around the axis of his knife arm to present a narrow sliver of a target. His knife snaked forward, curved under her guard, and rested with the point wedged beneath her chin.

Kaydu stared at him, wide-eyed, while her knife hand opened of its own volition, to offer the knife on the flat of her palm. Llesho flicked his eyes once, groundward, and she let her knife drop. Only when she stood unarmed before him did he shift his own knife from its threatening position, but then her hand was flashing again, coming at him with a knife she had secreted in the cuff of her wrist guard, and his own knife flashed up, in reflex, and he would have severed the hand from her body and followed up on her throat without thought. Master Jaks stopped him—slapped his arm down and held on when Llesho would have twisted the knife into his teacher's gut.

"Llesho!" Jaks called to him, and Llesho became aware that the silence had given way to a low rumble, that his friends stared at him with mouths agape, and that Jaks was gazing deeply into his eyes, as if checking him for fever. Then he realized that he still held the knife in his cramped fist, and he dropped it with a dazed grunt.

"She tried to kill me," he explained shakily, fighting the urge to vomit.

"I was testing you." Kaydu rubbed at her own wrist, shaking as much as he was. Jaks glared at her.

"I told you not to test him on the knife," Jaks reminded her with a warning in his voice. "He *cannot* overcome the reflexes trained into him. You would have been lucky to lose a hand. He might not have been able to stop even after you were disabled."

Kaydu studied him through adrenaline nerves. Llesho

recognized the feeling; he had it himself. "What did you do to me?" he asked, stunned at what he had almost done, at what Jaks intimated he would have done. Jaks shook his head slowly. "Not our doing," he said. "We couldn't reverse the early training, so we honed it. Your knife battles will still be to the death, but we wanted to give you a fair chance of being the one standing at the end of them."

"It seems you succeeded," Kaydu said, more matter-of-factly than Llesho could manage under the circumstances. "Can you teach it to me?"

"I wouldn't," Jaks told her, "even if I could. And your father would have me killed if I tried."

"Why?" She almost seemed to be sniffing at the scent of the secret, but Jaks smiled knowingly and shook his head.

"Ask your father," he said, with a warning glance at the fighters watching them in their various stages of arrested sparring. She relaxed into a gesture of submission then, and bowed to Llesho with the time-honored formula of respect. "The teacher becomes the student."

Llesho gave Master Jaks a look that told him he would not settle for nonanswers. But first, he had to ease the fears of the guards who had seen the fight, and would now hesitate to engage with him in his own practice sessions. "However," he said, "the student handles the trident and the spear like a rake and a hoe."

Somewhere in the crowd someone snickered, remembering the insult to the skills of the Thebin pearl divers. He smiled, with deliberate mischief in the grin, and bowed to the guards in their training class and to their teacher. When he looked around, Master Jaks had disappeared. From across the narrow watercourse, Hmishi and Lling were watching him with solemn, dark eyes. Llesho didn't bother to smile at them—no point in it, since he had no consolation to give them, not even the secrets that would only have made them more afraid. With a last bow, he withdrew across the footbridge and rejoined his companions.

"Where is the infirmary?" he asked.

"That way." Lling pointed to an airy building with white cloths blowing at the windows, down another path and across another tiny bridge. Llesho decided that, pretty as it was, he could quickly get quite sick of all the water standing in the way of a straight line to anywhere.

"Do you want us to go with you?" Hmishi asked, but he had taken a protective stance at Lling's shoulder, and Llesho could see the hesitation, the stubbornness in the set of Hmishi's chin.

It hurt that his old friends looked at him with fear and mystery in their eyes, but he could think of nothing to say that would make things the way they were before. He shook his head, and answered with an effort, "No. I just want to visit a friend."

They did not ask him who that friend was, or how he came to have friends other than themselves in the governor's compound, when he had been there just two days and had spent all of that sleeping. He wondered if they were afraid he only had unearthly answers for all their questions now, but watched them go without a word. Then he headed for the infirmary.

The infirmary reminded him of his brother's clinic, and almost he could remember the feel of the cold mountain air on his cheeks and the awkward weight of a too-large broom in his hands. Adar had taken a very literal approach to serving his people. There were no mountains in Farshore, of course, and the breeze blew warm and thick with green and growing things. But each place showed the hand of a healer of the soul as well as the body. The floor and walls were pale, scrubbed wood, the screens left open to the light and the air. The bitter tang of healing herbs and the sweet smells of soothing medicines mixed with the smell of scrubbed wood and boiled linen. He half expected to see Adar himself at the polished workbench, and the reminder of how impossible that was pricked tears at the back of his eyes.

Bixei was sitting up in bed, Kaydu's monkey asleep in the circle of his legs, when Llesho found him.

"There you are!" he said when Llesho poked his head through the open window. "I was beginning to think you were dead!"

"Not dead, just sleeping." Llesho popped through the window, not bothering to look for the door, and flung himself at the foot of the bed. Bixei winced, and the monkey leaped away as if it had been shot from a springboard, screaming monkey obscenities down at them from his new perch on a crossbeam in the rafters.

"Sorry," Llesho said.

"No big deal," Bixei answered. "But you will have to apologize to Little Brother if you don't want him throwing excrement through your window at night."

"Manners like his mistress," Llesho commented.

Bixei was holding onto his bandage protectively. After a moment during which Llesho ignored his questioning frown, Bixei shrugged. "Habiba has a woman apprentice and all her potions smell like flowers," he complained, wrinkling his nose.

"She's not likely to poison you, though, which is an improvement," Llesho said, and Bixei laughed in agreement. "Her cures don't hurt as much as Markko's, that's for sure. But she has a temper. I heard her peeling the bark off Master Jaks. He was meek as a babe while she blistered him with her tongue. When she was done, he slunk away like his knuckles were smarting. Wouldn't give you up to her, though, no matter what."

Llesho heard the question in the gossip, but he

didn't know what to say. "I was just sleeping." Didn't seem worth fighting about to him.

"Little Phoenix—that's Habiba's apprentice—said that you'd been badly mistreated, that you needed care. Jaks said you needed your Thebin friends more, that you would need them around you if you were ever going to feel normal and safe again."

Bixei was watching him for a reaction. When he didn't get one, he pushed a little more. "So where are they, your Thebin friends?"

"They're around."

Oh, hell. He'd kept it together, hadn't thought about it or let it tear him down until now, but suddenly he couldn't stop the shaking. He wrapped his arms tightly around his stomach and glared out into the infirmary while he fought the tears under control.

"What did he do to you?" They both knew Bixei meant Markko, and the months spent in his workroom.

Llesho shook his head, embarrassed enough for one day. He still wasn't sure if they were friends or enemies, or if Bixei would believe him. After all that had happened to him, the months in Markko's workroom were such a little thing. . . .

In spite of his effort at control, Llesho started to cry, tears falling silently and unstoppably down his copper cheeks. "I was afraid all the time. That he would misjudge the dose and kill me with his poisons, or that he wouldn't, and I'd have to go through it all again, puking up my guts on his floor while he took notes on how long it took for my legs to uncurl from the back of my head.

"Sometimes, he threatened to burn me for a witch if I didn't give him the healer Kwan-ti, but I didn't know where she had gone."

He never would have given the healer up to Markko. Not ever.

"Sometimes I wondered," he said to the distance,

as if he could see the past like a play acted out on the surface of his eyes. "If Markko himself did not invent the Blood Tide, for his own purposes. Maybe it was all a game to destroy Lord Chin-shi from the start and Kwan-ti never mattered to him at all, except as a name to burden with his own crimes. "

"I was afraid of him, too," Bixei admitted, offering what comfort he could, though the shock that widened his eyes made it clear he had never guessed how bad it was for Llesho. "I don't think that makes either of us weak."

The image of Lord Chin-shi dead by his own hand in the dirt of the arena filled Llesho's mind with questions, and a warning. "I think that makes us smart."

Jaks chose that moment to make his presence known at the same window Llesho had entered through earlier. "I think you are right," the teacher said. He rested his forearms on the windowsill, but did not pull himself through as his student had done. "Has Bixei been telling tales again?"

"Half the compound must be telling tales about your arguments with Little Phoenix," Bixei returned. "You were loud enough that I'm surprised you didn't wake Llesho out of his trance."

Jaks looked uneasy. "Trance may be more than a joke, so don't repeat it, please."

Bixei hung his head, though Llesho wasn't sure whether he did so out of submission to his teacher's will or out of resentment. Jaks held out a bit of news as a peace offering: "Master Markko has disappeared."

"Was he a spy for Lord Yueh?" Llesho asked.

"Yueh may think so," Jaks answered, "but I doubt Markko considers himself a servant to any man. Lady Chin-shi has also disappeared. It is unlikely she still lives."

Llesho knew what that meant. Lady Chin-shi had been Markko's champion, against her husband. But

Markko returned no feelings of loyalty to his patron, who would have become an inconvenience and an impediment to his escape once his mischief had been done.

"There's my other patient. You have brought him to me after all, Master Jaks?"

A small golden woman with straight dark hair entered the infirmary through the door and tsked at the monkey chattering in the rafters. She wore the plain coat of an apprentice healer, so he wasn't surprised when Master Jaks introduced her.

"This is Little Phoenix. She assists Habiba in the matter of cures and potions in the governor's house."

"I won't hurt you." She took his face in her hands and stared into his eyes. "I hadn't heard that Lord Chin-shi used torture on his slaves," she commented to the weaponmaster, who had dropped back as if he wished to escape this part of the conversation. For Llesho's benefit, she added, "Open your mouth and stick out your tongue."

Llesho clenched his jaw around the black pearl caught between his teeth, but Master Jaks twitched an uncomfortable acknowledgment. "His lordship learned, to his regret, that one welcomes such as Master Markko to the bosom of his home at the peril of all he holds dear.

Llesho paid attention with both ears to the healer's question and Master Jaks' answer. He'd only thought of it as misery when he'd been going through Master Markko's torment, hadn't given it a name or known that it showed.

"Perhaps, if he is fortunate, he will carry the lesson into his next life, where it may do him some good—your tongue, boy." She managed to scowl at both of them while tapping her foot impatiently. Llesho slid his tongue out, but kept his teeth as close together as he could. He opened wide when she took advantage of the small opening to insert a wooden wedge and press his mouth open wide.

"You're lucky he has a brain or a heart, or can stand on his legs at all, Master Jaks. The monster has been feeding him poisons; you can see by the discoloration here, and on the roof of his mouth." She gestured with the stick in his mouth, but withdrew it before Jaks could take a look. "Fortunately, he comes to us with protections of his own. Den's work?"

Jaks shook his head. "Not until the very end."

"Someone, then, has done you a favor. If he relied on the protection of his master, he'd be dead by now. I don't know what Markko was thinking, but this boy should be dead." Taking the stick out of his mouth, she nudged his chin up with the palm of her hand, asking Llesho neither for an explanation of Markko's thinking nor for the source of the pearl between his teeth.

"He needs pure food and warmth and rest, maybe a tincture to leech the poisons from his bones. And I want him here, under observation, for tonight at the least."

"No. I'm going home." Llesho stopped breathing, brought up short as he surprised himself. He did not see in his mind's eye the house he now shared with Lling and Hmishi when he said, "home." Didn't see the barracks at Pearl Island, or the longhouse where the pearl divers slept. He saw Thebin's high, sere plain, its stunted trees twisted in the thin cold wind, and the snow, drifting to the roofs of the scattered farms and cottages. In memory he looked out at the city from the balcony of state at the Palace of the Sun. He saw temples to the gods of a hundred different faiths. The largest, devoted to the Goddess of the Moon and the symbolic home of his mother the queen, glowed in the rose of a sunrise spearing through the mountain passes to the east.

Somehow, Master Jaks saw where his mind had taken him. "It appears that Llesho has other plans," he said, but the set of his mouth and the hard determination in his eyes promised more.

"And Bixei?" Llesho asked.

"That boy is going nowhere," Little Phoenix complained. "He has dressings to change, and wounds that need healing."

"We don't know who we can safely trust here," Bixei seemed to be weighing something in the way Master Jaks centered all his attention on Llesho. Finally he decided. "Somebody's got to watch the pearl diver's behind out there."

So. Friends, then. Something settled quietly into place for Llesho. He gave the other boy a mock frown and a tart, "Keep your eyes *off* my behind."

Then he grinned. With Bixei at his back, and his Thebin friends around him, he could ignore for a time the sense of powers closing in on him. "*Girls* fight in the governor's army," he said with glee.

"No boys?" Bixei demanded, even as Master Jaks was advising, "They are women. I'd suggest you remember that if you want to finish your training with all your parts in working order."

Little Phoenix took pity on him. "Yes, Bixei, there are men in the guards as well, but you will have to ask for the first date." She ruffled his hair affectionately. "The rules of the governor's house don't permit active guardsmen to take advantage of the novices."

"Kaydu can take advantage of me if she wants," Llesho volunteered just to make his teacher take that playful swat at his ear. Bixei looked doubtful.

Jaks seemed to understand his hesitation. "I've never seen a will that didn't find a way," he offered. Something seemed to pass between them then, assurance and warning, and acceptance of both. Then Bixei gave one sharp nod.

"All right, then. I'm ready to leave."

Little Phoenix glared at Master Jaks, blaming him for the flight of her charges.

"Not a bit of sense if you put all your brains together. Well, take him if you must, but bring him back in the morning to check those wounds. Habiba will have all our heads if we bring infection into this house."

"Yes, Mistress Little Phoenix." Llesho knew when he had gotten off more lightly than he deserved, and he bowed deeply. Even Master Jaks at the window gave a respectful nod of his head.

Bixei could not bend without pain in his leg, but he dropped his eyes in an appropriate display of submission. With Llesho supporting him under one arm, he walked slowly back to the novice house they would share with the Thebin pearl divers turned provincial guards.

"I've never seen anything like this," Bixei said as he looked around the water gardens. Llesho didn't say anything. He was thinking about his mother's gardens, hardy plants that defied the winter and the hard land that ran with water only during the spring thaw. Jaks said nothing, but set his lips in a grim line. Llesho wondered what gardens the teacher saw in his head, and if he missed wherever his home had been before slavery and the arena brought him to Farshore.

"Where are you from?" Llesho asked his teacher, filling the silence. The question broke half a dozen taboos between slaves, but the infirmary seemed a place out of time somehow, and made many impossible things seem reasonable—like asking a weaponmaster a personal question.

"Farshore."

Bixei gasped, but Llesho met his gaze levelly and said nothing more. Slaves came from three sources: conquest, prisons, and birth to a slave. Bixei had been born into slavery. He struggled to better his condition in the arena, but none of his actions revealed any fragments of a lost past. He'd assumed that Master Jaks, like himself, had been captured in a battle or raid, but Farshore had been a part of the empire since before Llesho's grandparents were born. That left prison.

There were hundreds of laws that could lead to indenture or slavery, including treachery and treason. Unbidden, speculation tickled at Llesho's mind. He looked at the six tattooed rings on Master Jaks' arm, visible marks on his body that warned all who saw him of the six men he had murdered as an assassin. Her ladyship had shown no sign of disapproval when she spoke of Master Jaks' kills. Nor did murderers find their way to the slave markets, being considered too dangerous. So how had the man come to be a slave and a weaponmaster? Why had Llesho trusted him from the first moment he set eyes upon him? That wasn't even a question. He had known Jaks, not personally or for the skill that named him master, but by the uniform he wore and even the rings on his arm. The king of Thebin had trusted his family and his nation to this man's kind, of course, and had lost it all—nation, family, life itself. Could Llesho afford to trust again?

Jaks said nothing, daring him to ask. Not today, he decided. Not until I understand what plots the governor's lady is scheming and how a mercenary assassin turned weapons teacher fit into them. Knowing might make the asking easier, but Llesho thought it might just make the trusting harder. So he waited.

Chapter Fourteen

WITH Llesho awake, and Bixei added to the novice house, alliances shifted and clashed in ways that drove Llesho out into the night just to avoid the quarreling. Bixei, in his usual way, wanted to lord it over the house because he was older by a year, and bigger than the Thebins. Hmishi looked to Lling for direction. Lling wanted them all to shut up so that Llesho could rest, but Bixei wouldn't listen to a girl even if he knew she was right. Llesho left them to bicker among themselves, hoping they'd come to some sort of agreement before he came back. Putting the din of his housemates behind him, he drifted down the flagged path toward the practice field, silent and empty at this time of night. Perfect for thinking.

The fight with Kaydu had shaken him. If Master Jaks hadn't stopped him, he would have maimed or even killed her. It wasn't her fault, or even her failure of skill. Kaydu, after all, had thought they were sparring, and did not fight as she might in a battle to the death. That mistake had almost ended her life. Until the fight with Kaydu, Llesho hadn't realized how completely focused on killing his knife training had been. He had heard the warnings, but Master Den and Master

Jaks both had taken care never to let him get the upper hand in their sparring practice. Just when he thought he was getting close to a win, one or the other of them would disarm him before he could do any damage. He hadn't realized that the only follow-through he had was deadly. Jaks believed that Llesho had already killed. If it was true, he was glad he didn't remember.

He shivered at the reminder, but something rattled loose in his mind in spite of his heartfelt prayer to forget: a guard, dressed like Master Jaks in figured leathers and a beaten brass belt and wrist guards, but with a bloody smile where his throat should have been. A Harn raider lay across the body, his eyes wide and glassy, Llesho's knife buried in his back. The guard's name was Khri, and he'd shoved Llesho behind a wall hanging that draped soft folds across a window overlooking the palace gardens. Beside the window was one of the fragile chairs scattered about the halls for the convenience of the old men and women who advised the king. Hidden by the draping of the wall hanging, Llesho had climbed up on the chair. He drew his knife from the soft belt where his scabbard always hung, and waited until the battle for the hall had turned its back on him. Then he'd struck.

At seven summers he hadn't had the strength to stab a raider through his heavy clothing, not even with a knife as sharp as the Thebin blade he had carried. But the chair had slipped and sent him flying after the knife. With trained instinct, he'd turned the blade sideways and felt it slide between the raider's ribs. The man had died, blood bubbling from between his lips. Too late to save Khri. Too late to save his father. Or his sister. Maybe too late to save his mother. The memory got all mixed up in his head with Lleck, floating in front of him in the bay, telling him to find his brothers. Not too late to save them, maybe.

When Master Jaks said that he had killed, Llesho

had wanted to deny it, to separate himself from all the violence and mayhem that had marked his life, right up to the Blood Tide and Master Markko's poisons and Lord Chin-shi, who had treated him kindly one night and then died at his own hand. With the new memory, however, had come the tactile recall of blood slick on his knife, his fingers, and the pure fire of rage that had lit his young heart. If he'd been older, if he'd been trained in all the weapons of a warrior, he would have raged through the palace with the wrath of the ages, cutting down the Harn raiders like wheat in a storm. After all these years, the desire to fight his way to the throne room and stop the slaughter returned to him so powerfully that he pulled the knife from his garments and slashed around him in a wide swath, imagining the necks of raiders in its path.

"Whoa."

He stumbled, didn't recognize the voice until Kaydu added, "It's only me!" Then he dropped the hand that held the knife like it was made of stone.

"I'm sorry," he said, and bowed low to her. "I didn't know anyone else was out."

"I'll leave you alone if you want."

He shook his head and Kaydu walked past him to the center of the footbridge that led to the practice field. Dropping to its wooden surface, she let her feet dangle almost to the water.

"Where is your monkey?"

Kaydu gave a soft laugh. "He would say that he keeps guard over my possessions, if he could speak. Actually, though, he is sleeping in the rafters of the guardhouse, enjoying his monkey dreams."

Llesho thought it would be impolite to let his relief show. Little Brother had not, so far, made a favorable impression on him. He sat down next to Kaydu on the bridge, but kept his feet tucked up under him while he watched the carp come up and nibble at her toes.

"I'm not supposed to feed them," she said, aiming a bread crumb at the head of the largest fish. Distracted, the carp chased after the bread, as did his fellows. Llesho said nothing, but took the bit of loaf Kaydu offered him and sent a crumb after the fish as well. Kaydu clucked at him and mockingly chastised, "You will make that old fellow fat as fat if you don't stop that. I'll have to dig him a new pond!"

"I can't imagine your father saying such a thing!" Llesho chuckled in spite of himself.

"Nor can I," she admitted. "He is more likely to say, 'Actions have consequences, daughter. Decide if you can live with the last step before you take the first step.' The governor, however, is more down to earth, and cares more about his fish than philosophy."

"But you don't agree with him?"

"Oh, his excellency is right, as always. The old carp *will* get too fat. And we will need to deepen and widen the pond to keep him." She grinned at Llesho. "It's a game between the two of them, carp and governor. I am on the carp's side."

"You are very strange," Llesho pointed out to her. But he threw another bit of bread at the carp, making his own allegiance known.

"Comes of being the daughter of the governor's witch," she said, a reminder that he didn't need, then asked him, "What were you doing when I came along?"

"Avoiding my housemates," he admitted. "I am hoping that by the time I return, the trumpeting and beating of chests will have ended, they will have decided on a winner and a loser, and I can sleep in peace."

"You're supposed to be getting rest, not running away from quarrels. Little Phoenix will have their heads if she finds out."

"But she won't. Find out, I mean. Will she?"

Kaydu studied his face for a moment before she

shrugged. "Not from me. That isn't what I meant anyway. What were you doing with your knife?"

"Remembering." He pulled it back out of its scabbard and weighed the heft of it in his palm. "Master Jaks was right. I killed the Harn raider who murdered my guard. Khri was a lot like Master Jaks. Looked sort of like him, wore the same decorations on his wrist guards. No tattoos on his arms, though."

"Master Jaks is a very dangerous man," Kaydu pointed out.

Assassinations. He wondered if she knew. "So was Khri. I couldn't save him, but he gave me time to save myself. Since that's what he was dying for, I guess it was enough.

"I was only seven," he added. "I couldn't save anyone but myself. They assassinated my father, killed my sister, and threw her body on a rubbish heap. The rest of us they separated and sold. Still—" he held the Thebin knife up, watched moonlight play along its blade—"it could have been worse." It had been, for Khri. "If the governor's lady keeps her word, next summer I will leave here a free man, a warrior."

"Who are you?" she asked.

Llesho blushed and dropped his head. For eight summers he'd kept his secrets to himself, but he couldn't remember to keep his guard up around her. Now he'd said too much, and he couldn't figure a way out of what he'd revealed.

"Nobody," he said.

"I don't think so." She rejected that with a skeptical eyebrow, raised and waiting for a better answer. Too late, he remembered what Lleck had always said, that lips once opened could be shut, but the words couldn't be stuffed back inside and forgotten. Words always had consequences. Seemed like the old minister had a lot in common with Habiba, the governor's witch. Both were better at philosophy than practical advice, like what did you do when a pretty girl who could beat you at tridents set the words tumbling like rose petals offered at her feet.

"Once, maybe I was something," he admitted. "Now just another Champion of the Goddess." Even here in Farshore they knew about the Champions, half priest, half knight, and all mad, who wandered the length and breadth of four empires committing strange acts of chivalry and daring in the name of the goddess. It was considered a sin to send a Champion hungry from your door, but no one sent out invitations, and they were considered well rid of when they went on their way. Kaydu laughed, as she was meant to do, but she hadn't stopped thinking.

"Thebin's Deliverer," she said. "That's what my father calls you. Master Jaks tells him not to count his worms and call them fishes."

Llesho's head dropped. From the moment the governor's lady had appeared disguised as a peasant in the weapons room at Pearl Island to watch him with the knife, his secrets had belonged to others. Perhaps not all of them, however. He met Kaydu's serious gaze with one more dire. "Retribution," he said. He slid the knife home and met her curious gaze, held it. "Don't tell."

"I won't."

She got up and left so quickly that he didn't register what direction she had gone. With a deep sigh he did the same, turning toward the novice house with considerably slower feet. When he arrived, peace had descended; his three companions waited for him in the dull glow of the stove.

"We talked," Bixei said, but Llesho noticed that Hmishi had a puffy wedge under his eye that was growing darker by the minute, and blood dampened Bixei's bandages.

Lling had no signs of bodily damage, but she watched Hmishi with that short-leash expression that meant she wasn't taking any more nonsense from the males in this group, not even from her own. "We figured out that you are the only thing we have in common," she said, and he didn't like the way she said it.

"I won't—" he began, but just then Kaydu popped her head in the door, and followed it with a bedroll and a small bundle that chimed out of tune like the bell of a clapper wrapped in cloth.

"Who's she?" Bixei asked. Hmishi and Lling were passing horrified glances as if they thought the others in the room couldn't see them.

"I'm Kaydu," she said, unrolling the bundle and taking out a wind chime, which she hung in the open window. "And I'm moving in with you." The wind stirred the chimes, and she gave them a satisfied nod before spreading her bedroll on the floor by the door.

"I suggest we all get some sleep now. The morning will be hard enough on you babies." She gave the Thebins a grin with too many teeth showing, but no one moved. Instead, they looked to Llesho, who stared belligerently back at them.

"I'm tired," he said, and dropped into his bunk with a sulk coming on strong. He did not ask for this, did not want this, and didn't even know why it was happening to him. But he'd be damned if he'd let worrying about it keep him awake. He closed his eyes with stubborn determination. For all his display of resting, however, he was the last left awake, long after the glow in the stove had dimmed to gray ash. Eventually, however, his body gave in to the orders his brain was sending, and he slept to the peaceful sound of the wind chime in the night.

Llesho spent a restless night haunted by the specters of Harn raiders drifting like shadows through the halls of the Palace of the Sun, their horsetail decorations hanging motionless down their backs. In his dreams,

Llesho walked the same halls with blood on his hands, looking for water to wash them in. At each stop he came upon the body of someone he loved or knew—his mother, Master Den, his guard, Khri, his brothers—and knelt and tried to wash his hands in their blood, like a ritual that never ended. He did not know if he washed away his sins, or bathed in the guilt of surviving when all about him had died. Huddled at the base of the East Gate he found his companions, Lling and Hmishi, Bixei and Kaydu, all dead with the marks of their wounds drying in the harsh wind. The governor's lady stood over them with a terrible fire in her eyes.

He moaned and pulled out of sleep to find his companions still alive and gathered around his bed in the chill dawn light.

"You were calling out in your sleep," Kaydu told him. Little Brother had found her, and he lay curled in her arms, watching Llesho out of deep, dark, accusing eyes.

Bixei fixed a sharp look on him. "What language was that?"

Llesho glared at him. "I don't know," he said, "I was asleep at the time."

"High Thebin," Lling said. She stood her ground, though her voice shook. Hmishi had already dropped to his knees, his head to the floor, where he set up a low keening that seemed to wrench from his throat. Even Kaydu bowed her head to him, though Bixei looked from one to the other with the growing anger with which he always met confusion.

"You must be mistaken," Llesho objected. His Thebin companions would not meet his gaze. Kaydu twisted an eyebrow in a show of ironic disbelief, although he was actually telling the truth as far as he knew it.

High Thebin. The language of priests and the law. The language of his Thebin gods, of prophecy. No one used High Thebin for normal conversation, not even in the palace, though his companions wouldn't know that. Llesho had forgotten all of it he'd ever known years ago in the pearl beds. Lleck, perhaps, would have continued his education in the high language, except that it had been too dangerous with a witch-finder in the longhouse and politics in the overseer's cottage. He wondered what had dredged the language from the back of his mind, and didn't like the only answer he could think of: the gods were angry that he had not yet rescued his brothers. Pointless to ask what he had said, though; no one else in the room spoke the language. Llesho was considering what the governor would do to him if he escaped the compound when a servant appeared and bowed in the doorway. For a moment Llesho wondered if his excellency, or his witch, read minds, but he shuddered the notion out of his thoughts. Coincidence.

"His excellency the governor wishes the presence of the young gentleman Llesho at his convenience," the servant said, and waited patiently for Llesho to dig himself out from under his blanket.

"I will follow in ten minutes," he assured the servant in a less than steady voice. The servant bowed again and departed with his message.

"I don't know what you are thinking," Llesho said to his companions, who continued to watch him as if he might sprout wings and fly. "But it will have to wait." He pushed through them, grabbing his clothes as he passed, and headed for the outhouse and the baths in that order. Maybe he'd learn something in his audience with the governor that would clear up why he was here. And why he had suddenly started dreaming in High Thebin.

When he arrived in the audience chamber, Llesho saw that Kaydu had arrived ahead of him. She stood beside her father's chair at the left hand of the governor.

Master Jaks stood a little to the right, watchful but not participating in the debate at the center of the room. The governor and his lady had abandoned their high platform seats of state for straight-backed chairs set in front of a large table on which maps were spread. The governor looked up absently when Llesho was announced and motioned to him to come forward and study the map.

"Tell us all you can about the Harn," he said without any warning, and Llesho felt his mouth drop open.

"Bumpkin," he chided himself, and stood a little straighter. He sneaked a sideways look at Master Jaks, who seemed impassively approving, so he took a chance and put on his "royal" mien: spine stretched, shoulders back, chin out, and rested his fingers splayed over the map. "What do you want to know?" he asked, and added, to qualify his answers, "I was very young when the raiders came, and I don't remember much of what I did see."

Habiba, the governor's witch, spoke up then. "You will," he said. Llesho caught his level gaze, and could not look away. This, he thought, is what it must be like to meet the cobra. With a purposeful gesture at the map, Habiba released him, and Llesho discovered that he could breathe again.

Her ladyship interceded with a mild reproof for the witch. She smiled at Llesho, and he trusted that less than he had the stern-faced judge she had shown him in the weapons room. "Start with what you know, child."

He let out a deep sigh, ordering his thoughts, then pulled himself together again to address the company. "They are evil."

He thought about the evil he had encountered since then, great evil in the slave market, and petty evil in Tsu-tan the witch-finder, and the evil of a grasping poisonous spider in overseer Markko, and they all shared the same feel, like slime on the eyeballs just from looking at them.

"They live out on the plains, in tents, and raise horses. They hate cities. They hate beauty. They measure their worth against each other—who has the most wealth, the most horses, the most kills. When they kill, they cut off the hair of their victim, and tie it like a horsetail, and sew it to their battle dress." Llesho's mind had passed out of the governor's audience chamber at Farshore, and wandered again the halls of the Palace of the Sun, echoing with the terrified screams of the victims and the lust-filled cries of triumph of the Harn raiders, who shouted with joy and exultation when they killed. "I saw a Harn raider kill my lady's first attendant in the throne room. He cut off the braid of her hair with its jeweled decorations still in it. Then he sat himself on the throne—" Llesho stumbled, almost said, "my father's throne," but kept that part of his secret. They knew he came from the palace, but perhaps they did not know on what pillow his head had lain. "He sat on the throne, stitching the braid to his chest while the lady herself lay dying at his feet."

When he looked up, the governor flinched, but her ladyship met Llesho's ravaged shock with the cold calculation he remembered. This time he found it comforting; she did not shy away from the horror of his story, but took it in, and measured his worth in his survival. He remembered the look on Khri's face when his guard had tucked him behind the curtain with a warning to be still, and he found something of that same determined acceptance of the deadly battle in her ladyship's eyes. Oddly, she reminded him of Kwan-ti for a moment. But Kwan-ti was gone, along with everything that had ever given the young prince comfort in exile, including now friends and shiftmates, driven away by the strange language that escaped him in his dreams.

Her ladyship acknowledged all his losses in the tilt of her head, but gave him no pity, and so he was able to go on.

"They killed anyone who opposed them and stripped the palace to the bare mud walls. Then they gathered together everyone who was left. The babies and the very old—anyone who could not walk to the slave markets on their own feet—they murdered in the square, and threw their bodies in piles like garbage. The rest of us they herded like their horses to market."

Habiba slipped a quiet question into his reverie: "I thought that Thebin had no slave markets."

Llesho nodded. "Thebin was free, ruled in the name of the gods of the earth and the goddess in heaven. We walked to Shan."

Kaydu answered his claim with a snort. "That's impossible. Shan is thousands of li from Thebin. No child could walk that far."

"Not impossible." Habiba set his elbows carefully on the edges of the map and buried his face in his hands for a moment, as if to wash away all expression. "Most Thebin slaves are seized out in the provinces and brought to market in carts or by river. To the Harn, they're just property and receive the care necessary to bring a profit. They didn't really care if anyone from the holy city survived to reach the market, however. The Long March served as a warning to others who would oppose them.

"We were ten thousand when we left Kungol, the holy city," Llesho continued, "and fewer than a thousand when we came to market in Shan. Of those, the Harn decided half were unfit, and slit their throats. The rest of us, they sold, dispersed throughout the empire as a reminder as much as for the money, I think."

"But you survived," Habiba prodded, though he would not meet Llesho's eyes.

"Yes. I survived." Llesho kept his chin high as a prince of Thebin must, even when his heart was shivering into pieces at memories he could not bear. He would not tell them how, though he figured they could guess. Must have guessed, because the governor looked away, and Master Jaks had disappeared completely somewhere inside his own head. Kaydu still stared at him as if she did not yet believe him. Only her ladyship met his glance without flinching or looking away. It felt like he was falling into her eyes, swimming in depths as dark and hidden as the sea. She did not ask, and he did not offer, that he had lived on the lives of others, eating their food when his own ration would not keep a flea alive, and passed from hand to hand, carried when the guards could be distracted to other parts of the long trail of dying Thebins. He deserved no credit for surviving, buying his own life as he did each day with the lives of his people.

Her ladyship did not condemn him, though he saw in her eyes all the deaths his life had cost. "If you wish to be a general," she said to Kaydu, though Llesho knew the message was for him, "learn this lesson. When everything is lost, down to the last hope of the soul, a good leader will lay down his life for his people. A great leader will continue to live, to give the people hope in spite of the despair that may have seized him."

He would have told her that he had earned no praise for surviving for his people, since they had not let him die. But her ladyship set a hand upon her husband's sleeve.

"Yes, dear." He wiped a tear from his gray face. "That is enough for now, I think. You may go."

Llesho bowed low to depart, but her ladyship detained him. "Meet me at the dinner hour, in the grove," she said. "It is time you learned the art of archery."

Llesho wondered if she meant before or after dinner;

she seemed to read his expression if not his mind, because she smiled and added, "We will dine on peaches from the orchard."

With a final obeisance, Llesho took his leave.

Chapter Fifteen

THE grove where Llesho met with the governor's lady smelled of peaches and ripe plums in the late afternoon sun. Since he had neither bow nor arrows, he came with empty hands and waited, watching the golden coins of sunlight dapple the grass beneath the trees. He did not wait long, however, before the sound of chimes reached him, and the lady entered the grove carrying an empty bowl. One servant came ahead of her, ringing the bells that heralded her arrival, and four servants followed. Two carried bows as proudly unbent and almost as tall as the lady herself, and two bore elaborately embroidered quivers, each with twelve arrows in it. The lady set the bowl on the ground beneath a tree and smiled at him.

"We will work for our supper tonight," she said with a smile. Then she motioned forward the servants. "You will learn the Way of the Goddess with the bow."

Llesho blushed a deep crimson. The Way was sacred to his people, the path of the goddess known only to her handmaidens and her chosen consorts. As a prince of the sacred blood, his own life belonged to the goddess, who might accept or reject him as her consort during the vigil celebration of his sixteenth natal day. That day approached, but he had not yet offered his manhood as husband in heaven, nor did he know how he would do so when the time came.

As an unfledged prince, he had no right to anticipate the pleasure of his goddess by learning her Way, and it shocked him to find the secrets of his own culture in a Farshore orchard. "I did not know the people of Farshore followed the goddess."

"My lord the governor allows me a small shrine at the back of his gardens, as he wishes in all things to please me." Her ladyship spoke as if this will to her pleasure came as her due. Her explanation left more questions than answers between them, not the least of which was how one who knew the sacred Way of his culture could offer the knowledge to him as if it were no more than gladiator training for the arena. Therefore, he bowed his head very low, and his voice shook with terror when he objected, "If you worship the goddess, then you must know that what you suggest is improper for me to learn."

"The Way belongs to all people who believe," she chided him, "Don't let the ignorance of priests who crave their own power blind you to the truth." As a slave, her remote glance reminded him, he had no right to question his master's wishes.

"As you wish." He bowed to her again, in proper submission, and offered his silent repentance to the dead priests of the Temple of the Moon, and to the goddess whom they served.

Her ladyship returned his bow with a nod of acknowledgment, and began her instruction.

"The bow is like the will. The man who does not bend, who cannot yield, stands alone and apart from nature. He is powerful only when he bends his will to the string."

She took the first bow in her hands and pulled a coil of twisted gut from a deep pocket in her outer coat. "Choose your bow as you would choose a warhorse," she said. "It must be strong and sure, and yet, must bend to your will."

She showed him how to string the bow she held and then handed him the second bow and a second coil of gut. "Likewise, the man must bend his will to the bow, become the yielding string that subdues the bow to its flexible strength."

Llesho fumbled the task. No bolts of lightning descended from the blue sky to strike him dead, so he let himself relax into the bow, bending his own soul to the will of the goddess as the bow bent to the string.

Next, her ladyship took an arrow from the quiver offered by a waiting servant and held it out on her extended palm.

"The point, or head of the arrow," she said, making a graceful gesture with her free hand to draw his attention to the stone chip affixed to one end of the arrow, "must be cunning and sharp. Making arrowheads requires rare skill. You may develop the knack, but it is better to acquire them from a maker than settle for second best, even if they are your own. The true archer never pollutes his arrow with spell or potion, but trusts to the well-cut stone, the clear eye, and the strong arm.

"The shaft—" She ran a finger along the wooden length of the arrow. "It must be perfectly straight. Learn to carve your own, for only then can you be certain that your arrow will follow the flight of your heart. Be careful what prayer you carve into its woody flesh; your heart should be as straight and uncompromising as the shaft of your arrow.

"Fletching—" She held up the arrow between two fingers and directed his attention to the feathers at the nether end. "It stabilizes the arrow and gives it flight. Learn the language that the fletching speaks: hawk feathers for war; dove for peace. Fletching of swan's feathers swear the true love of the archer.

"Think of the completed arrow as an egg. All that the bird will become in flight is contained in its birth. If the wings are unformed, the bird will not fly. If it is too easily buffeted by the wind and turned off its course, it will never reach its destination. If its beak does not harden, it cannot crack open seeds, and it will die. So you must ensure that each arrow is perfect, like the egg, so that the arrow's flight will be perfect, like the bird's."

She did not demand that he learn to construct arrows on the spot, fortunately, but moved on to the next step. Putting the strung bow in his right hand and an arrow in Llesho's left hand, she stood at his back and wrapped her arms around his arms, her hands around his hands, so that they clasped the curved wood before them with their entwined fingers. "You can fight the bow," she said, "or you can be the bow," And she fitted the arrow to the notch of the string and pulled.

"You can let the arrow go, or you can release your heart with the arrow, and be its flight—" He could feel her smile skim his ear as she let the arrow fly into the tree beneath which her bowl was positioned. And into the bowl fell a peach, freed by the arrow. "Try it."

Llesho took his own bow in his hand, and set an arrow, pulling back on the string. He felt as if he were pulling against his own weight in the bow; it did not yield.

"You are trying to force the bow," her ladyship corrected him. "You must caress it, not overpower it. Become the bow and find it in your will to *want* to bend. . . ."

She did not touch him, but her voice caressed him like fingers on his spine. Llesho took a deep breath, let it out again, and let the feel of smooth wood bow and taut gut string sink into his being. "Like the willow," he thought, "bending before the storm, enfolding the stream—" and as he thought, he drew back on the string until the arrow poised on a line with his eye, and he felt the goal in his nerves and his being, the stem of a ripe peach high in the lady's tree. *Fly,* he thought, and felt his spirit fly, spin unerringly out into the universe, twanging by the stem of the peach which fell as he passed it, reaching out to the top of his flight, and curving back to earth.

When he returned to himself, the bowl held a second peach, and the governor's lady had fixed a sharp but approving eye on him. "Can you tell me where the arrow fell?" she asked.

Llesho nodded and closed his eyes. "There," he said, and pointed to the place where the arrow had plunged to earth, its head buried in the ground, its fletching upright like a banner.

"Again?" she asked, and he nodded, unable to form thoughts into sentences while he lived the graceful curve of wood and the teasing tension of the string. Carefully he set the arrow, and studied the tree. Then he closed his eyes, pulled back on the string with two fingers bracketing his arrow—his heart—and let himself fly. His body did not relax back into itself until the peach hit the bowl with a soft thunk, and the lady at his side laughed.

"Tomorrow, on horseback," she said. Llesho could not tell her that he had never ridden a warhorse, but only the shaggy, ill-tempered Thebin pony that had hated its caparisons as much as Llesho had hated the thin beaten plates of his child's armor. They had been but poor reminders of an ancient time when the Harn would not have dared to cross the Thebin border.

He'd cross that bridge tomorrow—an apt metaphor, he realized, given the number of bridges scattered about the governor's compound. Her ladyship walked over to the peach tree and sat beside her bowl of peaches.

"Tell me about Pearl Island," she said, holding a

peach out to him. He sat beside her, his legs crossed in front of him, thinking he might be falling under a spell she cast over the orchard. Then he remembered the cold, sharp expression she had worn when Master Jaks had tested him on the Thebin knife. He took the peach, therefore, but decided to remember that she was, after all, the governor's lady, and a dangerous person by any lights.

"What do you want to know?" He bit into the peach, so sweet and ripe that the juices spurted on his chin, and he ducked his head and wiped his face with his sleeve.

She spoke casually when she answered, as if she hadn't seen the sticky juice decorating his chin.

"Tell me about your life. How you came to be in training as a gladiator." She did not ask him about Thebin, and Llesho was grateful for that. The governor's questions had felt like poking at unhealed wounds, and he wanted to think of anything but the bloody body of his dead father, his sister bleeding out her life on a pile of refuse.

"I don't know." Llesho shrugged his shoulders, almost as embarrassed at the question as at the mess he was making of the peach. "At first, I lived in the longhouse with Lling and Hmishi, and the others who worked in the pearl beds. We aren't from the same part of Thebin, but we got along once Hmishi and I fought over who would be leader."

"Who won?"

"Lling, of course." He laughed. "She is smarter than both of us, and she fights dirty. And winning really mattered to her; she wouldn't give up until we admitted she had won."

"Good for Lling," her ladyship said softly, but with real admiration in her voice. "What happened to the pearl beds?"

Llesho shrugged, but he felt his entire body grow cold. "I don't know," he said, "I was gone by then, into the training compound to be a gladiator. Sometimes, when a diver stays below too long, he begins seeing visions, If he survives the first time, he is likely to do it again, and again, trying to get the visions back, until he drowns—"

"And you saw visions?"

He nodded.

"And were they the figments of an oxygen-deprived mind?" she asked him, and he stared at her, afraid to answer the question. She would think he was mad, or a witch, if he gave her the truth, and know he was lying if he didn't. While admitting to being a witch didn't seem as deadly in the governor's compound as it would on Pearl Island, he was no Habiba, and didn't want her getting funny ideas about him. She honored his privacy, or accepted his silence for her own reasons, and brought him back to the original question: "Even in the training compound, you must have heard rumors about the pearl beds."

When she looked into his eyes, Llesho remembered what she had said about the feathers on the arrow: her glance pierced him, like a hawk, and he wondered what war he had stumbled into.

"Yes," he said, nodding. "Lord Chin-shi, they said, was afraid of witches. Master Markko, the overseer, convinced his lordship that our healer, Kwan-ti, was a witch, but she disappeared before he could gather evidence to prove any crime. Soon after that the Blood Tide came and killed everything in the surrounding sea. Master Markko declared that Kwan-ti had created the Blood Tide to punish Lord Chin-shi for his actions against her."

"Kwan-ti disappeared before the Blood Tide?"

Llesho nodded. "The Blood Tide came soon after. But I never saw her commit an evil act. I don't think she was able to do evil, even to save herself."

"I think you are right. But if not Kwan-ti, who ruined Lord Chin-shi with the deadly tide?"

"Did it have to be a person?" he asked in return, "Might it not have been a freak of the sea itself?"

"No, Llesho," she answered carefully, and he wondered if she thought the truth would frighten him or turn him against her. "The sea behaves in certain ways, according to its nature and the seasons. To create the Blood Tide, someone had to change the nature of the very sea—to poison it with devouring life that does not occur naturally in these waters—where it touched upon Pearl Island. Who do you think would have wanted to do something like that?"

Llesho remembered Lord Chin-shi's chambers, his lordship's pressing questions and his own regret that he had no answers to give. He had fallen asleep while Lord Chin-shi struggled through the night to find an antidote for the poisoned bay. Lord Chin-shi had failed, losing everything, and had died by his own hand. Llesho could not help feeling that the failure was somehow his own. "I think Lord Chin-shi believed I might be a witch, or that if Kwan-ti was truly a witch, she had taught me her spells, and that perhaps I could stop the Blood Tide," he said. "But I'm not, and I couldn't."

"You could have, Llesho," she said, and touched a tentative hand to his cheek. "You are the favored of the goddess, had you but known to entreat her."

"No," he said, shaking his head, denying it to himself as much as correcting her ladyship's misunderstanding. "My only talent seems to be surviving disasters; I can't do a thing to prevent them, and for all I know, something about me calls disasters down on my head. But I don't have anything to do with it. It just happens."

"Surviving is perhaps the greatest talent of all, child. But if not Kwan-ti, who killed Chin-shi's pearl beds?"

Her explanation of the tide had shed a different light on Lord Chin-shi's fall. If fate and the sea had set the plague on the oyster beds, the worst any of them had done was let it happen. He knew that Kwan-ti had not seeded the plague when she left, but she might have been healing the bay, holding off disaster until staying even a day longer meant her death. Freed of her restraining touch, the poison had quickly taken hold. And Llesho knew about poisons.

"Master Markko," he said. "His workroom smelled of poisons and rot, and dead things." He truly didn't want to think about Markko, or the workroom where the overseer had chained him to the floor. He didn't want to see Lord Chin-shi dead in the sand of the arena, either, but that had happened, too.

"I think Lord Chin-shi was himself a witch," Llesho ventured, "but he couldn't find the cure for the pearl beds."

"Not a witch," the lady corrected him, "but certainly an alchemist, which is much the same thing and probably what your Kwan-ti was, more or less." She stood up then, and handed the peach bowl to a servant while Llesho jumped to his feet.

"Master Markko has passed to Lord Yueh, who held many of Lord Chin-shi's debts," she added.

It made sense, all except for why she was telling him, which he asked her pointedly.

"Because you need to know," she answered as if it were the most obvious thing in the world, though he couldn't imagine why. "I hope we are not already too late."

She left him there with one of the bows, and a quiver of arrows. He watched her go, unable to drive from his mind either their conversation or the fear that seemed to grip her at the last. Too late for what?

In the weeks that followed, the novices trained together in weapons and in unarmed combat. Her ladyship herself led them in archery on many days, and Llesho found that he excelled at the weapon. As he grew in skill he found his thoughts moving more deeply and more slowly, whereas his reflexes reacted like lightning. Kaydu taught a sharper, faster, dirtier form of hand-to-hand than Master Den had done, and she included deadly moves that grew out of forms that assumed a larger opponent with intent to kill.

Master Jaks took up the teaching of armed combat without the rules of engagement that governed the arena, but that was suited to working in pairs and groups to attain one goal. Extraction and infiltration became a part of the training, skills that no gladiator would need, but that turned them into soldiers capable of moving at the forefront of a massed troop, or running and fighting in small bursts of guerrilla action. Or working as assassins in the enemy camp.

It seemed natural that the novices should train together. They soon learned each other's strengths and weaknesses, and forged a purpose with Llesho at its center. Kaydu joined them when she could free herself from her own teaching duties, acting as student and as teacher under Master Jaks' instruction. Llesho grew confident in wielding his small cadre as a force, sending Bixei to the front with a glance when strength and intimidation might avoid bloodshed, unleashing Kaydu for stealth attacks; she could move soundlessly through dry reeds, and her combat skills fit her like her skin. Lling he begged with his eyes to talk them out of trouble, or to hold ground if talk did not work.

Hmishi, it turned out, was the fiercest fighter of them all, but only if the life of a companion was at risk. In practice his moves were hesitant and laden with apologies and the wounded pain of doing harm to others. When, in exasperation, Master Jaks pulled him in front of the troops at practice and told him to fight or die, Hmishi had stumbled and mumbled, absorbing the jeers of the guards and the curses of his teacher. Then a knife caught him in a deep downward slash across the cheek, and he realized that Master Jaks had meant every word. They weren't playing at tridents with their muck rakes anymore, and Master Jaks would kill him dead where he stood rather than let him be a burden on his team.

Kaydu said later that Hmishi would probably have died rather than hurt his teacher in that artificial setting of make-believe combat, but Llesho had refused, utterly, to lose a friend to that sort of game. He would not let them make enemies of each other, and he knew he could never trust Master Jaks again if Hmishi died at his hand. So he lunged at the master, latching on to his knife arm, and clinging to it while he shouted to Hmishi to run, to get away. Master Jaks had shaken Llesho loose and turned on him, a dreadful light in his eyes. Growling deep in his throat, Hmishi had attacked with a savagery that almost took the master down before he tumbled out of the way and set himself for defense. They battled then in earnest, Master Jaks' years of experience and cunning matched against the force of Hmishi's will focused on the death of his opponent. Master Jaks would have died in that battle if three hefty guards had not risked Hmishi's blade to knock him down and hold him while a fourth disarmed him.

"I don't care who you are," Hmishi had screamed, straining against the arms that held him down. "If you hurt him, I will kill you. Anywhere. Anytime. I will kill you."

For Llesho, time slowed to a frozen agony. Nothing moved but the blood dripping from the cut on Hmishi's face, and from another, shallower mark under Master Jaks' ear. Llesho thought he might walk unseen among them, like a wraith among mortals, tasting their blood and choosing who would live and who would die. He wanted to kill Master Jaks himself then, for what they both had done to his friend. But Master Jaks was watching Hmishi with relief touching the edges of a tension that had become a part of him over the weeks of training.

"You're ready," he said. "Have your face seen to,

and be prepared to march. All of you. We leave for Thousand Lakes Province in the morning."

Ready. Tomorrow would be Llesho's sixteenth birthday. In Thebin, he realized, he would be going to his purification rites now. The eve of his natal day would have been spent in silent meditation and prayer, fasting and offerings of incense and fruit in the Temple of the Moon. His brothers had told stories of how the scent of the fruit would come to fill the world as the night lengthened and their hollow stomachs complained. And he'd heard the servants laughing at the bites in the plums they found after Adar passed the eve of his sixteenth birthday sampling the offerings.

But the jokes and the ceremony were only the surface of the rite. During the long night, the betrothed prince became the true husband of the goddess in all ways, and received from her hand the bridegroom gifts of the spirit that would mark his soul forever. Those gifts brought with them powers of sight and the shared dominion over the living realm. Or the goddess would pass over him, and he would leave the temple in the morning changed only from a boy to mortal man.

Llesho had no expectation that the goddess would choose him as her husband, but he did not want to enter into this new phase of hardship in his life still a boy. Tonight, therefore, he would observe the rites of the god-king to prepare for both journeys: into manhood, and then into the unknown. He left his companions on their way to the cookhouse, and followed one of the compound's many pathways, over several of the ethereal bridges, to the small shrine deep in her ladyship's gardens. Bowing low to the gods who lingered about the place, he drew his Thebin knife and lay it on the altar, the length of the blade stretching from knee to knee of the seated goddess. With an abject kowtow that she might accept him in his unworthiness, Llesho settled himself in the proper form for meditation, and began his long watch alone.

Chapter Sixteen

AS the darkness settled around him, Llesho's doubts seemed to curl themselves in the corners of the shrine, peeping out at him with hot, fierce eyes. The priests were dead, none left to call the goddess to her husband with their prayers, and her ladyship's shrine was small and far from the gates of heaven where the goddess dwelt. How would she find her betrothed, how would she even know to look for him, so far away and with none to herald his time?

With an effort he set aside his misgivings. Only rats lurked in the corners, attracted to the cool shelter of the stone altar. Like them, he must put his life in the hands of the goddess and trust to her decision. Sitting cross-legged in front of her stone image, Llesho had lost himself in the silent meditation of his past life that made up the long night of passage for a young man entering manhood. His mother in her library in the Temple of the Moon, holding him on her lap, and his father, sitting in judgment on his throne in the Palace of the Sun, the two sides of heaven always in each other's gaze across the city. The Long March, and slavery, Lleck speaking to him from beyond the grave, and Lord Chin-shi desperate to heal the dying sea, and spilling the blood of his regret upon the sand. Her ladyship, watching him at weapons, questioning him at the side of her husband, teaching him the forbidden secrets of the Way.

Sinking deeply into his own mind, he sifted through the details of his life. Where had he failed, and where had he striven to serve with all he had to give Her whom he worshiped? In the balance, did he prove wanting, or would the goddess cast her favor upon him? At midnight he was disturbed by the presence of another in the shrine: her ladyship, come with gifts of fresh peaches for the goddess.

"Peace is the most precious gift the goddess may offer us," she said, holding up a piece of the fruit so that it glowed a rich gold in the candlelight. "Some say it is the one gift that man only appreciates when looking back in longing after he has rejected it. Others say the gift has no value except as a reward for strife. What do you believe, Llesho?"

She offered the peach and he took it, considering its soft richness, so unlike the cold white woman who offered it. "I believe," he said, "that each gift is a test, and with each test met we go a little farther upon the Way of the Goddess. And we cannot know what the purpose of the gift or the test is until we reach the end of the Way."

"Even peace?" she asked him.

Remembering the Harn descending upon Thebin, Llesho nodded his certainty. "Especially peace," he answered.

Her ladyship studied him for a long moment, with eyes as sharp as Llesho's Thebin knife. Then she let out a sigh, so gently that Llesho almost could believe he hadn't heard it at all.

"Know the goddess loves you," she said, and rested a cold hand over his heart. Llesho bowed his head, and heard but did not see when she stood and departed.

Alone again with the night and the rats with their glowing red eyes, he tried to settle into his meditations again, but the lady's words had disturbed him. The goddess might love him, as she loved all that lived within her dominion, but the night grew long, and she did not come.

In the deepest dark, when even the moon had set, meditation turned to memory and turned back on itself to mingle past and present in troubled patterns. He was grown, as now, but at home in the holy city of Kungol, alone and lost in the twisting mazes of the Temple of the Moon. From every wall remembered images of the goddess smiled down at him, but now they wore the face of her ladyship, the governor's wife. Somewhere in the distance, he heard his mother cry out, but when he tried to reach her, her cries seemed to grow more distant instead of closer, and the images on the walls seemed to grow colder. Through the dream-laced memories wove the screams of the dying, and the smell of smoke from the burning marketplace in the city.

"No!" His own voice broke the self-imposed spell of his meditation, but the sounds of pain and anger remained. The shouts of the watch summoning the guard and the slap of running feet were real. Here, now, in the governor's own gardens, it was happening again.

Llesho rose awkwardly to his feet, knees and ankles protesting the hours spent in their strained position. Grabbing his knife from the altar of the goddess, he hobbled to the door of the shrine.

Fire glinted from the rooftops of the wooden houses of the compound closest to the road. A soldier wearing the neck chain and wrist guards of the governor's house guard ran by, stopping long enough to push him back from the open door with a hand to his chest.

"Get back inside," she ordered him. "We're under attack!"

"I can fight!" Llesho returned, and raised his knife to show that he was armed. An arrow whipped past his ear and he ducked as it embedded itself in the thick lintel.

"Find your squad, then," she said, and ran to join the fray.

Llesho slipped out of the shrine, keeping low, his knife held lightly in his steady fist. This time he was not a child; he had both the skills and the strength to defend himself. But the guard had been right: he had to find his squad. Master Jaks had trained them to fight as a unit, and he felt naked without his friends at his side.

Crouching in the shadows of the reeds and low plant life that bordered the lawns and canals, he made his way back to the house he shared with the other novices. Before he could pull himself over the threshold, however, a voice he dreaded sounded nearby.

"Search everywhere—I want the Thebin!" Overseer Markko's insistent shout came from a more solid mass of shadow just steps away, silhouetted by the rising flames. "He's here somewhere!"

Llesho froze, paralyzed by that voice. Master Markko had gone to Lord Yueh at the death of Lord Chin-shi, but what had driven Yueh's army to attack the governor's compound? Why was Master Markko looking for him? To kill him outright, or to throw him into chains again? What did the overseer, or his new lord, know or suspect about Llesho's true identity that they would seek him out in the midst of battle?

Llesho had no time to ponder the answers to his questions; the sounds of fighting were getting closer. Suddenly, a hand snaked out of the window of his house, grabbed him by the arm, and pulled him into the large room. Bixei. Lling and Hmishi stood back to back in the center of the room with their knives drawn. Kaydu was missing.

"Where have you been?" Bixei hissed.

"The shrine in the garden," Llesho hissed back. "Where did you think I was? Opening the gates for Lord Yueh?"

Bixei didn't have to say anything; it was clear on his face that the accusation shocked and offended him. "What, then?" he asked.

They looked at each other, and it was clear they each had unanswered questions. Lord Yueh's armed guard wouldn't be tearing the governor's compound apart to find a common slave, but they had all heard Master Markko order his troops to look for Llesho.

"Who are you?" Bixei pushed for an explanation in spite of the danger they were in, "What does Markko want?"

Llesho uttered a single Thebin curse. He didn't want to know what kind of rumors had spread. "We can talk about this later." If there was no later, explanations wouldn't matter anyway. "If you want to live, we are going to have to fight or run *now*."

The attack had come through the main gate, the only way in or out that Llesho knew. "Where is Kaydu?"

Little Brother chose that moment to swing from the roof by his tail and pop through the open window with a chittering rebuke for their tardiness. Their young instructor followed him. "I'm right here. Let's go. Jaks has horses waiting." She disappeared again.

Llesho ran for the window and would have been first out, but Bixei held him back. "In case of ambush," he said, and darted out the window after Kaydu. Llesho followed, and turned around as Lling, and then Hmishi spilled out of the novice house. Kaydu said nothing, but gestured for them to keep low as they crept along the side of the house, hidden by the reeds and bushes.

Kaydu moved so silently that Llesho was surprised to hear the clatter of heavier feet when Bixei followed her over the footbridge. He tried to imitate Kaydu's silence with no success, but had to turn around to be certain Lling was still behind him. She was, and Hmishi next to her. Hmishi stumbled and came up again with a sword in his hand. Already a battle had passed through here, leaving its scattered dead and their weapons behind. Lling hunted around until she, too, had a sword in her right hand, switching her knife to her left. Bixei gathered up a spear, and a short sword which he wedged into his belt.

Llesho remembered his own knife in his hand, and realized—damn!—he'd left his scabbard by his bed, along with the few possessions he had acquired while at the governor's compound. Once again, he was starting out with nothing. But he was starting out alive. Llesho scrounged among the dead as well, and found a short spear that he took up in his free hand. He had begun to think that they would make their way clear when a sound to his right was followed by the flare of torches.

The oiled parchment screens of a small house burst into flame. A shout rose from the fire, and shadows formed around it, resolved in the light into men on foot. Yueh's men, dark against the fire that backlit them, had seen Llesho's squad. Soldiers ran toward them brandishing weapons. Bixei caught the first across the ribs with the staff end of his spear, turned the long weapon quickly and finished his man with a lunging stab to the breast.

Lling and Hmishi slid to either side of Llesho, swords poised high, knives pointed low. They joined the battle with a flurry of clashing swords, vanquishing their attackers, who fled with screams on their lips that they had been bested by demons. Llesho gave a grim laugh, but did not count his victory too soon. A horse loomed out of the darkness. Its tall rider urged the beast up on its hind legs to lash out at the Thebins with its sharp front hooves.

With an enraged howl, Hmishi leaped to the defense, driving his sword into the rider. The sword passed through the man, who tossed him aside and laughed with the sound of ice breaking in his voice. Master Markko—Llesho recognized him even in the dark—bled from no wound, though Hmishi's thrust should have sliced him in two.

"You are mine, Thebin!" The magician pointed a short spear at Llesho, and cold terror pierced his heart. Frozen, he could not have moved, except for the warmth radiating from the short spear he held in his own hand. He raised the weapon between them, and it seemed to glow in the light of the silver moon. "Never again, witch!" he shouted, and Markko's spear burned and shattered. The magician growled his wordless rage and brought his horse around to attack, but the animal bucked and fell, screaming, with the point of a spear buried in its flank.

"Move!" Bixei shouted, and Hmishi was pushing him, and Lling was pulling her knife out of the gullet of a soldier who stared up at the sky with blank, dead eyes.

Kaydu ghosted up to Llesho and whispered, "This way—Jaks has the horses." They had entered the peach grove, the smell of the ripe fruit cloying over the sickening reek of blood and burning flesh and sweat and fear. Llesho followed the direction she pointed, moving deep into the darkest corner of the grove.

Around them, troops were mounting up, too many for Llesho to judge in the dark, but it felt as if the whole household must be saddling to fly. Shadowed by a thick growth of trees and hedges, Master Jaks awaited them with their mounts. Fortunately, their warhorses were intelligent and trained to battle; the creatures stirred restlessly at the smell of blood on the hands and clothes of Llesho's squad but did not balk when they gathered their reins and mounted. Llesho noticed with satisfaction that someone had strapped his cavalry-style short bow and a quiver of arrows to his saddle. The governor's lady had been as good as her word, and his squad could ride now, and shoot from the saddle as well as on foot. They might need to before this night was out.

Kaydu took the lead of their small party, finding their place at the center of a longer train of mounts and pack animals moving quietly in single file through the grove. Llesho allowed his horse to fall in step behind her, with his three companions following. When he saw where they were heading—toward a place of thicker shadows in the garden wall—he wondered if it were a trap.

"Master Jaks!" Llesho turned around in his saddle to throw a whisper into the black on black murk, but he received no answer. There had been no sixth horse waiting; Jaks was staying behind. Llesho smelled blood, and saw the face of his teacher on the dead corpse of his bodyguard, and he knew that Jaks would die if he did not come now. Unthinking, he communicated his distress to his horse, which quaked under him in fear of the night and its shadows, and the dark emotions of its rider. Llesho rested a calming hand on the horse's neck while his thoughts spun in turmoil. He knew right to the core of his being that the memory-vision was true. Time itself skittered out of control, the past and future colliding in the vision of Master Jaks, dead. The house guard could not hold the compound against the fires of the attackers, and Master Jaks would give his life to hold the attackers at bay for their escape.

"I'm not through with you yet," he muttered to himself. Turning his mount out of the column, Llesho headed back toward the low fires that marked where graceful houses had dotted the watery space.

"Where are you going, boy?" An outrider caught his horse by the bridle and stopped him, staring hard into his face until it registered who Llesho was. "The midnight gate is the other way!" He turned his horse around to lead Llesho back the way he had come, but Llesho pulled back on his reins to bring his horse to a stop.

"Where is Master Jaks?" he said, using his best imitation of his father.

The outrider jerked his head in the direction of the burning compound but continued to urge Llesho's horse toward the bottom of the orchard.

Llesho dug in his heels and refused to be moved. "I am not leaving without him." He kept his jaw firm and hoped the man couldn't see the shaking of his hands in the dark.

"The lady will have my head," the outrider muttered, but he turned his horse. "He went this way—I'll take you." They rode back, into the chaos and the fire, toward a tight knot of grunting bodies and clanging swords. The fighting was on foot and the outrider made quick work of it. He swept into the fray with a blood-curdling battle cry, cutting down one attacker and sweeping another under the hooves of his charger. Then he angled his horse between Master Jaks and the fires lighting a hundred battles like the one he had just fought.

The outrider slipped from his horse and held out the reins. "His excellency wants that boy out of here, and the boy says he won't go without you." With that he was gone, lost to sight in the fray.

Jaks lifted himself into the saddle, swearing softly under his breath. "Now, Your Highness?" he asked. The words dripped with sarcasm, but even so they served as a reminder to both of them.

Llesho tilted his chin at the exact angle to receive his title, letting Master Jaks know in the doing of it that he read all the levels of anger and submission in his words. If they were going to use him for their own secret agenda, however, they would have to accept him at his rank, and not as just another stone in their game. He would not go quietly to anybody's slaughter.

Master Jaks dropped his head. "I know," he said, and Llesho thought that maybe he did, too.

Together they entered the shadows at the bottom of the peach grove, and passed through a hidden gate that opened to the country northwest of the city. Outriders galloped up and down the line now, and when the last of their party had come through the gate, the order to ride hard came with the slaps of the outriders on the rumps of the trailing horses. For a moment Llesho felt wrenched in time, a small boy again, and Jaks was wearing the bloody uniform of his dead bodyguard and the travel stained clothes of the long march.

But the horses stirred restlessly, reminding him that he was not alone, and not helpless. He had an army at his back. And, if they were fleeing by dead of night, at least they were running toward help, and not into greater danger. Llesho kicked his own horse to a faster gait and quickly found his squad again.

"We ride for Thousand Lakes Province," Kaydu informed them, "Pray that we are not too late."

Gradually, the outriders herded the refugees into a tighter, more defensible group plodding slowly toward the inner provinces. Llesho fretted anxiously about their pace. Once the decision to flee had been made and acted upon, he wanted to put as much distance as possible between their makeshift caravan and Lord Yueh's troops. But the outriders kept them at a pace that protected the mass of the household and the servants who had fled on foot. Gradually, however, fatigue ate away the desperate compulsion to run that coursed through his bloodstream.

Farshore lay on a sandy flat, but beyond the city limits, to the west, the foothills stretched north and south as far as the eye could see. Llesho felt the road angle upward into the hills and fell forward over the neck of his horse to balance himself into the ascent. His legs were sore from riding, and his horse was setting down its feet with the heavy indifference that spoke of exhaustion louder than any words of its human rider could do.

"How far to Thousand Lakes Province?" he asked Kaydu.

She shook her head, eyes grim, and curled one hand around Little Brother, who rode tucked close to his mistress' body, his arms clinging to the rise of her saddle. "Too far. More than five hundred li."

Llesho looked around them at the shuffling horde pressing into a narrow line again on the mountain road. His nose wrinkled, assaulted by the moist warmth of animals and humans, fear mixed with the dust of the road in a pungent taunt at his sinuses. He remembered another long march, staggering through the night until strange arms swept him up, passed him on, as the road stretched in a neverending blur of light and dark, hunger and thirst. Out of memories he'd long tried to submerge, images arose of bodies dropping by the wayside, beaten into the dirt by the hooves of the Harnish horses. So powerful were the old feelings that Llesho braced his body for the staggering jolt of a horse stumbling over a human obstacle in its march.

I can't do it again, he thought. But he said, "When Yueh realizes that the governor has escaped, his army will follow us."

"The governor didn't escape," Kaydu said, and her voice choked on the words. "He stayed behind, to keep Yueh occupied in the capital. Her ladyship leads us."

Llesho wondered if her father had stayed behind as

well. Kaydu's set face did not invite the question, and Bixei was looking at him as though he'd been struck. "What makes you think it was Lord Yueh who attacked?"

"I heard Master Markko call out—" Llesho began his answer just as Kaydu interrupted. "There is a resting place beyond this pass, with grass for the horses and a stream for water. The hills will hide us from Yueh's scouts and spies. Her ladyship will stop for the night when we reach it, and we can talk there."

Lling was riding at Llesho's shoulder, listening quietly to their conversation. At the mention of rest, she sighed, but didn't relax the watch she kept on the road and the hill that rose at its shoulder. "He'll know that at least some of the governor's household escaped. Will he send an army after us?"

"Probably," Kaydu admitted. She did not say aloud what Llesho already knew from past experience: they could not escape at their present rate of travel. Already the very young and the less hardened among the household suffered from the journey. "But enough of the house guard stayed behind that Yueh may not realize we have escaped until he has searched among the dead for our bodies. With any luck, they've bought us some time to regroup and make plans. If our scouts report back that we are followed, we may have to run, but her ladyship will want everyone to rest while they can."

If it came to a midnight scramble, those on horseback might have a chance, but Llesho knew about being frightened and weak and on foot. Most of the people who slept tonight at the resting place in the hills would die tomorrow or the next day or the next, running from certain capture into the arms of exhaustion, hunger, and thirst. Armies did not march with children and the sick in tow. Those who did had no chance of outrunning trained and hardened fighters.

When the outriders passed the word that they were

stopping ahead, Llesho wanted to urge his own companions to continue, to outstrip the reach of Yueh's army. He had his own purpose set upon him by the ghost in the pearl beds: his brothers to find, and his country to save. But a child stumbled as he passed, and he scooped her up and set her in front of him on the horse, and when the outrider called a halt and directed them down into a hollow cradled in a circle of hills rich with the scent of pine trees, he set the child down with her mother and followed his companions to a grassy plot they chose for their camp. They dismounted and led their horses to the bottom of the hollow where they found the stream Kaydu had promised. Hmishi took the reins from his companions, and followed them as they made their own way to the stream and water. When they had drunk their fill, he staked the animals in a soft stand of grass and began to unbuckle their saddles.

After a moment in which they all stared dumbly as Hmishi worked, Lling sighed and offered, "I'll get wood for a fire." Bixei dragged himself to his feet and followed her into the nearby forest to help her look for fallen branches. Kaydu tucked her sleeping pet into a sling she wore around her neck and hunted for stones to ring their fire pit. Llesho sat, thinking. He was deep in the puzzle of their survival when Kaydu interrupted.

"Anything I can do for you, Your Highness?"

"No, thank you," he said, so caught up in wrestling with the problem in his head that he didn't notice her sarcasm, or the pointed hint that he should rouse himself to help set up the camp.

"Would you mind explaining that answer?" Bixei asked the question. Kaydu looked uncomfortably like she was just confirming what she already knew, but she silently dropped down beside him on the grass. Lling and Hmishi had also finished their self-appointed chores, and they, too, watched him, more frightened than they had been when they fought Master Markko and Yueh's provincial guard for him.

Not now, he silently begged. He was too tired to deal with questions, too tired to stand and face them but unwilling to try to explain while they were looking down on him—it felt too symbolic.

"I'm nobody, just Llesho," he said.

"Where were you when Master Markko attacked?" Bixei demanded, but Lling stopped him with a hand on his arm.

"Not selling out the governor to my worst enemy," Llesho answered sarcastically. He stared down at the grass between his feet, pulled up a leaf, and twisted it around his finger, contemplating how quickly friends became strangers in the presence of a secret. "Tonight is the eve of my sixteenth summer." He tried to sound as if it meant nothing when he added, "By custom, that time belongs to the goddess."

In Kungol, the royal family had played out its most intimate existence for the honor of the people: the royal chambermaids would hang the first marked sheets of prince or princess from the celebrant's bedroom balcony. Royal couples consummated their marriages while a choir of monks at the bedside intoned the heavenly praise of the families brought together in the union. If he had grown to face the eve of his manhood in the Palace of the Sun, like his brothers, all the males of the royal family and their priests and retainers would have escorted him to the Temple of the Moon for his vigil. They would have sung ribald songs of his prowess with the goddess. In the morning trumpets would have sounded with the gay dances of the wedding feast while he rode through the streets to his breakfast at the right hand of his father. All of Thebin would acknowledge him as the husband of the goddess, or jest about his luck as a free man, ungifted and unwed, but a man nonetheless.

In his captivity, Llesho's determination to complete

the sacred rites of adulthood in her ladyship's garden shrine seemed foolish and self-important. Certainly the goddess had not come to him in the night, had not accepted him as a man and a husband of the Thebin royal line. With Kungol a thousand or more li away and Thebin in the hands of the enemy, he didn't want to share the ceremony of meditation and fasting, or his failure, with strangers. It embarrassed him now to think that he had tried to complete his ritual of manhood alone and in a foreign land that still saw him as a boy and the property of another. No wonder he had been found lacking—the body he offered to his goddess was not his to give. But he had already said too much. To his Thebin companions, the ritual identified him as a prince of the Royal House more completely than anything else he could have said. Lling and Hmishi understood at once the import of his words, and dropped to their knees with bent heads. Just exactly what Llesho did not want in the middle of a crisis.

He gave vent to a disgusted sigh before he ordered, "Get up! The Harn rule Thebin now; I have no claim on your allegiance."

"What are they doing?" Bixei crinkled his nose in confusion, but he was determined to understand what everyone else seemed already to know.

"He's the king of Thebin," Kaydu answered for him, and looked at Llesho with a newfound uneasiness.

"I *was* a prince," he answered, exasperated, "more recently a slave, and soon to be dead if Yueh's troops catch us here."

"But the old king is dead, they say," Lling dared to correct him; Hmishi still trembled at his feet.

"I have six brothers, all older than me," he answered, grateful to see that Bixei had finally sunk down beside them. He seemed unconvinced, but he was listening. "And any one of them may be the chosen of the goddess." He did not add that he had not been so chosen.

Bixei fed a branch to the fire. "The deadfall is dry enough. We shouldn't lack for a fire," he said, and added, when Llesho had begun to think he had escaped the conversation, "Is it true? About being a king?"

"A prince," Llesho corrected him. "And not that since my seventh summer. Now I am a slave like any other."

"It could be true." Lling gave him a disapproving frown that for some reason reminded him of his mother, though the two looked nothing alike.

"There *was* a Prince Llesho, seventh son of the king and the lady-goddess in the capital. Half the babies born that year were named in his honor."

"She's right," Hmishi explained to Kaydu and Bixei. He still watched Llesho carefully as if he might turn into a dragon and fly away, but Llesho hadn't struck anyone dead yet, so he risked the conversation. "I always figured Llesho was one of the namesakes, but I suppose he could just as well be the prince as a farmer's son with a name above his station."

"Is that why Yueh is after us?" Bixei asked. "Did he know about the prince thing already?"

Kaydu shrugged. "Maybe. Markko must have suspected. Llesho made himself as obvious as the lighthouse on Farshore Point when he had visions in the deep and then petitioned to be a gladiator. Something was going on, and he'd want to get his hands on it, whatever it was."

"Do you think we brought any food? I'm starved." Hmishi distracted their companions with a more immediate concern. He rummaged in the blanket roll he'd taken from his horse and drew out a flat spiral of chewy bread. "Food. Somebody knew we were going to be on the run."

"Her ladyship knew," Llesho told them.

Hmishi frowned, not quite following. "That Yueh would attack the governor's compound?"

"I think so," Llesho agreed. "And I think she knew who I was before anyone else did. She came to Pearl Island for my first weapons test."

Bixei's eyes grew wider. "She did?"

Kaydu nodded. "It makes sense. My father said she was most particular about keeping Llesho out of Yueh's hands. And she is always very cunning at knowing what to keep hidden."

Llesho didn't question the comment. The governor's lady had many faces, and more people than Llesho knew it. "Jaks was expecting an attack. He told me to be ready to ride."

"The governor knew what Yueh was up to," Kaydu confirmed. "He just didn't expect Yueh to make his move so soon. Father thinks that Lord Yueh subverted Master Markko years ago, waiting for his chance to strike. Lord Chin-shi already had gambling debts, and Lord Yueh bought them up and demanded payment. Markko's witch-hunt was to cover his own evil magic; he probably created the plague that killed the pearl beds himself, so that Lord Chin-shi would have no way to pay the debts.

"Lord Yueh seized Pearl Island and its properties in payment; Habiba anticipated him, though, and made his purchases in the governor's name before the contest."

Bixei was still troubled. "No one would start a war over one slave, even the former prince of someplace I've never heard of."

"I don't know why her ladyship wants him," Kaydu said, "or even *if* she wants him. But she won't let Yueh have him."

"It doesn't matter," Llesho protested grimly. He didn't like the conclusions he'd drawn, but he was pretty sure he was right.

"If it doesn't matter," Bixei pointed out, "you can raise the tent."

"You don't get it," Llesho snapped. "I've done the Long March before. I know how fast we can move, even when the pace is forced with whips and jackals. We can't escape a trained army, and I don't see her ladyship imposing a death march on her people with torture."

"But if the governor is still in Farshore—" Lling objected, remembering the conversation on the road.

"Yueh can't let her ladyship reach Thousand Lakes Province. She would report his treachery, and her father would have to offer his own guard to rescue his daughter's husband. From Thousand Lakes Province she can send messengers to the Emperor and beg him to come to the governor's aid as well." He looked into the eyes of each of his companions in turn, until he was certain that he had their full attention. "Lord Yueh won't be safe until we are dead, or returned to him in captivity. And I, for one, don't intend to let Master Markko get his hands on me again."

"What can we do?" Hmishi asked him.

Run, Llesho thought, *run now, as fast as we can, and don't stop, ever.* But he dropped his head back against the saddle he leaned on and shut his eyes.

"I don't know," he said, because he could not admit to the cowardice that whispered, "Run," into his ear. "I don't know. But I've done the Long March before, and I won't do it again. I'll make him kill me first." He didn't open his eyes, but felt the tension of his companions.

"It's better to be alive," Kaydu objected. Kaydu, the daughter of a witch, who had never been a slave. If Master Markko had any say in it, she would see her father burned alive in the same marketplace where Yueh sold her body.

He did open his eyes then, dark with bleak memory. "No," he said, "It's not." He closed the coffins of his soul, let them think he was sleeping. Let them think what they wanted as long as they didn't require his presence in their schemes. But they fell quiet, and Llesho found himself lulled by the crackle of the fire and the scents of the night—grass and horse and pine, human sweat and exhaustion blunting the pungent odor of fear.

Chapter Seventeen

HE must have slept, because the sky was gray and the grass was damp when a hand shook him. "Llesho!" Master Jaks shook him again. "Find yourself a bush, and then follow me."

"What?" Mornings made him stupid, but Master Jaks answered as if it had been a real question.

"Her ladyship requests an audience."

Llesho figured he must be stupider than he thought, because he couldn't detect any irony at all in his teacher's voice.

"Just a minute." He rolled over, cracked open his eyes enough to see that his companions still slept soundly. Lling and Hmishi had moved closer to each other in their sleep, and foolish as it was to let it happen, the sight twisted in his heart a little bit. At first, out of the modesty that grew between diving mates, he'd worked hard to keep Lling from intruding on his thoughts. Later, after the ghost of Lleck had appeared to him with a reminder of his duty, he'd determined to go to his vigil night with a clear heart to offer his goddess. Now, when he found himself free of every obstacle between them, Lling herself was turning to another.

Master Jaks followed the direction of his thoughts

with a wry quirk to his mouth. Llesho answered with a pointed glare. Maybe someday, when he was as old as his teacher, he'd be philosophical about it, but right now he didn't want to hear it. Didn't want to be up before it was time either. Even Little Brother still slept, his tiny paws curled under his chin, his tail curled lightly around his mistress' throat. Not an immediate threat, or a general call out to mount and ride, then; a more personal disaster pulled him out of his bedroll.

Wondering why catastrophe seemed never to arrive in the wake of a full stomach and a good night's rest, Llesho staggered out of the sleeping camp to water the bushes. He returned a moment later, only slightly more awake, to follow Master Jaks between the ragged knots of sleeping refugees to her ladyship's tent.

Someone, he realized, had been preparing for their flight long before they had actually left Farshore. The tent was as large as the governor's audience hall, with yellow silk walls and a red and blue striped awning for a roof. Inside, the floor was covered in thick carpets. Graceful hangings separated the private parts of the tent from the public area where her ladyship sat upon a high seat, surrounded by her generals. He wasn't overly surprised to see Master Jaks take his place at their head. Minions of less determined station, with the opaque eyes of spies, hovered nearby, in shadowed corners. In her ladyship's right hand, resting across her lap, she held the ancient spear that Llesho had last seen on Pearl Island.

As it had then, the spear sent a chill through him, and he felt a faint dislocation when he looked at it: nausea, like the way he felt in the pearl boat on a stormy sea. At her feet he saw a map he had at first mistaken for a carpet. He tried to focus on the map instead of the spear, and found that his stomach settled and the map stayed where it was without troubling his vision.

Tall, narrow tables scattered at her ladyship's left and right held the remnants of a meal: a teapot and cups, and various ornaments that the lady fondled thoughtfully before turning the sword's point of her gaze upon Llesho.

"Tea?" she asked.

When he answered, "Yes, please," she put the short spear aside and poured with her own hands from the pot into two unmatched bowls. One was of jadeite, so thin that the light of early morning shone through its intricately carved design, laying patterns of light and shadow on the table. The other was of finely thrown porcelain, with gilt around its rim and decorated on the bowl with a portrait of a lady in a garden.

Her ladyship waited, as if she expected something of him, and Llesho hesitated, his hand poised over the porcelain cup. But the jadeite bowl called to his touch with the whisper of old memories he knew were not his own. Slowly he let his hand drift over to it, and gently he traced with his fingertips its carved designs.

"I know this cup," he said. The smile that stretched his lips felt alien to his mouth. He could not know it was the smile of a man long dead, but when her ladyship looked into his eyes, her wistful sigh fell strangely on his ears, as if for that moment she saw in him a memory he did not share.

When he had finished his tea, she gestured for a servant to wrap the jadeite cup safely for the journey. Then, taking the package, she held it out to him. "Take it with you. Keep it safe for your children."

"I couldn't," he answered, and left it sitting on her outstretched palm.

"It is yours. It always has been." She tucked the bundle carefully into the folds of his shirt. "The governor is dead," she informed him, and Llesho wondered at her control, to drink tea with a fallen princeling with the wound of her husband's death still fresh on her soul. "Yueh moves on Thousand Lakes Province, with Master Markko at his right hand. Habiba rides before us, to warn my father of the coming storm. I wish we had more time, but our fortune is cast, and we can but play out the fall of the rods."

Taking up the spear she had set aside, she looked at him out of eyes grown cold with the baleful mystery that made him cower within the shell of his own body. He let himself relax only a little when she turned to the map between them.

"Tell me again about the Harn."

His throat went dry. He had thought the lady would ask him about Lord Chin-shi, or Yueh, or Overseer Markko, but instead she studied the map before her avidly for the more distant danger. Llesho darted a glance at Master Jaks, who said nothing but showed no surprise at her question, either. There would be no escape from that direction.

"I was just a child." What could he know of value to the governor's lady? "I don't understand what you want me to do."

"You are a prince, and the beloved of the goddess." She touched a single finger to his breast, and he burned there, falling into eyes large and dark as the pearl Lleck had pressed on him in the bay.

As if thinking of it woke the pearl from its hiding place, it throbbed as if it were trying to regain its original size. The small pain distracted him and he pulled back, disturbed by how easily he fell under the spell of her gaze.

The lady nodded, as if something in his response settled the doubts in her mind. "When the time comes, you will act according to your birth and nature."

He knew by her actions that the tense was not a mistake, that she didn't speak to the pearl diver or the novice gladiator, but addressed the scion of a house as noble as her own. In spite of his exhaustion, his spine straightened, his chin came up, and he returned her level glance, aware only at a distance that the ache in his jaw had subsided.

"They use promises of riches and shared power to lure their spies." He didn't know why he told her that first of all the things about the Harn he knew or guessed. When she closed her eyes and bowed her head, he saw that it was what she feared but had expected. Yueh. It made sense. The Harn were a plains people who went on horseback more often than afoot and had no temperament for cities. They ruled by indirection, putting the traitors of one captive people in positions of power in the captured lands of another, so no fellow feeling would grow between the conquered and their overseers. The Harn themselves came and went at will, took what they wanted in lives and wealth, and returned to the smooth round tents that sprouted like leather-cased mushrooms wherever they passed.

Her ladyship gestured to the map at their feet. Llesho fell to his knees to study it more closely, and he felt the breath of Master Jaks leaning close over his shoulder, following the play of Llesho's fingers across the map. He recognized bits of it from school in Thebin, but that had been years ago, and much of what he hadn't forgotten had changed.

"Thebin," she gestured with the point of the short spear in her hand to a dusky orange blotch scarcely bigger than his two fists set side by side. "Harn proper—" a large sweep of green for grasslands, Llesho supposed, lapped around Thebin on the north and swept up to a yellow square, perhaps a little bit larger, to the east. Yellow dominated the eastern portion of the map all the way to the blue that Llesho figured must represent the sea. "And the Shan Empire," he supplied.

Shan was the name of the capital city and the empire it directed. Trade routes, he knew, had always run along the length of the yellow—the Shan Empire—through Thebin, and into the red that represented the unknown kingdoms at the end of the trade roads to the West. Trade passed up and down the road for the three months of summer and stopped again when snow blocked the mountain passes through Thebin for the ten months of winter. Llesho had lived seven summers in Kungol, the Thebin capital and holy city, and he still counted the years of his life by the imagined ebb and flow of caravans through the passes.

Sixteen summers, and most of them spent far from home. But the sights and smells of the caravans, and the bustle of the trade centers, remained with him still. The mountain passes had made Thebin rich, but that all changed when the Harn came. Now the horsemen controlled the western end of the trade route. And he saw what he had not realized before. Marked on the map, the city of Shan rested not a hundred li from the border between Harn and the Shan Empire. As far south of Shan as it was west of Farshore, the Thousand Lakes Province, outlined in red stitching on the map, lay like a glistening jewel set above the Thousand Peaks Mountains. And on the western side of those mountains, lay the green of Harn.

Somewhere behind him, Llesho heard the grunts of servants and the rumpling of silk being taken down and folded, the denser sound of rugs being rolled. The sun must be up. The thought slipped through his mind, and with it the knowledge that they must ride soon, or die. But he could not take his eyes off the map. He reached for it, slid from his chair to kneel, and touched his fingertips to the line of embroidered mountains curving in a crescent along the western edge of the Shan Empire. He stopped when his fingers came to the dusky orange of Thebin. The map could not show how high the mountains thrust into the clouds, or how airless those highest peaks were—how no man but a Thebin born could travel them. Children of Heaven they called themselves, who alone could reach for the garden palaces of the gods whose seed had set in the soil of the Thebin people. Outlanders stayed to the relative lower altitudes of the capital city, following the three major passes through the mountains. Llesho longed for the heights.

"You look like you are seeing God," her ladyship whispered, and Llesho looked up at her with a tiny smile, sharing the secret.

"I am god." Or should have been. He could not meet her eyes at the thought. His ritual had failed.

Master Jaks didn't bother to hide his skeptical snort, but her ladyship nodded, as if his words hadn't surprised her.

"Can you save us?" she asked.

Llesho shook his head. "I cannot even save myself. The goddess did not come." He didn't think she would understand his explanation, but she took his chin in the curve of her fingers and lifted his head, kissed each eyelid closed against her piercing gaze.

"Yes," her ladyship said. "She did. You are alive."

Cool as a goddess, she terrified him. But her kiss sparked fire in his body, desire rising at the touch of her lips. He reached a hand to stroke her skin, and blushed with embarrassment when she withdrew into her chair. "I'm sorry," he said after a long silence. *I am not a man. I don't know what to do.* He didn't say it, didn't know himself which of the myriad things he had to regret he meant: for the death of her husband, or because he could not save her from her own fate? For reaching out to her, or for not knowing what to do about it if she had moved into his touch instead of away?

Llesho could feel the army of Lord Yueh entering the foothills in pursuit of the weary refugees, could hear the beat of distant hooves on the grasslands, and he knew what troubled her ladyship because it had started the same way in Thebin. Travelers harried on the road, minor raids on outlying farms, spies bribed with promises. Yueh pressing from the east, the Harn pressing from the west, and Thousand Lakes Province between them, peaceful, fertile, free. But none of those things for long. He turned to leave her ladyship with her knowledge of doom, but she stopped him with a word.

"Take this." She held out the short spear to him. He shuddered but did not take it. "Like the cup, it belongs to you."

"It killed me once," Llesho objected, though he didn't know how he knew. His arms wrapped instinctively around his middle, feeling the jade cup nestled in its wrappings under his coat. "I think it means to kill me again."

"I cannot keep it for you any longer." She held it out, watching him through eyes that held no hope, but endless calculation, and he took it from her, though he believed he would have been safer accepting a viper from her hand. Then she offered him what he wanted most in the world: "You are free now, of all but your own quest. Find your brothers."

He didn't ask—she saw the need in his face, and gave him this prize with no promises in exchange.

"The records are in Shan and so is the one they call Adar." Adar. Llesho bowed. Adar. The name slid through his mind like sunlight and peace, and he wanted his past back so much it hurt to think of it. But he let none of that show.

The servants had taken the tent down around them, had packed up most of the rugs and waited for her ladyship to finish the audience so they could pack the last of her furnishings. "Our paths divide here." She physically withdrew, hiding her hands in the sleeves of her robe. "Go now. Take my prayers with you, and my general, Master Jaks, for guidance and protection on the road."

Master Jaks protested with a deep bow and a request for a word with her ladyship. Llesho left them together, to find the camp in an equal state of hurried preparation. When he reached his own companions, they had packed his blanket roll and saddled his horse.

"We are ready to ride as soon as we receive the signal," Bixei told him, but Llesho shook his head.

"We ride now," he said. And to Kaydu, "Can you guide us to Shan?"

"I've never been that far," Kaydu objected. "My father had hoped that Master Jaks would ride with us as our guide."

"I don't intend to give him that option."

"Why not?" Kaydu studied him for a long minute. "Master Jaks has sworn on his honor to see you home. The governor accepted this debt of honor in his contract—to deny him would be to dishonor him."

"The governor is dead," Llesho informed his companions. "And Master Jaks owes the greater debt to his lordship to keep his lady safe. Either way he chooses, Master Jaks must sacrifice his honor. Unless we take the decision out of his hands."

Kaydu closed her eyes to hide her sorrow, but a tear leaked from under her lids and ran down the side of her nose unhindered. "I see." She nodded and pulled herself lightly into her saddle, but Hmishi took the reins of Llesho's mount and refused to move. "What is in Shan?" he asked.

"Prince Adar."

Lling's eyes opened wide. "The healer prince?"

"My brother. I ride to find him, and the others."

Hmishi stood out of the way then, and cupped his hands to help his prince into the saddle. Lling scrambled onto her horse without another objection, but Bixei stayed where he was. "I can't leave," he said, "Stipes . . ."

"I know," Llesho agreed. Yueh had purchased Stipes for the arena, but he would use every trained fighter he had to invade Thousand Lakes Province.

Bixei would not leave Stipes to the enemy. "Tell Master Jaks that if he delivers her ladyship safely to her father, then all his debts of honor are paid. My own fate is in the hands of the goddess. Good luck."

Llesho set the short spear from the lady at his back, though it made him tremble to touch it, and turned his horse. Kaydu nudged her own mount with her knees, urging him to the front of their little band.

"This way," she said, and guided them to the bottom of the clearing. Little Brother caught up with them at the stream, chattering indignantly to be taken up with his mistress. Kaydu pulled the sling from her pack and wrapped it over her shoulder, holding it open for the monkey to scramble in and make himself comfortable for the journey. When he had settled, they crossed the stream and entered the forest that rose on the other side.

PART THREE

THE ROAD TO SHAN

Chapter Eighteen

THROUGHOUT the morning Llesho's tiny band pressed more deeply into the forest, making brief stops only to water and graze the horses in the occasional grassy breaks in the trees. When the path grew too steep for them to ride, they walked alongside their animals, leading them by the reins. By midafternoon, however, the horses were stumbling with exhaustion and the humans were doing no better. Llesho would have urged them to continue, staggering until he dropped, but Kaydu pulled him up short with a tug on his arm.

"Enough," she said. "We will rest here, and eat. The horses need a break as badly as we do."

Llesho stared at her, not understanding. He had only one model for such a journey—walking until his legs gave out then going on, carried in the arms of another until that one dropped in the dust of their passage.

"If we stop now, we can travel again for a few hours before the sun sets, and make better time for the rest." Kaydu was watching him for some sign that he understood, so he nodded and dropped to his knees.

Only then did he hear the rush of water over rocks. A stream, and fresh, from the sound of it.

Rest. Why hadn't he thought of that himself? He wasn't, after all, a Harn raider. Not a very good prince either, apparently, but he'd have to pretend for a few minutes longer. His three companions—four, if you counted Little Brother peeking out of his sling—were watching him expectantly. Lling spoke up in the silence.

"Should we scout the area, post a guard in case Lord Yueh's men have followed us?" she asked.

Kaydu took the suggestion for a call to informal council, and shook her head. "We can take turns at guard duty," she said. "We can fight if we have to, but we'd do better to run if Markko has sent a party to track us." She looked at Llesho. They were all weary, but they could probably push on, except for him. He was the only one of them carrying a child's memories of the Long March on his back. Once again others were making decisions based on his survival above their own.

"We have to know if Master Markko is following." Llesho hardened his voice to keep the words from shaking on his lips. "And if he is, we run until we fall, and then fight until we die."

The looked their unspoken questions at him, and he returned their gaze with his own bleak glare. "I will not be his prisoner again."

Hmishi tipped his head in silent obedience to his prince and slipped away, into the trees. Lling needed more convincing. She was Thebin, and she would follow wherever her prince led. Her analytical mind, however, craved reasons.

"He's a powerful magician," Llesho explained, "with a particular interest in poisons."

Her eyes went wide. Wordlessly she picked up her bow and a quiver of arrows. Scouting for a secure lookout point, she picked a tree and climbed high into its branches.

"What did he do to you?" Kaydu asked.

"Terrible things," Llesho answered with a shudder. "But if that were all, it was nothing so bad that I would risk your lives over it."

"Then why?" Kaydu persisted.

He wished Lling was there to do the explaining. From Llesho himself, to someone who did not know the ways of Thebin, it sounded . . . he didn't know how it sounded, but he didn't want to see the disbelief on her face.

"Tell me."

He shrugged as if it were nothing—only my life, the life of my people, he thought—and struggled to find a way to tell the outlander the most private secrets of Thebin's theocracy. That somehow, the governor's lady had already known.

"I am Thebin's seventh prince of my father's body," he said, and Kaydu waited.

"In Thebin, princes are wedded to the goddess on their sixteenth birthday. The prince is then considered a man full grown, but he is also a godling. If the wedding night goes well, the goddess may reward her new husband with gifts."

Kaydu waited still, expecting something more. When it didn't come, she offered, hesitantly, "According to my father, many lands have rituals of symbolic union with their gods and goddesses—"

"Not symbolic," Llesho blushed. He would explain in words even an outlander could understand if he had to, but he could not, would not look at her.

"The prince takes his vigil in the temple, and the goddess comes to him. Dressed in the flesh he most covets. And they . . . she . . . if he pleases her body, he will find himself changed in the morning. Not that anyone can see, at first," he rushed to explain, "but gradually, he develops some gift, a skill or power from the goddess. Adar is a healer. Balar centers the universe. Lluka sees the past and the future." He laughed a short, familiar snort. "Three of my brothers fell asleep and did not please the goddess. They are ordinary men. They say, of course, that they pleased Her best of all, and their gift is to live in peace within their own heads."

He wondered what peace his brothers had found in the years since the fall of Thebin, but Kaydu stirred restlessly.

"What do the religious beliefs of Thebin have to do with Lord Yueh's traitorous magician?"

" 'The seventh prince is blessed beyond measure,' " he quoted, " 'most favored of the goddess, his gifts are beyond compare.' Yesterday was my natal day. I was in the shrine when the attack began, but there wasn't enough time to complete my vigil." He pleaded with her to understand, "The goddess did not come! Or I thought not, but her ladyship says she did, and that she was pleased with me, though I did not give her pleasure as a prince must. But if she has given me the powers of the seventh prince, then better that you kill me now than Master Markko have the shaping of them. Because he is evil, and everything he touches he bends out of true. I don't know who he serves—not Lord Chin-shi, who is dead, or Lord Yueh, who carries the serpent at his breast and believes he is the master when he is just another servant of Master Markko's ambition.

"Somehow, Markko knows what I am. If he captures me alive, he will wield my soul like a weapon, and my people will die. Your people will die as well. Better to kill me here, now, than let that happen."

He let himself fall back against his saddle and shut his eyes, recognizing the light-headed drift away from his body that he felt in times of greatest weariness. In that state of separation from his surroundings he didn't really care that she didn't believe him. As long as she let him sleep. He didn't mention the promise he had made to the ghost, though, figuring one shock at a time was all either of them could handle.

"Damn!" Kaydu's voice, drifting out of dreamy distance, surprised him. "My father knew Master Markko was powerful," she explained when he cracked a heavy eyelid to look at her; and even from the far place where he floated he could see the worry in her frown. "How strong *is* he?"

Llesho thought about that. "In Thebin, there is a saying. 'Apprentices do magic. Around masters, things just happen.' Also, 'A good magician leaves no tracks on dry ground. A bad magician leaves no tracks in the snow.' To a Thebin, magic you can see is poorly done. It is difficult to tell a great Thebin magician from someone with no gifts at all who stands, by some coincidence, near the center of great moments.

"Markko isn't Thebin, of course, but if he knows what I think he does, and if he has set in motion the deaths of Lord Chin-shi and the governor, and her ladyship's flight for Thousand Lakes Province, as I think he has, then he is very, very strong."

"Stronger than my father?" she asked him, and Llesho saw the fear within the question.

He shrugged, his shoulders rubbing against the leather of the saddle propping his head. "I don't know, I'm not a magician myself, I just know the sayings."

"Among the witches of Shan, there is also a saying," Kaydu told him. "A good witch should always wear a bell around her neck."

"The question is," Llesho suggested, "how much between them is difference of philosophy, and how much a difference of art?"

"My father should wear a bigger bell," she admitted, and he figured that meant that he didn't let all his workings show. Good. Maybe Habiba had a chance. If so, maybe they had a chance, too. The thought gave him some comfort.

"Wake me in an hour to take my turn at guard duty," he mumbled, then rolled on his side and fell soundly asleep.

Llesho woke to the snuffling of hot breath against his neck. "Stop it," he insisted. Still more asleep than awake, he took a random swipe at the direction from which the annoyance seemed to come. His hand connected with a hard snout, slid down over long, sharp teeth. Not Kaydu, then. He opened one eye, and gulped. A bear stood over him, its muzzle wet and its fangs still colored with the blood of its last kill.

"Don't move," Lling instructed in hushed tones. She stood next to the tree she'd been sitting in, her bow drawn taut, arrow seated, waiting for a clear shot. Standing over Llesho's terror-frozen body, the bear shook its head at her. Opening its bloody maw wide, it roared a challenge across the grassy clearing. Kaydu jerked awake at the deep-voiced growl. She rolled away from the bear, coming to her feet with a short sword in her hand.

The bear pushed at Llesho's shoulder with its nose, whoofing a mournful tone in his ear. It was a very small bear, he realized, scarcely more than a cub; he wondered if the mother was around somewhere.

"Lleee-sshoo!" the creature sneezed. It sounded like his name, in spite of the bear spittle running down his neck. Looking into the glowing coals of the ferocious creature's eyes, Llesho found an ageless wisdom there, and perhaps a hint of rueful humor as well.

"Where is Little Brother?" Kaydu drew their attention to the fact that the monkey would have awakened them with his own high shrieks if he'd still been alive. Lling pulled her bowstring a little tauter.

Llesho sat up, his arms outstretched protectively.

"Wait!" he cried to his companions, and the bear raised its head, gargling a high-pitched growl of gratitude.

"Let me kill it," Kaydu whispered, though Llesho figured the bear had better hearing than any of them. Nobody moved, especially not Llesho, and she could not reach the bear without endangering its protector.

The bear sneezed again: "Lrlrl-eck!" it spewed at Llesho, and took a swat at his head with the pads of its paw.

"He could have taken your head off, Llesho," Lling hissed at him.

Llesho shook his head. "Could have, maybe. But he didn't. He retracted his claws before he hit me." He reached out and touched the bear. "Lleck?"

The bear tossed his head in a semblance of an affirmative, and emitted another high gargle of support before nuzzling at Llesho's hand with his nose.

"See! He knows me!" Llesho reached up to scritch behind the bear's ear. "He's just a baby," he said, and added, for Lling's benefit. "It's Lleck. I don't know what he is doing here in the body of a bear, but I know it's him."

The cub howled his agreement, bobbing his head up and down to emphasize the truth of Llesho's explanation. "Ll-iiiiing!" he said, and the sound of her name, coming from the wide open jaws of the bear, so startled her that Lling let the bow fall to her side, and gaped at him.

"Is it really Lleck?" she asked Llesho.

Released from the immediate threat of death from his allies, the bear who had been Lleck lumbered across the clearing in the direction from which they had come, then galloped back again. He repeated this dance several times, honking a series of high, panicky tones answered by the hysterical chattering of a monkey high in the walnut tree where Lling had been hiding. At least for the moment, Lleck was freed of suspicion of eating Little Brother for lunch, but the horses tossed their heads and added their nervous whickering to the clamor. Something was coming.

Llesho jumped to his feet, reaching for the knife and sword fastened to his saddle, just as Hmishi crashed through the low brush around them.

"Yueh's . . . men . . ." Hmishi gasped. "One of his forward scouts, dead, back there, mauled by an animal—" He pointed back in the direction he'd come from, then stooped with his hands on his knees, whooping for breath. The bear cub who had once been Lleck the minister joined his noisy warning to Hmishi's.

"Goddess!" Hmishi swore and reached for his knife, but Kaydu shook her head.

"Llesho has strange allies." She shrugged, as if the explanation made no sense to her either, but was nevertheless the only one she had, and started toward the horses.

"No time to run." Hmishi pulled her up short with the warning. He drew his bow and arrows and turned toward the sound of men on horseback shouting to each other and to their animals as they crashed through the forest. Lling moved up to Hmishi's right flank and Kaydu stood at his left. Lleck the bear ran awkwardly across the clearing and disappeared into the afternoon shadows creeping over the forest.

Llesho stood a little apart from his companions, his knife and sword both drawn and held at the ready. A scream arrowed through the clearing, and another, despair and terror gurgling to a wet end that sent a chill through the lonely young defenders. Then a horse broke from the forest, an ax swinging from the fist of its rider. Llesho ducked and raised his sword, but the rider was already falling, Lling's arrow in his throat. The horse, a roan bred for battle on flat open territory, reared up in terror, froth flying from her nostrils, her eyes rolling with her panic. Hmishi reached for her dragging reins, but she tossed him aside and crashed away into the forest again. They heard an animal scream of terror, and the fading sound of her hooves growing more distant.

Then the next and the next of Yueh's soldiers were upon them, and Llesho had cut the legs from under the horse that thundered by him, and finished off the fallen rider with a knife to his breast. Kaydu dragged the next from his seat and crushed his windpipe under her foot as she swung a sword in the path of the soldier who followed him.

Llesho heard the high battle cry of the bear cub at his side, darted a quick look to where the creature stood at the center of the clearing, blood dripping from his muzzle and bits of flesh and hair and cloth hanging from the claws of his outstretched forepaws. A mad light shone in his beady black animal eyes and the straggling few soldiers left alive turned and fled in terror at the sight of the savage beast fighting at the side of the magician's enemies. They were trained to fight and kill human beings, with capabilities no greater than their own. Only the fear of their master, following hard after them, could have induced the soldiers to confront the young witch and her Thebin team.

The bear was more than their terror could endure, and so they ran, not back to report to their master, but scattering for escape in every direction, the bear cub snapping at their heels. It seemed as good a plan as any to Llesho, who rapped out his order, "Mount up, we move *now!*" and reached for his own saddle. His hand slid on the pommel, and he gave the wet red smear an annoyed frown for a moment, before checking his hand for the source of the blood.

"Llesho!"

He turned at Lling's call, and noted her sudden pallor. She reached a hand to him across the clearing. "You're hurt," she said, and ran to his side. He didn't remember being wounded, but an arrow pierced his breast. Lling's words seemed to cut through the fog of adrenaline and shock, and Llesho realized that it hurt, deep in his chest. Suddenly, it hurt a lot.

"Lling?" The clearing tilted, trees turning sideways in his vision. What was happening to him? He fell to his knees, sat back on his heels with a grunt as the jolt shivered pain through the arrow jutting out of his chest. His comrades gathered in a claustrophobic circle around him, and Llesho glared up at them. "Stop it," he said, "I'm not ready to have my throat cut yet."

"Nobody's going to cut your throat," Lling responded tartly. Llesho didn't notice what Kaydu was about until the pressure against the arrow brought him back to himself.

"We can't take it out now; you would bleed to death before we could find help for you." Kaydu snapped the shaft off an inch or so from where it entered Llesho's tunic. He screamed, a high shrill sound that tore at his throat. A part of his mind that stood outside his body wondered what animal was being slaughtered in the forest. A prince, the part of him in agony answered himself. A prince is dying. The daylight dimmed, and he fought unconsciousness while the pain thrummed in him like the arrow was a live thing, digging its way through muscle and bone.

"Lord Yueh, or his servant, won't be far behind his scouts. He'll send a bigger force when the patrol doesn't come back," Kaydu said. He knew what that meant: ride or die.

"We ride," Llesho gasped. "Help me to my horse."

Hmishi and Lling each slipped under an arm and grabbed hold of Llesho's belt.

"One, two, three," Lling counted, and on the mark of three, they hoisted him to his feet, then to his stirrup. He managed to swing his own leg over the horse's back, and Kaydu settled his foot on the other side.

When he was set, Kaydu teased Little Brother from his walnut tree but did not tuck him back into his sling. Instead, she took his hat and coat so that he would look like the wild monkeys that populated the forest, and slipped a thin band around his body, under his arms. "Find Father," she instructed. "Give him this message."

She tried to lift him from her shoulder to a low branch of his hiding tree, but Little Brother clung to her neck, his little face grave and fearful. Kaydu sighed heavily, but she untangled the monkey arms from around her neck and chirped at him in the strange language they shared.

"Llesho is hurt," she murmured, "Find Father, bring him," and this time Little Brother leaped into the tree with a shrill stream of monkey curses. As they watched, he scurried out to the edge of his branch and flung himself into the next tree, and the next, his cries disappearing into the answers of the wild monkeys shaking their branches as he passed.

Llesho peered into the forest. His vision blurred, and sweat ran down his brow into his eyes. Something within him was drawing him farther away from his surroundings. He hoped to see the bear cub that had warned them of their danger but he didn't have the strength, and his companions lacked the time, to search for the cub.

Kaydu took the reins of his horse and led them out of the clearing. After a while, when their camp had fallen behind and only the deep woods surrounded them, Llesho thought he heard the sounds of an animal in the underbrush. He could see nothing but the occasional sway of a branch in the windless air, however, and gradually his sight faded to a twilit gray tunnel down which he staggered for an eternal afternoon. When he felt himself falling into the darkness, he called out to his old teacher, Lleck, though he had no idea how much of Lleck remained alive in the mind of the bear cub, or how much of his teacher had reverted to the wild nature of the bear. In the clearing they'd needed the savagery of the bear, but now, with his own life fading with the daylight, he missed the wise teacher.

"Help me, Lleck," he called, and the sound of his voice reminded him of other times, another march. When his horse stumbled, and he fell from his saddle, he struggled to rise lest he be trampled underfoot. "Mama," he thought at first, but remembered she was dead, "Adar!" he called for the brother who had soothed his fever when Llesho was a child. Healer king. *Adar, where are you?*

Chapter Nineteen

UNTIL their flight from the governor's compound at Farshore, Llesho had never seen a mountain or a forest. There had been the tangle of sand-loving trees and vines that crowned the hill at the center of Pearl Island, of course, and Llesho had once thought of that as a jungle or wood. But nothing had prepared him for the cycle of life and death played out in tones of black and gray in the night forest. Vaguely, through the fever that radiated from the arrowhead lodged in his chest, Llesho remembered that he'd once thought the forest must be silent at night, not this rackety clatter of birds calling and monkeys chittering and a thousand different kinds of insects chirping to each other with the clicking of their wings.

The sounds at a distance were a comfort. Those same creatures had fallen silent where they passed; that they resumed their nightly concert meant Master Markko's soldiers were not following yet, would not be looking for them until morning when his patrol did not return.

But the skulking hiss of predators keeping pace with their party over the leaf fall on the floor of the forest, and slinking from tree to tree overhead, raised the hackles of Llesho's neck. He sweated hot and cold by turns, fear and the oppressive heat of the forest confusing his damaged body. The creatures knew by smell that he was weak and waited only for his companions to let down their guard, and then the jaws of some huge cat or flying monster would seize him. Llesho could feel the prickle of anticipation in his legs, his shoulders, his neck. His flesh seemed to reach for the tooth and the beak in the eager rise of the hairs on his body.

As his fever rose, the sounds blurred, changed, and he heard skirts brushing through the grass, the cough and wheeze of old men driven beyond their strength. In Llesho's mind, the wail of a predator celebrating its kill mingled with the death cry of its prey, and he heard it as the curses of the guards and the death of another child strangled for its misery on the Long March. A keening wail for his mother and his father, dead and lost to him forever, started in the back of his throat. He wanted his brothers to hold him and tell him it was a bad dream, but no one came. He pressed onward through the night, through the pain and the numbness that was creeping across his shoulder and down his arm, and through the terrible, terrible grief of a seven-year-old child with the blood of his first murder still on his hands.

He knew he must not let his screams out, that if he started screaming the guards would come and they would stop him with their huge hands wrapped around his throat, and his eyes would bug out, and his tongue would turn purple, and they would throw him by the wayside to appease the jackals that fought with each other and yapped their selfish demands for the carrion left in the wake of the Long March. He did not want to be set upon his own feet, gradually to drift to the rear, where the lions who paced the human herd roared their challenge and watched for the weak, the small, the sickly, to fall behind. He had seen a lioness attack a child fallen on the trail, how quickly the tawny cat sneaked up on them and snatched the child away before its mother rightly knew her precious burden was gone.

"The lions," he whispered to his companions. Better prey than carrion. "The lions, not the jackals." And then he fell.

"Llesho!" A voice he recognized—Lling—called to him, too late. He heard the sound of horses, and cringed within himself. The guards would take him, and they would strangle him for the jackals. "The lions," he murmured in his fever.

"Llesho, it's me, Lling. Can you hear me?"

Small hands with hard calluses brushed the hair from his forehead. "He's really sick, Kaydu. I don't care how much daylight we have, he can't go any farther."

Daylight? "Dark," Llesho objected, "Adar?"

He wanted Adar, wanted his brother, the healer prince, to hold him and tell him it was just a dream, a nothing fever that he would bathe in herbs and whisper gentle prayers over. But Adar's hands were soft as were none of the hands that touched him now, and the air was too thick to breathe, not the cool, sharp air of Adar's dispensary, tucked into the high mountains overlooking the Great Pass to the west. He coughed and felt liquid bubbles shift in his chest, coughed harder and couldn't stop. Another voice in the darkness—not Adar, but male, and scared, muttered, "He's coughing up blood, prop him up so that he doesn't choke to death."

They moved him, and he screamed. He couldn't help it, though he knew it was dangerous, and the guards would come. A breathy "Shhh" warned him, but he couldn't hold it in, couldn't even form the thought to fight it, and the scream went on endlessly, until even Thebin lungs held no more. Llesho gasped and struggled for air that he sucked in with desperate rattling wheezes, but his blood was filling up his chest cavity faster than his indrawn breath could replace itself. He coughed and choked and vomited blood on himself until the hands on his shoulders rolled him onto his side and a voice above him swore softly. "Oh, Goddess, what are we going to do?"

"Make him drink," Kaydu said, and something fell next to him, was picked up and offered, and he reached for it with his lips like an infant reaches for his mother and the water poured over his mouth, and he tried to swallow, but felt the water coming back up thicker than it went in. *Oh, Goddess.* If this was her favor, then Llesho did not ever want to anger her.

"I'll go for help," Lling's voice, close to him, said, and he muttered, "Adar," through the chattering of his teeth. He was so cold all of a sudden; he felt his body shiver convulsively, and he grasped at the tunic of the person who held him. "Cold," he managed, and Kaydu was arguing with Lling, "Where will you go? Who do you expect to find out here but Master Markko's men? You know what he said about being taken again—he'd rather be dead."

"That doesn't mean he *wants* to be dead. I'll ride ahead. We're on a path, there must be a village somewhere."

Lling went away then, and someone put a blanket over him. The blanket smelled like horses, and he tried to cringe away from the hands that held it there, but the voice he knew as Hmishi hushed him with soothing words, and the words turned into a song, the prayer song for a sick child. He knew the words:

Free this child of his pain,
Let him laugh and sing again.
Lady of the crimson west,
From his fever give him rest.

It was a simple prayer; Adar knew much better ones, with harmonies sung with the lower throat voice while the upper nose voice sang the rhythms, broken by the ring of finger cymbals between the choruses. For state occasions, the birth of a prince or princess, or a plague, prayer wheels and gongs would join the song, and the entire order of healers would sing together in polytonal synchrony. Llesho had listened with wonder as his brother led the healing monks in petitioning the goddess to ease the birth of their sister. They'd been too successful for Llesho's young taste, and the little princess had been stubborn and loud from the moment of her birth. Llesho didn't want to think about that, though, because then he would have to remember that she was dead on a garbage heap somewhere and not even given the honor of a funeral. How would she ever find her way back to the world if she didn't know how much she was missed, how they had mourned her?

Why hadn't Adar saved her, if he was alive? He was a healer, after all, and knew all the chants and songs, and all the ways of herbs and the power of touch that only the most gifted healers practiced. Why hadn't he saved their sister? "Adar! Adar!" he called, while the voice over him broke from its song to whisper, "Hush, hush, hush."

"Hot," Llesho fretted, and pushed at the blanket.

"Take it off him," the voice of Kaydu said, and he could see her, standing over him with a sour frown on her face.

"But he was cold a minute ago," Hmishi objected.

"Fevers do that sometimes, if they are high enough," Kaydu answered, still frowning, but she didn't sound as severe as she had a few moments ago, and Llesho was grateful when the blanket was taken away. He was still too hot, but without the blanket to hinder him, his restless limbs could move. "He'll complain that he is cold soon enough," she continued. "When he does, use this—" she handed over a headcloth so fine he could see her face through it. "Drape it over his shoulders, to comfort him, but don't cover him for warmth. Let the air cool his skin."

But neither of them was Adar, and as the chills seized him again, he called out for his brother, gasping his cry, "Cold, Adar, cold."

Hands that were not his brother's covered him with a wisp of cloth and he wrapped his hands in it and curled himself around it, trying to warm himself in its folds, but he couldn't get warm, couldn't get warm, and he rocked himself, and the arrow bit deeper when he moved.

"Lions," he said, "lions, lions, lions," and he would have shouted if he could, because they would not understand. He wanted to go to the lions now, not wait until he was food for the jackals, and he heard the wind in the grass, and the moans of the women and the old men driven beyond endurance in the Long March. And he heard the crying of the children, and knew he was one of them, but he was a prince and must not cry, must not cry, but his face was wet, not a prince after all, but a slave. Were slaves allowed to cry?

Horses then, and Lling, saying: "There is a village about a mile down this track. I found a healer. She said she would come."

Then Llesho heard the robes of a woman stirring the underbrush, the smell of herbs and sunshine on her hem.

"The boy is sick?" she asked. Kwan-ti. He looked up at her and smiled. "I knew you would come," he said, and closed his eyes. He was safe now, though she was not Adar, and he had thought her dead.

"Are you a healer?" Hmishi asked, and Llesho would have laughed at him if he could have. Didn't he recognize Kwan-ti, their old healer from Pearl Island? But Lling did not correct him, and Kaydu was explaining Llesho's wound as if to a stranger.

"An arrow, here." Kaydu gestured to her own body,

to a spot just above her left breast. "We did not take it out, afraid that he would bleed to death, but the wound has sickened, and he has fever and coughs up blood."

"He's conscious some of the time," Hmishi said. "But he makes no sense when he talks."

"We'll see what we can do." The healer knelt down at his side and touched the stub of arrow jutting from his chest. It should have hurt like fire piercing his heart, but it didn't. All he could think about was the cool touch of her fingers, and the scent of mint and honeysuckle that clung to her like a perfume.

"The village is more than a li distant, his condition too serious to carry him so far," she said, "But I have a small house here in the wood that I use when I need to replenish my supplies. It's just this way—"

Llesho did not open his eyes to see what she did, but her hand disappeared from his chest, and he guessed she must have pointed, for she added, "The first bit is uphill, but it is only a short hike, and then the way is level. Lift him onto a blanket, and we will each take a corner. You can come back for the horses when we have a roof over his head."

Hmishi's hand on his shoulder tightened, and he heard his friend say, "You did not ask who we are, or how our companion came to have an arrow in him."

Why did Hmishi sound so suspicious? Surely he knew the healer as well as any of them. "Kwan-ti," Llesho called out to her.

"She's not Kwan-ti," Hmishi murmured a quiet warning, but the healer contradicted him with a mild rebuke:

"It will not hurt to let him think I am someone he knows, and if he wishes for her presence, perhaps it will help him. Come, before it rains, or worse. Your attackers may have reinforcements nearby."

She moved away briefly, but after a moment returned. "We have to lift you now," she whispered. "It will hurt, but just for a few minutes, and then we will try to make you more comfortable, yes?"

He nodded to signal he was ready, and she favored him with a smile in reply. "Now," she said, and his companions lifted him and set him on the blanket. He gasped, still shocked at how much the wound could hurt when he moved, but he stuffed his fist in his mouth to stifle the scream. He would not give their position away to the guards. But he couldn't quite remember what guards he was watching out for, so he let his head fall to the side, and escaped the pain into a dark well of oblivion.

Chapter Twenty

"YOU'RE going to be all right, Llesho, but this will hurt. I'm sorry."

Kwan-ti's voice reached him from somewhere in the fog that dimmed his eyes and clogged all his thought processes. He thought she was wrong, though. He could feel Master Markko's poison burning in his veins, and he knew he was dying. Llesho smiled at her anyway. The bed was soft and smelled of sweet grasses, and when she spoke, her voice held the dark at bay. The paste she smeared around the arrow jutting from his chest chilled him to the bone, but with that icy contact, the pain went away.

"Kaydu, Hmishi," Kwan-ti called to his companions in the voice that demanded instant obedience. "Tie these."

Soft clothes wrapped Llesho's wrists and upper arms, wrapped his legs and his torso so that he couldn't move.

"No!" He started to panic, but Kwan-ti settled him with a hand on his forehead.

"I have to take the arrowhead out, Llesho.

"Lling, bring the knife from the fire, and plenty of cloths. Kaydu, bring the tub of hot water, and Hmishi, bring the jar, there in the window." She never stopped stroking his brow, but Llesho heard the scurry of footsteps away from his bed and back again, felt cloths draped over his shoulder, heard the hiss of a hot knife in water.

"Hold him," she said, and the knife pierced Llesho's breast, cut deep, past the blessed ice of the surface, into the pocket of infected, rotting flesh, and deeper, until the tip of the knife scraped bone, and Llesho was straining against the restraints that held him, screaming as if his throat would turn itself inside out. Oh, Goddess, what had he done to deserve this? Why wouldn't she just let him die in peace?

Hands left him. He heard footsteps running, and a door opened and banged shut again. The hands that remained still held him immobilized for the healer's knife, but they shook. It must have been Lling who sobbed at his feet, because he recognized Kaydu's voice growling prayers and imprecations at his head, subsiding after a while into a muttered string of words, "Finish it, finish it," over and over like a mantra. So Hmishi must have run from the house.

Then the arrowhead was out, lifted away, and Kwan-ti called for boiled cloths and stroked the weeping slime from his body, dipping into the wound itself to clean out the poison.

"Could be worse," she muttered through gritted teeth. "Just a bit of fecal matter smeared on the tip of the arrow. A soldier's trick, not the work of a magician. Deadly enough if left untreated any longer, but we caught it in time, I think. Now, hand me that jar."

Kwan-ti's hands went away. Llesho heard the grind of a stopper being pulled from the jar in question. Kwan-ti smeared something into the wound that crawled over his flesh like jackals over carrion. With a sick moan, Lling followed Hmishi out the door.

"What are you doing?" he demanded. "What is it?"

Llesho squirmed while she pasted a cool mash of leaves and moss over the mess and wrapped a bandage tightly over the whole strange patch in his flesh.

"Something to help clean away the dead flesh," she answered, the cool humor in her voice at odds with her earlier tension. "We'll leave the packing in until the maggots have done their work, and then we'll see what we have."

Maggots! If he'd had the strength, Llesho would have been beside his friends outside, vomiting his disgust along with his dinner. But he hadn't the strength to lift his head nor had he had any dinner. When he reached to tear away the bandages and their foul infestation, the soft ties still held his arms trapped at his sides.

"Relax, Llesho." Kwan-ti's fingers left cool traces where she touched his forehead, and he found himself sinking back into the bed of sweet grass and herbs. "Your own dead flesh was producing the poisons that were killing you," she explained. "My little ones will eat the corruption and leave the healthy flesh to grow strong again. They are less painful and more sure than my knife, and they will not injure the living body as the knife has done."

As she spoke, Kwan-ti bathed his side, his arm, his neck. The feel of the damp cloth against his skin distracted him from the crawling sensation beneath the bandage. When she had finished and left him to rest, Llesho lay awake, waiting for the sensation of fat white maggots to gnaw through to his heart. It seemed like an eternity before he decided to let the terror go. If he had come so far only to die hideously at the hands of a friend, he'd rather not know. So he gave in to the pull of exhaustion and fell into a deep sleep haunted by dreams of Harn raiders storming through the palace and the Long March. In his dreams he heard the mocking cries of the jackals drawing near.

When he woke again, sunlight cast soft beams through the pollen that floated in the air of the little house. His companions had carried him here in the dark of night, he seemed to remember. He didn't know if the house looked east or west, if it was morning or afternoon. He had no idea how long he had lain between normal sleep and fevered delirium in the healer's house, or how long it had been since he had eaten. He heard the murmur of soft voices nearby, and the chink of cups on saucers, however, which triggered the juices on his tongue. He was hungry. Starving, in fact. He could eat a bear.

Which reminded him that he hadn't seen the bear cub since their battle with Master Markko's scouts in the woods. Had something happened to him? Was it really the spirit of Master Lleck, his old teacher and his father's minister, or was that just another of his fevered dreams? Very little seemed real to him right now. Not his life as a pearl diver or as a novice gladiator, or his training as a soldier in the governor's compound. His recent experience with the infected wound seemed to have stripped everything away but the Long March. He wondered if that meant he was dead, or that his whole life had been a dream while he marched across an endless grassland in the arms of his dying people.

If the bandage still covered his left side, he bargained with himself, that would prove with the evidence of his own body that he was alive. He didn't know how he was going to test this theory, since Kwan-ti had ordered his arms tied down and Kaydu had tied the knots. When he lifted his right hand experimentally, it moved freely—in fact, it seemed to float above him of its own accord. Llesho had to speak sternly to it in the privacy of his mind before it would settle over the bandage.

The cloth was still there, bound tightly around the place where Kwan-ti had carved out the arrowhead, so, perhaps he was still alive. The crawly feeling of flesh-eating vermin was gone, however; that could mean they had transformed into some other form of creature now invading his body for the kill, or that

Kwan-ti had removed them while he had slept. He wasn't sure he cared which was true, so long as he could keep this feeling of floating free of his body and its pain.

"You finally decided to rejoin us!" The healer had noticed his hand drifting above his eyes. She filled a cup from a kettle that simmered over a three-legged brazier by the window and carried it over to him.

"Drink, boy. You need the nourishment."

She gave him an encouraging smile, but Llesho could not hide his disappointment when he took the cup from her hands. She wasn't Kwan-ti at all, but a stranger. With his head cleared of the fever, Llesho wondered how he could have mistaken her for the healer on Pearl Island. This woman was much older, her face seamed with the effects of weather and time. Her gait was steady and quick, but her back was bent forward so that she seemed always to be getting a little bit ahead of herself, as if her head could not wait to arrive where her feet were taking her. She had a cheerful smile, and eyes . . . she had Kwan-ti's eyes as surely as Llesho breathed air and drank tea.

"Kwan-ti?" He barely breathed the question, though he knew, logically, that it couldn't be true.

"If that is who you wish me to be, young princeling." There was more to her answer than the wry humoring of a sick patient, but he couldn't read the truth of it, or why a woman of the Celestial Empire of Shan would call him by his title, even as a pet name.

The dusty, unused sound of his voice had drawn the attention of his companions. Lling reached his bed first, with Hmishi close behind, exclaiming their surprise and encouragement so that he could not dwell on his questions.

"Llesho!"

"You finally woke up!"

"I thought you were going to sleep forever!"

Llesho smiled, drunk with that haze of good feeling

between the breaking of a fever and the measuring, in the ache of movement, the losses the body had suffered.

"Give him space to breathe," the healer warned. "Don't get him excited; he's still weak."

His two old companions withdrew a few steps, punching each other in the shoulder and bobbing on the balls of their feet. But he did not see Kaydu anywhere in the cottage.

"Where's Kaydu?"

Lling shrugged her shoulder. "She was afraid that we might be trapped in this cabin if Lord Yueh sent reinforcements after us. So she left, late last night, to scout the area."

"When I went out to tend to the horses this morning, I thought I saw dragons in the distance—two of them, flying too high for me to be certain. Mara says that she will be safe enough, since the local dragons haven't eaten people for several generations." Hmishi twitched a shoulder in a companion gesture to Lling's shrug. Neither wanted to think about what might have happened to Kaydu alone in the forest with dragons in flight and enemy soldiers on the ground.

Only the healer seemed unconcerned. "I am Mara. I would have introduced myself when we met, but you seemed to need someone else in my place, and I didn't want to disturb your recovery with a little thing like a name."

She eased herself down onto a low three-legged stool beside his bed and urged the cup to his mouth. "Don't forget to drink," she ordered him, but Llesho put up a hand to stop the cup from coming any closer.

"Kaydu," he said.

"Will be fine. She's a smart girl, and full of tricks. Don't you worry." Mara, the healer, held out the cup again, more insistently, and this time Llesho drank as he was told.

He expected something sharp and smelling of iodine, as Kwan-ti's potions often did on Pearl Island, but this was sweet and light and smelled of flowers good enough to eat. When he would have drunk too fast she tilted the cup away from him with a warning, "Slowly, princeling, your body isn't used to taking nourishment any more."

By the time she had spoken her warning and he had nodded understanding he really didn't have, he was ready to drink again. When she offered the cup, he slurped noisily, trying to take in as much as he could before she took it away. His childlike cunning made her laugh.

"Definitely improved," she decided. "And well enough that I can afford to leave you in the care of your traveling party for a few hours. I have patients I need to see in the village, and they will have missed me by now."

"What do you want us to do?" Lling stood between the healer and Llesho's bed, looking down at him with concern hunching her shoulders.

The healer offered her the cup. "Get as much of this into him as you can, slowly at first, then let him set his own pace. If I am not back by evening, he can have some of the boiled fowl from the icehouse."

She stood up and stretched out her back. Hmishi drifted over to listen as she gave her instructions. "He should sleep most of the day, but if he gets restless, you can prop him up on pillows—don't let him try to sit on his own. When he needs to relieve himself, bring him the jar—he is not to get out of this bed until I say so!

"If he isn't careful, he will tear the healing flesh." She smiled to take the sting out of the warning. When she was certain she would be obeyed, she untied her apron and hung it on a hook. She put on her bonnet and tied it under her chin. Then, taking a cloak of mottled green from the peg beside it, she issued her final warning, "Don't chatter too much, you will tire him. Remember, a relapse is always harder to treat than the original fever."

With that she opened the door and went out, closing it softly behind her.

When the healer had gone, Lling moved purposefully out of his range of sight, and Llesho heard a clatter on a staircase he could not see, followed by footsteps overhead. Lling soon returned with a huge bolster full of goose feathers, and Hmishi lifted him up so that she could put the bolster under his shoulders. When his two companions had settled Llesho against the bolster, they sat cross-legged on the floor next to his bed. They could talk this way without looking down at him, and Llesho could see them without craning his neck.

He knew they were waiting for his questions, but first he gave a luxurious sigh and took stock of his surroundings. The house appeared to be small but comfortable for its occupant. He dismissed the upper loft, which he could not explore in his present condition, and which must contain few dangers to concern him if Lling could root around up there without setting a guard. The main floor was one tidy room with a single door and one large window with its shutter propped open with a stick. When he was sitting up like this, he could see most of the room. A fireplace and a table and chairs stood at one end, with shelves knocked into the wall next to the fireplace. In the corner by the door sat a three-legged stool and the low, grass-filled bed. Through the window, sunlight filled the space and left the silhouettes of pine boughs brushing the floor.

The light troubled him. He'd been awake for long enough that the quality and direction of it should have changed, but it stayed bright and soft as early morning. He didn't want to let go of the delicious weightlessness he felt basking in the warmth of it, but they had been running from danger, and he didn't think that danger had gone away just because he needed time to heal.

"Where are we?" he asked. "How long have we been here?"

Lling took the first question. "We've come about seventy li from Farshore. We were moving away from her Ladyship's party at an angle, but we are still a hundred or so li from the outer border of Thousand Lakes Province, more than twice that far from the provincial capital. If her ladyship kept ahead of Lord Yueh, the refugees should have passed the border two days ago, and by now her ladyship's father must have sent his own troops to escort her home. They may be watching for us along the frontier, but Thousand Lakes Province can't do much for us unless we cross its border, which we don't plan on doing if we can help it."

If the refugees had already covered more than seventy li, he'd been asleep too long. Hmishi confirmed that assessment as he answered the second question. "We brought you here three days ago, I think. It's hard to keep track." The tremor in his voice gave him away. They had given up hope that Llesho would ever awaken. He wondered what had kept him asleep so long, but could remember only the fading dreams of another life. Which was real? he wondered. Was he sleeping now, dreaming of friends and feather pillows? Would he waken again to the Long March when he hit the ground, another Thebin subject dead beneath him, another taking him up in her arms and walking on?

He thought he could hear the whisper of the long grass in the distance, and shuddered. This was real: Lling and Hmishi, Kaydu gone to scout for trouble, and the sunshine casting bars of bough-patterned light against the old and weathered floor of the house in the woods. But this reality, he remembered, had a monkey in a coat and hat in it, and a bear cub that said his name, which sounded as unreal as any dream. He closed his eyes, too confused to take it in, too frightened of the alternative if this world wasn't real. He'd almost died in this world, too, of course, and he wondered if the goddess left any path open for him on which he lived to reach his majority. She must have been really pissed off at him for the interruption of his birthday vigil.

Lling gave him a moment to regain his composure, then laid out their choices. "Our next step depends on what Kaydu finds during her reconnoiter. If Lord Yueh was pursuing the refugees and the scouting party stumbled upon us by accident, his army may not have stopped at the border. Thousand Lakes Province may be under attack even now, and we will find no sanctuary there. If the scouts were looking for us—" she did not say it, but they all knew she meant Llesho—"it is unlikely that we can outrun a trained army."

Again, Llesho knew he was the obstacle to their escape. The others could run, or hide, but Llesho couldn't sit up under his own power, let alone escape a pursuing army.

"Sky Bridge Province is closer," Hmishi continued, "not more than thirty li to the south, but the mountain passes are more difficult there. We would have to trade the horses for donkeys, and any spy who learned of it would know immediately that we had changed our route."

"We'd be moving away from Shan and not toward it," Llesho objected, still determined to reach the capital city and find Adar as soon as possible.

"But we'd be heading *toward* Thebin. Whatever plan we make will have to wait on Kaydu's report."

Llesho nodded his agreement, though what he expected to accomplish with just the four of them, all too young for legal freedom and Llesho with a hole in his chest, he didn't rightly know.

Lling focused her gaze on the edge of Llesho's

bandaged side where it had escaped the blanket. "We don't have to decide yet," she said, "not until Kaydu finds out whether Master Markko is still looking for us, or if Lord Yueh has pulled off all his men to attack Thousand Lakes Province. In the meantime, Llesho needs to heal."

Waiting sounded like a good idea to Llesho; he needed his friends working and thinking together when they went after Adar. He didn't have the energy to persuade them to go to the capital city of Shan anyway—didn't think he'd have much luck trying when he couldn't stand up under his own power. But he wasn't sure that they could stay where they were either.

"Do you think Kaydu is coming back?" he asked, and meant not, *Has she betrayed us to our enemies?* but, *Has she been captured?* and, *Do we have to run now, before her captors find us, and while I am not yet sure which world I live in let alone what route we should take to freedom?*

Lling frowned in a way that made Llesho think she had figured out the shades of meaning in the questions he was really asking.

"We're as safe as we can be," she said. "Or we have been, until now."

Until now. Llesho wondered about that. Lling answered his frown without waiting for the next question: "We are still free, more or less, though Mara—the lady healer—hasn't had much chance to betray us to Lord Yueh. She has stayed with you night and day since she brought us here."

Thus the "until." Whatever Kaydu's fate, Lling didn't think she'd give them up to Master Markko or Lord Yueh. The healer, Mara, however, could be reporting them to authorities in the village at this very minute. Those local officials might hand them over to anyone happening by with a provincial government badge on his cap.

"You don't trust her?" They both knew which "her" he meant. Llesho wasn't sure he could ride yet, but he could send his companions on ahead, out of harm's reach, if he had to, and find his own way out of Lord Yueh's trap. There was always the one final escape open to him, though he regretted the pain and exhaustion he had already invested in recovering from his injury.

Lling wouldn't meet his eyes, but raised her eyebrows in question at Hmishi, who hesitantly took up the answer.

"I think she would do anything in her power to keep you from harm," Hmishi began, "but she's not Kwan-ti."

The first part of Hmishi's answer surprised him. Llesho had already figured out the second part for himself. "Has she told you who she is?" He didn't mean the name, of course, but Hmishi repeated it anyway.

"Her name is Mara, and she says she is local to the village, and only uses this house when she is foraging in the wood for herbs and fungi to use in her medicines."

"But the house had all the signs that someone had been living in it recently," Lling observed. "No dust on the tables, the bed made with grasses still green from the plucking when we arrived. And there were fresh fruits and vegetables in the bins."

"She had the medicines she needed for your wound right to hand," Lling added.

Llesho did not look happy, but he admitted, "I know it doesn't make sense, and you've both seen a lot more of the healer than I have, but I trust her." He glared at his companions, defying them to contradict him. "It was something about her touch—I could feel it. I think that's why I mistook her for Kwan-ti. There was something about her touch that just felt like a true healer." They couldn't object, however;

they had all grown to like her, and for many of the same reasons.

"At first, when she cut out the arrowhead, I thought we'd made a mistake," Hmishi said. "She seemed as cold as her blade, and even more unbending. I couldn't even watch, but she didn't flinch once, not even when you screamed that horrible scream and only the cloths tying you down kept you from rising right out of the bed."

Llesho remembered that part, dimly, and it still had the power to turn his stomach. His companions seemed to feel the same way, for they had turned matching shades of green.

"And when she did that thing with the—" Hmishi couldn't finish, just shuddered in revulsion, and gestured loosely at the bandages. Llesho remembered that part, too, and was regretting that he'd drunk so much of the healer's potion so recently. He had a feeling it wouldn't be pleasant on the return trip.

"I'd heard Little Phoenix mention the use of the carrion eaters as a battlefield treatment for rotting wounds," Lling interrupted, "but I'd never actually seen it done. Hope I don't again."

Hmishi shook his head. "I don't have to like it, but I can accept that it was necessary."

Llesho knew he wasn't in the best shape for logic, but even he could see that Hmishi was making a better argument for distrusting Mara than for trusting her. "So you like her, even though you don't trust her and think she might be trying to kill me?"

He didn't like the sound of that, but it was how his tired brain chose to phrase it.

"It was afterward," Hmishi said. "She bandaged you and then gave us all instructions for keeping you cool. She told us what to say if you cried out in your sleep, and asked us to watch you while she cleared her mind. And then she went outside.

"We were all nervous then," Lling said, "because

we thought she had gone to find Lord Yueh's men, to hand us over."

"So I followed her," Hmishi admitted. "I would have killed her before she gave away the location of this house, but she only went as far as the trail. She brushed away the marks of our boots and the horses' hooves, and scattered fresh branches to erase all the signs of our camp. She was angry. It took me a few minutes to realize that she was praying while she worked, and that she was addressing heaven in that tone of voice mothers use when you leave the gate open and the goats get loose in the vegetable garden.

"She was furious because you'd been so hurt—I've never seen a healer threaten the gods before, but that's what she seemed to be doing. So, I don't think she is going to turn us over to Master Markko, or to Lord Yueh's soldiers."

Hmishi shrugged, unwilling it seemed to explain why he would trust their safety to the curses of a madwoman. "I wasn't sure of her skills as a healer until yesterday. Your fever broke, and today you woke up. I don't think she is likely to poison us, not after spending so much time on making you better. But I don't know how safe she will be, or us, if the villagers tell Lord Yueh's men about this house."

Llesho could feel the smile stealing over his face. The sunlight would never make *sense,* but perhaps there was a *reason* for the eternal morning. "I don't think anyone will find this place unless she wants them to." Still smiling, Llesho drifted into a peaceful sleep.

Chapter Twenty-one

LLESHO rose out of troubled dreams to find that the sunlight had faded into evening. He'd missed another afternoon and so, apparently, had his companions. Hmishi and Lling lay asleep on the rug by the fireplace, tucked up close to each other as if to ward away the cold.

"What time is it?" he called. "Is anybody here?" It gave him a moment of satisfaction when the sleepers started up with foggy expressions of guilt on their faces.

"Sorry. Fell asleep." Hmishi rubbed his eyes in an effort to look more alert. "Do you need something?"

"Have you noticed something strange about this place?"

Lling gave him a slow smile. "I like it here," she said around a yawn and a stretch. "It's warm, smells nice—"

"Nobody whacking at us with swords or pikes," Hmishi added.

"What about the missing afternoons?" Llesho would have asked the question but a commotion at the door drew all three Thebins to their feet.

"Home! And not before time, as I see." Mara entered

the cottage trailing a dirty and bedraggled Kaydu, who looked around the little house with suspicious, darted glances out of eyes that seemed charged with feral nerves. Little Brother crouched on her shoulder, his arms wrapped around her neck, but made no sound.

"Kaydu—" Llesho began, just as the healer spoke up, chiding him with a "tsk" in her voice.

"You should be resting. I thought you two had sense enough to keep him lying quietly."

"We did."

Llesho slumped back on his feather bolster, more wary than ever but resigned to wait until they were alone again to discuss this matter of lost time. It seemed more important now to find out why Kaydu looked like she'd been on the Long March and why she slumped onto the three-legged stool with relief when her glance fell upon him propped up in his bed.

"I couldn't find you! I thought you must be gone, or dead—"

"None of that!" The healer interrupted Kaydu's stammered plea with a sharp order, "Out! Your father taught you better than to track mud into a house where the injured are healing."

Kaydu took a deep breath, as if she wanted to argue the point, but no words came. Taking belated notice of her disarray, she shuffled out the door again, Little Brother still clinging to her neck, while the old woman's tart promise followed: "You can talk all you want when you've had a wash at the pump."

When Kaydu had gone, Mara shook her head, as if in disapproval of the returned scout, or at some news from the village that troubled her. She hung her bonnet on its hook and took up her apron with a reverent hand, stretching and sighing with a shake of her head as if she was setting her day aside with her cap. After completing the little homecoming ritual, she dragged the three-legged stool over to Llesho's bed and dropped down onto it. Her smile couldn't hide the weariness that deepened the lines between her eyes, but she seemed genuinely pleased at his condition. "You look better, Llesho. Did you behave yourself today?"

"If you mean did I sleep the day away, yes. I didn't have much choice about it."

"I don't suppose you did. But you needed the rest, and I wanted to take no chances that you would do something foolhardy while I was away."

Until she said that, Llesho had not suspected the delicious drink his friends had pressed on him all day. When he realized that she had drugged him, he blushed, a little angry at her for tricking him, but more at himself for not suspecting the potion. Adar had taught him long ago how foolish it was to judge a medicine by its sweetness. But Kaydu's anxious glances needed his attention now.

"What happened to Kaydu?" He asked. "Have Yueh's soldiers found us?" His companions, at least, might escape—

"You are safe for the time being." The healer made a sour face. "No one has seen any soldiers in the village yet, though some of my patients reported strangers creeping around asking questions about comings and goings at the crossroads. I didn't tell anybody you were here with me, however, not that they would have talked to the spies if they knew. We are not a trusting people hereabouts."

Llesho kept to himself the reminder that Lling had gone into the village to seek help in the first place, and that Mara herself had trusted his companions enough to bring them into her home and heal his wound without question. He figured she had ways to protect herself.

Something had unsettled Kaydu's mind, which not even Yueh's surprise attack and their flight under cover of darkness had managed to do in the past. He didn't want to know what had put her in this state, but suspected that, in the absence of the enemy, she'd run afoul of the protections of the healer. She had left to find the pump easily enough once she'd assured herself that Llesho was safe, though. He didn't think she would have done that if Mara posed a threat to them, but he wasn't quite ready to give up his own suspicions yet.

"I did hear a strange tale about a bear cub," Mara continued. "The villagers say that the creature takes careful nibbles of food offered from the hands of small children, and that he says, 'Thank you' when he is done, but one can't believe everything one hears."

She tilted her head in a question, giving him the opportunity to come clean with his story, but he wasn't ready to grant her Lleck's secret yet.

When he said nothing, she added, "The village elders didn't believe the story either, having their own experience with bears. They were gathering a hunting party to find him and kill him." She saw his look of dismay and her smile developed a wry pucker. "Fortunately, this particular children's story followed me home."

Llesho tried to rise from his bed, torn between chagrin and the need to see his teacher, even in his new form. But the healer pushed him down again. "He's outside. Master Lleck's manners, like those of your guide, currently leave much to be desired. You must trust to the forest to keep him safe, at least until tomorrow."

"You don't mean Kaydu to sleep outside as well!" he demanded.

"Of course not, child! I am sure she will be her usual self as soon as she has had a good wash, and then she may come in and visit you and sleep by the fireplace or in the loft as she chooses."

Only then did Llesho realize that not one of his three human companions remained in the house.

"They are having a chat with your furry brown friend." Mara seemed to read his mind, although the question, and the fear, had marked themselves pretty clearly on Llesho's face.

Fortunately for his peace of mind, he didn't have to rely on her assurance about their safety for long; the door opened onto growing shadows, from which Kaydu tumbled, looking more herself with the mud washed away and fresh clothes replacing her damaged ones. Hmishi and then Lling followed, with Little Brother chattering in her arms. They all talked at once, in a shorthand that left unspoken the experiences they had shared while Llesho had lain unconscious from the effects of the tainted arrow. He felt a sudden pang of jealousy, that they had formed a unit while he slept. They had seen and talked with Lleck while he lay on his bed like a wet noodle. Mara seemed greatly distracted by the sudden clamor, but she focused keenly enough on the door when Lleck tried to sneak past under cover of their commotion.

The healer was on her feet faster than Llesho could see her move, elbows akimbo, her hands in tight fists perched on her hips. "Not in my house, master bear!" She glared at him, tapping her foot all the while.

The bear cub uttered a mournful cry and ducked his head so that he could cover his eyes with a forepaw.

"That won't work on me, you old reprobate. We settled that on the way home."

"Please?" Llesho asked weakly from his bed. He needed to know that, however changed, his old mentor was still safe and whole.

The healer turned her glare on him, but Llesho didn't flinch or look away. He had to see Lleck. If he couldn't do it in the cottage, he would get out of bed and sleep in the forest, whatever it did to the wound healing under his bandages.

"Stubborn," she remarked. "I almost feel sorry for him."

She measured the determination in Llesho's face a moment longer before throwing her hands in the air and leaving his bedside. "Just a quick hello," she insisted. "Then it is outside for him. He'll be more useful as a guard if he can roam a bit, and I'm not cleaning up after a bear in here. Bad enough with the four of you."

Embarrassed that she had seen through their covering commotion so easily, his companions likewise moved away from the door.

"Kaydu, please bring the chicken from the icehouse."

Kaydu dropped her gaze and backed nervously out the door as Mara gave further instructions, "Lling, there are carrots and potatoes in the root bin in the cellar; would you please fill this sack with equal numbers of each." She held out the sack, and when Lling had taken it, picked up the water bucket. "Hmishi, you may bring water from the pump."

Lleck waited until his human companions left the cottage to do the healer's bidding, then he lumbered in over the doorstep.

"Llle-sshhooo!" he wailed, and Llesho held out a hand to him.

"Lleck!"

The cub neared him suspiciously and sniffed his hand. Lleck's muzzle was cool and moist, his fur soft. Llesho pulled himself up in his bed enough to wrap his arms around the bear's neck. "Lleck," he sighed, and dropped his head on top of the bear's low skull, resting his forehead between the laid-back ears. After a long minute he raised his head and let the cub lick the salt from his cheek, whuffling in his ear.

"I'm not heartless, you know," Mara commented while she set two lamps on the table. She trimmed the wicks, then lit them. One she hung from a hook near the bed, and the other from a similar hook above the table.

"A house is no place for a bear. He really will be more comfortable out-of-doors." She cast him a chiding look, then shifted her attention to the shelf by the fireplace, from which she selected first a handful of herbs dried in jars and then some spices twisted in little packets.

"I need to know he is not just a dream," Llesho tried to explain how he felt about the miracle that had brought his dead teacher to his aid in the forest. Even with his arms around the bear cub's neck he could not shake the fear that none of it was real. What if he hadn't wakened from his delirium at all, but still lay dying by the roadside?

"I know, boy." Mara sighed. "That's why the old reprobate is sitting by your bedside and not outside as he ought to be."

Kaydu returned with the fowl, already plucked and boiled and waiting for dish-cooking, and Lling returned with the carrots and potatoes.

"But bears are solitary creatures by nature; to keep him near, you must not hold him too close." Mara took down her big, sharp knife and talked while she energetically chopped the vegetables.

Returning in time to hear this last comment, Hmishi set down his filled bucket. "He's not really a bear, though," he insisted, with a doubtful glance in the direction of Llesho's animal companion.

"You're wrong, Hmishi." Mara's expression seemed more sad than anything else when she corrected him. "In this lifetime, he *is* a bear. He fights the impulses natural to this new form because his spirit still yearns to protect the princeling as he could not protect the king in his former life."

"If you can make the afternoons disappear, why can't you change him back into Lleck?" He had determined not to speak out about his suspicions until he was alone with his companions, but Lleck's presence at his side gave Llesho the courage to confront the healer with her magic.

"I don't know what you mean, Llesho," Mara answered. "Sleep is the only thief of time in this house. Sick people often take strange fancies, however, and I recommend that you put this one right out of your mind." She stirred some broth into the pot, filling the room with delicious odors that went right to the heart and warmed the body from the inside.

Kaydu sat up straighter. "He's right," she said. Her voice had grown stronger now that she had cleaned her face and put on fresh clothes, as if the whole weight of civilization shored up her flagging courage. "You are doing something to our minds, or to the flow of time. How many days have passed in this house while I have been gone? Far less than for me out there, I'll warrant, or you would have shown more surprise when I turned up on your doorstep. Instead you greeted me as if I had stepped out that door just yesterday."

"It was just yesterday," Hmishi pointed out.

No one was listening to him, however, because they were watching Mara, who wiped her hands on her apron and directed a sorrowful frown not on Kaydu, but on Lleck, the bear.

"I have some small powers, to aid in healing, or to give rest. I did not shape the mysteries of this glen, but I have the power to enter into them and to protect those in my care by use of them. Even here, day passes into night, however, and no matter how he might wish it otherwise, Lleck will live out this turn of the wheel as a bear is meant to do."

"But not today?" Llesho objected, his arm still tight around Lleck's neck.

"Yes, Llesho, today. He will catch and kill his own dinner, and sleep in the arms of the trees tonight. But no harm will come to you as long as he is nearby."

Lleck dropped his head, accepting Mara's words with a low cry, "Lleee-sho!" He gave his pupil's face a farewell lick and walked slowly to the door.

When he was gone, Lling wrinkled her nose, a question in the gaze she passed from the healer to Kaydu. "Lleck must think we are safe or he wouldn't leave Llesho for anything. I trust him, if not you. But how long *was* Kaydu gone?"

"Time doesn't mean much in these woods," Mara returned to her cooking with a smack for Hmishi, who plunked himself down at the table and snatched a bit of carrot that escaped her flashing knife. "One day is very like another, just as one tree looks very like another if you aren't familiar with the forest."

"Six days." Kaydu had returned to the three-legged stool, her arms dangling between her knees. "I found my father."

"And Little Brother." That still bothered Llesho.

"And Little Brother. Habiba said that Master Jaks is furious with us, and is likely to blister our hides for sneaking away without him, but that Lord Yueh caught up with them before night on the day we sneaked away. We were probably safer alone than we would have been if we'd stayed behind. Master Jaks led the counterstrike and saved her ladyship, which he could not have done if he had come with us, so Father is not as mad as Master Jaks. They are on their way, but they can only travel as fast as their horses. Father said not to wait, but to run as soon as we can."

Hmishi held out a bit of carrot that had escaped the pot. Kaydu's pet abandoned Lling to take it from his fingers. "Maybe they should leave their horses behind. You seem to have made better time without one."

Lling sidled closer to Llesho's pallet, her hand falling to her belt, where her sword usually hung. "That would only work for Habiba. Master Jaks can't travel the witch's road, can he?"

"I am beginning to think you are fools, the lot of you," Mara waved her stirring spoon at them to emphasize her anger.

"You may not understand Habiba's gifts to his daughter, but you still need them. Didn't you ever wonder *why* Master Markko wanted so badly to rid Pearl Island of witches?"

Llesho didn't have to wonder. "The Blood Tide," he said. "A witch might have saved the pearl beds."

"Very likely one did, until it became more than her life was worth. As graceless a thank you as I've ever heard, but accepted. Can we return to the matter of escaping Master Markko's clutches now? Have you anything else to tell us?"

Llesho wondered at the pronoun. When had Mara become a part of their quest? But Kaydu looked worried, and not about the healer.

"Lord Yueh went after her ladyship, but Master Markko followed *us.* I saw him at the crossroad, trying to pick up our trail. He almost caught me, but I hid in a fox's abandoned den until they had searched the area and moved on. Then I reported back to Habiba and returned here, but I couldn't find the clearing or this house. I would still be stumbling around in the woods, except that I hid myself to watch by the road, and when Mara left the village, I followed her.

"You'll feel better with a good meal in you."

He'd recognized everything she'd put in the pot by its smell if nothing else: rosemary and thyme, and a bit of lemon-flavored grass that made the whole dish smell like a country garden. Still, he hesitated, wondered if the healer had drugged the food as she had the potion.

"Come now," the healer reminded them, "if I wished you harm, I had only to leave you where I found you."

"Or you may have your own reasons for keeping me here," Llesho suggested.

"I might. But since I must fatten you up if you are to make an attempt to escape my clutches, it would seem that our immediate goals are the same."

She was making fun of him. He might have resisted the food anyway, with a thought to self-preservation in the presence of magics he did not understand, but his nose overruled him. It tasted even better than it smelled—fowl braised with the vegetables in a thin broth of the herbs with a dash of spice. Mara brought a chunk of bread out for dipping in the broth so that not a drop of the delicious flavor was wasted. In spite of his stomach's uneasiness with solid food, Llesho felt better. He sank into the now-familiar curves and dips in his grassy bed with a full stomach, jostled only slightly when Lling sat down beside him and leaned against his pallet for support. Hmishi remained at the table, his head resting on his arms, and Kaydu sat on the three-legged stool, staring thoughtfully into the fire. He was too comfortable, he decided, to work up a suitable terror about Mara's intentions, and closed his eyes. He had almost fallen asleep when the mournful cry of a bear rose from the forest. Lleck, defending the little house, he thought with a smile. But the tone of the bear's complaint changed, grew more angry and more desperate.

Llesho tossed in his bed, aware that he had in fact been sleeping, and that Mara tended him with cold compresses. "You are safe, Llesho," she crooned. "No one will find you here."

The cry of the bear cub subsided into whuffling plaints of curiosity, and then faded entirely.

"No one can hurt you under this roof; you are in the land of dreams now."

With Mara's words echoing softly in his last fading thoughts, Llesho drifted off again. When he awoke, his companions had disappeared.

Mara was standing over the table with her arms sunk to the elbows in a bowl of yeasty dough the color of butter. He knew that for sure because a pale yellow brick of the stuff sat on a plate beside the kneading board.

"Your friends are out with Lleck, scouting. They

will be back soon, looking for breakfast." She extracted one hand and peeled the dough from her fingers, then reached for a jar of raisins, sprinkling in a generous handful before punching the dough back down and covering the bowl.

"Do you think you can stand?" She gave him her full attention, fists braced on hips, a measuring frown on her face.

"I think so." The wound itched more than it hurt under its clean white bandages, but lifting his head was an effort. His limbs, too, seemed to have developed a will of their own while he'd slept.

Mara nodded. "Time you tried, at least." She wiped her hands and arms clean with a damp cloth and walked briskly to his bedside. "Let's see what you can do."

Llesho sat up and swung his body around so that his back rested on the wall and his legs dangled off the side of bed. He stopped there, dizzy for a moment, and closed his eyes. When the room stopped spinning, he opened them again. Mara watched him calmly, evaluating his progress. Llesho figured he wasn't supposed to see the urgency lurking behind the calm, but it goaded him forward anyway. He pushed off the bed with his arms and stood up under his own power, though he swayed on his feet, almost overcome by nausea.

"Good. Let's try for the door, shall we?"

Llesho wondered if the healer had lost her mind. He was disoriented and dizzy; he couldn't imagine lifting a foot off the ground and not replacing it with his butt. The healer had already taken a step backward, however, and she had a tight grip on his elbow, which didn't leave him a lot of choice in the matter. One step, then another, and Llesho reached the open door, where the sun shone on his face and the scent of pine sap and morning fizzed in his nose. He smiled in spite of himself. It was a beautiful day.

"Outhouse?" he asked.

The healer quirked an eyebrow at him but pointed at the little cabin a few yards away at the edge of the clearing. "Do you want help?"

He didn't dare shake his head, or he'd be on his face at that instant, but he said, "No. I can manage."

She released his elbow and Llesho set off. The outhouse seemed to get farther away as he staggered toward it, but finally he made it, and without falling in the process. It took almost more courage than he possessed to let go of the door when he was done and totter back to the cottage. In spite of his misgivings, he made the return trip successfully, with less vertigo, but no breath left to spare. When he finally dropped onto his bed again, he felt as if he had run all the way from Farshore, but he felt vaguely proud of himself as well. Mara hadn't expected him to manage this much on his own, but he'd proved himself stronger and more determined than she thought. He wasn't certain why that was important to him, except that she seemed to expect greatness of him and he was pretty sure he'd disappointed her so far.

Mara hadn't been idle during his trek to the edge of the clearing. She had prepared a tray of buns with raisins enticingly bursting from the dough and had pulled open the door to a bake oven over the fireplace. She slid the tray into the brick cavern and closed the door again before acknowledging his prowess: "You'll be keeping up with Master Lleck in no time."

"Do we have even that much time?" Llesho asked.

She didn't pretend to misunderstand. "Not as much as I had hoped. But maybe, enough." Mara grinned at him, all teeth, with a warrior's glint in her eye. "The Harn underestimated you once, and so did Lord Yueh. I hope I am not counted in their number when the day is done."

"I could say the same," Llesho pointed out. The

healer knew far too much about him and his business, and he wondered who she really was and what side she was on. He also wondered where his companions had got to, but a commotion at the door answered the second question.

"The same about what?" Lling asked. She entered the little house with an arrow held as far from her body as she could reach. Hmishi and Kaydu followed, keeping their own careful distance from the arrow while Lling finished her report.

"We found this in the bushes at the edge of the clearing. It looks like whoever shot it came upon Lleck while he was sleeping."

Mara took the arrow with equal care and sniffed at the tip. "Did it break his skin?" she asked.

"He says not," Hmishi answered. "He had blood on his muzzle, but I got the impression it wasn't his blood. I expect whoever shot the arrow is limping today."

"Can Lord Yueh's men find us here?" Kaydu asked with a darted glance at the door. "I thought they gave up and went away."

Mara set the arrow on a shelf with great care. She looked worried. "I would say Lord Yueh's lackeys could not find this place," she said slowly. "But if they have Master Markko with them, and if it is the magician's intent to find Llesho, then I can't be sure. Markko's power is strong, and not always predictable."

"Then we ride," Llesho decided.

Kaydu frowned at him. "You're not strong enough."

"I'm not strong enough to stand against him, and I won't be his slave again. Ever." Llesho turned Kaydu's objection around on itself. He couldn't fight yet, but maybe he could ride. If the choice was that or capture, he would take his chances with a horse, even if it meant he would die.

After a long minute spent studying his face, Mara nodded her reluctant agreement. "But tomorrow is soon enough." She went to the window and whistled a strange, quavering note. Then she waited. Soon a bright-eyed swift fluttered into the room and came to rest on her outstretched finger. She whistled again, and the swift pecked at her knuckle. Then it took to wing with a warbling cascade of notes to which Mara listened sharply before she turned away with a sigh. "Let's see what the wind turns up first. In the meantime, there are warm buns to eat."

Llesho took a deep breath, and a smile bloomed on his face without conscious thought. The rich scent of raisins and cinnamon filled the air, and his mouth watered. His stomach wanted filling, and as Mara reached into the oven with a heavy cloth to remove the buns, Llesho's fingers itched for the drippy feel of hot butter and soft bread. Hmishi did more than yearn, however, and his darting theft earned him a cuff on the ear.

"Sit and eat like a civilized being, Hmishi, or I'll send you out to forage with Master Lleck."

Hmishi dropped the bun onto the plate as if it had burned his fingers, which it probably had. Then the healer turned to Llesho with a question, "Would you care to join us?"

Hot buns in front of him was an even better incentive than Yueh's magician behind him. He pushed himself off of the bed and tottered to the table to the applause of his companions.

"How long have you been able to do that?" Lling asked him, and Llesho blushed. "Just since this morning," he said. But he'd resisted temptation long enough and abandoned discussion for the more serious work of putting as many buns inside his stomach as he could comfortably hold, and then finding space for a last greedy mouthful.

"That much effort deserves a nap," Mara observed. Her tone was broadly disapproving, though her smile told him that she didn't disapprove at all.

Llesho did need a nap, though. He made it back to his bed with no help, but was glad to lie down at the end of the short walk. When he woke up again, night had fallen. The fire in the fireplace had dropped to ashes and embers, and his companions had found their own temporary beds. All but Mara, who stood at the window in secret conversation with an owl. Llesho couldn't make out what she said, but he could hear the terrible sorrow in her voice. He sat up, uncomfortable at the thought that she might think he was spying on her, and wished he could help with whatever had upset her so.

"Mara?" he asked when the owl had flown away.

"Shh," she turned from the window. "Sleep now. You will need all your strength in the morning."

The healer passed a hand over his eyes, and Llesho felt a heavy weight pulling his eyelids down, down, until the darkness was complete.

Chapter Twenty-two

LLESHO had awakened to the sound of birdsong while the sky still closed its darkest night around the cottage. Mara stood at the window, a jar forgotten in her hand while she listened intently to the shrill cries of a swift that had lit on the sill. After a moment the healer trilled a reply and the bird flew away.

"Kaydu! Wake your company, and hurry!"

She resumed her search of shelves and cupboards with renewed urgency, reaching with more speed than care for a jar of salve, a twist of paper filled with a yellow powder, a small bottle of oil with cloves and peppers floating in it, half a dozen pouches of drying herbs that crinkled when she thrust them into her pack.

"What?" Kaydu rolled from her mat into a defensive crouch with a knife in her hand. "What is it?"

"What's all the noise?" Hmishi struggled upright, with Lling right beside him. Llesho said nothing about the single blanket that had covered them.

"Your Master Markko is on the outskirts of the village. Privy, and pack. Hmishi, get the horses." She thrust another packet into the pouch at her waist. "Llesho, can you ride? There are branches and tarps for a drag travois if you don't think you can manage."

They both knew there was more to the answer than pride. If he slowed them down, he gave Master Markko an advantage. And Master Markko would kill them. So he said, "I'll ride."

Hmishi ran for the horses, with Kaydu to help him, while Lling threw their few possessions into a pack. The healer stood in the doorway of the house, her pack over her shoulder and her eyes pinched as if she were trying to see through the trees to the threat beyond. Lleck poked his nose past her skirt in a thwarted effort to reach Llesho, but subsided with a moan when she did not let him pass.

"You can't mean to travel with us, healer!" Lling glanced up from her packing with a worried frown. "We are riding into danger, and you don't even have a horse."

"One finds danger staying or going." Mara straightened under her pack and pinned the Thebin with a ferocious glare. "I choose to find it in Shan, where my daughter now lives.

"As for a horse, we will be traveling difficult terrain today; I will keep up well enough on foot. And tomorrow, Master Lleck's paw will be healed enough that he can carry me."

The bear cub moaned his objection to this plan, but Mara ignored him. It was more difficult to ignore his prince.

"How bad is it?" Llesho asked—no, commanded—pinning her with his sharpest, most imperious gaze. He thought she might put him off, or lie, but she didn't.

"Lord Yueh's men attacked the village last night," she said. "There may be survivors scattered in the woods, but the carrion birds are feasting today."

"Then it isn't any safer to stay behind." Master Markko had powers of his own. He would penetrate the mysteries of the glen for his new lord, perhaps already had.

"It seems your small war party continues to grow."

"I didn't know that's what we were."

"Oh, yes." A long staff rested against the doorjamb, and she wrapped a hand around its middle, leaning into it to take some of the weight of her pack off her feet. She seemed more substantial with the wooden shaft in her hand, and the house seemed less so. Llesho shook his head with a silent warning not to let his imagination run off with him, but he couldn't quite shake the queazy sensation that the ground had tilted. He still felt light-headed, but decided, wisely or not, to keep that to himself.

Hmishi drew up next to the cottage with the horses saddled and ready. Mara gave him a satisfied nod before setting off down the path that led away from the cottage. "We can eat when we are well away."

When they came to a turning in the path, Llesho looked back. The clearing was there, more tangled and thorn-shrouded than it had seemed when they had ridden through it. He could not see the little house at all, and wondered if it had ever really been there.

The road wound steeply through the mountains with dark forest pressing in on either side. By Farshore standards it was little more than a glorified trail and only wide enough for two to ride abreast. Two wagons could not pass each other, but one must withdraw to a lay-by carved out of the dark woods until the other had gone past. The authorities in each district took their responsibility to maintain the route seriously, however. The road was smooth and clear of encroaching underbrush, and the company made good progress. Llesho wondered what would happen now, with the governor dead and his ladyship put to flight, but order still held out here where news traveled slowly.

By late morning the party had settled into a steady pace. Lling and Hmishi led the way on foot, walking the horses that needed resting in rotation. Llesho followed on horseback, accompanied by Mara, who walked at his side to watch him for signs of exhaustion or weakness. Kaydu rode behind, bow strung and arrows at the ready. They all knew a single bow would not protect them if Lord Yueh's army came upon them, but it might give the party the moment they needed to scatter into the forest. With Little Brother riding on his back, Lleck tracked them from the shelter of the trees that overhung the road. He barked the signal for friendly travelers once or twice but had no cause to howl a warning of enemy soldiers on the road.

With more bravado than sense, Llesho had assured his friends that he was strong enough to travel. Mara had seen through his claim. She'd bound his upper arm to his side and tied his forearm in a sling against his middle to support his wounded side. It was enough to dull his awareness to a throbbing discomfort. Llesho reminded himself that he didn't trust her, really. He wouldn't be surprised when it turned out that she had saved his life for her own purposes, much as Master Markko had kept him alive only to poison him again and again. Until she showed her true intentions, however, it wouldn't hurt to take advantage of whatever comfort she afforded him. So he surrendered himself to his exhaustion, drifting in and out of a light doze while his horse plodded on, his reins in the hands of the healer.

The sun had nearly set when Llesho slid out of his saddle with the thought that he'd had it good when he didn't remember the afternoons. Mara had insisted they halt for the night after Llesho had nearly fallen from his saddle as she strode beside him. She'd led them to a stopping place with fresh water and enough cover to protect them from any but a determined search. As he dropped numbly to the mossy ground, Llesho had to admit that the problem wasn't his companions or the mysterious healer, or even the forces of Lord Yueh. Llesho was the problem: a relatively useless former and completely unnecessary prince of a vanquished country. All he had to do was surrender and his companions would be free.

Hmishi cast him a concerned frown as he unsaddled Llesho's horse.

"I'm sorry I got you into this," Llesho told him.

"My father sold me to the Harn for the price of a loaf of bread when you were six years old," Hmishi answered. "I don't see how even you can take credit for that."

"But—"

"Did you kill the pearl beds or cause Lord Chinshi to take his own life? Did you attack the governor's compound in the dead of night? You were not the cause of my problems when I was six years old, and you are not the cause of them now. Or do princes tax evil the way they tax grain?"

With a skeptical smirk on his round dark face, Hmishi dared him to agree, but he was too tired to explain. He didn't think Hmishi would listen anyway. It didn't seem worth the effort it was taking to keep his eyes open, so Llesho let his eyelids slide shut.

"Do you need Mara?"

"I'm fine."

After a long pause, Hmishi led the horse to the little stream that flowed nearby. Llesho was almost asleep when a boot nudged him gently in the side.

"What now?" he asked with more snap in his voice than seemed appropriate, given his remorse a few short minutes ago. He opened his eyes with an apology ready, but Hmishi just winked, a rueful grin plastered on his face. Sort of like the mud plastered all over his boots and leggings.

"Boggy springs," Hmishi explained with chagrin as

he rubbed at his leggings with a fistful of spongy moss. "Lling and Kaydu are going to mark them out so we can move about safely. Just don't go wandering in the dark."

That explained why Mara had seemed so sure when she announced that she had found them a perfect campsite for the night. Anyone trying to sneak up on them was likely to sink knee-deep into quicksand. The warning seemed irrelevant, though.

"Do I look like I plan on taking a moonlit stroll?" he muttered. He rolled over onto his strong arm and closed his eyes, putting an end to the discussion.

Cradled in soft moss rooted in a rich mulch smelling of green woody things, his exhausted body began to relax, only to discover a new set of discomforts. He realized that he had a full bladder and an empty stomach, and he'd have to do something about both before he could sleep. Neither seemed urgent enough to force movement back into his leaden muscles, however.

"He's not moving!"

Hmishi's call drew the attention of the healer as it was meant to. Llesho heard the swish of her skirts, then felt a cool dry hand on his forehead.

"Can you move, Llesho?" she asked him softly, brushing the hair from his eyes with a gentle fingertip.

He would have told her "No," but he couldn't open his mouth, or move his tongue to form the word.

Her hand left his head, and he heard more rustling about as she searched her bag of medicines. "You can rest soon," she promised him. He would have told her that he was resting already, but she crushed a pinch of leaf between her fingers and waved it beneath his nose. Tears sprang to his eyes, and his nose twitched at the pungent odor that assailed him, but he found he could move his head again, and after a moment could uncurl his whole body and drag himself back to his feet. He swayed between them until Mara gave him a nudge in Hmishi's direction.

"Find him a tree," she ordered Hmishi. "We'll be ready to eat when you come back."

Llesho had to admit he felt much better when he returned to the camp, but the gnawing at the pit of his stomach had turned into a determined demand for food. He sat with his back against his saddle, and Lling handed him a bun and a thick slice of cheese while Kaydu portioned out some fat berries she had picked in the forest.

"Cold collation tonight," Mara explained as each drank his or her fill from a pot of fresh springwater she handed around.

Kaydu nodded her agreement. "We light no fire and set guards, two and two, until morning."

"I would offer to serve first watch, but Llesho is not the only one whose heart outpaces his body." Mara smiled, giving Kaydu the point. "I must have sleep now, I am afraid, if I am to be any use later."

Llesho wondered if the healer referred only to her turn at watch, or to other uses of her powers that might sap her hoarded energy. When he would have asked, however, Mara had disappeared into a blanket the color of the forest floor, shades of green and black that changed as she moved in her sleep. Only the low snore that punctuated her rest gave her presence away.

Sleep seemed a really good idea, and Llesho slid down where he sat, embarrassed when Lling drew a blanket over him. Not too embarrassed to smile his thanks before he closed his eyes, though. He pulled the blanket up tight around his ears, curled on his good side in the moss again, and felt the tension flow out of his muscles. Tomorrow would be better. He could feel it in the clean exhaustion, so different from the fevered crash of his failing body a week ago. And if he lay really still, he could imagine that the moss that held him was a soft puddle of velvet, the hem of his mother's gown. He used to curl close to rub the soft fabric against his face and listen quietly to the murmur of her voice and the silver call of her laughter. The memory put a smile on his lips as he slipped into sleep.

Hard midnight held the forest in its dark hand when the whisper threaded its way into Llesho's sleep. It nagged him out of dreams of winter in the palace, when the caravans had gone and a blanket of snow wrapped Thebin in a hushed, expectant peace. Llesho woke breathless from racing down the long hall in search of his brothers, but he could still hear Master Markko's voice.

"I'm here, waiting for you, boy. We need each other, you and I. Together we will rule heaven and earth."

The words made no sense. Llesho was a runaway slave. No one but Llesho and the spirit of his teacher knew that Llesho's journey did not end at Shan, but truly began there. Most of the time he didn't believe that he would succeed in his quest to regain Thebin. He couldn't figure out why Master Markko would care about Thebin or its princes anyway. A thousand li and two imperial powers separated Llesho's country from Farshore, and that didn't count the seven li straight up the side of a mountain range to the plateau where Kungol stood.

His companions slept on, undisturbed by any sound, and Llesho wondered if he had imagined the voice in his dreams. But no, there it was again, sweeping over his mind like the mirrored flame of a beacon tower. "You are mine, body and soul, boy. You cannot escape your destiny. Didn't I show you that on Pearl Island?"

Llesho shuddered. The voice was in his head, and he felt the iron collar on his neck, the chains that weighed him down with despair. He could never escape those chains; they drew him from his bed in the moss, choked him when he would have resisted, and he followed the voice, and the pull at his throat. One step, two, past the huddled lumps of his companions wrapped in their blankets. Dimly, Llesho recalled that they had agreed to keep a watch, but he counted four sleeping bodies. When he stumbled over the last, however, the pain in his toe made him gasp. A log! He wondered if all the rumpled blankets hid firewood, but one of them moved and snorted in its sleep. After a moment Llesho released the breath he held and moved again, quietly, toward the voice in the forest.

"Where are you going, Llesho?" Unyielding, Mara stood before him. She wore a shawl over her shabby dress, wrapped tightly around herself and held in place by both of her arms crossed firmly under her breasts. She looked younger in the moonlight, or ageless, and terrifying, as if she were living stone come to life in front of him.

"I need to find a tree." He stammered out the lie and hung his head, unable to meet her eyes.

"The chains are gone, Llesho."

He did look up then, and met her grim-faced challenge: "He cannot make you come to him, he can only hope that you are fool enough to heed him when he calls."

"I'm not a fool." He wasn't sure of that, now that the voice was gone from his head and he thought about what he'd almost done. But it still made a terrible sense. "If I go to him, he'll leave the rest of you alone. If I try to escape him, he will kill you all, and take me back anyway.

"Only if he catches you." She smiled at him, and he took no comfort from it at all. "Give us tomorrow, at least. Until we reach the river."

"I can't," Llesho pleaded with her to understand. "He's in my head." He hadn't realized that he'd raised his voice until his companions stirred and begin to sit up in their bedrolls, guilty to be caught sleeping when they had agreed to post a double guard. Llesho figured that was Markko's doing as well, but he kept his conclusions to himself, like a guilty secret.

Hmishi and Lling came to him and took up guard positions. Hmishi stood slightly in front of him and to his right with a sword bared in his hand. Lling settled behind his left shoulder, an arrow nocked below his ear.

"Are we being attacked?" Kaydu wanted to know.

"Not anymore." Mara was looking into Llesho's eyes when she spoke: Master Markko would not disturb his sleep again this night. The healer believed she could protect them from the mental assault of his pursuers. In the moonlight her dark eyes seemed to reflect infinity, and Llesho was tempted to trust that she was right. He gave her the barest hint of a nod, enough to know that he would take her advice for now.

She accepted his decision with an equally subtle nod. "Get a few more hours' sleep," she said to his companions. "We ride before daybreak."

Hmishi and Lling followed him back into the camp, but Kaydu joined Mara on guard, her face still troubled by her failure to fulfill her duty. He'd have to explain that it wasn't her fault. They were all easy prey for dark thoughts at midnight, and Markko had taken advantage of that. The magician had seized their wills before they knew what was happening. Given that her father had been the governor's witch all of her life, he didn't think Kaydu would have much trouble accepting as fact what Markko had done. He just wasn't sure what she would decide to do about it. And he was too tired to deal with it now.

"Sleep," he muttered to himself, and reached for the soft comfort of his mossy bed again.

Why is Master Markko so determined to get you back?" Kaydu wrinkled up her nose in displeasure, and Llesho understood why. During the night he had tossed and turned under the burden of his secrets, until he finally decided that they couldn't afford to hide things from each other if they hoped to survive. While they prepared for the morning's trek, he'd told his companions everything, starting with who Lleck was in Thebin and his apparition as a ghost in the pearl bay, how Master Markko had poisoned the bay with the Blood Tide and set the blame onto the healer Kwan-ti. He told them about the terrible months when the overseer had beaten him and held him in chains and used him as an experiment to test his poisons on. He admitted the sick dread he had of ever being returned to the master's evil workroom. Hmishi and Lling had known some of it, Kaydu a little as well, and Mara, they thought, none at all. Only the healer was not surprised to learn that Master Markko had come to him in his dreams last night, however. Mara had nodded her gray head to confirm his suspicion that Markko had affected them all, putting them to sleep when they should have kept watch.

By the time he was finished, Mara was stamping with impatience, but ignorance of Master Markko's power, and of his intent, could kill them more surely than an hour's delay. Llesho stared levelly into her eyes and then went back to stringing his bow and checking his arrows. He knew why they had fallen so quickly back to sleep after the midnight call, and he knew why Markko had made no return in his later sleep. He had no evidence, not even logic to back his intuition, however, so he accepted her silent command that he keep his guesswork to himself.

Kaydu had spoken aloud the question that had bothered him since he realized that Master Markko was still looking for him: Why? When she didn't get an answer, she offered her reasoning. "I mean, I know you were once a prince and all, but it's not like anybody is offering to pay a ransom for you."

Strategically, it made no sense, and she tried to explain that to Llesho without hurting his feelings, he was sure. She couldn't know that Llesho had asked himself the same questions ever since Markko had first snapped an iron collar around his neck. "Can you do magic or anything like that?"

"I can hold my breath underwater," he said with a perfectly straight face. "And I can, or could, execute a nearly flawless Wind Over the Mountaintops prayer form, though I tend to stumble in the middle of the related fighting stances."

Mara choked and made a display of holding her hands over her head and pointing to her throat. But she hadn't been eating at the time, so Llesho wondered. When she had settled a bit, she motioned to them to go on, and walked purposefully into the trees.

Lling jabbed him companionably with her elbow just then, declaring, "I don't know anything about prayer forms, but I've seen you fall over in the middle of a fight sequence."

Llesho nudged her back; neither of them let the moment turn into a full roll-and-tumble play session, but the momentary distraction relieved the tension. It couldn't drive out the feeling that someone was drilling holes between his shoulder blades with their eyes, though; he sobered quickly.

"I don't get it either," he said. "If I had completed the vigil on my birthday, maybe I would have some influence with the goddess. But I didn't."

"Maybe that was part of his plan," Kaydu suggested, "He may have feared he couldn't control you once you had successfully completed your vigil."

Her ladyship said that he had gained the favor of the goddess. Llesho didn't think that was a secret in the real sense, since he personally didn't think it was true. He squirmed a bit when he evaded the question, though. "For all I know, he just likes the idea that he has a prince on a leash instead of one of those fluffy dogs Lady Chin-shi was so fond of. I don't really care *why* he's after me. I just want to make sure he doesn't catch me."

"Then we had better get moving." Mara had returned with Lleck following her and she gestured in the direction from which she had come. "We are not far from the Golden Dragon River where the Dragon Bridge crosses. Markko is likely to know about the crossing himself, and he will make for it just as we do, so we shouldn't return to the road. I noticed this track, however—" she pointed to the ground near her feet where the grass seemed beaten down but otherwise no different from its surroundings "—and followed it to where it comes out on the riverbank just a stone's toss away from the bridge. Once we break from cover of the forest, we must mount and ride as fast as we can. It will be a run for our lives if we are to reach the river ahead of him, but reach it we must."

The forest growth was close on either side, with branches hanging to form a low canopy overhead and undergrowth grabbing at their legs as they passed. The company led their horses in single file, with Mara in the lead, and Lleck rumbling behind. In spite of their danger, Llesho found himself enjoying the stretch and pull of his muscles, the feel of his body doing work again. The sense of being watched had passed; Llesho wondered if Mara had something to do with that as well. He also wondered what good it would do them to cross the river if Master Markko was following right behind.

Determined to confront the healer, he dropped the reins. Horses were stupid, but they would follow where they were led, and there wasn't really anyplace but forward a horse could go in the thick wood. Before he had taken two steps, however, Kaydu had raised her arm to signal a halt.

"Mount up," she said.

Mara had slipped into the woods. She would wait

until Lleck came up to her position, then ride on his shoulders. Llesho set his foot in his stirrup and slung his free leg over the back of the horse, keeping his head bent low over the animal's neck. He darted a nervous glance around him, then took his bow in his hand, ready to run or to fight. They broke into the clearing.

Chapter Twenty-three

THE sun had not yet appeared over the treetops, but when the companions broke from the shelter of the forest they discovered the riverbank was already bathed in a golden wash of sunlight. Llesho winced at the sudden shock of bright light, but he had little time to adjust. Kaydu's voice rang in the still morning air: "Ride!"

She kneed her horse into motion, and Llesho did the same, snapped into action at the familiar command in her voice. Lord Yueh's troops, about fifty men on foot and a dozen on horseback, waited for them no more than a hundred paces up the riverbank. At first Llesho wondered why they did not leap to the attack, and then he saw that they were staring with amazement at the bridge that rose up in front of them. Llesho would have done the same if he'd had the time: Golden Dragon Bridge arched in glory high over the churning water below.

Ancient artisans had carved it in the shape of the legendary dragon from which the muddy yellow river took its name. They had given the bridge two ridges of scales across its back to keep men from falling off in dark or windy weather, with space enough for four men walking, or a good sized wagon, to pass between them. True to its name, Golden Dragon Bridge glittered its burnished glory in the sunlight. But the bridge shouldn't have been there at all.

According to legend, a war between the giants had, in an earlier age, destroyed the wondrous bridge. No man living had seen the broken remains. Supposedly, no one even remembered where the bridge had stood. Some stories said that when giants walked the earth again, the bridge would rise out of the mist of the river and the past glory of that age would return. Llesho didn't see any giants. The carved head of the dragon bridge, however, rested on the near shore, submerged to the realistically carved nostrils. Huge fringed lids shuttered its eyes, as if the masons and carvers had known that to portray in stone the living gaze of the dragon was to risk conjuring the creature itself out of myth.

The legend hadn't been completely wrong, however. Some great cataclysm of a former age had torn the bridge loose from its moorings on the far side of the river, because the arch disappeared under the water an arm's reach from the shore.

Mara crouched below a carved nostril of the sleeping dragon. She beckoned them to hurry when they would have frozen where they stood, in the same stupefied amazement that ensorceled Lord Yueh's troops. Llesho kicked his horse into a gallop; someone in the enemy ranks shouted, and he faltered, trembling, as Yueh's men parted. Master Markko made his way on horseback through the troops, looking for something. *Me,* Llesho figured. Their eyes met; he could not break that contact, but his body responded to his training even when his mind did not. As her ladyship had taught them, he fastened the reins to his saddle, controlling his horse with his knees, and drew his bow and an arrow from the quiver at his back.

Arrow nocked, he stood in his stirrups, body turning

to hold the gaze of his target. Steady, steady. Allow for the gallop of the horse—the changing distance and the uncertain elevation. He let the arrow fly, watched as Master Markko reached out and snatched it out of the air inches from his breast. Markko smiled, and the arrow burst into flames in his hand.

Bad move, Llesho saw. That sudden whoosh of fire had startled his horse into a faster gallop, but it had terrified Lord Yueh's soldiers, who scattered as if Markko had dropped the burning arrow among them. Those nearest their leader surged forward to overtake the fugitives, but those out of the direct line of the magician's fierce glare ran back into the forest from which they had come.

No point in wasting another arrow; Llesho tucked his bow into the strap of his quiver. He bent low over the neck of his sturdy little horse and urged it to close on the bridge that frightened the animal as much as it awed him.

But Mara was standing now, still dwarfed by the massive size of the dragon, but urging them to cross. Kaydu stormed onto the bridge first, Little Brother tucked into a pack strapped to her back. Hmishi and Lling followed right behind her, the hooves of their horses ringing like a demented carillon on the gold paving stones, and Llesho came next, pounding up the steeply sloped spine of the bridge until he was high over the river, looking straight ahead because he didn't have the nerve to check behind him for pursuit. And then he was on the downward slope, horse stretching out over the last broken arm's length, and there was water under them, no bridge at all.

The jolt of solid ground shuddered through him. A stone wall lay in front of them, with the twisted branches of fruit trees rising above it. A perfect place for an ambush, but they were out of choices. Whooping a battle challenge, Kaydu bent into the jump, and her horse leaped, leaped, and was over the wall.

Hmishi and Lling jumped next. Llesho gave his horse its head and it soared, cleared the wall, and ran out its momentum between the rows of fruit trees. When it stopped, Llesho saw that he was surrounded, with hundreds of soldiers closing in on him.

Llesho's stomach clenched like someone had reached inside with a fist and squeezed. He reached for his bow, but a hand stayed him: Master Jak's. Llesho hadn't seen or heard him, and he shivered, knowing that if the assassin-soldier had wanted it, he'd be dead. The six tattooed rings around Jaks' arm told their own story about that, but Llesho hadn't and still didn't want to think of his teacher as a man who sneaked up on people and murdered them for cash. Someday he would press the man for his stories, but not now. Now he would be grateful for this man's skills.

"How did you find us?" Llesho didn't need to ask how they knew to come. Kaydu was a few feet away, wrapped in the arms of her father. Little Brother chittered and screamed from a branch over their heads.

"How did you find the bridge?"

"A little bird told us." Jaks followed his gaze with a wry smile.

Llesho nodded. Mara had known and sent word by the swift he'd seen at her window. He wanted to thank her, but he couldn't find her among his companions or the soldiers who had come to greet them. "Where is she?"

Master Jaks looked back, toward the river.

"Alone? Markko will kill her!" He turned his horse and Jaks grabbed hold of his bridle.

"I can't leave her to face Master Markko alone."

"If Habiba isn't worried, doubtless she can take care of herself," Jaks reasoned quietly.

"Maybe." Llesho figured the magician would sacrifice the old woman to protect the surprise of his ambush; Habiba didn't owe the healer a life-debt, after all. Breaking his teacher's hold on his reins, he headed back the way he had come, hunching over the neck of his horse to absorb the jolt of the landing on the other side of the wall.

In mid leap, a warning stabbed through his head. The pain disappeared almost as soon as it had come, but he had already lost his concentration on the jump. The horse skittered under him, unsettled by his uncertainty. It bucked and rolled, and Llesho was falling, hitting the ground like a sack of rice. Master Markko's soldiers didn't notice their prey lying helpless on the far shore, however. They had their own problem. And Mara clearly didn't need his help.

With their leader driving them forward from atop his massive warhorse, Markko's troops had begun to cross the bridge. As they reached the very top of the arch, Mara had stepped out from the shadows by the carved eye and climbed up on the wide snout. She called something Llesho couldn't hear, and the great eyelid opened to reveal an emerald as tall as Mara herself. The bridge blinked, and then it writhed and contracted. Straight-backed and terrible as he had never seen her, the healer Mara stood at the center of the great golden head, her gaze locked with the magician's as the neck of the dragon raised her high above the river, higher than the arch of its great worm body. The loop of its back twisted and sank, tumbling screaming, terrified soldiers together with their panicked horses into the rushing river. Gradually the cries of the dying faded out of reach. Mara lifted her right arm straight ahead of her and pointed at Master Markko.

"You owe me a debt, Magician, but I will not collect it now. Consider yourself fortunate that I have business with this worm, or we would decide right here who of us is the stronger."

"My lady." Master Markko gave her a mocking bow and turned his horse. Before he rode away, however, he turned in his saddle and addressed her one last time, as if with an afterthought. "Caring is a weakness, my lady. Each delay finds you more encumbered than the last. And I grow stronger."

Mara did not answer him, and he settled himself in the saddle with a final laugh before setting heels to the flanks of his horse. When the magician was no more than a speck on the horizon, Mara signaled the dragon to carry her to the other side of the river and set her down on the riverbank.

Llesho remained where he had fallen, lying in the grass by the river. He was close enough to observe all that transpired, but both Mara and the dragon seemed too preoccupied with their own business to notice one insignificant Thebin in the dirt. In this he was mistaken, not counting on the sensitivity of a dragon's sense of smell.

The golden river dragon opened his mouth just enough for his long serpentine tongue to flick out and lick his massive chops.

"It's been a long time since I received payment in virgin blood." An occasional wisp of smoke escaped the worm's nostrils when it spoke, while his tongue explored the air for the taste of a scent. Llesho blushed to the roots of his hair when the dragon added, "I prefer girls, you know, though they've become more scarce than dragons. One wonders where the virgin boys come from."

"They grow a little more slowly," Mara answered with the same humor that the dragon offered in the question. "But they do grow, or there would be no young ones for you to ask about. As for this one—Llesho, stand up and bow to your benefactor. Dragons insist on good manners always—I still need him."

Llesho stood and bowed low as the dragon turned an emerald eye to study him. "Does he know?" the dragon asked. The great worm ignored Llesho to direct his question at the healer. This suited Llesho just fine, as he was shaking in his boots and didn't think he could utter an answer even if he had understood the question.

"That is not your concern," Mara answered him tartly. "Shall we get on with this?"

"Oh, very well. But wouldn't you rather owe me something less personal to be collected at a later date?"

"Life-debts must be paid in life," she said, and opened her arms to the dragon's tooth.

"NO!" Llesho cried, as the dragon opened his mouth and nipped at the healer. Revulsion released him from the paralysis of his fear and he dashed forward, sword drawn, but too late. The golden worm pierced the heart of the healer with his poisoned fang. She fell between them, dead, and Llesho followed her to his knees, reaching for her bloody corpse. With great delicacy the worm nudged him with his snout and Llesho tumbled in the grass. Even such a gentle push, for a dragon, felt like a tree had fallen on him. Then the dragon opened his mouth wide and swallowed the healer whole.

Llesho tried to scream, but the sound caught in his throat would not come out. He could not breathe, could not see for the darkness that seemed to cover the sun; he could only kneel where he had fallen and rock himself painfully, his sword forgotten at his side, his arms wrapped tight around his gut.

"Noooo!" The scream finally escaped its prison in his chest. "No, no, no, no." He moved his arms so that he could cover his eyes with his clenched fists, rocking and screaming, "No, no, no!"

"What are you going on about, boy?" Still licking his chops, the dragon loomed over him, and Llesho wanted to kill the creature, but he couldn't move. He noted that the thin tongue had missed a spot, and his gut turned over when he realized he was looking at the healer's blood.

"I loved her," he moaned, still rocking himself like an out of control cradle. That wasn't what he intended to say, and he wasn't even sure how he meant it. As a mother, perhaps, or even as a grandmother. She had reminded him of Kwan-ti and even Adar, his brother, a little, and he'd lost every one of them.

Llesho's declaration didn't seem to surprise the golden dragon nearly as much as it had surprised Llesho himself, but the creature had little patience with his continued distress. The dragon snorted, and Llesho felt the touch of heat, the smell of ash, on the breath of the great worm.

"No need for hysterics," the creature pointed out. "She'll be back."

Lleck had come back as well, but Llesho could take little comfort and less counsel from a bear cub with a tendency to forget his charge and wander off into the woods to hunt. "I don't need another bear or a monkey or a parrot or crocodile; I need Mara, herself."

"You don't have much faith in her, do you, boy?" The creature eyed him thoughtfully, as though he was deciding which morsel to take next from the platter at dinnertime. Llesho bowed his head, waiting for the devouring mouth to descend, but the dragon merely gave a pained sigh and belched smoke and greasy fire. Something the worm had eaten clearly did not agree with him. With a last sniff of disdain, the creature abandoned him; Llesho looked up in time to see its gleaming coils ripple the surface of the river and then it disappeared beneath the swiftly running current.

Long after the dragon had gone, Llesho stared at the place where he had disappeared, but the youth's thoughts were not on the worm that had only acted according to his nature. Disaster seemed to follow Llesho wherever he went, and he stood up, walked to the river's edge with a calculating question: if he threw himself in, let the river take him, would the rest of his friends have a better chance at survival? Perhaps no other governments would fall if he were gone. The world would turn as if he had never existed, which would probably be a good thing for the world. If he could be sure it wasn't already too late.

The brush of cloth sweeping across grass alerted him to a presence nearby and he turned. Habiba approached. The governor's witch, except that the governor was dead for buying Llesho away from Master Markko's control. Llesho wondered if the witch still had a job, but figured he'd always been her ladyship's anyway. Kaydu's father, and Llesho had almost gotten her killed today, with her father close enough to watch on the wrong damned side of the river. Llesho would have thrown himself at Habiba's feet, except that Habiba had come as close as he seemed to want, and then had dropped to one knee, his head bowed.

"You have given me two great gifts today, my prince," he said. "How does a man pay a debt greater than the value of his life?"

"I am not your prince. And you owe me nothing." Llesho did not look away from the river; he hoped the witch mistook his hopeless anger for strength of purpose. How could Habiba honor him? "Your daughter, Kaydu, could have died here today."

"But she didn't. You saved her. For that alone I would give you my life."

"I put your daughter in danger. Mara saved her, saved all of us, at the price of her own life."

"Kaydu is a soldier. She did her job. As her commander, you saw her safely home, at great cost to your own peace of mind."

Habiba paused, and Llesho thought he would get up and leave now that he had said his piece. But the witch spoke again, more wistfully. "All my life I have wished to see one of the great worms. Almost, it had become easier to believe they no longer existed than to accept that I was unworthy. Today you have shown me wonders I thought lost to the world forever."

"Mara did that. And Mara is dead." Llesho faced the witch with all the truth of his guilt. His eyes burned, and Habiba flinched, was himself the first to turn away. He watched the river as if he expected the golden dragon to surface again and invite him to tea.

"We live in an age of wonders, Llesho. Something died here today, but I think, whatever she was, that it was not your healer. You will see her again, if you don't do something really stupid like drown yourself out of self-pity."

"What can you know about it?" Llesho demanded, though he couldn't work up much fight. He didn't really want to die. It wasn't very heroic, but mostly he wanted to lie down where he was and sleep for a very long time. Maybe, if he slept long enough, the storm would have passed him by.

Habiba seemed to know what he was thinking, though. "You are, yourself, the eye of the storm," he said softly, and Llesho saw compassion in his eyes. "If you sleep, the storm sleeps with you, when you awake, the storm is with you still." He shrugged, a gesture of submission to the fates. "Some of those who ride in the wake of the storm always suffer, but without it we have no rain, no rivers, no life."

"I'm not strong enough," Llesho whispered. He wondered if he could have given his life in the healer's place, and had no answer.

Habiba put a hand on his shoulder. "Then today, the storm will sleep." In the sanctuary of the arm curved around his shoulder, Llesho permitted the witch to guide him back to the wall. He looked for a break to enter by, but Habiba used one hand as a balance and vaulted over with the agility of a youth. Llesho clambered after him with a great deal more effort and considerably less grace.

Chapter Twenty-four

LLESHO slid over the low stone wall. He would have fallen, but Bixei was there, waiting for him, and propped a shoulder under his arm to hold him up.

"Is he all right?"

That was Stipes, and Llesho wondered what the gladiator was doing here in the camp with the governor's witch. But Lling was tearing at his shirt, her fingers gentle but her tongue a good deal sharper. "Fool! If you've opened your wound again, Mara will have your guts on a platter."

Habiba put a hand on Lling's wrist, stilling her fingers on Llesho's bandages. "That can wait until we are more comfortable."

"No, it can't—"

"Mara's dead," Llesho gritted between clenched teeth. He pulled away from Bixei's support before he added, "The dragon ate her."

Lling's hand fell, her face going white with shock.

Bixei gave the newcomers a cautious frown. "What dragon?" he asked, as Hmishi objected, "I saw her at the bridge—"

Llesho sighed. "There *is* no bridge over the Golden Dragon River."

"No bridge. Then what—"

"Our enemies have spies everywhere." Habiba stopped the argument with a glare that cut like a knife. "Let's take this conversation under shelter."

They walked in silence after that. Llesho glanced sidelong at Stipes who strode with familiar ease at Bixei's side, but no one else seemed surprised at his presence. Stipes dipped his head in acknowledgment of Llesho's unspoken questions, but answers would have to wait, as Habiba had commanded. Any of the myriad birds calling overhead or the small creatures skittering in the grass might be under Markko's spell. Even the wind might carry their words away to the magician.

Master Jaks had set up camp in the orchard. Habiba led their party past lines of red felt tents tucked between the gnarled trunks of fruit trees. At the center of the camp a larger tent was stretched over stout poles. Its sides were furled, and under its shade Llesho counted half a dozen silent guards whose presence warned away accidental trespassers. Their drawn swords offered more persuasive arguments in the event of unfriendly approach. Master Jaks waited for them at a folding table strewn with maps. Two secretaries in the robes of their office hovered in the background.

Master Jaks spared the newcomers a brief smile, which Llesho did not return, and gestured to chairs set up in a rough circle around the table. By some unspoken agreement the others left the most comfortable chair for Llesho, who only realized what they had done after he had seated himself and planted his elbows on the chair's smooth wooden arms.

When they had all settled in, Habiba spoke in his most formal tones. "The governor of Thousand Lakes Province sends his regards to Prince Llesho of Thebin, Lord of the Eastern Passages and Wizard-King of the High Mountains. His lordship regrets that he could not deliver his respects in person, but begs the prince's understanding, as he must prepare the defense of his own people. The soldiers you see about you, however, he offers at your disposal, with most fervent prayers for success in your endeavor."

"Thank him for me, please, though I wonder if the emperor would recognize the right of the governor of Thousand Lakes Province to offer his protection here."

"I do not understand you." Habiba smoothed a hand down his coat, a weak effort at distraction.

"I think you do, Habiba." Llesho moved forward in his chair, leaning over the table to better read the message in the witch's eyes. "Where are we?" It wasn't the most important question on his mind, but the answer would shade all the others.

"The Golden Dragon River," Master Jaks replied. The faces of Llesho's companions hardened with the reminder of their loss, but Llesho refused to give in to the remorse he felt.

"It's a long river," Llesho pointed out. "I just lost another healer on it, so I am not in the mood to play geography games. Are we in Farshore Province, or Thousand Lakes?" He thought they'd strayed too far north to have crossed into Sky Bridge Province, but he couldn't be certain.

"I told you, she'll be back," Habiba objected softly. "It isn't always about you."

Llesho stared down the governor's witch. He felt a door open in his soul, to one of those caverns darker than he cared to look at, and he didn't bother trying to hide it. Habiba pulled back, frowning as if he'd been given something tough to chew. "Lately, it may seem so, I'll grant you that. But under cover of the storm, many agenda are at work. Including Mara's own, and her business with Golden Dragon."

"But still we play geography games. What province do we put to the storm today, Master Witch?"

Master Jaks gusted a heavy breath. "Until a month ago, this land was part of Farshore Province."

Whatever was bothering him, Habiba had put it aside, and he took up the explanation in terms of an imperial memorial:

"His lordship, the governor of Thousand Lakes Province, has extended his protection to the lands that border his own, and to the household of his daughter, who has come to him for refuge. Think of this orchard as a provincial mission of the governor of Thousand Lakes Province, sanctuary to all who ask it in the name of her ladyship, wife of the murdered governor of Farshore. Until the Celestial Emperor himself assigns a new governor to Farshore, it is within the lady's right to request the aid of her father, and within the duties and obligations of her father to fulfill her request wherever her ladyship's interests may find themselves."

Habiba extended his hand in a gesture that took in the orchard and the surrounding camp, demonstrating the unstated. The army that held it possessed the land they stood upon and that army owed its loyalty to Thousand Lakes Province.

"And Lord Yueh?" Llesho asked. "Master Markko did not pursue us to offer safe passage to the borders of her ladyship's lands. What claim has Lord Yueh made?"

"Yueh is dead." Stipes answered that one, which surprised Llesho. He'd wondered why Stipes had joined their counsel; now he knew. "Poison, I think, in his wine.

"I had already decided that I would run, if I could find Bixei, but I didn't kill Lord Yueh," he added when all eyes turned on him. The penalty for a slave who killed his master was skinning alive, a painstaking process in which the skin was removed slowly beginning at the feet and moving up his legs to his torso before the very eyes of the horrified victim. There were stories of executioners who could peel the skin off a man in one piece, toes to crown, and leave his victim still alive and bleeding in the sawdust when he was done. The sun got any survivors soon enough, or the cold. Or the vultures and the bugs.

Knowing her ladyship's feelings on the matter of slavery and adding that to what she must feel at the murder of her husband, Llesho didn't believe she would condemn Stipes to a horrible death for killing Yueh. Still, he could not suppress the shudder that passed through him at the thought of the terrible execution that awaited one who would commit such a crime.

Fortunately, Llesho was pretty sure the man was telling the truth and hadn't killed his master. "Did Markko have access to Lord Yueh's wine?" he asked. Master Jaks must know the story, and Habiba, if they had permitted the gladiator to join them, but Llesho looked to Stipes, who had been there, to tell it.

"Not that night. Markko learned from his spies that you had split from the main party. He took a couple of foot units and a few horse to find you, and Lord Yueh followed her ladyship's train. Her ladyship traveled slowly, with the aged and the young in her care, and we were soldiers on a forced march. We caught up to her easily enough, but Yueh hadn't counted on Master Jaks.

"He stood us off after the first attack failed, waiting for Master Markko to return with you. I think he planned to put her champions to the sword and take her husband's place as governor and as mate, but he fell ill soon after he dined, and never left his bed. In the morning, Yueh was delirious, his army in disarray. Few among Lord Yueh's forces fought for him willingly, and many surrendered without raising a weapon that day. I was lucky to find Bixei; he took me to Master Jaks, and I offered my weapons and my service."

There was something left unsaid in that last, and Llesho wanted it, down to the last promise: "To whom?"

Stipes dipped his head, acknowledging the hit. "To Master Jaks, actually. Don't know much about lords and such, but that Chin-shi was a foolish one and Yueh a bad one. And yours was a dead one," he added sullenly when Habiba turned a threatening eye on him. "By then, Yueh was a dead one, too; the healers could do nothing.

"But I trusted Master Jaks, had done so for more years than I care to consider. And Master Jaks says you are a king, so here we are." He shrugged, admitting he didn't understand what had gone on while they had belonged to different camps, but that he was willing to take some things—even outlandish things like a skinny pearl diver being a long-lost king—on faith from the right person.

Llesho turned thoughtfully to Master Jaks, who returned his level gaze from across the table. Master Jaks was his teacher, and he had trusted the man just as Stipes had. But Llesho had grown wary since the poison arrow had felled him. Master Jaks had served Lord Chin-shi, who was dead, under the direction of Overseer Markko, who now sought to capture or kill Llesho. Master Jaks had followed Llesho to Farshore, but now took into his escort Stipes, who was Lord Yueh's man, or had been until his lordship's timely death. Most damning, Jaks was an assassin; Llesho's eyes returned again to the six rings tattooed on Jaks' upper arm. Why was an assassin so interested in an exiled prince of Thebin?

Master Jaks followed the gaze. "They trouble you?" he asked, nodding his chin at the rings on his arm.

Llesho waited, while the assassin returned his study, looking for a crack in the stone of Llesho's eyes and finding none. With a little shrug, a tiny smile that

Llesho did not understand, Master Jaks rested his arm on the table, palm up, the gesture of surrender. "If my arm offends you," he said, "cut it off."

Not what Llesho had expected. He turned to Habiba for an explanation, or advice, but the witch said nothing, merely gestured to a guard who raised his unsheathed sword and set it lightly across the muscle, just above the first, and oldest, ring.

"Why?" Llesho asked.

"I wasn't always an assassin," Master Jaks answered, and gave the rings on his own arm a look of such loathing and hunger that Llesho would have drawn his own Thebin knife had a guard not already held the man in check with a sword resting on flesh. "A long time ago, I served Thebin as a hired defender."

"A mercenary," Llesho corrected. He had seen the device on Master Jaks' wrist guards long ago, that time with blood splashed on them from the Harn. Mercenaries, yes, but his guard had died like a Thebin to protect a young prince.

"A mercenary." Master Jaks accepted the correction. "My clan is poor; her sons serve others for pay. The less skilled take contracts as foot troops in the border wars of strangers. Those of breeding and skill hold positions in the great houses of the wealthy. My own squad served the Royal House of Kungol. My brother swore his life to the protection of the young prince, but could not save him."

He met Llesho's stony gaze with fire in his eyes—grim, grim fire. "I was, myself, sworn to the young prince's mother. I lay as the dead on the floor of her temple while the men of Harn tormented her and dragged her away. To my shame, I did not die of my wounds that day."

"You loved my mother."

It wasn't in the words but in the longing when

Master Jaks said them, and in the despair that crossed the landscape behind his eyes when he spoke of her torment.

"Everyone loved her. How could they not?"

Llesho saw in the rueful smile that Master Jaks had never overstepped his place at the foot of his mistress: no dishonor to the queen or her husband had ever been contemplated. The self-loathing at his failure would have been the greater for his feelings, however. Llesho understood about failure and regret. He didn't understand how one could honor the holy queen of Thebin with the rings of an assassin on his arm, and he said so.

"You prove your love of that holy woman of peace with the taking of lives for pay, as an assassin?"

Master Jaks flinched, as even the sword resting on his arm had not made him do. "There are few professions open to a member of the elite guard who has failed so disastrously in his charge. But I have kept myself alive, when I could wish only to join my brother in death, for the day when I might restore honor to my family and my clan, If I have dishonored my quest, I offer my death. Let my blood wash away the stain upon her pure honor that I served. You would be doing me a favor, one I have wished for many years. If you want to win in the coming battle, however, I can offer my service. With two arms or with one, I pledge my life, and the lives of those men who follow me, to restore her house to its rightful place, and for my brother's honor to protect her son in all things."

"You will do with one arm what you could not manage nine cycles ago with two?"

A glint behind the fire, a deepening of the lines around Master Jaks' eyes, told more than the words: "I know more now." He hadn't been a paid assassin then. With rueful, dangerous humor, Master Jaks followed the length of the sword with his eyes. He'd abased himself enough with his confession. Llesho wasn't ready to fight this war on his own, and he thought maybe the boy even knew it. "Better with two, of course."

Llesho gave the slightest flick of dismissal with his fingers, and the sword lifted. No emotion broke the impassive obedience of the guard, but the man's whole body eased. So it hadn't been just for show. Some, though. And it wasn't over yet.

"By the laws of Shan, I cannot take your pledge, " Llesho pointed out with ice in his tone. "I am a slave."

He had his manumission papers in his tunic, of course, but, until his seventeenth birthday, her ladyship could free him only by adopting him. When offered the opportunity, she had declined. Now, having recognized his lineage, any such act on the part of Thousand Lakes Province must appear as a first move in a political game neither her ladyship nor her father could afford. Shan itself would move against the province. And Llesho would be no closer to freeing his brothers than when he was diving for pearls off Pearl Island.

Too much had happened. Llesho knew, in his head, that he had come a long way in more than physical distance from the bay where the spirit of Lleck, his teacher, had appeared to him and sent him to free his home. But he was no wizard-king, and in his heart, he felt only the weight of his losses. Given his track record on this quest, he doubted he'd live long enough to see Kungol and his beloved mountains again.

"His lordship the governor has interpreted the manumission status of a young royal under the law that governs the succession to the governorship." Habiba reached out a hand and a secretary set a sheaf of papers into it. "If a governor should die before his orphaned heir reaches the legal age of majority, the law allows for the appointment of a regent.

"His lordship did not wish to be seen as motivated

by political ambitions in the appointment of the young prince's regent. Accordingly, he has charged me to invite your own recommendations for the role of your adviser."

No one stirred at the table. The silence was so complete that Llesho could imagine no one stirred in the whole camp. He studied the faces of his companions, but each kept his eyes downcast and his counsel to himself. He could have wished for Kwan-ti then, or Mara, or Master Den, or Lleck—any one of the people he had grown to depend on for their wisdom who had died or disappeared from his life, leaving him storm-tossed without an anchor. He sorely needed their advice now; if any one of them had been at the conference table, he would have landed the regency in their laps and been done with it. But they weren't—even Lleck the bear had not followed him to this camp—and Habiba, while clever and deep, was too much her ladyship's creature. And Master Jaks. Master Jaks, with the six rings tattooed on his upper arm, one for each paid murder he'd committed, would be no fit regent for the spiritual leader of the Thebin people, even if Llesho never had another spiritual thought in his life. Stipes was a fighter, not a thinker, and he was Yueh's anyway, or Bixei's, if he had his choice. The rest of them were no older than he was, or not by much, and no smarter.

The more he thought about it, though, the more he rejected the notion of anyone making his decisions for him, law or no law. It was his quest, his country he had promised to free. The decision was easy after all.

"Adar," he said. "My brother."

Habiba smiled and handed him the papers. "Her ladyship thought you would decide as much. She persuaded her father to complete the appropriate forms appointing Adar as your regent in absentia."

Adar. Llesho brushed the sheaf of papers with his fingertips. He needed to find his brother, to prove to himself that he was on the true path to the liberation of his people and not on a fool's journey. The papers appointing his brother regent until succession should be decided at Kungol reminded Llesho of Farshore's own problems.

"His lordship the governor left no heir, did he?"

"He did not," Habiba answered. "His family line having failed, the emperor will appoint a new governor in his place. Lord Yueh would have petitioned for the post if he had lived, I am sure."

Llesho nodded, thinking. The emperor, far away in Shan and with only the word of easily bribed advisers to guide him, had awarded Lord Yueh the governorship of Pearl Island. Yueh had received clear title to all the holdings that belonged to the island, including the dying oyster beds of Pearl Bay, in payment of debts left owing after the death of Lord Chin-shi. With Lord Chin-shi's overseer Markko as his adviser, Lord Yueh had attacked Farshore. Now Lord Yueh was dead, and Markko had turned back after his defeat at the jaws of the dragon on Golden Dragon River. Llesho didn't think the deaths of three governors were coincidence.

"Lord Yueh had a young son, did he not?"

"Still does," Stipes confirmed. "At least, the son still lives, though just a babe."

"Will the Emperor name his mother regent?" Llesho directed his question to Habiba. As the adviser to a murdered governor himself, the witch would know better than any of them what would happen next in the matter of continued government.

"I doubt it." Habiba considered his answer. "Her ladyship of Farshore produced no heir for the governor. If Markko acts true to form, he will lay a claim against Farshore in the name of Lord Yueh's young son, and petition to be named regent under the guidance of the boy's mother. Everyone knows that Lady Yueh was much younger than her husband, and that she was a quiet, shy creature. Markko's deference to her wishes will be seen for what it is: an opportunity offered the mother to visit her child upon state occasions. She will have no say in his upbringing, and certainly none in the rule of Farshore, which Markko will want to consolidate with Pearl Island in his own name."

"And how long will the boy live?"

"At least a year," Master Jaks suggested. "It will take Markko that long to marry the widow and get her with child. Then Yueh's child will die, and Markko will petition to claim the post in his own name, for the son his wife carries."

Between them Habiba and Master Jaks had outlined Llesho's own conclusions. It left one question unanswered, however. "What does he want with me?"

"The trade routes through the passes above Kungol?" Master Jaks guessed.

Llesho shrugged a shoulder. "Then he'd do better attacking the Harn. I couldn't give him Kungol if I wanted to."

"He may wish to control your power of persuasion with the goddess," Habiba suggested.

Llesho snorted an unpretty laugh. "He'd have done better to wait a day to attack Farshore if that's what he wanted. The goddess didn't come. I didn't see her. I'd rather believe that the attack came before I had a chance to finish the ritual than that the goddess did not choose me. If she was able to find me at all so far from home, however, it's more likely the goddess found me wanting and rejected me. No special influence there."

Habiba looked at him strangely, but didn't say anything. There seemed little left *to* say. Llesho had his own quest, but Thebin seemed very far away and his enemies formidable. He wasn't smart enough to defeat Markko, wasn't strong enough, and his so-called "mystical powers" weren't going to impress the magician. Aside from having a ghost tell him what to do and a dragon eat his healer, he didn't have any magic. And like his luck, it seemed that if it weren't for bad magic, he'd have none at all.

He did know that he was too tired to think about it now. He rose from his chair, but when he turned to bow politely to Habiba, he found the witch on one knee before him again, along with Master Jaks and the secretaries and Stipes. Bixei had moved to stand next to Kaydu, and together with Hmishi and Lling the four companions stood to attention, his personal guard awaiting his next order.

"I need to rest." He was also hungry, he realized, and in no condition to make more difficult decisions. Given his current temper, he was lucky Master Jaks still had two arms.

Habiba took that as permission to rise, as did his companions. "Kaydu can show you to your tent," he said. It was accepted that his companions, who once again included Bixei, would not leave his side, and equally clearly understood that no other company was welcome at this time. Except for one person, who wasn't available.

"I wish Master Den were here," Llesho said.

"Who is Master Den?" Lling wanted to know. Before Llesho could answer, Bixei volunteered the information, "He is here. Don't know why he didn't attend the meeting just now, but you can probably find him in the laundry after you've had something to eat."

"The laundry? Here?"

Bixei laughed. "He brought two huge cauldrons with him on a supply wagon, and he's had Gryphon Squad hauling water from the river all morning. By now he's probably knee-deep in soap suds!"

A darkness at the edge of vision that Llesho hadn't even noticed until now suddenly lifted. He smiled: a real, full smile, for the first time in so long he couldn't even remember when it had last happened. Den was here. Maybe he had a chance after all.

Chapter Twenty-five

"THEY'VE assigned us one of the large command tents." Kaydu led them through the bivouac lines. When the smells of food warned them that they were passing close by the cook tent, Bixei left the group with a murmured promise to bring something to eat for them.

"Something hot," Llesho requested absently. He felt cold from the inside out, the chill escaping in fine tremors that shook him in waves, like a fever. He followed Kaydu along a row of round felt tents.

Men and women in the leather and brass of fighters stopped in their mending and polishing to stare as they passed. Kaydu glared, sending them back to their tasks with unanswered questions still lurking in their eyes, but no great desire for answers. Llesho was just as glad; what few answers he had satisfied no one, least of all himself. He wasn't up to sharing them, but turned his thoughts inward, fighting the cold that crept over his heart. Mara was dead in his place, though Habiba seemed to think she had survived the dragon's poison tooth and fiery gullet somehow. The other deaths, and Kwan-ti's disappearance, he could blame on events that flowed around him but were not themselves a part of his own story. Local politics, far from the eye of Thebin and no fight of Llesho's, took their toll, and he could do little more than survive them. But Mara had called up a dragon to rescue him, and then had offered her life to the creature in exchange for his own. He should have—

"Stop it." Lling punched him in the arm, and he realized that she'd been talking to him, and he hadn't heard a word.

"It wasn't your fault." She called him on his guilt-ridden brooding, angry at him for it. "According to Habiba, she isn't dead anyway."

"He said she'd be back, not that she wasn't dead." Llesho emphasized the distinction. "Lleck is back, too. Does that mean he didn't die of the fever on Pearl Island?"

"Where is Lleck?" Hmishi thought to ask just then. "I didn't see him cross the bridge . . . Or . . . Dragon . . . Something."

"He clearly had better sense than to cross a rushing river on the back of a legend," Llesho suggested.

"I didn't think kings *had* temper tantrums," Lling snapped.

Llesho looked at her, too tired for any of this. He wanted to escape, to dig a deep, deep hole, and crawl in and hide. But they weren't going to leave him alone; Master Jaks had made sure of that. "They probably don't," he agreed, thinking about his father, who had often laughed, and sometimes cried, and in court would stroke his beard in thought before handing down a wise and balanced ruling. "But since I will never be a king, I don't see your point."

"But Jaks said—"

"A thousand li of Harn grassland, filled with Harn raiders, stand between me and a crown," he pointed out. "And somewhere between here and there, I have six brothers, each of them older than I am and more suited to the throne. So I am still just a minor prince in exile, as I told you before."

"You are the seventh son of the king of Thebin, though," Hmishi pressed him.

"Favored of the gods," Llesho quoted. "Is that how it seems to you?"

"Well." Lling put an arm through his, and Hmishi took the other. Together they leaned into him. "You've got us. I'd say that counts as blessed." She grinned at him, daring him to contradict her.

He tried to laugh but could only manage a tight smile, until the smell of soap bubbles hit his nose.

"This is it," Kaydu said, tugging him toward a command tent, red like the others, but bigger, and tall enough to stand up in.

"Later." Llesho followed the sound and the smell he had grown to love because they reminded him of Master Den.

He found the washerman, loins bound up and knee-deep in a steaming vat of soapy water. The traveling washtub was made of knee-high oaken staves bound in a circle as wide across as a spear, with an oaken floor in sections set clinker-style, one board overlapping another to make the whole watertight, on the grass. Long strips of bandages hung from lines that festooned the fruit trees, and bright red tent cloths lay spread upon the grass to dry. Llesho stood beneath a cherry tree, letting the smell and the sound ease into his soul and loosen the rock-hard tension in his muscles. He realized suddenly that it didn't hurt to smile and let his lips have their way, skinning back in a toothy grin he'd forgotten was ever a part of him.

"Kick your sandals off and get in here, boy, or have you forgotten all I've taught you?" Den set his fists atop his broad hips and huffed a steamy breath for emphasis.

"I'm a prince now," Llesho reminded him with a

haughty sniff. He was toeing off his sandals when he said it.

"You were always a prince," Master Den corrected him with an answering grin. "You had to learn to be a washerman."

Llesho dragged his leggings off and dropped them in a heap over his sandals, and followed with his tunic. The washerman's grin faltered, and Llesho was suddenly self-conscious about the wound still raw on his breast. But Master Den taunted him with another mock challenge, "Unless you've forgotten everything I taught you."

In nothing but his own smallclothes, Llesho climbed into the vat. "I haven't forgotten a thing," he promised, and meant much more than how to stir up the wash.

"And well you shouldn't, young prince." Master Den gave a meaningful look to the Thebin knife hanging in its sheath from a cord around Llesho's neck. He gave a broad smile then, and opened his arms. "It's good to see you again, boy."

Llesho gave his teacher a hug. "I thought you must be dead, too," he whispered, and Den set him at arm's length so that he could look deep into his eyes. "I am not dead. Hold onto your faith, Llesho. The world is a more wondrous place than you can yet imagine."

"I could do with a few less wonders. The last one ate my healer."

"Perhaps she is a wonder, too." Master Den gave him a nod to signal the end of meaningful conversation, or perhaps the beginning of a lesson, Llesho could never quite tell when the washerman was teaching and when he was making small talk. "But now we have bandages to clean, and then boil, and tent cloths to prepare for the hospital."

He stepped out of the vat, and Llesho followed; each took a coarse rake and began to dredge the soaking cloths. Working in comfortable unison they draped the waterlogged bandages over the spokes of a wheel, the axle of which ended in a crank. When each spoke was lined with long bandage cloths, Llesho grabbed their loose ends, and Den turned the crank, twisting the bandages and wringing out the dirty water. Then each bit went into a bubbling cauldron for a brief but important boiling to kill any putridity that might still inhabit the weave, and onto the lines it went.

Llesho bent and stretched, thinking of nothing but the regular motions of duties he remembered from a time when his road seemed clear and the risks belonged to him alone. While he worked, the hot water of the vat and the steam from the cauldrons loosened the muscles that had grown rigid with a soul-deep cold. He wiped sweat from his brow with the back of his hand, and felt his shoulders uncurl from their customary hunch around his wound and his heart.

"Father says you need rest," Kaydu insisted, her frown expressing the disapproval of his humble toil that she hesitated to speak out loud.

"Are you scolding the prince, or the washerman for detaining him?" Master Den asked with laughter barely restrained in his voice. Kaydu didn't know Master Den, of course, and she didn't like that tone of voice from a stranger.

"He's been wounded," she snapped back. "He shouldn't be pulling at that shoulder."

Master Den acknowledged her with a wise nod, a twinkle hidden in his eye. "His wounds run deep, but even the deepest wounds heal, give the opportunity to do so."

While Den and Kaydu challenged each other for the right to determine his well-being, Llesho scratched idly at his damp belly. His damp, empty belly. "Is there anything to eat?"

"Bixei brought your dinner. It's getting cold in your tent right now."

"Cold is good," Llesho decided, "unless it is fish heads in porridge." He shuddered a little, and Den laughed.

"No fish heads," the washerman said. "The fish are known to curse the fishermen in their own tongue hereabouts."

Llesho figured he meant the Golden Dragon River, which had already shown itself to harbor stranger creatures than he had ever wanted to meet. No, he wouldn't want to fish in that river.

"Do you have any cheese?" he asked. "And a bit of bread?"

"Llesho!" Kaydu snapped.

She wanted to protect him. Llesho figured he was making that difficult for her, and that at the least he owed it to his friends to make it as easy as possible for them to keep him alive.

He raised his head, instinctively setting his shoulders and tilting his chin with the quiet poise of a prince. In his eyes lingered the fear of a terrible pain waiting to claim him if he gave himself time to think. Kaydu dropped her gaze, suddenly embarrassed to be ordering him about, and guilty for reminding him of that pain that lay in wait for him.

"You do that very well." Den might have been mocking him, or . . . something.

"I'm sorry," he apologized to Kaydu, "but I need this." He had missed his old master more than he was willing to say in front of his companions.

She nodded, not looking at him, and turned to go.

"I'll watch him, Kaydu." Den made his own peace offering. "He won't come to any harm tonight."

"I know," she said, and turned to Llesho. "But one of us will be on guard anyway. Just in case. Bixei wants to talk to you. He's been really worried since we parted with her ladyship's train. He has asked for first watch. I'll send your dinner up with him."

"Thank you." The debate had drained much of the warmth out of his bones, and Llesho felt his muscles tightening up again.

"Cover up; we've done enough for one day." Den threw him a patched linen shirt and a pair of coarse breeches, reminders of another time. "Perhaps you would like to do prayer forms with me?"

Llesho nodded, then realized Master Den couldn't see him with his head under his shirt. He found the open neck, popped his head through, and answered, "Yes, Master, very much," while punching his arms into sleeves, and pulled on the breeches just as Bixei showed up with his dinner.

"Dinner can wait." Den bowed, his hands clasped. Bixei grinned in answer and set himself next to Llesho, their old positions in the training yard on Pearl Island. Following Den's lead, they performed the Flowing River form, to thank the Seven Gods for their timely rescue across the Golden Dragon River, and the Twining Branches form to honor the orchard that sheltered them. Somehow, Jaks had joined them, and Stipes. For a brief span of minutes, they fell into old routines that were, Llesho reminded himself, no less dangerous for their familiarity. A gladiator was called to die as often as a soldier in battle, for the price of a wager or the whim of an audience.

But in the forms, Llesho could forget all the dangerous roads that had brought him here. The pieces of his heart tumbled, found their proper places, and clicked together in the moment. Body and mind, motion and a soaring heart joined in the fading sunlight. Llesho reached through the forms, became the twisted shadows of laden branches, honored the grass that bruised beneath feet in Wind through Millet. The grass offered itself in answer to the prayer forms, releasing its sharp green scent around his legs, its touch a reminder of life infinitely renewing all around them. Fingertip breezes soft with the perfume of ripe peaches kissed his cheek and whispered through the strands of his hair. The earth rocked them gently, the universe cradled them, and the evening flowed with his muscles, one with all the living men and gods.

Llesho offered plums to the lady goddess in his mind. She was his bride, and he felt her kiss in the kiss of the breeze, her touch in the warmth that flowed through his body. He knew that he could wait for her, as she waited for him. When he finally came to rest, with a bow to his master, he noticed that his companions were staring at him with guarded wonder.

"Did I do something wrong?" he asked, ducking his head in embarrassment. He meant by that, *Did I do something strange to call attention to myself.* It was one thing to have a private moment with the universe, and quite another to share that moment with all one's closest companions.

Den shook his head, his own little smile accompanied by a shrug of the shoulder. "Nothing to be ashamed of," he promised. "But it is becoming more and more difficult to forget you are a prince."

"Does that mean I can't join you in the washing anymore?" he asked, the first thing that came to mind. Master Den said nothing, just watched him with the same gentle smile, but Master Jaks sat down hard on the ground, laughing till the tears ran down his face.

"You scared the hell out of me, boy." Jaks shuddered at a memory Llesho didn't share. "I thought you would die on that river." He shrugged, helpless to explain away the feelings that had escaped him. "Didn't realize you had influence with the local river dragon."

"Not my influence." Llesho winced at the thought of Mara facing the dragon. But Habiba didn't seem disturbed. And there were all those missing afternoons. . . . "I don't think I'm meant to die yet."

He reached for the bread Bixei had left under the nearest peach tree and tore off a chewy bite, grabbed the slab of cheese resting beside it, and munched thoughtfully, leaning back against the tree trunk. Llesho had always understood the responsibility a king owed his subjects. Not since Khri had died to protect him from the Harn raiders, however, had Llesho felt the weight of responsibility a prince owed his protectors. He had to stay alive or the sacrifices of Khri, and of the Long March, and of Mara were for nothing. If he had died on the river, Khri's brother would have gone to his grave with a blood-debt unpaid. Llesho understood about brothers. Looking at Master Jaks that way was a revelation.

"You will have your chance to complete your contract." This time he meant it, in the full knowledge that he owed his debtor as much as the mercenary-assassin owed him. With a single dip of his head, Jaks acknowledged the solemn promise in Llesho's demeanor.

Done. Llesho returned the bow with a jerk of his chin, and blinked. Thinking took as much energy as running from Master Markko, and he'd had more than enough of both to last him a while.

"You need a bed, and rest," Bixei took his arm.

Llesho struggled to his feet and let Bixei lead him to his tent. The clothes he wore were soft enough that he didn't worry about taking them off, just let himself drop on the pallet prepared for him and fell into the welcoming darkness.

Morning came with the sunlight spilling red through the tent cloth and the smell of fresh bread and hot porridge rich with peaches. Llesho opened his eyes and found Bixei kneeling by his bed with a steaming bowl of breakfast in his hands. "I told you this would wake him up," Bixei said to someone behind him.

Llesho sat up and craned his neck. Kaydu sat cross-legged on her blanket with a bowl of her own in front of her. "Llesho liking his breakfast is not exactly news," she answered with a sniff.

"Who likes breakfast?" Lling popped into the tent, followed by Hmishi, both with steaming bowls in their hands.

"I do," Llesho took the bowl from Bixei while the two newcomers settled themselves on the floor of the tent.

They ate in silence for a while, then Bixei cleared his throat. "We're going on to Shan?" he asked.

Llesho shrugged. "I promised Lleck that I'd find my brothers. Adar may be in Shan, so that is where I will start the search. But no one is obliged to follow me."

"Who's Lleck?"

Hmishi finished his porridge and set down his bowl. "Lleck was Llesho's teacher. Now he's a bear."

"A what?"

"Never mind that." Llesho waved aside the discussion. Whatever Lleck was now, he'd exacted a promise from Llesho, one he intended to keep. "I think we'd all be better off if I did this on my own."

"Like that would work!" Kaydu gave him a crinkled frown over her porridge. "We barely made it this far with the four of us. If it hadn't been for Mara, we'd be Master Markko's prisoners right now."

Llesho didn't need reminding. Mara was dead and wouldn't be coming to their rescue any time soon.

"If you act like you're unbeatable, you usually don't have to fight," Bixei added. "I learned that when we defeated Lord Yueh on the road."

Lling finished her porridge and flicked out a dainty tongue to lick her fingers clean. "Habiba said we are to go in state," she reminded them with a waggle of her eyebrows. "That sounds a lot more comfortable than straggling into the capital with my clothes in rags and my hair in snarls."

"And we'll have more time with Master Den." Bixei had assumed his place among them again, but he darted an uncomfortable glance at Llesho. He was hiding something, and Llesho wondered if he could trust Bixei now. "Out with it," he demanded, unwilling to wait until whatever it was bit him in the backside.

"It's Stipes." Bixei dropped his head. "He knows it won't be like the old times. This is war, not the arena, but he asked me to remind you that he was first to befriend you in the practice yard, and he would be at your side to see the end of the story, if you would permit it. He had no choice but to serve Lord Yueh. He was a slave. But he never spied for Markko, and he has never compromised his honor for personal gain. He says." Bixei looked up at Llesho, pleading: "All that I have known of Stipes tells me that he speaks the truth. And I have missed him."

Perhaps he should have doubted more, but Llesho did trust Stipes. He wondered, though, about Bixei. "If you had to choose," he asked, "to let Stipes fall, or to give your comrades into Markko's hands, what would you do?"

Bixei hesitated, as Llesho expected he would. In a matter of Stipes' life or Llesho's, Bixei would choose to honor his sworn oath to protect the prince of Thebin. Given what appeared, on the surface, an equal choice, the outcome was not so certain. But Bixei had already chosen Stipes over his comrades once. Llesho couldn't leave decisions of loyalty to the field.

"Stipes will remain in Habiba's guard, under Jaks' command," Llesho decided. "You, Bixei, will act as liaison between Habiba's camp and ours here. Where will you bivouac?"

Bixei stared at him, stricken, then slowly processed the question. Not *Where will you sleep while we are in camp,* as it appeared on the surface, but, *show here, now, where your allegiance lies.*

"I'll bivouac with my comrades, and take my turn at sentry duty with the others." He acknowledged

Llesho's purpose in asking the question with a rueful smile. "Stipes will understand."

Llesho set his empty bowl on the pallet beside him and rubbed at his head. He knew he was just postponing the day of reckoning with Bixei, but with any luck none of them would ever have to choose. In the meantime, he was pretty sure he'd awakened late and missed prayer forms, but it wouldn't hurt to wander down to the temporary laundry and say hello to Master Den. Stipes, on the way to Llesho's tent, met Llesho himself on the way out.

"Pardon, Your Highness, but Habiba has ordered that we strike camp and be ready to move by midmorning. And Master Jaks asks if he can be of service."

"It's a little late to be throwing titles around, Stipes. I'm the same person I always was."

"Begging your pardon, Your Highness, but you're not," Stipes objected.

Llesho had turned back to his tent, but Kaydu shooed him away with a scornful whoosh. "Time you learned how to act like a prince," she said in support of Stipes. "And princes don't strike their own tents. Go, find Master Den, or Jaks, or whoever, and do what princes do in the morning."

Weapons practice. "Ask Master Jaks if we will have time on the journey to renew our study of the martial arts, if you please. At his leisure, of course."

When Stipes had made his deferential bow and departed, Llesho left his companions to pack their new wealth and went in search of Master Den. He found the washerman under the same trees, his tubs and cauldron empty around him and the last of the tent cloths and bandages spread out to dry.

"Llesho! Come here, boy. You're the very thing. Would you take that end—there you go."

Llesho picked up the trailing ends of the tent cover

that Master Den was folding and mirrored the washerman's moves, coming toward him when Den moved forward, and away when Den pulled back, until the tent cloth was no more than a dense square the size of a dinner plate. They went on to the next, comfortably working together, while Llesho wondered if this, too, would soon change. Would Master Den, like Habiba and Master Jaks, soon press him to behave more like a prince, and less like a washerman. Not knowing just made him more and more tense, so he took a deep breath and plunged in.

"You aren't treating me any differently . . ." And let Master Den make of that what he would.

"Would you like me to?" Den returned the question with one of his own, but then offered an answer that unwound a bit of the tension pulling Llesho's mouth into a frown.

"I thought you would have had enough of that from the rest of the camp. Would you prefer that I treat you like a hero, or like a prince?"

"Like an apprentice washerman, if it is all right with Habiba," he answered, and began rolling the strips of clean bandages with a will.

"It is not for Habiba to say," Den reminded him. "And when you are finished with that roll of bandages, I need your help to break down this washtub."

"Yes, Master," Llesho answered the washerman, who himself hid secrets of his identity. He joined Master Den in pulling up the floor of the tub in three pieces, and discovered that the rim of barrel staves folded into a bundle and stowed snugly in the wagon alongside the cauldron. They had just finished loading the various tent cloths and Master Den's own bedroll when a boy just a bit younger than Llesho brought round the cart horses to lead into harness.

"Your own mount will be waiting for you," Master Den reminded Llesho, who bowed to take his leave.

"Would it be all right if I joined you tomorrow morning for prayer forms?" he asked before he left.

"Who can say what tomorrow will bring?" Master Den mused. "But if I rise in the morning, and a certain young man should happen to be near, he might, if he had a mind, perform his prayer forms in company rather than alone."

In his weakened state after his wounding and later, in the confusion of running from Markko and his men, Llesho had forgotten the comforting ritual of prayer forms. He bowed, in part to hide the deep wine color pulsing in his cheeks. Torn between guilt and embarrassment, he resolved to make up for his negligence, starting the very next morning. And for once, he was glad to abandon his teacher.

Chapter Twenty-six

AFTER the council held on their arrival, Llesho expected that his squad would join Habiba and Jaks at the head of the massed guard. But Habiba had wisely explained that marching on the capital of the Shan Empire with a deposed prince in their company might stir up more concern than they were prepared to face on the journey. Instead, he set them somewhat forward of the center in the order of march, an anonymous cluster of very young soldiers lost among the horse guards.

As they left the orchard behind them, Llesho turned for a last glance back at the Golden Dragon River to his left, imprinting the memory of the sun sparking off the tiny frothed peaks of the swiftly running current. He'd seen wonders on the river, but would have traded the dragon in all its glory for one more glimpse of the old healer, Mara, sound and scolding him to be still so that his wound would heal. His flesh scarcely twinged at all now, but the newer wound of Mara's loss was a deeper, sharper hurt.

They advanced at an easy pace that maddened Llesho. He didn't think Master Markko had given up the pursuit; the magician would find a way to cross the river, perhaps already had, and then he'd be after Llesho and his band of friends again. Llesho had an army with him now, and they had a witch of their own, of course. He wasn't sure who practiced the stronger magic between the two, but thought perhaps Markko would hesitate before attacking if he knew Habiba had ridden against him. He had enough grudging respect for Master Markko's skills, however, that he wanted as many li between them as possible.

Ahead lay Shan, the imperial city. Caravans from the north had brought stories of Shan to Thebin. The gods might set Kungol down in its entirety in the emperor's gardens and have room left over for his tiger preserves. Llesho didn't know how he was going to find Adar or their five remaining siblings when he got there, but Habiba had them going in the right direction at last. He wanted to move faster. If he had magic of his own, he would make the li disappear, and they'd be walking through the mighty gates of the capital city by nightfall. But he didn't have magic of his own, and Habiba didn't seem inclined to use the skills he had, or to press the company to haste.

Kaydu rode ahead of him, and Lling and Hmishi guarded his flanks. Bixei rode behind. When Llesho had reminded him that his liaison should travel with the leaders of their force, Bixei had responded that Stipes would serve as their link to Habiba and Jaks; for himself, Bixei would stand ready to ferry messages from Llesho to the commanders at the head of the column. And until there were messages to carry, he would keep his place and guard his companions' backs.

The column had taken up a journey song. Llesho didn't know the words, but his companions picked up at the chorus and the mournful plaint wove its lines of home and sorrow into his dark thoughts.

As I march from the home I am leaving
by the cottage door, holding our babe,

my sweetheart is quietly weeping
for the sweet boy she sends to the grave.

As I march from the home I am leaving,
by the fence post, clutching her shawl,
my mother stands quietly grieving
her sons, she has given them all.

As I march from the home I am leaving,
in the cornfield, swinging his scythe,
my father stands anxiously yearning
like his son, he would follow the fife.

But the drums and the pipes now are silent
and the tunic of red turns to rust
and the fields are now sown with the fallen
in the twilight, in blood, and in dust.

And I long for the home of my fathers,
for the smiles of my sweetheart and babe,
to bring home the sons of my mother,
let our leaders, and gods, point the way.

The mood of the song reflected his own dark thoughts, but the rhythm kept the measured pace of the march. Slowly, however, the meaning of the song found its way into his heart. He'd lost mother and father, brothers and home, and much of his own innocence when he was little more than a babe. Since he'd taken on the burden of Lleck's oath, he'd lost comrades-in-arms. But he wasn't alone anymore. He traveled with an army, and with the promise that his brothers were alive.

While the marching song reminded him of the grief of parting, it also reminded him of his goal: he was going home. He would rescue his brothers, and together they would free Thebin from the Harn. They would do it. He found his head tilting upward, out of his moody slump and seeking the sunshine. His shoulders drew back, as if a weight were not lifted, but had settled properly where it belonged. As the words of the song said, he would return the sons of his mother to their home. Markko was an obstacle, but he wasn't the goal, and Llesho couldn't let his fear of the magician take over his thinking so that he forgot what he'd set out to do. That didn't mean he could forget the forces pursuing them, but he had to let go of the dread he'd built up of the magician over the months he'd spent as his captive. To do that he had to know more about the overseer.

He pulled his horse up slightly and fell in step next to Bixei. "Back when I first entered the gladiators' compound on Pearl Island, you were Markko's assistant."

"I was not in league with him, nor did he tell me any of his secrets." Bixei looked sideways at him, uneasiness crossing his features. "I carried messages, nothing more."

"You were afraid that I would take your place."

"As a messenger, I could leave the compound pretty much whenever I wanted. I'd just tell the guard at the gate that I was carrying a secret message, and they'd let me go." Bixei looked down, and Llesho wondered if he was hiding some guilt about his actions, but Bixei's eyes were as clear and true as they had ever been when he met Llesho's gaze again across the necks of their horses. "I would never betray you. You annoyed the piss out of me when you first showed up. You were too short and too skinny, ridiculous for the arena, and I couldn't imagine why Markko had accepted you for training. I thought perhaps he found you pretty, though he never seemed interested in boys before. I was afraid that, if you were his favorite, Markko would give you my place, and I'd be stuck behind the palisades again. But even then, I would not have betrayed you."

Llesho had never thought much about how others saw him. He'd been born a prince, and had taken the devotion of his people and his large and loving family for granted. Then he'd lost it all and hadn't cared what anyone thought of Llesho the slave—that wasn't him, and the people whose opinions mattered weren't there anymore. Whether he wished it or not, however, it seemed that he was about to learn as much about himself as he was about Markko. He found himself cringing at Bixei's word-picture of him.

"But you learned fast," Bixei continued, "like you'd been born to the forms, and sometimes, in weapons practice, especially with the sword and the knife, it was hard to tell where the weapon in your hand left off and your body began. Master Den had that skill, and sometimes Jaks. Madon, too, if sorely pressed. I thought it was odd that you didn't practice in the yard with your born weapons more often, but I figured Jaks wanted to raise your skills in a broader range of weapons."

Bixei shrugged. "I suppose I should have been more jealous when you proved you could hold your own in the practice yard, but Stipes said you were all right, and I didn't envy you having Master Den breathing down your neck. And, sometimes, when you were using the knife and the sword, you would have a look on your face that . . . well, just say that I never wanted to find out what put it there. And I never wanted to be your practice partner when I saw it."

"Master Den never let anyone but himself practice knife with me," Llesho admitted. "Not even Master Jaks. When Habiba took me to the governor's compound at Farshore, I nearly killed someone in practice. That's when Master Jaks explained that I only knew how to kill with the knife, not to wound or to hold back for a practice match, and that to try and change that would ruin me. Since then, I sometimes dream that I killed Master Den in practice. It gives me the cold sweats just thinking about it."

"How did you get that way?"

Llesho shrugged. "Goddess knows. Master Den says I was trained to it as a child, but I have no memory of it. Lately I've begun remembering more. I was only seven, but I remember killing a man with my knife, so I guess Master Den is right."

"Is that why you were sold into slavery?" Bixei asked. "I mean, you were a prince and all, but . . ."

"The man had just killed my personal bodyguard, and would have killed me if he'd seen me first. He was a Harn raider. They attacked the palace, killed my mother and father and my sister, and sold the rest of us into slavery. I don't feel guilty about killing him, exactly, but I want to throw up when I remember how it felt to drive a Thebin war-knife between a man's ribs."

Bixei nodded. "You were different when you began weapons practice—"

"I'd forgotten a lot about the attack on Kungol, our capital city, until I held a war-knife again. Then it all came back." Llesho didn't mention that her ladyship had watched him in the weapons room that day, that she had known even then who he was.

Bixei nodded. That made sense. "By then, I realized that you weren't interested in taking my place in the team; you had a plan of your own, and whatever it was, it worried Master Jaks.

"I don't know why Markko treated you the way he did—he never was cruel with me, never interfered with my life or with Stipes. I knew about his workroom, of course, but other than carrying a potion to a patient now and then, I had nothing to do with that part of his business."

They both fell silent for a few moments, listening to the song of the soldiers as they marched. Then

Bixei went on. "I'm not saying that Markko was ever a decent overseer. But a lot of things changed when you showed up, Llesho. You spent years diving for pearls on the same island, but I don't think anyone in the training compound knew you existed. And then suddenly Master Markko wants you, and you are making Master Jaks nervous, and Master Den is alternating between treating you like the village idiot and like his most prized chick.

"I never saw Master Den take weapons practice with anyone until you showed up, and suddenly he is a master at the knife and sword. I never, I mean never, saw anyone handle them like Master Den did, not even you, and until you came, I would have guessed he didn't even know how to hold a sword."

"I think his stories are all true," Llesho offered. "I just don't know how he managed to do all those things, or how he came to be the washerman in a stable of gladiators."

"Me neither," Bixei admitted. "But I just wanted you to know that things were different before you showed up. So part of what Master Markko has become was always in him, but part, somehow, has to do with you. And I think, I *think* that he sees a power in you—whatever it is that has Master Jaks and Master Den and her ladyship and Habiba in a stew."

"It's the prince thing." Llesho tried to convince himself as well as Bixei that was all there was to it. "If today the Harn can take Thebin and hold the passage to the West hostage, tomorrow they may decide to take Shan and the eastern end of the trade route."

Bixei, unfortunately, didn't take the bait. "That might explain Master Jaks, and even her ladyship," he agreed, "but not Habiba or Markko. Markko wanted to study you and use whatever power he saw in you, but he couldn't figure out how to reach it. And I think it finally got to be too much for him. Chin-shi wasn't the greatest lord in the empire, but he wasn't the sort to let his overseer dissect the slaves for his own education. I think that's why Master Markko made the deal with Lord Yueh."

"There's just one problem with that theory." Llesho shuddered. He could too easily imagine himself spread out on the long, sturdy table in Markko's workroom, his guts revealed to the curiosity of the poisoner. "I don't have any power. If I did, Mara would be alive. Madon would be alive. I wouldn't have taken an arrow in my chest, and I wouldn't have spent weeks recovering from the fever."

He didn't add, *We wouldn't be in this mess if the lady goddess had found me pleasing in her sight,* but said, "Master Markko has what he was looking for. With the governor murdered by Lord Yueh's soldiers, and Lord Yueh himself now dead, Markko will hold Pearl Island and Farshore. He has all the power he can possibly want."

"Not all," Bixei pointed out. "And it's not me you have to convince. Markko isn't likely to believe you don't have some mysterious powers, because he's already committed everything to capture them."

"I don't understand." Llesho muttered the comment to himself, but Bixei picked it up and answered: "Ask Master Den. If you can make any sense of what he says. Whatever Master Markko sees in you, Master Den saw it first."

With that, Bixei dropped back to take the rear again, leaving Llesho with his thoughts.

Chapter Twenty-seven

IF someone had asked which of his companions Llesho expected to unsettle his thinking the least, he would have answered, "Bixei," without a moment's hesitation. Which just proved once again that he'd taken on this quest thing with his eyes half shut, and hadn't opened them yet. Half the company he traveled with apparently considered him a magical talisman of some sort, while the other half—probably thought the same thing by now, except that they hadn't yet told him so. It made him wonder if they weren't right, and he was just too stupid to realize it. He was smart enough to know that he didn't want Master Markko to be the one to unlock his mysteries, though.

The magician was following them, he was sure of it. Habiba had to know it, but he held their pace to a slow and steady advance, as if no danger followed them nor anything of importance awaited them ahead. Habiba wasn't riding beside him, but Kaydu made a handy substitute, so he complained to her.

"Can't we move any faster?" Llesho pressed when Kaydu dropped back to ride beside him.

"Not if we want the wagons to keep up," she answered. "Father will not risk the wagon teams to an attack on an undefended rear. He doesn't want you to greet the emperor's ministers with anything less than the full honors of your position, and the tents and supplies are carried in the wagons."

"I'd rather arrive without the tents, but within this lifetime," Llesho grumped. An image flashed in his mind, of himself, in a cage lashed to the back of a wagon, with Master Markko riding beside him, gloating. He didn't think it was his own imagination, but how had Markko got into his head?

Without thinking about it, he'd been urging his sturdy mount forward with insistent pressure from his knees. When the horse obediently picked up the pace, he tugged impatiently on the reins, holding their place in the line. The horse, which had coped patiently with Llesho's nervous energy to this point, gave a frustrated snort and a little sidestep, bucking as if he'd been bitten by a fat green fly. Llesho sailed into the air and crashed down hard on his tailbone.

"Ouch!" he shouted, and grunted a humiliated complaint, "I can't feel my butt!" The images of himself in chains were gone, though, pushed out by the sudden awareness of the pain in his backside, for which he was grateful at least. Now all he had to do was figure out how to manage it without falling off his horse.

Hmishi snorted, but he slid off his horse and offered a hand. "Your butt's still there," he assured Llesho, "though you may regret it by the time we stop for the night!"

Llesho glared at him and remounted, gritting his teeth as his nether regions renewed their acquaintance with his horse.

"More stubborn than a packhorse," the voice of a soldier snickered behind them. His wounded expression earned Llesho no support from his companions, however. Lling sniffed scornfully instead, and muttered, "It's only the truth."

Embarrassment reddened his dusky skin to the

color of an aged wine. "I have to find Master Jaks," he said, and urged his horse out of the line.

His companions surely knew he had no more business with the officers at the front now than he'd had just minutes ago, when he'd argued the pace with Kaydu. But it gave him an excuse to escape their knowing glances, and his horse needed to work off some of the nerves it shared with its rider.

Master Jaks was not to be found, and Habiba, riding at the head of the line of soldiers with Stipes at his flank, greeted him with a polite nod, and a sympathetic smile that for some reason made Llesho even angrier than he was already. Muttering some courtesy he did not mean and forgot as soon as he'd finished saying it, Llesho turned his horse and headed back down the line. Without quite realizing it, he found himself moving toward the rear where Master Den followed with the wagons, willing to trade the watchful attention of his guard for the curious glances of the men of the line. He had not gone far, however, when Stipes caught up with him, a wrathful glare on his face, and a sharp word on his tongue.

"Your guard is responsible for your safety," he began. "They can't protect you if you insist on running off like an irresponsible child."

"There are a thousand troopers on this march, Stipes. If the whole of Habiba's forces cannot keep one man from snatching me away, I don't think the five of you will make much difference."

"And you don't want to see us dead like your bodyguard in Kungol Palace," Stipes snapped back at him. "But Lling and Hmishi would die to save you from nicking your finger on your dinner knife, and Kaydu and Bixei aren't far behind, for their honor if not for love of you."

It hurt to hear the words said aloud. He hadn't understood it as a child—his people falling dead by the wayside so that he would live. Now he carried the guilt as a warning as well as a memory.

I don't want anyone dead for me. No point in saying it, since Stipes already had, so he glared back at the man. "And you? What are you doing here?"

"What do you think?" Stipes shrugged. "Habiba and that girl, Kaydu, have fixed it so that the only way I can keep Bixei safe is to keep you alive. So I'm doing it, even if I have to drag you over my horse's rump like a saddle pack and haul your ass back to your place in the line."

Think cold thoughts, Llesho told himself. But the hurt still sneaked onto his downcast face. He didn't want that responsibility. He heard a sigh from above him—Stipes, taller to begin with and riding a bigger horse.

"You've got friends, Llesho, whether you want them or not. Give them a break."

That was the problem. Llesho grabbed the reins of Stipes' horse close by the bit. When the two horses settled, closer than either of the animals would have liked, Llesho met Stipes' gaze and held it. "Friends die," he said.

"Remember that the next time you decide to do something reckless." Nodding an end to the conversation, Stipes tugged his reins out of Llesho's hand and turned his horse.

Neither said anything when they slipped back into place with their companions, although Llesho, even deep in his own thoughts, could not ignore the silent communication going on around him. "I won't go off on my own again," he growled when it had gone on long enough. "Far be it from me to permit my death to get in the way of true love."

He'd used as much sarcasm as he could summon, and Bixei responded with his usual sneer. Llesho hadn't expected the furious blushes that heated the faces of his two Thebin companions. He remembered them lying close together in the healer's cottage, and it made him unaccountably angry, in an unfocused way—left out more than wanting Lling for himself. He'd kept himself as a gift to the goddess, who didn't want him, and now he found himself on the outside in his own company. He wondered if he was supposed to start plying Kaydu with poetry and sighs now.

She answered his curious look with a disdainful tilt of her head. "Don't even think it."

She seemed to have read his mind. Since the others were snickering, however, he figured his speculation must have been pretty obvious. He hoped his relief wasn't as easy for everyone to read, but Kaydu's indignation, and the renewed laughter around him told him it probably was. Tucking his head into his collar like a defensive turtle, Llesho turned his attention forward, wishing he hadn't just promised not to run off on his own. Stipes gave him an encouraging slap on the shoulder before cutting out of the line to return to Habiba's side. Llesho'd done something right, apparently. He didn't know what it was, but he was glad to know the humiliation wasn't for nothing. Even embarrassment passed the time, however, and soon the troops ahead were breaking formation, spreading across a field of beaten grass to make camp. That night his companions held Llesho close to their own campfire.

They could not stop him when he rose at dawn to take his place at prayer forms before breakfast, however. Master Den led the exercises as he had in the training compound on Pearl Island, and each day that passed found more of Habiba's army joining them. Most were strangers, but Bixei and Stipes were there, standing next to each other as they had in the practice yard of old, and Master Jaks took his place in the line close to Hmishi and Lling. Gradually, Llesho's newly healed body relearned how to sketch the forms on the wind, muscles acting in harmony with each other and the earth, wind, fire, and water.

He should, perhaps, have helped with the eager recruits from among the Farshore troops, but he felt a selfish need to experience the separation from thought the exercises could bring. The forms flowed through him, shaped him as they had not done since Markko had made a prisoner of him.

Master Den called out the forms: "Red sun."

Llesho closed his eyes and lifted his face to greet the newborn day. Muscle moved against muscle, action against action; his arms stretched to meet the first light bathing the meadow, filling his mind with physical sensations.

"Wind through Millet." Master Den moved with the words, and Llesho followed. Feet touched grass, became grass, the sharp scent of green life rising in the wind that touched him, parted for the blade of his arm.

"Flowing River." Llesho's body moved with the breeze that flowed around him, with him, like a river. In the Way of the Goddess, all life flowed the great river, Llesho, and the earth he stood upon, and the gods he worshiped, were all a part of each other. Markko's chains, her ladyship's plots, could not break him if he flowed with the river of all life. "Butterfly," and Llesho moved free of the flight in darkness and the arrow searing his flesh and all the other horrors he relived in his dreams at night and in his waking reveries.

His escape from his own dark thoughts ended when Master Den completed the last of the forms and performed his bow of respect to the assembled company. Instead of leaving, as he usually did, before Llesho could free himself of his comrades and ask for a private word, Master Den remained behind as the company broke up. Master Jaks stood by him, and Llesho waited impatiently for the two teachers to finish their low conversation. Neither of his masters looked at him, but—sensitized by the prayer forms—Llesho felt the hairs on his neck prickling the way they did when others made him the focus of their secret attention. The conversation ended, but before Llesho could speak up, both men had departed, leaving him feeling foolish. Bixei and Stipes said nothing, but followed him to breakfast with their own silent conversation of eyebrows and frowns.

When he returned with his companions to their tent, Llesho found that Kaydu had already started to break camp. Together they made quick work of it and distributed their light gear among the five horses. Kaydu held his bridle as Llesho mounted up. "Stay close today," she warned him. "There are rumors in the camp that make me nervous."

"What does your father want you to tell me?" Llesho's temper was already short and he didn't like being kept in the dark, or fed information in tidbits, like a child. Kaydu's father was leading this march, after all. Her intelligence could hardly be called rumor.

"My father has told me to keep you alive," Kaydu snapped back at him. "It would help if you didn't make it so hard to follow orders!"

Before Llesho could decide how to answer, he was distracted by the forceful "Uhum!" of a throat being cleared behind him.

"Do you mind if I join you?" Master Den asked with a bland smile. He wore a travel robe and carried a light pack on his back and an ironshod stave in his hand.

"Yes," Llesho could have bitten his tongue when he heard his ill-considered answer. He'd been wanting to talk to Master Den for days, and now that the opportunity presented itself, he was rejecting it out of temper.

However, Den didn't go away. He ignored the hasty answer with a wink, though his smile remained as meaninglessly polite as ever. "I felt the need of a bit of exercise; thought I'd walk a bit today."

Llesho glared at him. "It will be a dusty walk so far back among the troops," he pointed out. "You might want to travel with Master Jaks at the head of the line."

The soldiers ahead of them began to move, and Llesho nudged his horse into motion. "I think I'll be comfortable here." Master Den clasped the bridle and walked beside him.

"Your sudden desire for exercise has nothing to do with the mysterious rumors Kaydu was about to explain, I suppose?"

"Rumors? Must a man find nothing but questions and suspicion just because he takes a walk with old friends of a morning?" Master Den grinned at him as if he hadn't expected Llesho to believe him, but wished to invite his pupil into the conspiracy.

Llesho declined the invitation. He figured at the rate he was going, he'd be lucky if his companions didn't tie him up and toss him to the wolves before the day was out. But he wasn't seven years old anymore; if Master Den was going to be there, Llesho had a whole list of questions, and he wasn't waiting any longer for answers. "I assume you will have no trouble talking as you walk?"

"What do you want to know?" Master Den spoke as if he had not been avoiding Llesho for days, as if the answers were always his for the asking. Llesho shook his head, but determined not to waste this opportunity on pointless arguing, especially now that Kaydu had posed him a new question.

"What is the truth behind the rumors Kaydu talks

of?" Llesho shook his head when Master Den took a deep breath, a sign that Den was going to tell one of his long tales in which his answer might or might not appear in some form Llesho would spend the whole day trying to untangle. "You are here, beside me today, when I haven't been able to get a word with you since we left the Golden Dragon River. Why now?"

"Habiba's spies have seen Markko following, and he is traveling fast."

"And we still move as if we were on parade?"

"You have heard the proverb, 'to the swift go the spoils'?"

Llesho nodded. That was the point, wasn't it?

"It isn't always true." Master Den smiled, the kind that twinkled in his eyes as well as tilting his mouth. "Did I ever tell you the story about the falcon and the turtle?"

Habiba called a halt at noon to rest the horses and feed the troops on cold rations at their stations. During the pause, Master Jaks appeared on a large battle steed with armor plates attached to its chest and withers. Jaks tried to make light of his appearance at the middle of the line, but his eyes remained watchful and grim. When the line moved again, he fell into place next to Llesho, offering the defense of his person on the exposed flank. Master Den took the more defended side, walking at the head of Llesho's smaller horse with a pace that never faltered. Stipes had joined Bixei guarding their rear. Kaydu, with Little Brother peering nervously out of the pack where he'd tucked himself to hide, rode at the head of Llesho's guard, Hmishi and Lling to either side of her.

"How long?" Llesho asked Master Den. He didn't need to explain himself. The question was obvious, and Den did not pretend to misunderstand.

"Soon." His glance flicked to Master Jaks, who nodded agreement.

The shadow of a low-flying bird passed over them, and Master Jaks amended his answer: "Now."

Calls passed through the line as sergeants brought their squads to a halt and gave the command for battle formation. Kaydu glanced at Master Jaks, who directed the formation of a circle of pikemen around Llesho's squad. He called for archers to take their positions inside the circle, prepared to shoot over the shoulders of the pikemen, ranged a double line here, and here, where he expected the greatest pressure from Markko's attack. Llesho's own guard set themselves at the fore of the line of archers, their horses protected inside the circle. When all was in readiness, Master Jaks returned to Llesho's side and drew his sword. Llesho considered his choice of weapons, and decided on his bow and arrow.

They had scarcely taken their places when a dark line appeared over a low rise in the landscape. An army, no bigger than their own but driven by fear of their leader, plunged forward, battle cries shouted as they ran. Llesho tensed and focused his gaze on the rise, where a figure sat astride a restless warhorse. Master Markko, proclaiming himself in the horned helmet of a warlord.

Llesho shivered. He sensed the sharp gaze of the magician pass over him and halt, then turn back again. If an arrow could have reached so far, Llesho would have turned away that searching gaze with a well-fired bolt, but at this range he could only call attention to himself.

"Hold on, boy," Master Jaks muttered at his side, and Master Den held the head of Llesho's horse, quieting the animal's nervous dance.

Markko was flying down the hill then, his charger striking sparks off the ground beneath its feet, and a bird, huge and lethal, flew over their heads to meet the enemy. It circled overhead, calling encouragement in the deep-voiced cry of a roc. Kaydu shouted a salute to the bird, a magical creature, and would have followed him, Llesho thought, but Master Jaks called out a reminder, "Hold your post."

Then Markko's forces were upon them. The defensive circle Jaks had ordered bristled with pikes, their staffs planted firmly in the ground and their blades tilted out at the horsemen thundering toward them. They had only seconds to wait. The cavalry reached the circle, but the horsemen could not force their mounts to close with the sharp-toothed fence of pikes. Turned aside, the horsemen met the harrying arrows as Habiba's cavalry darted in for the kill and moved away again. Markko's foot troops followed the scattering horsemen; driven mad by their master, they flung themselves upon the pikes to clear the path for their fellows. Llesho set an arrow and fired. Fired. Fired again, until his quiver was empty. The bird was gone from the sky, but Lling was at his side, one arm tied with a makeshift bandage, the other flinging a fistful of replacement bolts into his hand. She had gathered the arrows falling into their circle from the enemies' bows; Llesho recognized the strange devices marked upon them as he shot again, again.

And then the circle was breached, and the fight turned inward. Llesho dropped his bow and slid from his horse, drawing his sword from its saddle scabbard and his Thebin knife from where it rested at his breast. On foot he moved like a demon, protecting his own belly with the knife in his left hand while he carved at the enemy with the sword in his right. Master Jaks, still on horseback, whirled his sword over his head, striking terror into all who saw him, while his battle horse fought under its master with tooth and hoof. Careful as a mother the mare picked her way around Llesho, snapping at Markko's soldiers, kicking out at them and beating at them with her frantic feet when they fell.

Master Den held his position to Llesho's right flank,

warded off an attack with his stave, cracked a head like an egg, and swung around to brush the legs out from under the nearest attacker while knocking the breath from a third with the rising end of the stave.

Bixei was down, Stipes standing over him with a two-handed sword held out in front of him, Hmishi at his back slashing with a long knife and jabbing with a short-handled trident.

"Close up! Close up!" Master Jaks ordered, shoring up their broken circle and drawing it more tightly around Llesho and his guard. Master Den accepted the surrender of Markko's troops left inside the newly re-formed circle. When they had been disarmed and placed on good conduct, Jaks called for retreat: "Back!" He whirled his sword once overhead, and pointed to the fallback position with his blade. Stipes got a shoulder under Bixei's arm and they moved, the pikemen holding their defensive formation. When they met the circle behind them, their numbers swelled, the two circles interlaced, filling in the weak places around Llesho without leaving a break for the enemy to exploit.

Markko was driving his army in a wedge directly at Llesho's circle. If he succeeded, he would divide Habiba's army in two parts. As the circle fell back, Markko pressed forward, until he faced his prey down an alley of his own troops. "I will have you, boy," he said, a snarling grimace of a smile contorting his face.

Llesho froze, aware suddenly how thin his defense was, just a single band of pikemen between them, and Markko dug his heels into the flanks of his horse, lowered his head over the animal's armored neck, and charged.

The pikemen set their pikes and braced for the onslaught, but at the last moment, Markko urged his horse faster, up, higher than a horse could jump, and the warlord flew over the blades bristling beneath the belly of his steed and landed lightly inside the circle.

Master Markko raised a strange weapon of his own devising, a tube shooting sparks of fire and smoke and tiny slivers of crystal sharp as knives from the end. In confusion the defensive circle broke. A picked squad of Markko's followed and joined him in the fray.

"Get down!" Hmishi called.

Under cover of the billowing smoke, Lling knocked Llesho to his knees.

"Pretend you are dead!" she demanded, and pushed him to land with his face in the dirt. Then she fell on top of him, her bandage convincingly stained rust and crimson from her reopened wound. Llesho wondered what had happened to Kaydu, if she'd managed to escape, but a vulture landed on his shoulder and gave the back of his head an imperious peck.

"Cawuuuiet!" the bird squawked, and Llesho wondered if he had gone mad, or if the bird had really told him to be quiet.

"Wha—" he began, but the bird snapped up a strand of his hair and gave it a warning tug.

The smoke was beginning to clear. Through closely lidded eyes, Llesho saw that Master Den had suffered a myriad of tiny cuts which he seemed to be ignoring as he scrambled among the fallen. Stipes had dropped Bixei to the ground only to fall after him, clutching at his eye while blood gushed from between his clenched fingers. Master Jaks was down, on his back beneath his horse, his eyes wide and unseeing. The horse stood quivering but steadfast over her master.

Hmishi crouched at the side of his Thebin companions. His knife lashed out, not at the warlord, but at the legs of his battle horse. The animal screamed and fell to its front knees. Mad with its pain, the horse struggled to rise again, its eyes reddened and rolling wildly in its head. Master Markko sprang free of the animal as it crashed to its side, thrashing with its legs as it tried to rise. Hmishi struck quickly and the animal was dead, its throat cut, the blood splashing the fallen Thebins.

It could as easily have been human blood. Llesho had to remind himself that he was unhurt, and ought to do something more than lie about playing dead. Like stand up and *be* dead, he figured, and stayed where he was. Somehow, Master Markko seemed to have turned the day in his favor, and Llesho could only hope that he would be overlooked in the carnage. A faint hope, with Markko seeking him, but it was enough to keep him facedown in the dirt.

Above him, Llesho heard a terrible cry, and he cringed where he lay, afraid to open his eyes. A deep growl from closer by answered the first cry, and Llesho felt a weight suddenly lift from his heart. Freed of his terrible fear, he turned his head and peered over his shoulder, into the sky, where two beasts—he knew for a fact such beasts did not exist in nature—fought tooth and claw in the air overhead. One was a huge bird, a roc, if such a thing could actually exist. It uttered a challenge, the most desolate sound Llesho had ever heard, as if it contained within itself all the grief of the battle and its losses, and called them forth in a mourner's wailing cry. The other, a creature out of night terrors, was a rodent-faced monster with the haunches of a horse and stiff gray hair instead of feathers covering its broad leathery wings. A long naked rat's tail whipped out behind it. The creature had clawed feet and claws at the joints of its wings, long, fanged teeth and angry red eyes. When it opened its mouth to answer the roc's cry, Llesho had to cover his ears to stop the piercing pain it released instead of sound.

The creatures tangled overhead, the fanged monster grappling the bird with its tail while its claws ripped at the roc's breast. The roc darted its razor-sharp beak at the monster, and when it pulled back, the ends of a bit of flesh dangled from its mouth. The monster emitted another of its soundless screams and began to tumble from the sky, its shape blurring as it fell: now it was a creature out of nightmares with the hands, the face of a man, now it became a man with leathery wings covered in gray hair, now a creature with the hindquarters of a beast and the arms and breast of a human, its human mouth open in a scream that did not stop through all its transformations, until it had fallen to earth.

The roc followed it down, transforming as it did into the witch Habiba, dressed in robes the colors of the bird's plumage. But Markko was gone; no sign of him remained except for a splash of steaming blood where he had fallen, and the remnants of his scattered army.

"You can get up now. And you did well, my daughter." Habiba tapped the vulture on its long, curved beak, and the bird unfolded, grew arms and legs, and a familiar face.

"Thank you, Father." Kaydu did not have the success of her father in transforming her clothes with her body. She gathered her discarded uniform that had fallen on the battleground while Habiba bent over the heap of Thebins.

Llesho didn't notice until Habiba started to sort them out that Hmishi had joined them on the pile. "I'm all right," Hmishi insisted, but his eyes darted wildly in his head, unable to fix on anything.

"Concussion," Habiba informed him. "Lie still until I can spare someone to escort you to the hospital tent."

The magician raised Lling with his own hands, and examined her arm before he declared her serviceable if damaged, and able to make her own way to the hospital tent.

With the weight of his companions removed from his back, Llesho was able to rise on his own power and survey the damage. Markko had disappeared and left behind his army—the fallen where they lay, and the defeated wandering the battlefield in confusion and terror.

The field was silent now except for the cries of the wounded, but the ground was muddied with the blood of the dead and churned by the hooves of the horses into a thick black muck. Squads of her ladyship's army passed back and forth over the sucking mire, searching for their own wounded, and marking out the dead for burial.

Closer to hand, Stipes sat cross-legged in the dirt, Bixei's head in his lap. He still held a hand to his damaged eye, but his blood had caked and rusted his fingers in place so that he could not have comfortably moved them if he chose to, or if he'd even remembered that he held them there. Bixei's eyes were closed, but his chest rose and fell in rhythmic breathing.

His own wounds forgotten, Master Den sat quietly at Jaks' side. Jaks' eyes were open, fixed on a distance living eyes could not reach. Whatever the soldier-assassin was seeing in the afterlife, it did not seem to frighten or dismay him. Tenderly Master Den wrapped a cold hand in his broad, warm grasp.

Llesho wanted to pound at Habiba with his fists, to scream at the man and curse him for the devastation that surrounded him, but he found he could not break through the hard, numb shell that separated his bleeding emotions from the outside world.

"What happened?" Llesho demanded an answer from Habiba with the cold authority of a prince. He didn't feel the tears leaving trails in the dust on his face, so he didn't try to hide them.

Habiba looked at him for a long minute. Then he picked up the splintered remains of an arrow and drew two parallel lines in the bloody dirt, added a few lateral lines between them.

"Our column," he said, and put a circle midway between the front and rear. "Kaydu's squad."

Next he drew a triangle, its apex driving at the circle. "Markko sent his army at your position—we knew he used birds for spies and would have your location pinpointed. When he attacked, we knew he would try to divide our army and pluck you out of the middle. So we let him try."

He drew two more lines, showing how the column had not truly broken at Llesho's position, but had bent toward the flanks of Markko's army like the blades of a scissor closing. "The emperor could not authorize imperial troops to take part in the battle without consulting his advisers and considering the messages sent to him by either side of the conflict. Fortunately, in his capacity as governor of Shan Province, the Celestial Emperor has no such limitations. Shan provincial troops moved in to close off Markko's escape—"

Habiba added a final line to his drawing in the blood-soaked mud, joining the two halves of the column at their widest separation to mark out the base of a triangle enclosing Markko's wedge. Then he threw the bit of shattered arrow away from him and stared at Master Jaks, lying motionless on the ground. "He knew your position was the key. Markko must be lured in, but he could not be permitted to break through. Master Jaks chose to hold the position himself."

"Did the others know?"

Habiba brought his gaze back from the dead assassin, but settled his focus inward, as if he could not face Llesho with the answer. "Kaydu, yes."

She had put her clothes back on, but when Llesho glanced up at her, she turned away as if she still were naked.

"Anyone else?"

"Stipes may have guessed. As for Master Den—" Habiba shrugged one shoulder, an admission of helplessness Llesho did not credit. "The question should be, perhaps, 'did he choose to know?' I don't have an answer, though."

Stretcher bearers had reached them at last, grim-faced men who looked at Habiba nervously and then waited while he gave directions for the care of his charges: Bixei and Stipes, and Hmishi, to the hospital on stretchers. Lling might follow on foot, but should have her arm seen to. Master Jaks should not go to the mass grave of the line soldiers; the bearers must return him to his tent, where he would be prepared for the burial due his courage and his station. Llesho wondered what rank a former slave and assassin might command. Master Den would not leave the body, although Habiba asked him to go to the hospital to have his own wounds tended.

When the stretchers had moved away, trailing their walking wounded, Habiba put a hand on Llesho's left shoulder. "And now, there is someone you should meet."

Kaydu joined them, walking a little behind, still unwilling to intrude herself on Llesho's grief or ask his forgiveness.

"You should have told me," Llesho stated.

"Perhaps." Habiba accepted the reproach, but his tone held no real agreement in it. Llesho was a pawn. He'd always known that—why else would her ladyship take such an interest in a deposed and rather pathetic princeling with some hint of magic about him, but no clue how to use it? Why else would Markko chain him like a dog for his amusement? He had not, until now, however, understood how dangerous a pawn he was.

Habiba interrupted his brooding. "General Shou," the witch said as he pulled back the cloth that covered the entrance to his own tent. The general stood in the glorious armor of his rank, but the splendor of his appearance was marred by a streak of dirt smeared across one cheekbone and ending on the bridge of his nose. More smudges of dusty sweat marked the arm he offered. Llesho clasped it, felt the firm grip of the general's hand above his own wrist.

"The emperor offers his grief for your losses this day, but extends his joy that you have survived the battle." The general released Llesho's arm after he delivered his message.

"We can only hope that the gain will be worthy of the loss," Llesho answered.

The general raised an eyebrow. "We can, perhaps, do more than hope." He turned on his heel and left the tent.

Kaydu had not entered with them, so Llesho found himself alone with Habiba, who was the first to break the tense silence between them.

"Kaydu will have a tent prepared for you. Clean up and rest as much as you can. We petition for an audience with the emperor tomorrow morning."

"I have to go to the hospital," Llesho answered. "And I must see Master Jaks." His voice broke on the last.

Habiba, thankfully, did not comment upon his loss of control, but only said, "He would not be sorry to die protecting you. If he regretted anything, it was that he could not see you safely home."

Llesho nodded, but could not speak. He brushed by Kaydu, afraid that she would want to offer her own apologies and demand his forgiveness when he only wanted to weep for the blood of his teacher on his hands.

"We did what we had to do," Kaydu shouted after him. She did not sound apologetic at all, and Llesho did not stop to challenge her on it. If he opened his mouth, he would scream, and he wasn't sure he would ever stop.

Chapter Twenty-eight

HIS first impulse was to find the tent where Master Jaks lay and give the dead man a piece of his mind. A prince owed his life to the living, however. Llesho knew he shouldn't have yelled at Kaydu, who had done her duty and deserved better for it. Much as the drama of the gesture might appeal to him, he also knew that he would not rather be dead in Master Jaks' place. Nor would the man have thanked him if he were, any more than his brother, Khri, would have seen Llesho dead at seven summers to save his own skin. He had a mission to complete, a people to free, and Master Jaks was just one of many who had already died and would die in the future to make that happen.

He had to stop thinking of them as friends. They were tools, weapons in his battle. A prince took care of his sword because his life depended on its readiness. Only a fool sacrificed the battle to save the sword. His heart didn't buy his argument, but he pulled the reins in on his anger and changed direction for the pale blue of the hospital tent. First the living.

Stipes had lost the eye. He lay on a woven rush mat rolled out on the blue canvas floor, a cloth soaked in a potion to ease the pain held in place by a bandage tied around his head. Bixei lay on the next mat over, still unconscious, but breathing steadily.

"He took a nasty bump on the head." Hmishi sat cross-legged on a nearby pallet, a cup of some sweet medicine in his hand, and continued the healer's report, "But his eyes are clear behind his lids. If he wakes, his brain should not be addled."

If. The healers offered hope and took it away in the same breath. Lling stood nearby, leaning on a well-tethered tent pole. Her arm rested in a proper sling now, with a clean bandage on the wound. She glared at him, measuring her anger against his own. "Are we going home?" she asked him.

Llesho knew what she meant, and so did Hmishi, who watched them both over his potion. Not Pearl Island or Farshore or Thousand Lakes Province, but Thebin. Had the pain and the death been worth giving to his cause? He nodded once. "We are going home."

"All right, then." She walked away, and Llesho watched her go.

"She's worried about Bixei," Hmishi tried to explain away her anger. "He should be awake by now. The healers believe that the mist from Markko's weapon may contain a slow-acting poison, and that Bixei somehow took a greater dose than the rest of us. They call for Master Den, but he doesn't come," Hmishi continued with a shrug. "I don't know what they think the laundryman can do. . . ."

Llesho sometimes forgot that his Thebin companions had not met Master Den until Habiba's forces came to their aid at Golden Dragon River. They could not be expected to see him as Llesho did. But even those who had worked with him in the gladiator days couldn't be said to know Master Den. Perhaps Jaks had, but he wouldn't be telling anyone now. Habiba guessed something, as the healers did. But Llesho figured even they underestimated the teacher.

"He won't leave Master Jaks." Laundrymen, in that, had more freedom than princes. Which explained much about Master Den's choice of rank in the world.

"Not even if the living need him?"

Llesho stole a glance at the unconscious form on the nearby sleeping mat. He tried to see Bixei as a tool, but his memory played tricks on him, fed him images of the training yard and the cookhouse. If Markko had poisoned them, Lling might be unconscious by nightfall. Hmishi, too, and Stipes, who had already lost an eye in Llesho's battle, for a country he'd never heard of. Llesho might never see Thebin again, except in misty dreams the dead clung to.

"He wouldn't leave us here to die while he wept over his dead," Llesho assured him, though he wasn't certain it was true.

"He might tell that to the healers," Hmishi complained.

"He will." Now that he had satisfied himself about the condition of his living, Llesho's mind had turned, Like Master Den's, to his dead. "I'll be back later."

Master Den looked up when Llesho entered the unfloored tent—white for mourning, with the grass still green underfoot—and gestured for him to come forward.

"Jaks is waiting for you," Den said. For a moment Llesho's heart beat faster in anticipation. It was all a mistake, and Master Jaks had merely been stunned and found the premature grief at his death a sorry joke, but nothing more.

No. Not alive. The body lay still and cold beneath a winding sheet of cloth white and fragile as chestnut blossoms in the spring. Den had removed the soldier's bloodied leathers and washed away the dirt and sweat of battle with water in which sweet herbs and flowers had been steeped. Master Jaks might have been sleeping,

Llesho thought, but no hint of breath animated the peaceful shell of flesh.

Teacher and slave, gladiator and assassin, soldier: what other words identified this man who lay so silent on the pallet before him? Did any of the names matter now that the man was dead? Only the wounds hidden beneath the white cloth and the six bands of the assassin on his arm remained to tell the harsh tale.

"He loved you as his liege and lord," Master Den said.

Llesho nodded. How could he explain how angry that made him? Jaks was gone before Llesho rightly understood him, and for what?

"I'd rather be a slave with a live friend than a free man with a dead servant," he said.

"It wasn't up to you. That's a price kings—and princes—have to pay."

"What would a washerman know about being a prince?" Llesho snapped. He didn't need that kind of pointless drivel from one who was grieving more than any of them.

"Nothing," Master Den answered with a sour smile. "Nothing at all."

"The healers think Markko used a poisoned vapor during the battle." Llesho did not look away from the dead soldier, but still he was aware of Master Den nearby.

"You look well enough to me," Den answered. Llesho waited, and finally, the master bowed his agreement. "If you stay with him, I will go to your comrades."

"It would ease their minds." Llesho added, not quite as a plea, "Bixei is still unconscious."

"He'll wake up." Den reassured him. Not like Master Jaks, who would never wake in this life. Llesho heard the sound of the tent flap pushed aside, and then he was alone with Master Jaks.

"I did not give you leave to go," Llesho said to the

absent spirit of his master, and found his anger rising again, becoming a white hot rage. "If I have to stay and see this through, what right have you to abandon me just when the fight begins? What am I suppose to do now? Who can I trust—"

Llesho's gaze fell upon the six bands around the arm of his teacher. Assassin. He reached a hesitant finger to stroke the first dull blue band, remembering his early doubts. Six times this man had murdered for pay. Llesho wondered who those souls were. What had they done to deserve such a fate, and how had Master Jaks justified his actions with his honor? Did all men walk such a tangled path from birth to death as Master Jaks had done?

"Fate has taken everything from me." Foolish, Llesho knew, to blame Master Jaks for that, but he did. "Home and family, Lleck and Kwan-ti, Mara, and now you, are all gone. And I am left with lesser folk who look to me for answers I do not have. What am I supposed to learn from this?

"Tell me, damn it!" he screamed at the corpse. Horrified at his own actions but unable to stop himself, he curled his fist and slammed it down upon the breast of the dead man. Again. "Tell me!"

A sudden gasp spasmed under Llesho's fist, and the eyes of his dead teacher flew open, animated with fear and confusion and pain. The dead mouth dragged air down a dead throat, and the dead chest, so mortally wounded, rose and fell unevenly.

"Master Jaks?" Llesho froze, paralyzed by his own conflicting feelings. It had all been a mistake. Jaks was alive.

The blue lips struggled to shape a word, and Llesho bent low to hear what Master Jaks wanted to say to him.

"What . . . have . . . you . . . done?" the voice, so near death, whispered.

Looking into those clouded eyes, Llesho saw agony,

not only for the wound that once again bled freely, staining the pure white sheet, but for something only those eyes could see, that now was lost.

"I don't know." Llesho fell to his knees, lay his head upon the heaving breast, and wept. "I'm sorry. I'm sorry," he cried.

"I . . . can't . . . stay . . . here . . . !" Master Jaks' tortured whisper cut Llesho to the heart. He had not meant to cause his teacher pain, only to demand recognition of his own anguish. But it was too late, to late for any of it. And he realized how selfish his desire to hold his teacher in this world past the time appointed for him was.

"I know," he said. He opened his fist, lay his outstretched fingers on the wound in Master Jaks' chest, but already the bleeding had slowed, cooled. When he looked up, the eyes were fixed again, and he realized Master Jaks had stopped breathing.

"Tell the goddess for me that I love her still," Llesho asked of his departed teacher. "But I do not understand what any of this was meant to teach me." Gently he closed the staring eyes.

"Llesho?" Master Den had returned, and now he dropped a heavy hand on Llesho's shoulder.

"He's dead," Llesho said.

It seemed a pointless statement, but Master Den looked from the body, soiled with fresh blood, to the princeling with tear tracks marking the battle stains on his face, and gave a deep and mournful sigh.

"Yes, he is. Bixei is awake, however, and demanding food and an accounting of what followed his own fall. The rest of you will survive this time as well: Markko's poison was not strong enough to kill in the open air of battle."

"He will fix that the next time," Llesho said, allowing Den to push his thoughts to surviving. "Markko never makes the same mistake twice."

"If it *was* a mistake. He wants you alive."

Llesho remembered the image of himself, a captive in a cage, that had come to him on the battlefield, and he shuddered.

"Is any of that blood yours?" Den asked.

Llesho shook his head. "I wasn't injured at all."

"That is a matter for debate," Master Den observed. "But it appears you will live. At least, you will if I let you get some sleep. Kaydu is waiting for you outside. Clean yourself up and let her take you to your tent. Eat. Rest. Visit with your friends if you must, but leave tomorrow to Habiba and the new day. It will get better."

Llesho wasn't sure if the last was true, but he found Kaydu waiting for him as Master Den had said. He ate what she handed him, though he didn't notice what it was. When she took him down the row of red tents and opened the flap into the one assigned to him, he followed her in and fell on his camp bed without complaint. Then he pretended to sleep so that he wouldn't have to talk while she kept guard.

Gradually the campfires faltered, until he could no longer see the peak of his own tent above him. He was surprised to find that his mind did not replay the day's battle in the darkness. In fact, while they would not let him sleep, neither did his thoughts circle endlessly on the memory of his losses. His mind was quite, quite blank, and he felt grateful for the emptiness until the sun grayed the corners of his tent.

In the morning, Jaks was gone, buried secretly somewhere on the field of battle. Llesho could not make out one freshly turned grave among so many in the churned ground. Kaydu, still at his side, said nothing; Llesho did not guess at what she saw on the bloody field. Or under it.

"If his friends can't find him, neither will his enemies," Master Den explained. "And they won't be able to desecrate his body if they can't find it."

Llesho shrugged. Once the spirit abandoned it, the body meant nothing. A soldier deserved freedom at death: not dirt in his face, but the high mountains overlooking Kungol, where his bones might be picked by the birds and his spirit might begin its journey that much closer to heaven. He would have taken Jaks to the passes in the West, but Thebin and her mountains were a thousand li away. Lowlanders had different customs anyway. So he accepted Master Den's assurance that all had been done as Master Jaks would have wanted, and followed him to the command tent. Habiba waited for him inside.

"Good morning." Habiba gestured to a folding seat open for Llesho at his right hand. He addressed the teacher with an ironic smile. "The yarrow sticks are in the air, Master Den. Have you come to see how they fall?"

Master Den eased himself into a solidly built chair that seemed designed for his personal use, a luxury Llesho had never seen his teacher indulge in. "The Changes can only reflect what rests within us already," he reminded their host, offering the words with his own subdued challenge.

Kaydu frowned at Master Den and wrapped her arms around her father's neck as if she would protect him from the washerman's barbed tongue.

Habiba patted her arm. "We'll keep it civilized, I promise," he said. She hesitated, but took her father's frown as dismissal and joined the watchful guards who stood at the entrance to the tent.

When they had all settled in their places, Habiba returned his attention to Llesho.

"Have something to eat." He gestured at the low camp table in front of him, where a map lay, held in place at one end by a bowl of plums and figs, and at the other by a plate of biscuits. Llesho did as he was directed, accepting a biscuit.

"We are here—" Habiba waited for Llesho to settle

himself, and went on, "—at the border where Thousand Lakes Province meets the frontier of Shan Province." He drew an imaginary line with his finger on the Thousand Lakes side of the border. "Scouts report a large force of imperial guards await us on the Shan side of this line."

"You sound worried about that." Llesho took a bite of his biscuit to cover his surprise and gain himself a moment to think. "Would the Emperor direct General Shou and his provincial guard to help us, and then send his imperial forces against us the next morning?"

"If he wanted Markko and her ladyship both off the board," Habiba conceded with a curious smile. "In his capacity as provincial governor of Shan Province, the emperor might assist us to defeat the greater threat. Calling upon his power as Emperor, he might choose to send his imperial troops against the survivor while he was weakened from battle."

"But we aren't preparing for battle," Llesho noted. The whole of Habiba's forces seemed to be catching their breath, tending to their wounded and their dead, collecting undamaged arrows from the field of battle, and otherwise healing the injuries to men and equipment inflicted in Markko's recent attack.

"Of course not," Habiba acknowledged. "Her ladyship and the governor of Thousand Lakes Province remain the loyal servants of his supreme excellency, the Celestial Emperor of Shan and Its Provinces."

Llesho detected irony in Habiba's representation of his master's position, but couldn't figure out what was behind it. Not treason. Habiba did not act like a man engaged in a desperate conspiracy; rather, he looked like he had a secret that brought him some reassurance.

"I have sent an emissary to the commander of the Emperor's force," Habiba went on, "begging his protection for our small band, which comes to petition for the safety of Thousand Lakes Province."

Master Den nodded solemnly, a gesture that belied his ironic answer: "A message that has the advantage of being true on the face of it. Markko has already murdered three lords in his bid for control of all the eastern provinces, and has attacked our party on the very border of Shan Province itself."

"The emperor already knows this, of course," Habiba agreed. "His spies have been busy on all sides of the border. But he also knows that Markko has left the consolidation of his conquests to pursue a boy who has declared himself a missing prince of the mysterious kingdom of the West."

"I have done no such thing," Llesho objected.

"Others have done it for you," Den said. "And now, his imperial highness will have his look at you, and determine for himself whether he will risk his empire to acknowledge the claim."

Habiba agreed. "With the Harn harrying his borders on the west, and Markko gobbling up the provinces to the east, and both declared enemies of this newly discovered prince, I don't think he can afford to help directly. He may, however, conclude that a boy who still lives in spite of such powerful enemies is not to be tampered with. So you will ride at the front today, and in attire suited for a traveling prince."

"I have the clothes I stand up in, and not much else," Llesho pointed out to him.

"We had hoped to rescue you with less trouble," Habiba admitted, "but we left Thousand Lakes Province with this part of the plan in place. Master Den has, in his supply wagon, the necessary garments for an audience with a provincial representative to the emperor."

"We can fix you up, no problem there," Den agreed.

Llesho was beginning to feel like a puppet, and he wondered if it was safe to let Habiba pull his strings. Without Habiba, of course, he'd be dead now, or in

Markko's hands, but Llesho still didn't trust the man or his motives. Oh, he was sure that Habiba served her ladyship honorably and well. From the first, however, Llesho had wondered why her ladyship took such an interest in him.

As Habiba himself had just pointed out, allies could quickly become enemies when one didn't understand the politics that bound one to the other. Llesho was on the point of asking Habiba directly what her ladyship wanted of him when Kaydu joined them, followed by a stranger in the uniform of an imperial messenger.

The messenger shook out her hair and gave a short bow to Habiba, then a deeper bow to Master Den. Of Llesho she gave no formal recognition at all, although he noticed that she examined him minutely out of the corner of her eye.

"Lord Habiba," she said, "in the name of the Celestial Emperor, Ambassador Huang HoLun invites you to a parley to discuss matters of great import to you both. Will you attend upon him for tea?"

"I am, as ever, the humble servant of his divinity, the emperor. Please tell Ambassador Huang that I shall attend upon him within the hour. And I bring gifts from the West." Habiba tilted his chin in Llesho's direction.

Betrayal. Habiba's words struck like a bolt of lightning and Llesho clung to his calm. Habiba couldn't mean what he seemed to say. As a slave Llesho figured he was fairly useless; he had some training as a gladiator, a bit more as a soldier, and some experience as a decent pearl diver, for which there was little call in the inland capital. The Harn had sold him once, but they might be inclined to cut off his head if the emperor returned him to them. He figured that her ladyship hadn't put her witch to all the trouble of getting him this far alive if she intended to hand Llesho over to assassins, though. Much easier to whack off his head at Farshore and send it off in a box. Less likely to attract the attention of Master Markko that way as well. He was pretty sure, however, that Master Den wouldn't let anything happen to him so early in whatever game of nations the powers about him played.

As if thinking his name could conjure his attention, Master Den chose that moment to speak. "Please convey my respect to your master. Tell him for me that he chooses his envoy well." He smiled at the girl. And she smiled back.

Oh. Den knew this girl. Liked her. And she knew him. Llesho had never fooled himself into thinking he was the only student Master Den had ever mentored, but he'd thought the others had been men like Stipes, fighting on the side where he found himself. The girl bowed and departed, leaving Llesho to wonder whether Master Den would defend old loyalties or new ones.

"It is time," Habiba said, "to put the pieces in play. Llesho will ride in the place of honor, at my side. That will give Ambassador Huang pause. And Master Den—"

"I need no guard, of honor or otherwise," Den cut him off. "Huang HoLun knows that I am a simple man, and he will expect nothing more."

"Then we will overset his expectations. I want Kaydu where I can see her as well, and any of the young prince's guard who are well enough to ride. We depart at noon."

"As you say." Master Den made much of pulling himself out of his chair, grunting and huffing in a way that alarmed Llesho. So when he called, "Give me your arm," Llesho came willingly to offer his support.

When they were out of the command tent, however, Den straightened up, and he set a finger to his lips, warning Llesho to silence. Llesho watched the shifting tensions in Den's face, trying to read some explanation for his strange behavior, but Den signaled, "Wait."

Suddenly, two crows flew from the command tent: the witch and his daughter. As birds, the two wheeled in a great arc across the sky, then turned in the direction the messenger had gone and quickly disappeared.

When the two were well and truly out of sight, Master Den urged Llesho forward. As they walked between the rows of low red tents, Den let him ask his questions. To Llesho's own surprise, they did not start with Habiba.

"What am I?"

"You are Llesho, seventh prince of Thebin. Beloved of the goddess," Master Den answered as if he were reading from a scroll. It wasn't what Llesho wanted to hear.

"That's nothing but titles, of no interest to anyone outside of Thebin, and of little concern to most Thebins either. I want to know why Markko wants me so badly. He's not interested in Thebin or the route to the West; he wants *me,* the way he would want a particularly poisonous root. Why?"

"You will have to ask him."

Llesho gasped with the shock of that answer, pierced through with a terrible chill. "Is that what Habiba plans? To hand me over to his enemies after expending so much effort to keep me out of Markko's hands?"

"No, boy." Master Den softened his tone. "No one here will hand you over to anyone willingly. But the emperor may have some purpose in seeing you publicly declared, or he may wish to see you quietly, in secret. That choice Habiba can give him. If it comes to more than that, rest easy. I would put my own life between you and a danger such as Master Markko, no less than Master Jaks has done."

Llesho didn't feel reassured by that speech. He didn't want the responsibility of Master Den's life any more than he wanted to risk his own life on Habiba's good intentions.

Master Den hadn't finished with Llesho's question, though. "As for the rest, how does an evil man turn something precious and good to his own twisted use? I don't know. Only Master Markko himself, or someone as evil as he, can answer your questions. So you must decide, either to forgo this understanding, or to confront Master Markko when the time comes, and ask him.

"I do know that you are good, that you are the beloved of the goddess, and that you have felt her touch on all your long journey." He put up a hand to stop Llesho when he would have interrupted.

"The goddess can be a terrible mistress to one she loves. The hearts of those who rule above see into the past and the future as no man can. They see more deeply into the hearts and souls of their creatures. And their reasons—we who are only human cannot fathom their reasons. We can only trust that, harsh as their judgment may seem, their love is true, and their purpose just."

"You mean, it will all turn out in the end? That's not enough. Too many people have died for a vague hope that our struggle has meaning, somewhere. If the goddess truly loves me, why doesn't she tell me what I am supposed to do?"

"Perhaps she has." Den sighed again. "It will have to be enough. The Way of the Goddess is seldom simple, least so in times such as these." He turned without another word and walked away, but his step was heavier than it had been.

Llesho followed. He thought perhaps he had hurt his old mentor, but he couldn't figure out how, or what he had done. They went first to the hospital tent, where Bixei was up and about, offering attentive care to Stipes one minute, and fretting the healers to distraction the next. When Master Den appeared, the healers were of one mind: "Take him!"

"I can't leave!" Bixei objected. "What if Stipes needs me while we are gone?"

"Go!" Stipes raised a foot and gave Bixei a not-so-gentle push on the behind. "The worst that can happen is that I bump into a post, and you have a duty."

Bixei lingered anxiously for a minute, then joined Llesho and Master Den with an embarrassed flush creeping over his cheeks. "I didn't mean to fuss," he confessed.

"I know." Den smiled at him. "Where are your companions?"

"Lling and Hmishi went off to find out where Kaydu had set up our camp. We were going to bring Stipes back there to recover."

"Stipes will have to recover among the healers for a little while longer," Master Den informed him. "But for the moment you have a reprieve. Wait until your companions return, and fetch them to the laundry wagon. Tell them we are going calling."

Bixei looked to Llesho for an explanation. Llesho said nothing, just made a sour face at the teacher and pointed west. "The wagons are that way."

So Master Den wasn't the only one being difficult. Bixei sank to the canvas floor beside Stipes' pallet and added Master Den to his list of things to worry about. Llesho was already on it.

"And now to dress you." Master Den drew Llesho away to the laundry wagon, piled on one side with trunks of cloths for repairing tents and for bandages, and on the other with chests Llesho had noticed only in passing. Master Den fussed with the chests until the four companions joined them. Bixei had found Kaydu in her human form, and had brought her along as well.

From one of the chests, Master Den drew Thebin breeches and embroidered shirts and caps.

"Where did you get this?" Lling squealed with delight as she put on the proper uniform of a past age, when the people of the high plateau had been ruthless warriors, before the goddess had come down from heaven to favor the Thebin kings. Hmishi was just as pleased with his uniform, but showed it only with a quick duck of his head to hide his smile. None of them expected an answer. Kaydu wore the uniform of her father's army. Bixei considered his companions thoughtfully, and then asked, "Do you have a uniform like Master Jaks'? I know I can never be as good as he was, but he should be represented, don't you think?"

Master Den smiled. "Yes, he should. And it would not surprise me if someday the student surpasses the teacher." With that he brought out leathers and the beaten brass wrist guards, the match of those Master Jaks used to wear. When he added a cloak, Llesho experienced a little shiver of recognition. In his features Bixei looked more like Master Markko than he did the dead weaponsmaster. In the dress of the mercenary assassin, however, he took on the watchful carriage of the guards who had died for him when he was a child and he would have snatched the cloak away as a bad omen. But Master Den looked at Bixei with pride, and Llesho knew he had to do the same. This was the truth of Bixei, as the embroidered shirts had become the truth of Lling and Hmishi. These three existed to protect him. He could only serve them by making their sacrifices worthwhile.

While Llesho was admiring his companions, Master Den had unearthed a chest covered in leather and bound with brass. From the silk-lined interior he drew a shirt and breeches like his Thebin guards wore, but of a finer fabric. Llesho stripped off the trainee's uniform he had been given in the governor's compound at Farshore; he felt as though he were shedding a false skin with it, reclaiming Thebin with the fine woolen shirt and breeches. Next Master Den pulled out a pair of soft boots encrusted at heel and toe with gold filigree that gleamed with a polished sheen in the sunlight, and a sleeveless Thebin coat embroidered in gold-and-crimson thread crossed with blue silk. Llesho pulled on the boots and slipped his arms through the slashed openings at each side of the coat, settling the shoulders with a familiar shrug.

"Now you look like a fine young prince of the High Mountains," Den assured him with a pleased look. The last item, a heavy leather belt, he wrapped around Llesho's waist with a satisfied nod. They were far from Thebin, however, and Llesho could think of no way that Master Den would have acquired the court dress of a prince of just Llesho's size on Pearl Island.

"Where did you get these?"

Master Den shook his head. "All in good time." He led them back through the line of tents, Lling at the left side of the prince and Hmishi at his right, with Kaydu and Bixei following behind.

Soldiers who had paid them no notice when they had passed on their way back to the launderer's wagon now stopped their mending or their gossip as they passed. Llesho tilted his chin up, refusing to show the nerves that were twisting his gut. A suit of clothes might convince the soldiers of the line, but alone it was not likely to impress the emperor's representative. He'd have to act like a prince as well.

Llesho didn't remember much from the part of his life he'd lived in his father's court. He did know, however, that before state appearances, the Master of Protocol had always taken him aside and explained what was expected of him. And his brothers, whichever of them was home at the time, would watch him to make certain he did not shame himself or the court. Yet here he was heading into the most important appearance of his young life—based on this meeting, he might gain the help of the emperor for his cause, or find himself clapped in chains and sold again in the marketplace—and there was no protocol officer in sight.

"What is it, boy?"

Llesho took a deep breath and let it go in a long, expressive sigh. Was his terror so obvious that his teacher could read it in his face without a word spoken? He didn't know what Master Den could do, but Llesho took the question as an invitation to unburden himself of some of his fears. "I don't know what to do." He did not add, "I don't know why you are doing this, or what Habiba—or her ladyship—hopes to gain by espousing the cause of a long deposed prince."

Master Den clapped him on the shoulder with a snort of laughter. "You forget, Llesho, I've seen you when you feel threatened. You are more haughty at those times than the emperor himself. Even dressed in rags you carry yourself like a prince. So be the prince you are. Beyond that, speak as little as you can; let them wonder. You can manage that, can't you?"

"I. Yes." Head up. Meet the challenge with a level gaze that judged everything and apologized for nothing. And trust no one.

It was Den's turn to sigh now. He dropped a heavy hand on Llesho's shoulder. "Your father would be proud of you."

"Thank you, Master." Llesho bowed his head, hiding the shine of tears in his eyes. His father was gone, and he didn't know how Master Den could have known him, or how the teacher could choose the one compliment that could bow him low with his grief while at the same time instilling a greater determination to do justice to his father and the line of Thebin kings. For Thebin, Llesho knew, he could do much.

They had reached the command tent; Habiba's guards came to attention when they announced Llesho and his party. Habiba waited for them inside the tent. The maps had been stowed, the dishes of food taken away. A simple wooden box now sat alone on the table.

"Prince Llesho. I have something that belongs to you. Her ladyship bid me return it to you, should the opportunity present itself." Habiba stroked the wood of the box on the camp table. The witch had never called Llesho by his title before, and he did so now with no hint of a smile.

Once you bought me fresh from the arena, a shop-worn prince for small change in that marketplace, Llesho thought, but did not say aloud. He did, however, returned the solemn bow.

Habiba opened the box. From it he drew a silver coronet, which he offered to the prince between outstretched palms.

"Where did you get that?" Llesho asked, surprised at how much it hurt to look at the slender circle of precious metal. Not quite a crown, nevertheless it signaled to any who saw it that the wearer was of royal blood. He'd worn one like it on his small head during the most solemn court occasions before the Harn had come. It was too big to have been his own as that child; it must have belonged to one of his brothers.

"Her ladyship obtained it from a Harn trader," Habiba answered. "I did not ask her why, or question her decision to return it to one who had the right to wear it."

She had always known, from that first day in the weapons room at Pearl Island. She had suspected even earlier, though Llesho didn't know how long he had lain in bondage while the governor of Farshore and his lady knew him for a wronged prince. He could not decide whether he was grateful that they hadn't murdered him as a gift to the conquerors, or angry because they had left him to suffer under Markko's hand for so long.

"If I may?" Habiba lifted the coronet over his head,

and Llesho bowed his acceptance. Habiba lowered his hands and set the coronet on Llesho's head. The weight of it settled over Llesho like a benediction, and he felt his fate shift beneath his feet. The sensation struck with such force that it made him dizzy, and he might have fallen had Lling not reached out a hand to steady him.

"Are you all right, my prince?" she asked.

He nodded, and realized that Master Den had the right of it. He *was* a prince, and Llesho had only to be himself to prove it. He found himself whispering a prayer to the goddess, that she might find him worthy in her eyes.

"To horse, Your Highness?" Habiba urged them all. "Ambassador Huang awaits."

"It's time," Llesho agreed. He had much to fear from the coming meeting, but none of it would be what he expected. Whatever happened, however, he would greet it with the dignity of a prince.

PART FOUR

SHAN

Chapter Twenty-nine

HABIBA'S sergeant at arms would have put Llesho on a war steed taller at the shoulder than Llesho's head, but he refused, choosing instead the short and sturdy horse, so like the beasts native to Thebin, that had carried him from Farshore. His guard had likewise rejected the more impressive mounts for their old companions of the trail. Like warriors stepping through a crack in time, they stood at the right hand of the magician, Habiba.

Master Den complained about mounting any horse at all, but was finally persuaded onto the back of a fat and complacent mare who took his weight with a single snort of indignation before sidling up to Habiba's left. The honor guard, twenty of Habiba's soldiers in the livery of her ladyship and Farshore Province, fell in behind the leaders.

"An auspicious number to honor a visiting prince," Habiba explained to Llesho, "but not so many that Ambassador Huang HoLun might consider our purpose a threat."

That was certainly true. Habiba's scouts had reported that the emperor's guard, a force in excess of five thousand men, waited in readiness not more than a li distant, camped in a wheat field left fallow for the season. The witch had accepted the information with a little shrug. "We are seeking the Celestial Emperor's help, not contesting his rule in his own province. If he decides against her ladyship's petition, we have lost before we have begun."

The thought did little to comfort Llesho.

The party of petitioners crossed the field on which their own army camped. Too soon, the forest that marked the boundary between Thousand Lakes and Shan Province was before them. Two by two, the party entered the wood, following a narrow but well-marked path that wound between tall trees whose thick branches blotted out the sun. Llesho shivered as his horse stepped into the shadows. The forest was too still, and he wondered what had startled the birds and crickets into silence. Perhaps the emperor's ambassador had decided to resolve the puzzle of a deposed prince with an anonymous arrow from behind a tree or from hiding in the brush that crowded close against the path.

Kaydu rode ahead with Bixei to scout the way, and Habiba followed, riding at Llesho's side, offering themselves unprotected at the head of the party as a sign of trust and good will. Llesho recognized the message his own place in the order of march sent the ambassador waiting up ahead. Habiba recognized Llesho's rank as superior to his own and equal to the lady's in whose name he traveled. Her ladyship's witch did not speak, but watched the forest to right and to left with dark and vigilant eyes. Llesho found himself darting quick glances to either side as well, wondering whether Markko had survived the recent battle unscathed, and where he had gone to regroup his forces. Master Den rode after them, alone, with Lling and Hmishi behind. The twenty men of Habiba's guard followed last.

Llesho held himself a little straighter. The short

spear her ladyship had returned to him remained hidden in his pack, but he displayed his Thebin sword in its saddle scabbard near his knee. Habiba had said nothing about the knife he carried beneath his shirt. To Llesho, the Thebin knife even more than the coronet signaled his rank. So he reached under his collar for the cord around his neck and removed it, clasping the scabbard to the belt that wrapped his Thebin coat. *Now* he felt like a prince of the House of Thebin, beloved of the goddess and successor to his father's throne. Without giving it any thought, his head came up, and the hesitation cleared from his eyes.

"Your Highness," Habiba addressed him with a smile. "I am happy to see that you have joined us at last."

Llesho responded with a level, almost threatening stare. "I know what they think of us in Shan. To them, we are barbarians, seduced by the riches of the West and brought to our downfall because we grew weaker than our savage neighbors."

Habiba looked surprised at Llesho's description of how imperial eyes must see Thebin. He was about to be more surprised.

"They're wrong," Llesho finished. "We are barbarians, perhaps, but captivity has made us stronger."

"Thebin was once known for its cunning." Habiba seemed to approve.

"I know nothing of that," Llesho answered with a sardonic twist to the words.

"I'm sure you don't."

They had reached the edge of the forest, and Habiba gave his attention to the open field before them. Llesho did the same. Waves of low grasses filled in the faint reminders of plowed rows. Now, however, the fallow ground sprouted silk pavilions like bright yellow mushrooms in the sunshine. Three men on horseback waited for them at the side of the forest trail. The central figure, dressed in the heavy coat of an imperial marshal at arms, moved forward to greet them. His two attendants, in the uniforms of the imperial horse battalion, waited with their hands on the hilts of their swords.

"Huang HoLun, Ambassador of the Celestial Emperor the Great God of Shan, sends his greetings to Habiba, servant of her ladyship of Farshore Province," the marshal pronounced, "and bids him come forward to offer tribute and receive the blessings of the emperor's house upon him." He said nothing of Llesho, but his eyes did not leave the Thebin prince until Habiba drew his sword in the ritual of allegiance.

First Habiba kissed the blade. Then, reversing his hold on the weapon, he extended the hilt to the emperor's marshal. "Her ladyship extends her worshipful prayer that the emperor's ambassador will accept her humble servant as his own, and lend an ear to her piteous plea. The emperor's governor of Farshore Province lies murdered, his state and all his holdings seized by enemies who press even now to lay waste to her father's realm."

"Ambassador Huang will speak to you on these and other matters," the marshal agreed. He did not add any kind wishes of the ambassador's that might have assured them of a favorable hearing, but turned his horse and, with a last backward glance at Llesho, headed for the largest of the bright yellow tents waiting for them on a small rise in the field.

"He knows who I am, but he didn't say anything about me being here," Llesho frowned after the departing marshal, wondering what he was to make of the greeting that ignored him officially while giving him all the attention of the man's stare.

"He knows who you *say* you are, surely," Habiba corrected him. He kicked his horse into motion, setting his small party to follow the marshal before adding, "Your dress and your bearing have made that clear. And he showed great interest in you, but no surprise."

"You're not the only one with spies," Llesho suggested.

"No, I'm not." Habiba narrowed his eyes, as if he could see through the yellow silk and into the heart of the delegate. He hadn't expected so guarded a reception, and Llesho didn't like the idea that something had taken the witch by surprise. After a moment of tense thought, Habiba shifted into a waiting mode with a little shrug. "We will know soon enough what the ambassador makes of us."

There was something brewing beneath Habiba's impassive exterior. Llesho couldn't figure out exactly what it was, but he figured that, if the witch was suspicious, he was well advised to stay on the defensive. He let his hand drift to the hilt of his knife.

"Five thousand to our twenty." Habiba did not turn to look at him, but offered the reminder as if to the wind. Llesho took the hint—a dead prince was no use to his people—and let his hand drop once again to the reins. It was as well that he did so, for they had arrived in front of the yellow silk tent, and soldiers poured out on every side to surround them. Llesho slid from his saddle, leaving his sword where it lay. When one of the imperial guard would have taken his knife, however, he reached it faster, not unsheathing it, but holding it tight to his side with the flat of his open hand.

"It is a symbol of rank," Habiba explained, and the soldiers backed off, letting one of authority among them come forward.

"No one may approach the emperor's ambassador while armed," the sergeant of the guard instructed.

Habiba waved a careless hand. "He is but a boy, the knife a mere trinket, but important as a symbol. You understand?" he lied.

The sergeant turned to examine the Thebin prince, who looked younger than he was because of his short stature. Llesho smiled back at the sergeant with his most vacuous grin. *I'm harmless,* he thought at the man.

Quick as a striking snake, the sergeant made a grab for Llesho's throat. Just as quickly, Llesho had the knife out. If the sergeant had not anticipated the move, he would have been dead, but he clasped Llesho's wrist in both of his hands and managed to stop the knife with just the tip bloodied. The wounded soldier exerted pressure on the nerves that ran close to the surface of Llesho's knobby wristbone, but the knife did not fall. "Give." the soldier said. "Give!"

They stayed like that, frozen for an endless second, until Llesho's eyes cleared, and he realized that he was standing in the center of a shocked and silent circle, his hand still wrapped around his knife, while a bleeding soldier clung to his wrist as if his life depended on it. Slowly, Llesho realized that it probably did.

"I'm sorry," he whispered, horrified at what he had done. But he did not drop the knife, even now that he was aware of the painful pressure the sergeant was exerting on the nerves in his wrist.

"Please let me go!" he cried. "I'm not going to hurt you."

The sergeant snorted indignantly. "Let go of the knife first, then we'll see."

Llesho stared with growing horror from the knife in his frozen hand to the sergeant. "I can't," he said.

The soldier frowned, and glanced away to call for aid from the men who surrounded them. Habiba stepped forward, however, with both hands out to show that he carried no weapon.

Moving slowly so that he startled neither Llesho nor the tense guards who awaited only the command of their sergeant to cut down the Thebin prince, he slipped one hand over that of the soldier holding Llesho's wrist. "Let go, very slowly." He pinned the man with a hypnotic stare, and the soldier's hand relaxed. Llesho pulled away, but he could not escape Habiba's hold, which had replaced that of the damaged soldier.

"Now, give me the knife, Llesho. You can trust me . . ." Gradually, Llesho felt the soft, low words lulling him into a warm sense of security. Relieved, he turned his bloodied palm up, offering the knife. With no outward show of urgency Habiba took it.

"I hope that whatever you learned was worth the cost," he said to the sergeant, holding the knife out to him. The sergeant looked from the witch to Llesho and back again, his face set in hard lines. He didn't have to say anything. It was obvious to everyone who had seen it that the man had learned exactly what he wanted to know from the exercise, and that he treated that knowledge with deadly seriousness.

"I truly am sorry." Llesho sighed, certain that they had just lost something more important than his Thebin knife, but not sure what it could be. They *wanted* the ambassador to believe that Llesho was a true prince of Thebin. If the sergeant knew enough about the raising of young princes on the high plateau to test him with the knife, he had only learned what they wanted the emperor to know anyway.

Whatever it was, Habiba had his "making the best of a plan gone awry" face on when he held out a cloth to the bleeding sergeant. "Bind that up; you are dripping on your uniform," he said when the sergeant had thrust Llesho's knife into his own belt. "And watch that blade—it's sharp."

The sergeant gave him a dark look, but accepted the cloth. When he had wrapped it around the wound in his arm, he directed his soldiers to surround Habiba's party.

"Hold their guards here," he ordered the greater

number of his men, and marked out half a dozen to accompany Llesho and Habiba. "These two, come with me."

"These three." Master Den gave the sergeant a respectful bow marred only by the quirk of an eyebrow.

The sergeant laughed. "Master Den! Ill met as always! I should have realized you would be a part of this!"

"Not by choice, my lad, not by choice." Master Den shook his head mournfully, but he was smiling as he did so. "I'll keep an eye on things for you."

"Go," the sergeant concluded. "Before I change my mind and have you clapped in chains for the last time we met."

"A man shouldn't wager what he can't afford to lose," Den suggested with another deep rumble of a laugh. He fell in next to Llesho before the sergeant could respond.

When the imperial guard had the party sorted out, the sergeant held aside the tent flap and announced their arrival to the house guards standing at attention just inside. The first gave a deep bow and scurried away. He quickly returned, and gave the newcomers low and humble bows before gesturing for them to come forward.

The ambassador was a tall man, so old that his thin gray mustache hung down almost to his belt, and so slender that one could almost count the bones in his upraised hand. He had a mean and narrow face that gave him the look of a miser in spite of the sumptuous robes of rustling silk he wore. Llesho felt his heart sink as he took in the measure of Huang HoLun. *He will not help us,* he thought. *This Ambassador Huang will send us away with our story unheard, and the emperor will learn nothing of our plight.*

If his first examination of the ambassador sank his hopes in his chest, he soon had greater cause for fear.

"That is the boy. He belongs to Farshore Province.

And Farshore belongs to me." Master Markko stepped out from behind the ambassador's chair and rested a triumphant smile first on Habiba and then on Llesho. He did not seem to look at Master Den at all, but his next words proved that he had recognized the third man: "As for this one, I did not know that it was customary for the emperor's ambassador to meet with washermen, but I can save you the trouble with this one. He belongs to Pearl Island which, as we all know, belongs to me by right of Lord Yueh's last wishes."

"I see no washerman," Ambassador Huang answered in a high, testy voice. "These two are unknown to me, although you do not contest that they are who they say they are—"

"I contest not who, but what they are, Master," Markko pointed out the fine shading of difference between his own position and that of the ambassador.

"Yes, yes, but you have accused neither of washing laundry, I presume?"

Llesho would have volunteered that he had, in fact, washed laundry, but held his tongue. Master Markko seemed unhappy with the direction of the ambassador's discussion, which suited Llesho just fine.

"Then you can only mean Master Den," the delegate continued. "And Master Den is well known to me as the general who led the house guards of our present emperor's father. Master Den's strategy for the defense of Shan's borders against the Harn have protected the emperor and his people lo these many years, even as the Harn prey upon our trade routes to the south."

"You have been duped," Master Markko insisted, "by this man, who, until Lord Chin-shi's recent demise, washed the linen for Pearl Island's stable of gladiators, of which the boy here was a member in training. Both belong, by right, to me!"

"I know nothing of the boy," Huang agreed, though

his black eyes glittered when he said it, "but I believe I am correct about Master Den. I am not likely to have forgotten my old teacher, even after so many years."

"But . . . But . . ." Markko spluttered. "He cannot be the same man, he is too young!"

Ambassador Huang turned a bland stare on the traitor. "I am convinced that, having made a mistake in respect to the identity of one of my guests, you may have made equally serious errors about the others. By no deliberate fault of your own, of course, Master Markko. As it is, I find myself at a loss to make a judgment that will so profoundly affect so many who consider themselves under the protection of the Celestial Emperor."

Llesho flinched at the loathing in Markko's eyes. The old ambassador seemed not at all aware of the seething hatred directed at him. "Disagreements are so tiring!" Ambassador Huang complained petulantly. "I believe I must take a nap."

Master Den beamed complacently at the yawning delegate, looking as doltish as Huang HoLun himself. "I think we could all use a nap," he agreed cheerfully.

Shocked at his teacher's apparent loss of sanity, Llesho nevertheless succumbed to his mentor's suggestion. Try as he might, he could not stifle the gaping yawn that almost unhinged his jaw.

Ambassador Huang's black eyes twinkled at him. The old man might not be the doddering fool that he wished to appear, but Llesho did not let himself forget the cold-eyed calculation that had greeted them. Huang played his stones with apparent carelessness, but strategy informed every move.

"We should all rest now." The ambassador rose from his chair while pronouncing his plan. "This evening, we shall all of us return to Shan together. By sedan-post, we may arrive before midnight on the second day of travel, and then we may leave the matter in the hands of the emperor and his advisers."

Markko accepted Master Huang's decision with a bowed head, but Llesho saw that the magician's eyes burned with frustration before he lidded them to hide his anger.

"And now, Master Den, come. See me to my bed. We have much to talk about, many lifetimes to catch up on!"

The ambassador spoke as if in jest, and Master Den laughed as he offered his arm to the old man. But Llesho could not help thinking that the joke was on the rest of them. He wondered, not for the first time, exactly who Master Den was.

Chapter Thirty

LLESHO trusted his horse not to drop him, but put no equal faith in the arms and running feet of men like himself. He had never journeyed by litter, and the thought of doing so made him uneasy. The litters were designed for the comfort and reassurance of the travelers who made use of them, but on Llesho they had the opposite effect. Polished wood suitable for the finest furniture made up the pallet base, with low rails on all sides to protect the passengers from falling out onto the road. Brightly colored silk curtains hung from a sturdy frame suspended above graceful carved posts at each corner, preserving the privacy of the travelers within. On both sides, long carrying poles extended several paces beyond the front and back of the wooden floor. Llesho figured that, with the furnishings, it had to weigh more than his horse.

A dozen bearers stood in position next to the carrying poles of each litter while the ambassador's protocol officer sorted out their company. The ambassador entered the largest and most sumptuous litter. He insisted that Master Den accompany him so that they could catch up on court gossip, which sent his protocol officer into scandalized fits of temper. As the emissary of her ladyship and her father, both of whom had rights of provincial governorship by appointment and marriage, Habiba had precedence over Master Markko, who petitioned the emperor in his own right as regent for the dead usurper, Lord Yueh. If he wished to offer his protection on the road to Llesho, however, Habiba must cede his right by protocol, and accept the lesser station afforded the pretender to the Thebin throne. Llesho would be situated last in the order of travel to signify that the emperor had not yet acknowledged Llesho's status.

Finally, all parties agreed upon the order of march: Master Markko would follow the ambassador's litter in solitary dignity, and Llesho would bring up the rear, with Habiba as his traveling companion. Imperial foot soldiers would accompany them. Like the litter bearers, they would pass off their duty to fresh soldiers waiting at the relay points. The party's own guards would come after them on horseback.

"It's not safe," Bixei had insisted when he heard that they would be left to follow at a slower pace. They had gathered in the tent set aside for them by the ambassador.

"I can't believe you would go anywhere with Markko, let alone that you would leave your own guard behind when you did it. How do you know you can trust this Huang fellow?"

"He's the emperor's ambassador," Kaydu reminded them, but Lling shared Bixei's fear.

"The emperor did nothing when the Harn came," she reminded them. "For all we know, he may be in league with the raiders and wants only to see you dead!"

"My father would never let that happen!" Kaydu looked ready to strike.

Llesho stopped them with an upraised hand. "For good or ill, we are now in Shan Province, the very heart of the empire. If the emperor wishes us dead, he doesn't have to drag us all the way to the imperial city to kill us—he could have me murdered by any one of five thousand of his soldiers in this camp while I stand here talking to you. You might be able to avenge yourself on a soldier loyal to his duty before his comrades killed you all, but we'd still be dead. And the emperor would still be on his throne in his palace."

"So we leave you in the hands of strangers and hope for the best?" Bixei asked, not believing what he heard.

"I think," Llesho said, and paused, because he was puzzling it through as he spoke. "I think that her ladyship and Master Den—Master Jaks, too—wanted this all along, and Markko wanted us not to reach the emperor at all. I have to figure that those who want me here will keep me alive, at least until I find out why they thought it was so important."

"I think you're right," Kaydu agreed. "For whatever reasons, my father is determined to see you safely into the hands of the emperor. And he'll be sharing your litter. No one would dare to attack you while you are under his protection."

"Master Markko already has."

"We were not in the emperor's own province then," Llesho reminded the young gladiator, "and the emperor had not turned his head in our direction. We are now on imperial time."

Bixei muttered a grudging agreement, but added, "If you do run into trouble, we will be right behind you."

"I know it." Llesho gave each a handclasp to seal their friendship. They said nothing more, but accompanied him to his litter in silence, and stood by while he pushed his head past the silk curtains that swathed his litter.

There he stopped, frozen in amazement. "It will

never get off the ground," he swore. The inside of the litter was even richer than the outside! Thick down cushions covered in patterned silk lay scattered in heaps over the wooden flooring. In one corner a fat stand held a tall pipe bound about with brass and silver. Perfumed water already bubbled in its base, and the sweet grasses in its bowl sparked red before releasing fragrant smoke into the air. A basket of dainty tidbits for the road rested in the center of the litter, between two mounds of cushions for the riders.

"Of course it will." Habiba's voice behind him reminded Llesho that they had no time for gawking. Feeling inadequate to the luxury around him, he clambered inside. Habiba followed.

"Very nice," the witch approved, and began arranging his pillows into an impromptu nest.

Llesho did the same, and had barely settled himself before the litter began to pitch and rise. Llesho grabbed for the closest rail and held on tightly until the poles supporting the litter settled on the shoulders of the bearers. Habiba seemed untroubled by the jostling. He began to pick at the basket between them.

"Have something to eat," he said. "Even by post relay it will be a long trip."

Llesho considered the basket in front of him and shook his head, far too nervous to eat anything. "I'm not hungry."

When he'd started on his journey from the pearl beds, the empire was just another obstacle between himself and his goal: a map upon which he would find his brothers widely scattered but alive. In secret he would gather them around him, and in secret they would return to Thebin and somehow take their home back from the Harn. He hadn't considered how he would do that without an army or claim to his own name, and he certainly hadn't counted on setting the great empire of Shan on its ear as he passed through it. But sitting in imperial luxury, approaching the imperial city, with allies and enemies at either hand, it was all becoming too real.

As it often did when his quest began to overwhelm him, Lleck's pearl throbbed in his mouth like a bad tooth. On his road to Thebin Llesho had acquired gifts as well as allies—gifts that were supposed to mean something to him. The pearl, the spear, the cup all gave him feelings he should have been able to identify but which remained stubbornly out of reach. His knife, though, he could understand. And he didn't like what he knew. He was a trained killer, had killed even as a child. No wonder the goddess had not come to him! He thought, perhaps, he could not succeed without Her help, and would have wept for his captive country, with only an abandoned boy to care about the misery of his people.

Habiba frowned thoughtfully at Llesho as he chewed on a bit of fruit. Perhaps he knew what desperate thoughts passed through his head, but chose instead to remark upon the more obvious cause of Llesho's distress with a conclusion that seemed to amuse him.

"Thebin has a reputation for the riches its trade routes with the West brought. Surely you were accustomed to greater luxuries than this in the palace at Kungol." He waved a hand with a half-eaten peach in it to signify their surroundings.

"Not really." Llesho considered the silk appointments of the litter with the eyes of his younger self. By Thebin standards, it was overdone: too much surface glamour, but the richness of the cushions did little to muffle the jolt of the runners' feet. The motion passed up through the poles and bounced the litter like a skiff in a stormy sea. Llesho realized that in spite of the luxury that cradled him, the motion was making him sick.

Talking distracted him from his growing nausea,

however, so he let his mind wander back to his early home.

"Kungol lies just below the snow line," he explained. "Just below the point on the mountains where the snow never melts. It is cool all the time, and it can sometimes snow during the night even at high summer. Thick woolen rugs hang on the walls of the palace, and in winter rugs even cover the windows, to hold in the warmth. I had a goose down comforter covered in Shan silk when I was small, but everything else in my room was wool or leather." He shrugged. "The things that seemed most precious and rare in Thebin—wood is so scarce that we only use it for decoration and a few bits of furniture—are common to Shan. The things of their own country that Thebins value, like jade and amber, copper and bronze, we trade very little, and so they have the value of rarity in your world but lack the meaning they hold in mine. And I have heard what lowlanders think of Thebin dress—" He looked down at his own gaudy coat with a weary smile, knowing and sad. "Our cloth is too rough, our embroidery too garish, the cut of our garments barbaric."

"I take it that means no, you are not acquainted with such luxurious surroundings." Habiba grinned at him, a slash of sharp white teeth cutting through his whiskers like a secret spoken in the dark.

Llesho grinned back, aware of the lesson he had just taught himself. "It means that to a Thebin, this is not luxury at all," he answered. It wasn't true, exactly. All of the silk traded in the West passed through Kungol, and the Thebin people were certainly familiar with its worth. But they didn't covet such overnice luxuries as others did.

"Remember that when you meet with the emperor," Habiba said, and this time Llesho couldn't tell where his amusement was directed. He was about to ask when the bearers slowed their pace. Llesho heard tramping feet coming toward them—attack! His conversation with Habiba suddenly forgotten, he cursed himself for having left his bow and arrows in the camp. Ambassador Huang's guards had returned his knife for the journey, however; Llesho reached for it under his coat.

Habiba did not appear distressed. The witch finished his peach and threw the pit onto the road, and then took hold of the low railing that ran around the sides of the litter.

"We are about to change bearers; make sure you are secure."

Llesho gave him a wary look, but followed his example and reached for the railing instead of his knife. He did so just in time.

The newcomers had lined themselves up parallel with the litter and were beginning to match the slowed pace of the bearers. Suddenly, the litter pitched and tilted, bounced and jolted. "What are they doing!" Llesho wanted to know.

"We have reached the first relay station," Habiba explained. "The bearers we came with are trading places with the bearers who have been waiting at this outpost." The witch rolled with the uneven motion. He didn't look sick; he didn't even look uncomfortable. Llesho wished he could say the same.

"As we approach the city of Shan, the relay posts come closer together, so we should make very good time in our journey," Habiba finished his explanation and reached for a pear.

"How much farther do we have to go?" Llesho asked. At the moment, the length of their journey was the most urgent thing he could think about—that and the rolling pitch of the litter that carried them. He felt the color drain from his face.

"I'm going to be sick," he whispered.

Habiba threw down the pear. He reached for the water pipe and tossed it out onto the road as he had the peach pit, and then tucked the bucket-shaped base under Llesho's chin.

"Master Huang has shown you a great honor by putting the post relay system at our disposal," he chided while holding the bucket. "Only the most important officials on the most urgent business of the empire may command such travel. Is this any way to repay his kindness?"

"I would gladly decline the honor and ride to Shan on horseback," Llesho offered. His gut swung queasily in its own direction, completely at odds with the beat of the running feet that jolted the litter.

"But Master Huang could not ride so far, nor could Master Den," Habiba reminded him. "And we would have to leave our horses on the road in trade for fresh ones that we did not know as well, just as we have done with the bearers."

All true, Llesho supposed. But they had only a few li behind them. If Habiba were correct, most of the journey remained ahead, and already Llesho wished himself dead. He leaned over the bucket and was thoroughly sick.

When he had finished, Habiba handed him a silk handkerchief with a smile. "It is the simplest I have about me," he offered in a mild joke about the riches of empire. "Are you feeling any better?"

"Nooooo," Llesho moaned, and was violently ill once again. When he was through, he fell back on his cushions with a woeful sigh. "What is the point of all this haste if I wish I were dead already?"

Habiba shook his head. "The point? Why, putting you in front of the emperor as a live supplicant rather than as a dead pretender, I suppose. Or did you look forward to Markko plotting your demise at his leisure?"

"Do you think he'd kill me now if I asked nicely?" Llesho perked up. The possibility almost gave him hope.

Habiba gave him an exasperated sigh. With a finger tucked under Llesho's chin, the witch lifted the prince's head out of his bucket.

"How long have you felt sick?" Habiba asked him.

"Since we started out." Llesho wanted to ask how the witch managed to cope with the motion, but to think the words was to remind himself of how he felt, and that only made it worse.

Habiba frowned at him. "I could probably make you up a potion if we had an hour or two, and a fire." He considered Llesho for a long moment. "But we cannot spare the time.

"Look at me, Llesho."

Llesho looked, and flinched at the change that came over the witch. Habiba's eyes were wide and fixed; the irises almost vanished while the pupils grew to fill all the space with darkness. He closed his own eyes, but that only made the sickness worse.

Habiba gave him a sharp tap on the chin with one finger.

"You are not a prince yet, my fine young gladiator," Habiba snapped with more humor in his voice than the words merited. "Now do as you are told."

"What are you going to do?" Llesho asked in a whisper.

"Nothing to hurt you. Not after all the trouble I've had getting you this far! Now look at me!"

Llesho looked.

"It is night, very dark, and you are in your own bed in the palace at Kungol. There are no raiders; your guard stands watch at your door to keep you safe. Your bed is warm, the breeze through the open window brings the scent of snow off the mountains, and below, in the city, the bleat of camels and the bark of dogs fill the night with their music."

Llesho knew that none of it was real, but in spite of himself he felt his shoulders relaxing, his head growing heavier, his eyes closing . . .

"You are safe, you are comfortable, and you are so sleepy. You cannot stay awake any longer . . ."

When Llesho awoke, the litter had come to a halt, and beyond the tent curtains he heard the harsh calls of servants sorting themselves and locating their charges, From the hollow echo and the clack of wooden-soled sandals against paving tiles, he guessed they stood in a walled courtyard somewhere, but he didn't know how far they had come or why they had stopped.

"Where are we?" he asked groggily, but Habiba was not there.

"Come, come!" One of the servants pushed his head between the curtains and gestured for Llesho to follow.

Llesho shook his head. "Where are we?" he asked again.

The servant disappeared, muttering something about crazy Thebins, but he was soon replaced by Master Den.

"What are you still doing in there, boy? You can't see the emperor looking like that!"

Llesho paled in dismay, but climbed out of his litter as Den demanded. "Has the emperor come to meet us on the road?"

"We're not on the road, Llesho. This is the inner courtyard of the Celestial Palace at Shan."

"It can't be!"

It certainly didn't look regal. They had come to rest in a large walled courtyard with a cobbled square and plastered walls that rose well above Den's head. It was dark, with not even a moon to brighten the square. The few torches carried by servants did little to light the space beyond the circle of the three official litters, but from what Llesho could see, the courtyard was empty except for themselves. There were no plants on the edges of the wall and Llesho could see no trees bending their branches over it as might be the fashion in Farshore Province. Of course, with no trees or vines to climb, a spy or saboteur would have a difficult time getting over the wall. Kungol Palace, he remembered, hadn't had a wall at all. Who, after all, would invade the privacy of the goddess' own beloved family? Llesho found himself looking at the courtyard wall in a friendlier light.

A stranger—no, not a stranger, but General Shou; Habiba had introduced him after the recent battle with Master Markko—interrupted his thoughts with a slap on the back. "Indeed, you've been on the road for two days," General Shou confirmed. "Did Habiba put you to sleep? He's a sly one. You have to watch him every minute!"

He figured the general meant it as a joke, because the man laughed and slapped him on the back again, but Llesho decided to take it as a real warning. After all, he had lost two days to the witch's spell. What if they'd been attacked? He could have died without a chance to defend himself.

"As for meeting the emperor in your present state, I wouldn't worry," General Shou added, "even emperors have to sleep.

"If you have time during your visit, I'd like a chance to talk with you about Thebin."

That was more seriously said, and Llesho's curiosity perked up. "Do you know Thebin?" he asked.

"I visited it once, long ago, with a caravan to the West," the general confirmed. "That was before my duties kept me closer to home."

Spying, no doubt, Llesho figured, and whatever he'd seen hadn't persuaded the Shan Empire to step in when the Harn raiders attacked. He found it a little more difficult to be polite after that, but fortunately, General Shou turned his attention to the others in the party.

"I am very glad to see you again, Master Den." He slapped the master on the arm—something Llesho had never expected to sec. "Very glad indeed." He left them with instructions to have a comfortable night, and entered the palace by a small door from which a steady stream of guards and visitors in various degrees of official dress seemed to enter and depart.

"Come on, boy," Master Den called to Llesho, and together they followed the servants through a more imposing public entrance. Habiba, Llesho noted, had disappeared, as had Ambassador Huang. Markko strode before them like a conquering hero; Llesho wished he had his bow and arrow handy, or barring that, a snowball. But it was not yet winter, and a servant led Markko away before Llesho could devise a more pertinent attack.

Chapter Thirty-one

MASTER Den nudging him with a strong hand between his shoulder blades, Llesho followed a servant into a vaulted entry hall bigger than the audience chamber at Kungol. In front of them a broad stairway of inlaid marquetry rose halfway to the carved and painted ceiling, where it opened into a gallery that ran the length of the entry hall. The staircase resumed at either end of the gallery, disappearing into passageways at opposite ends of the hall.

The servant stopped on the first landing and wordlessly directed them past a sliding panel into a long corridor, dark except for a few scattered lamps set into the smooth plastered walls. When it looked like they could go no farther without bumping into a blank wall at the end of the passage, the servant turned right and disappeared.

Llesho followed and found himself in a narrower, darker passage that curved in a long arc, so that he could not see more than a few feet ahead of him. He stopped, unwilling to follow any farther until he knew where they were going, and Master Den bumped into him.

"What if it's a trap?" Llesho whispered urgently.

"It's the back way to the private bedrooms," Master Den assured him, and added tartly, "Some of us didn't sleep the entire journey away and are anxious to get to our beds."

Llesho began moving again, but he wasn't much comforted. "Where are Habiba and Master Markko?" He figured that the ambassador had his own home to go to, but he didn't want to bump into Markko in a dark corridor.

"They've been taken to official guest quarters in another wing of the palace," Master Den informed him. "They don't know where the guards have taken us, and they don't have access to the private quarters from their own rooms."

Master Den clearly had some connection to the royal household that would merit a personal invitation, but Llesho wondered why he hadn't been sent off with the others. The washerman who, if one were to believe the ambassador, had once been an imperial general, seemed to read his mind. "Official quarters are for those who have an official claim upon the empire. Until the emperor decides what claim he is willing to acknowledge toward you, it is better that you remain a guest in an unofficial capacity."

"You will be watched, of course." Master Den laughed under his breath. "And keeping you close like this is bound to make Markko nervous."

Llesho wasn't certain he wanted the overseer nervous—Master Markko was bad enough when he thought he had the upper hand—but he said nothing. The narrow passageway ended in a door which the servant opened with a big iron key that groaned in the lock. He threw the door wide and ushered them into a lavishly decorated hall lit at every point by lanterns with soft gold shutters. Creamy light gleaming off of gilt carvings dazzled Llesho's eyes, and he blinked away tears until his vision had adjusted to the glow.

Master Den followed him out of the passage and

the servant closed the heavy red-lacquered door after them with another impatient gesture to hurry. He led them just a little way down the elegant hall to a recessed alcove flanked by stiff-backed Imperial Guards. Elaborate panels carved with fantastic animals lined the alcove. The servant pressed on the head of a carved dragon, and a gilt panel slid aside, revealing a bedroom larger than Lord Chin-shi's room on Pearl Island, and decorated with more riches as well.

Again, the servant gestured without words that Llesho should enter. Leaving him to his own devices with a brief bow, the servant slid the panel shut after him. Llesho heard two sets of footsteps move down the hall, then another door slid on its runner. Master Den was nearby at least.

Alone, Llesho had a choice of only two occupations: he could think, or he could explore. His bladder made that decision for him: explore. Quickly. He passed over the lacquered cabinets and the tall standing chest, and ignored the bed big enough to hold his entire squad without crowding them. The room was lavishly draped with silken wall hangings covering greased-paper windows, paneled walls almost as sumptuous as the hangings that covered them. Some of those panels had to be doors: he'd come through one which had blended back into the decorative gilt and carving so that he could no more find his way out again than he could find the other doors that must be present in the room. When he had begun to despair of ever finding what he needed, however, he discovered the secret of the moving panels, and behind them, the door leading to the correct chamber.

More comfortable after a brief visit to the personal room, he explored more systematically. Besides the panel by which he'd entered and the door he had just used, Llesho found only one other functioning exit, and that was locked and bolted from the other side. He noted that the mysterious door had no locking mechanism on his side, and the absence of his personal guards suddenly took on a more ominous meaning. Assassins could come through that door any time they wanted to kill him in his sleep. Good thing he wasn't tired.

On a second round of exploring his bedchamber, Llesho opened the chest and the cabinets, noted items of Thebin apparel and others in the style of the Shan Empire, all in his size. Laid out among the elegant decoration of the palace chamber, the contents of his pack rested on the shelves of the standing chest. Displayed lovingly, like the votive objects of a shrine, he found the ancient spear that her ladyship had given him and the jade cup. Touching them sent a chill down his spine. Someone had gone to a lot of trouble to make him comfortable, had even recognized the value of the objects in his pack as relics rather than the tools of a soldier. The care they had taken hardly seemed necessary if they planned to have him killed immediately. He decided to take that as a good sign.

Even in daylight he wouldn't be able to see through the greased paper windows, but he stopped for a moment in his explorations of his bedchamber, struck by the silence. He could hear nothing of the life of the empire's largest and most powerful city, and the contrast with his father's palace struck him like a dagger in the heart.

Even in the darkest hours of night Kungol had hummed with life—groaning camels and bleating lambs, drunken caravan drovers brawling in the street—like the pulse of a living creature whose health a king might measure by the beat of it as he slept. How could an emperor know his empire when he could not even hear the cries of his city? Why did Habiba and Master Den think that such an Emperor would stoop to help the deposed prince of a conquered land a thousand li to the west, when he gave so little notice to the life just paces from his celestial throne? He would receive no help here; Llesho threw himself on the bed, determined to make his own way at dawn.

But the bed was comfortable, and he had been on the march for a long time. Despite his determination, he fell asleep and awoke only when the smell of breakfast pulled him out of his dreams. A bustling servant poured out his tea and opened the lacquered chest with a thoughtful frown. When Llesho returned from relieving himself, he found that the servant had laid out a set of ornate robes suitable to an imperial official. Llesho glared at the clothing, which looked too complicated for him to manage on his own and too uncomfortable for him to want to manage. The servant had already gone, so he ignored the clothing and focused on his breakfast.

While he was still nibbling a cake full of cinnamon, nuts, and honey, a man he identified from his medallion of office as a protocol officer knocked on his door and entered without an invitation. After a minimal bow, to show Llesho how little respect he was owed, the protocol officer stiffly recited his message: "The emperor is otherwise engaged. You may petition for an audience, but he is very busy. If he finds the time to see you, you will have two or three minutes to state your case in a public audience, and none at all alone. Be prepared with an inscribed memorial laying out your case and the outcome for which you petition: the Celestial Emperor does not suffer fools to live."

Llesho was tempted to comment that the continued existence of the protocol officer proved otherwise, but he kept his mouth shut. *Don't attract attention,* he warned himself. When the official had gone, Llesho wiped his hands on the silk napkin and prepared to dress. He ignored the Shannish robes laid out for him, and dug in the chest for something less noticeable to wear. The Thebin day wear tempted him, but it would draw far too much attention here on the eastern edge of the trade routes. Instead, he pulled on a pair of plain breeches and a silk shirt with a minimum of decoration, and found a pair of shoes more suited to walking than either his Thebin boots or the fragile slippers the servant had chosen.

When he was dressed, he left his room. The guards at his door did not surprise him, but neither did they follow when he turned down the hall, nor did they stop him when he tried to slide open the panel to the next room down the corridor. He was disappointed but not surprised when it didn't open. About thirty paces farther on he came to a staircase more modest than the one he'd taken the night before. Descending cautiously, he found himself in a small, octagonal chamber with a doorway in each wall. Two imperial soldiers stood guard at rigid attention, but they made no move to stop Llesho when he opened the first door.

"Just exploring," he explained.

The soldiers said nothing, so he peeked inside and found a small room with a few scattered chairs bearing no decoration, and a table with a large urn of hot water, a teapot, and a scattering of cups on it. Two of the chairs were occupied by soldiers, apparently waiting for their turn at guard duty or coming off the shift before and warming themselves with some tea before moving on. They stared at him, and Llesho smiled uncomfortably.

"As you were," he said, and closed the door again.

The next door opened into another small room, this one more carefully furnished, but still with none of the richness one expected of an imperial palace. Llesho guessed that the officers of the guard might take their rest or give their orders here.

The third door led into a long dark passageway that plunged deep into the palace. At the far end, Llesho could just make out by the light of a single lamp an iron staircase spiraling up to the level from which he had just come, and leading down into what must be an underground passage or chamber. The passage left him with the vague impression of dried and crusted blood, though he had seen nothing to support the terror that he felt just thinking about it. He stored the location for later, but closed the door on the passage with as much speed as he could muster with any kind of dignity.

When he opened the fourth door, he actually smiled. Here was another passageway, but one with natural light filtering in from slots cut high overhead. The passage followed the line of the palace wall, and Llesho guessed that there might be a hidden exit at the end of it. The soldiers did not stop him, so he entered the passage and closed the door behind him, leaving it ajar just enough so it would not latch and lock him in if he did not find another way out.

He needn't have worried. The passage led him through what must have been the palace's east wall, because the morning sun fell like bars of gold across his path. After he had gone more than two hundred paces, the passage opened out into a rough chamber that ended in a tunnel cutting into the ground beneath the palace wall. From this tunnel Llesho felt no air of death or decay, and he followed it. He was surprised to discover lighted torches all along the way—for all its apparent secrecy, it must be a well used route, a shortcut of some kind. The tunnel branched. Llesho considered for a moment, before taking the path with fewer torches burning down its length.

He didn't know what he was looking for, but it didn't take him long to find it: a door with a large iron lock with the key still left in it. Clearly an invitation, but to what? Llesho turned the key and pushed open the door. Nothing he had ever seen before had prepared him for the scale and the magnificence of his surroundings. He was outside the palace, the pink sandstone wall at his back rising to more than twice his height. On his left, the wall joined to a temple of many levels with seven curved roofs ascending like a ladder to heaven. The marks of the seven gods the temple served appeared in red paint above the heavy lintel.

Of course, the Emperor was himself a god, so his palace must be the greatest temple in the imperial city. The practical nature of the Shan people was well known, however, and Llesho had heard jokes even on Pearl Island that in the imperial city money itself was worshiped as a god. He didn't quite believe it, but looking up at the symbols of the deities worshiped here in the shadow of the palace, he was shocked to discover how many of the beloved gods of Shan were bureaucrats and money counters. *The goddess,* he thought, *would not bend her gaze upon such a city.* But one might buy the freedom of a brother here, where even the gods were worshiped for pay.

On his right stretched a massive building also made of pink sandstone. The building bore no marking to indicate its purpose, but the wide stone steps in front of it were filled with thc bustle of official looking men and women in robes of state with elaborate buttons of office on their hats. The buildings, together with the palace wall, formed three sides of a square in which the paving stones had been arranged according to the zodiac, with many signs of good luck and blessings worked into their surfaces. Llesho thought that ten thousand soldiers might fit into that square with room to hold a corps of drummers as well.

He stood in the shadows under the wall, trying to decide what to do. The city was alien to him, oppressive and cold and large beyond the scale men could comprehend. The few people in the square seemed busy and important—more likely to call out the guard than assist him if he asked for directions. Llesho hesitated to step out into the sunlight at all for fear that someone would notice he didn't belong there and sound a warning.

Although there were far fewer people around the temple than gathered on the steps of the offices of state, they seemed more varied both in dress and in their looks; a Thebin might not seem so out of place on those steps. Staying in the shadows, he worked his way around the palace wall and across the front of the temple, not stepping into the light until he had ascended the temple steps. From there he allowed himself to survey the city, which faded into a jumble of roofs around a square of green. A garden. Llesho turned toward that spot of comfort with purpose in his stride.

The Imperial Water Garden was very beautiful, restful and green with just the occasional hint of weathered cedar where little bridges arched over ponds and man-made streams. A few scattered willows drew the eye upward, but most of the water-loving plants huddled closer to the ground. Cattails and swamp grasses, water lilies and lotus, gave texture to the garden but drew the eye earthward to contemplate the stillness of a pond here, the gentle ripple of a stream moving over artfully placed stones in their path. At the center of the garden, a natural spring fed a waterwheel that spilled over a tumble of rocks to create a splashing waterfall which, in turn, sped the streamlets through the park. Under the waterfall sat a small stone altar with the symbol of ChiChu, the god of laughter and tears marked on its side.

Llesho considered offering a petition to the god, but thought better of it. Of the seven mortal gods, only ChiChu had used trickery to gain a place in heaven. When the six had demanded their unworthy brother be cast out, the goddess had chastised them for pride, and set the trickster among them as a reminder of their humanity. ChiChu often granted the requests that came to him, but he was likely to do so in ways both unlooked for and unwelcome to the supplicant.

Llesho found a bench nearby and sat. The park was

peaceful, and it was easy to forget his worries when the gentle breeze shifted the grasses in hypnotic patterns. He found it difficult to reconcile this refuge with the trading of cash-filled envelopes for heavenly favors on the temple steps. What was this city, where human lives and the favors of tax collector gods might be bought and sold, where tiny altars to the Seven might be hidden among the reeds of a public garden? Who were these people, who worshiped an emperor, yet turned their backs when the favored of the goddess fell to the invading Harn?

A shadow falling over him shattered his reverie. Almost as if it had a will of its own, Llesho's hand reached for the knife hidden under his shirt.

"I thought I might find you here." General Shou moved around the bench so that Llesho could see him. He wore robes of brilliant blue beneath a red silk coat. A crane embroidered in gold thread on each sleeve and a cap with a button of office completed his dress. The sleeves of his coat gave fleeting glimpses of copper wrist guards on each arm, the only clue that Shou was more than the merchant he appeared to be. The general's face settled into the petulant lines of a harried trader. If he had not spoken before he showed himself, Llesho wasn't sure he would have recognized him at all.

"I didn't know you were looking for me."

"You promised to tell me about Thebin."

"Oh. Yes." Llesho didn't add that he'd dismissed the request as diplomatic small talk. Or that the general's real interest made Llesho more wary than the pretend kind. What did Shou want?

"This is my favorite place in the city." Shou put a small offering on the tiny altar and sat down, letting the conversation fade as he contemplated the waterfall. It could have been strategy, let his prey grow comfortable with his presence before pouncing again, but Llesho thought not. The smile seemed free of artifice, and quiet joy seemed to radiate from some hidden center that Shou did not often reveal. That made him all the more dangerous, Llesho figured. Apt that a general who traveled about the city in the garb of a merchant should honor the trickster god; Llesho took that as a warning.

"It reminds me of the governor's compound at Farshore Province," Llesho commented with a gesture to indicate the garden. Idle chat. He would stay clear of his own concerns.

General Shou nodded agreement. "Her ladyship did not want to leave her home, and so her husband, the governor, promised that she could take a part of Thousand Lakes Province with her. He built the compound to remind her of her home among the lakes. This park, too, is a piece of Thousand Lakes Province."

"I thought you were from Shan Province," Llesho prodded.

The general shrugged. "I was born here in the capital city. But I was fostered for many years at Thousand Lakes."

"Then it's a lucky coincidence that the city has a park you can visit to remember in."

"Not luck, really," General Shou corrected him. "As the center of the empire, Shan must love all her children equally, and so there are many parks, each in the style of one of her provinces."

"And what province do you represent with the slave pens?" Llesho watched the emotion freeze on the general's face, and wondered what he showed in his own eyes. He was terrified again, shaking with it, so small and thin that he thought he must surely be culled before the market opened, spoiled goods that no one would buy. The trader had wanted to slit his throat to save himself the few coppers it cost to feed him. He remembered listening while the overseer of the pens and the trader argued his fate—he was too sickly to sell to the perverts, and too old to sell to the beggars' guild, though his size might give him a few years of good begging before he was turned out there. If he survived the exposure and the abuse.

Almost crippled by the lingering echo of past terror, Llesho crumpled in on himself, clutching his gut. Hopeless children with empty bellies still passed through the slave pens of Shan. Llesho had been luckier than most. If Lord Chin-shi hadn't wanted Thebin children to train as divers, the trader would have killed him and fed him to the pigs. If he'd been prettier, or younger, he wouldn't have lived out the year.

He didn't cry—not with the sensations hitting him like hammer blows—but he couldn't breathe either. And he didn't know how he was going to find his brothers if the thought of the slave pens alone dropped him to his knees.

"Are you sick?" General Shou asked him, setting a comforting hand on his shoulder. "Do you need a healer?"

Llesho shook his head, wishing the general would leave him in peace to regain his composure, or at least move his hand, which was making it hard not to scream between his clenched teeth.

Shou did not move.

"None of us are brave all the time." He seemed to be offering comfort, but when Llesho looked at him, he realized that the general didn't remember he was there at all. Shou stared into the waterfall, lines of suffering etching themselves into his cheeks.

"We do well enough at the moment," he said to the trickling water. "It's easier, really, to do what we must than to decide even on a cowardly course of our own. But later, when it is all over, even hardened soldiers cry at night."

Llesho stared up at him in amazement. He was a general, vigorous and energetic and a respected leader in battle. Surely he did not . . .

General Shou gave him a wry smile. "Even the emperor sometimes must take the room with the thickest walls at night, so that he doesn't disturb the sleep of those with quieter dreams."

Llesho doubted that, but he thought it was kind of the general to say it. And he thought perhaps the general might understand his problem.

"I don't know how all this happened, you know? I was a pearl diver for nine years and never received so much as an extra banana at dinner. Then Lleck died, and he made me promise that I would find my brothers and take back our home." He didn't mention that Lleck had been a spirit at the time—didn't think it would do much for his credibility, and it didn't matter to the story anyway.

"I thought, if I became a gladiator, I could travel, maybe win enough money to buy my freedom. I could look for news of my brothers in the cities we would visit for the games and return for them when I was free. We would travel secretly across the Harn lands and take back Thebin.

"I didn't know what plots and counterplots I was walking *into.* Since then, I've become a stone in a game that makes no sense and has nothing to do with taking Thebin back from the Harn. I can only assume Master Markko has gone mad. He seems to think I have some great magical power, and if he can't enslave it for himself, he wants me dead so that I cannot use it against him. The problem is, I don't have any magic, so I'm of no use to either of us in the way Markko thinks. Does that make sense to you?"

"Not on the face of it, no," General Shou admitted. "But you were young when you left Thebin. Perhaps Master Markko knows something about your heritage as a prince that you would have learned if your life had not so abruptly changed for the worse."

" 'Would have' isn't the same as 'did,' " Llesho pointed out. "My life did change, and whatever I would have learned or received as a prince, I did not learn as a pearl diver.

"As for her ladyship and Master Den, I don't know what they think they have to gain by sending me to the emperor. Thebin is a thousand li from here, and all that space is filled with Harn. If the emperor wanted to help Thebin, he would first have to conquer Harn, war band by war band, and he could never trust that those he left behind him in a conquered state would not rise up at his back or attack Shan in his absence."

"You'll make a good general someday, Llesho. I couldn't have explained the situation between Harn and Shan any better after years on the border."

"It's not that hard to figure out when you've made the Long March."

Shou didn't deserve sarcasm from him, but it was the only defense Llesho had. The emperor would certainly listen to his general, and Llesho had hoped that Shou would come up with a flaw in his argument and prove to him that her ladyship had been right all along. Instead, the general had just agreed that it was pointless to support Llesho's fight for Thebin. Praise was a poor substitute for hope.

"If you will direct me to the slave market, I'll be on my way."

"I love Shan, but I wouldn't trust her slavers to resist a Thebin boy on the streets alone." General Shou stood up and stretched out kinked muscles. "I'll take you there, and see that you get back safely."

"Thank you."

Llesho stood as well, and followed Shou out of the park. It seemed strange that someone with the responsibilities of a general would have the freedom and the inclination to humor the stubborn goals of a slave. If Shou felt inconvenienced, however, he didn't show it.

"You should realize I am only humoring you in this, Llesho." General Shou led them down a narrow, twisted street with ramshackle buildings stacked helter-skelter one on top of the other and leaning into the cartway on both sides. The general walked with a casual air, as if he had no particular place to go and no set time to be there. In spite of his apparent nonchalance, he kept a cautious eye out, and directed them around a pile of garbage heaped on the paving stones. Llesho copied the general's next action when he stepped out into the cartway to avoid walking under the narrow balcony overhead. He was glad he had done so when a pail of refuse cascaded over the landing they would have been passing just as it fell.

"It's been nine summers since Thebin fell, and almost as long since anyone from the highlands but ignorant farmers have come to market," General Shou pointed out, ignoring both the obstacles he avoided and the begging children to whom he absently threw coins without breaking stride. Harn traders walked among the passersby with hard, sharp eyes and a hand to their money belts. Llesho shuddered when those eyes glanced over him with silver in their evaluation and leering smirks for the general. He knew what they thought the man used him for, but their scorn was better than his fate if they found him alone.

I don't expect to find my brothers in the pens," Llesho said, "but there must be records."

"Maybe. But you can be sure they have been falsified to hide the identities of any slaves who might have the power to attract a following."

"One would almost think you disapprove that we were not killed out of hand."

The general shrugged. "I wouldn't have attacked Thebin in the first place, obviously, since I *didn't* attack her. But you're right: if I had, I would have killed her rulers and all their kin before I ever sat on her throne. It is bad policy to turn your back on someone with a grudge."

"Then I guess Thebin was lucky that it was Harn

that attacked, and not Shan." Not a comfortable conversation to be having in the heart of Shan's capital city.

"No doubt." General Shou did not seem to take offense. Or if he did, he had his revenge when they turned the next corner. "Here we are," he said.

Llesho hadn't needed the words to tell him. He recognized the place even before he saw it, by its stench.

Chapter Thirty-two

FORMALLY titled the "Labor Exchange," the slave pens took the more common name from the maze of stockades and livestock runs that ended at the slave block in thc market square. The place reeked of misery: rotting food and feces and the sweat of too many human beings, tainted with unendurable horror and despair and crammed together like cattle. Senses on overload, Llesho's memories assailed him like blows to the gut. He grabbed for the top railing of the nearest stockade, and rested his head on his hands; absorbing the blood-drenched horror opened old wounds in his soul.

"Prince Llesho of Thebin died here," he said. The slave market had obliterated the prince, if not the flesh he wore, had stripped him to the bone and rebuilt him as another person entirely. So many terrified children had passed down these chutes, and yet no one had raised a hand in protest when the innocent were sold like animals to be used and bred and slaughtered at the whim of whoever had the money to buy them.

A keening wail of mourning fought him for control of his throat. "My people," he moaned softly. "Oh, Goddess, what have you done to my people?"

In stark images of crumbling horror, the slave pens

reminded him that he was alone in this world. He'd known it since Lleck had died, of course, but sometimes the knowledge crashed in on him with the force of his need for allies, or friends. He felt a hand on his shoulder. He knew it was General Shou's, but memory of rough hands in the market made him flinch. What comfort could Shou offer him now, anyway?

"An empire with the rot of the slave pens festering at its heart cannot help itself," Llesho told him bleakly. "It certainly has nothing to offer Thebin."

"The old emperor is dead." General Shou withdrew his hand and rested his forearms on the top rail, next to Llesho. "His son now rules. Things will be different for Shan, but change takes time."

Change. Llesho stared at the holding facility leaning over its rotted foundation. The slave traders had called it the dormitory even though it had no beds—just an unswept dirt floor to lie upon. It had never been meant to shelter the wretched slaves, Llesho realized, but served to hide their exhaustion and hopelessness from potential buyers. They'd put men and women together. He'd thought at the time, with the mind of a small boy, they'd done it out of kindness, so that families might have one last night together. Later, when he'd come to understand what those anguished cries in the night had been about, he realized it was because the traders didn't care. If the females turned up pregnant in the morning, well, the buyer had made a bargain: two for the price of one. No. He couldn't expect help from Shan.

"It takes more than a day to change a world, Llesho. It needs a cause to raise the will of the people to change. Can you do this?"

General Shou's voice soothed the ache in his heart and the prickling unease that clenched his flesh. So many meanings in the question: "Can you offer Shan a cause to throw off the unclean trade in human lives? Can you walk back into that hell to save your brother?"

Llesho nodded. The last, at least, he could do. He just needed a minute to remember how to breathe. "The pens are empty."

"The next slave caravan is due tomorrow; the traders should be around somewhere getting things ready for the new arrivals and the sale to follow."

Llesho shot him a piercing glance and pushed away from the corral. "You seem to know a lot about the slave trade." Far more than Llesho found comforting.

Shou twitched a shoulder, not quite shrugging. "I keep my eyes open for the odd Thebin prince on the resale market. It's easier than fighting for them, or stealing them."

"Is that what you did?" Llesho asked him, thinking back to the battle with Master Markko, and Jaks lying dead. "You fought for me?"

"Not to own you," Shou clarified his statement. "But to see you succeed.

"Strategy, Llesho. When Markko attacked the governor's compound at Farshore, why didn't you stay and fight him there?"

General Shou used a tone of voice that Llesho knew well from his sessions with Lleck, and even the rare discussion with Habiba. No point in bristling at the suggestion of cowardice. The general was trying to teach him something, so he needed to answer the question as stated, not as pride interpreted.

"The governor ordered us to flee," he said, but Llesho knew that wasn't the answer Shou was looking for. "Farshore isn't my war. Thebin is."

That won him a slight nod. "And to save Thebin, you have to stay alive, and you have to stay free."

It was Llesho's turn to nod.

General Shou followed his first question with a second. "What do you think would happen if the emperor tried to shut down the slave market?"

"The slave trade would end," Llesho answered immediately.

"And the slavers?"

"Would be unhappy, but would have to find something else to trade."

"The Harn have a habit of turning their displeasure on the one who displeases them."

The Harn. Who stole or traded for human flesh to sell for money in Shan's marketplace. Who had laid waste to Thebin.

"The Harn control the high passes and, through them, all the trade that moves between Shan and the West. They hardly need to trade in human lives anymore."

"For the Harn, the trade value of the slaves they sell has always been secondary."

Llesho frowned. That didn't make sense. Oh. Yes, it did. The enemies of the Harn feared not only death in battle, but the public humiliation of the slave block and lives spent in misery. Better to be dead.

The Harn would not give up the trade peacefully, but that did not leave Shan free of responsibility. "If there were no market, there would be no slaves," Llesho insisted. "If Shan is willing to sell its soul for peace, the Harn have no need for battle. They have already won."

General Shou met his gaze briefly, then dropped his eyes again. "You shame me," he said.

"Shan shames you," Llesho corrected him. "I only point out what is already true."

"I know. But we cannot resolve the issue today. Did you have a plan for rescuing the prince, your brother?"

"I will need the price of a bid," Llesho pointed out.

"That is not a problem. I have more money than I have a use for."

Llesho shook his head. "I didn't come all this way to trade one master for another, for myself or for Adar."

"What do you suggest?" General Shou made it

clear in his tone that Llesho could offer no other solution. "You have won no purses in the arena, and wouldn't have the price of your own freedom if her ladyship demanded it."

"I have this." Llesho reached into his mouth and plucked out the pearl that Lleck had pressed into the space of his lost tooth. As he drew it out between his fingers, the black pearl returned to its original size, and he had to open his mouth wider to extract it. When he held it out to General Shou, the pearl almost filled the palm of his hand. "Will the slave traders accept the pearl itself as payment, or must I exchange it for money before I approach them?"

"Where did you get that?" General Shou's voice shook, and his face paled so quickly that Llesho thought the man would faint dead away in the gutter. Shou reached out to touch the gleaming black surface, but pulled back as if it had burned his fingers.

"Lleck gave it to me," Llesho said. "He was dead at the time. I was in the bay, and he put the pearl in my mouth to hide it, then told me to find my brothers. If it will pay for Adar's freedom, I consider it well spent."

"I think not," the general whispered. He closed Llesho's own fingers around his treasure, and slowly, as if he acted against his own will, he dropped to one knee and bowed his head over the fist Llesho clasped around the pearl.

"Adar shall be my gift to the goddess," he said. Rising from his obeisance, he asked, "Does anyone know that you have this?"

Llesho shook his head.

"I am sure Master Markko suspects," the general muttered. "It would explain his interest in you." Shou could not pull his gaze from the hand that held the pearl, and Llesho saw the troubled longing in that gaze, and the moment when that soul-deep inner conflict came to rest.

"Tell Master Den," the general advised him. "Explain how you came by it, and stand by his counsel. As for Habiba, Master Den will know what is best. Say nothing to anyone until you have conferred with Master Den."

Llesho hesitated. He hadn't wanted to share this secret with anyone, but Shou had caught him off-balance. He didn't know how he would buy his brother's freedom without the pearl.

"First, we must see to Adar," Llesho insisted. "And if we are not going to trade the pearl for his freedom, I am left without a plan."

"Fortunately, you have a general in your retinue, my prince. As I said, I have the price, and your brother shall be my gift to the goddess. More important, I have a plan for acquiring the prince without arousing suspicion. You will not like it, however."

"Strategy, General? I thought you honored a trickster god."

"If winning doesn't matter to you, we can return to the palace now," the general shot back. "I know very little about honor, perhaps, but a great deal about winning."

"So, what is this master plan?"

Shou looked away, and Llesho followed his gaze to the counting house, more solidly built than the dormitory. Llesho would have bet that the roof didn't leak either.

"The traders and the money counters will be preparing for tomorrow's shipment. They know me as a merchant and a slave owner. If I demonstrate an interest in Thebins, and ask about a Thebin healer, they may be inclined to open their records for the privilege of brokering the sale."

"I assume you have a role for me in this charade?" He wasn't stupid; he'd figured out his part in the game as soon as the general had spoken. It didn't even surprise him. But he wanted Shou to say it out loud.

The general threw down the challenge with a little smile. He didn't seem to regret a thing. "You will play my slave, of course. My dear slave. They won't find you on their books, but haven't I made much of the urchin once purchased in the market at Wuchow?"

General Shou's whole posture shifted; his expression grew soft and lost the keen edge that intelligence gave it. He stroked Llesho's face with a feather-touch of the backs of his fingers, and Llesho flinched like he'd been struck. But he resisted the urge to move away from the touch and even managed to drop his lashes provocatively.

Shou laughed. "I think that should do. Just try not to kill me before we've found your brother."

Kill him, no. But he had questions for this master of disguise—like why a general would need such skills. Answers would have to wait. Llesho didn't like it, but he couldn't afford to anger his only chance to secure Adar's freedom.

When he had last been to the slave market, Llesho had known only the dormitory and the holding pens, and the block in the market square. Unlike the parts of it he had seen, the countinghouse had a sturdy air. Inside, dark and solid wood gave weight to the entry hall. There were no chairs, but a gong on a small table invited the visitor to announce his presence. General Shou, playing the part of a merchant and slave connoisseur, struck the gong with its muffled hammer. A small woman with greased-back hair and a voluminous coat quickly answered the call, sliding open a panel to the inner chambers with a low bow.

"Your wish, good sir?" she asked, peering up at General Shou with a simper. She had the sharp, carved features of the Harn; Llesho's flesh crawled at the sight of her.

Shou took a moment to pet Llesho with a fatuous grin on his face before addressing the trader.

"I have developed a partiality for Thebins," he smirked. "And I am in the market to buy."

The woman gave Llesho a knowing leer, but schooled her features to a thoughtful frown before answering Shou's question.

"It may be difficult to serve the master if he wishes a match for the boy. The age is in demand across types, and one must make a profit where one can, you understand. Our entire stock, except for special orders, must go to the block. I could get you a good price for this one, though, and we can place an order for a set, if you'd like: two boys, or a girl and a boy if you prefer. Special orders, for which we must charge a premium, you understand, take at least six months to fill, but I am sure we could make an arrangement for resale of this one after the replacements arrive. Subject to the usual, of course. Contract is void if property is destroyed or damaged in a manner that negatively effects market value."

By the time the old flesh peddler had run down, Llesho was trembling under General Shou's hand. The general gave his shoulder a warning squeeze, but he needn't have worried. Llesho's rage and terror seemed to please the woman.

"He still has spunk. That's unusual. Some would pay extra for that, if he isn't broken before they take possession."

"I did not come to sell," Shou reminded her. "And I am not looking for another young one. The upkeep, you know. Eating all the time at this age, and far too much energy for an old man like me."

He smiled sweetly, and the trader replied with a flattering comment on the gentleman's youth, but quickly deferred to his taste. "Of course. What would you prefer, then, good sir?"

"I have several Thebins in my retinue, and would

like to purchase a healer of their kind to tend to their needs, and perhaps offer my house the novelty of his advice," Shou answered. "Medicine is an especial passion of mine."

"And Thebin healers are reputed to have a special knowledge of herbs that ease the mind," she added conspiratorially. "Of course, healers are likewise rare—even rarer than boys! Frankly, I don't expect to see one in tomorrow's selection. I could be wrong, though. Would you like me to send a note to your dwelling with the particulars about likely merchandise in the morning?"

"No need," General Shou answered. "I will send a servant for your list myself. In the meantime, perhaps if you have record of Thebin healers in the area, a current owner might be interested in a brokered sale?"

The trader considered him for a moment. "I have been a part of this market for more than ten summers," she said, "and can remember only two Thebin healers to cross our block. Three if you count a woman herbalist with a reputation for poisons."

"I would be interested in either of the two reputable healers," Shou agreed, and added, "I have an expert in poisons on my staff already, and would not trust such a sensitive task to a Thebin anyway."

"Wise, sir." She considered him thoughtfully, watching the glitter of jewels on the fingers of the hand absently toying with Llesho's hair. "If sir is not concerned about the price, perhaps we can be of service."

"I am very rich," General Shou flirted with his wealth. "And I can indulge my whims."

The trader led them down a hall so luxuriously appointed that even the clink of coins from the strong room whispered in subdued tones. Finally, she slid aside a screen and led them into an elegant room lined with shelves on which scrolls were piled.

"Have a seat," she invited him. General Shou took

the proffered chair and glared at Llesho when he would have taken another. Llesho bit off the comment that had almost leaped from his lips, and stood behind the general. Steeling himself to the intimate gesture, he rested his hand on the general's shoulder, which won him a sweet smile. The general placed a hand over Llesho's, holding it steady, and gave the Harn trader his attention once again.

"Here we have it." She ran a finger quickly down a list, explaining, "We keep a record of the special ones by skill and by origin. Crossing the two lists, I can locate your preferred merchandise. And here, two, like I said."

She lifted a scroll from a high dusty shelf and another from a shelf lower down, on which no dust had settled. "No," she corrected herself. "Not two Thebin healers, but one, a slave with the name Adar, traded some nine summers ago. The same came to block again about three summers ago, when the original buyer lost his property to debauchery. Had a reputation for being headstrong, as I recall, but that had been beaten out of him by the time he came to market again. Yeesss. That's the one. About thirty-five summers, so he is too old to pair with your boy for a pretty set, but we can work on that in a separate order for you."

Llesho shuddered for his brother. For much of the period of his bondage Llesho's treatment had been harsh and debasing, but until Markko he had never been singled out for personal humiliation by his owner. He had hoped that Adar had fared better. Now he hoped only to see his brother alive through whatever damage slavery had done him. The general's pressure on his hand warned him against voicing some protest.

"I am sure you will strike a fair bargain for me, Mistress Trader." Shou rose from his chair and bowed.

"Fair for rare." She reminded him that the price would be high.

Shou returned her a casual shrug. "I will not barter the boy, but your owner may state his price in gold or silver. You will, of course, add your percentage to the price."

"As you will, Master." She wrote out a note to confirm the commission and handed it to the general, then wrote another and called for a servant, who attended her at once.

"I will see you tomorrow, then, good sir?" She led the way to the front of the countinghouse, and opened the sliding panel into the entry room again.

"Tomorrow," General Shou promised, and with a last bow, he waited until Llesho had opened the door for him, and they departed.

"You did that very smoothly," Llesho commented when they were well away from the countinghouse.

"Is that a compliment on my skills as an actor, or an accusation that I own slaves.

"You tell me."

The general huffed an exhalation—whether of guilt or frustration, Llesho could not tell. Shou kept his face clear of all expression.

"If you are asking, do I own slaves, the answer is 'yes,' though I believe I have always behaved honorably toward them."

They had entered the market square. Llesho noted the noise and bustle at the edges of his awareness, but his senses had tunneled down to one focus: the slave block at the market's center leaked blood around the edges of his vision. "I don't see how you can use the words 'slave' and 'honor' in the same statement," he objected.

"Old customs are hard to break." It seemed that Shou was trying to justify his actions, but his next words were a surprise: "Lately, though, I have come to believe you may be right. For the most part, however, it was acting."

"I think that worries me more." Llesho didn't look at the general. He would see only the face Shou wanted him to, so looking for clues in the man's eyes or the depth of the lines above his brow seemed pointless. "I don't know what to trust of your motives. Have you lied to me as easily as you lied to the slave trader?"

"Not as easily or as well as I would have liked, obviously, or you would trust me more." The general laughed. "Are you hungry?"

For a moment Llesho wondered if General Shou had simply lost his mind. But he *was* hungry. Very. The smells coming from the food stalls on his left reminded him that he'd had breakfast a long time ago, and he'd eaten nothing since. The general gave him a shove in the direction of those wonderful smells, and suddenly Llesho's awareness of his surroundings opened up.

The market square was huge. He had thought so looking out on it from the slave block as a child, and his impression of its size hadn't changed much. Now, however, he was conscious of the excitement buzzing in the colors and the noise and the smells. This, much more than the square in front of the palace, seemed to be the center of Shan. They passed a booth where bits of meat were roasting on skewers over an open flame, but the general didn't stop.

"He has no butcher's bill, and his shop is remarkably free of rats," General Shou explained.

He went farther, toward a stall surrounded by customers pressing their demands for service. He waved a hand with two fingers raised at the fat old woman behind the counter, on which a variety of fillings sat beside a stack of flatbreads. The woman smiled her recognition, and had their order ready by the time they had cut through the crowd to reach her.

"Little Shou!" she hailed him. "I do not see you

for a full summer, and you appear at my stall hungry as ever and with an outlander at your heels! What have you been up to this time?"

"I've traveled the wide world 'round looking for the equal to your flatbread, Darit, and found only a friend to share your treasure with."

"I can believe it," she answered him with a laugh, handing Llesho a flatbread covered with a combination of hot and cold fillings that made his mouth water. "He's nothing but a stick—buy him two, before he fades away to a shadow."

"That wouldn't do at all," Shou agreed, pressing a few copper coins into her hand. He bit into his own flatbread and motioned for Llesho to take the extra that she had wrapped in paper for him.

She wished them enjoyment of the market and added, "Take him to see the performers over by the Temple to The Seven. The puppets have a play that reenacts the ascension of the new emperor, and a woman with a performing bear has drawn favorable audiences enough to annoy the cloth merchants."

"Why don't the cloth merchants like the bear dancer?" Llesho asked her around a mouthful of flatbread and meat.

"Her audiences block their entrances, so their business suffers when her bear dances. He is a very droll bear, however."

Llesho wasn't in the mood for watching bears dancing. He'd lost Mara to the dragon and Lleck first to death and later to the rapid current of Golden Dragon River, and the memory of his lost friends still hurt. That was all before he'd met General Shou, of course. The general couldn't know about Llesho's harrowing escape at the river, or his anguish at watching the healer give her life for his safety. So Shou headed straight for the knot of laughing people at the steps of a low, shabby temple.

Pushing his way through the crowd which had already begun to disperse, Llesho followed. When they reached the steps of the temple where the performers worked, the bear dancer had already gone. Shou stopped to chat companionably with a temple priest in threadbare garments who gathered up the offerings of the day from the worn wooden steps. No thick packets of cash changed hands here, but a flower, a bowl of rice, and one of vegetables fresh from a supplicant's garden. The priest interrupted his conversation to give thanks for each as he gathered it into his basket.

Llesho gave the area a quick scan—the bear dancer could not have disappeared so quickly—and caught a glimpse of her turning a corner between two vast warehouses almost before he recognized her.

"Mara!" He followed and discovered a short alley leading away from the market square. The alley had collected a few people on their way home, but Llesho saw nothing of the woman or the bear, who must be Lleck if he had seen the bear dancer aright.

"Llesho!" General Shou caught up with him and grabbed his arm, and he couldn't be a good enough spy to fake the near panic in his eyes. "By ChiChu, boy, don't disappear like that."

"I am not the trickster here," Llesho answered tartly, but he knew he owed the man a sensible answer. Unfortunately, he didn't have one to give. "I know her. The bear dancer. I saw her die."

He didn't add, *And if it is she, her bear used to be my teacher.* He had already given the man more wonder tales to believe than one afternoon could support, and didn't want to add any more fuel to that fire.

Shou peered down the alley as if he could see those few short minutes into the past and discover where the woman and her bear had gone, but his answer addressed the present. "Either you know her and she didn't die after all, or your friend is truly dead, and memory plays tricks on you."

"I saw her die at Golden Dragon River," Llesho repeated, "and I saw her slip into this alley just now."

"If your dead are walking the streets of Shan," the general said with a colder, harder tone than Llesho had heard him use before, "we had better find out why."

"How?" Llesho asked him.

The general's expression had closed around his thought. "Your companions from the road should have reached the palace by now," he said. "Perhaps they can shed some light on the question."

Llesho didn't know how his friends could help him. They hadn't seen the Dragon swallow Mara whole, and hadn't seen her in the marketplace either, but they had known Mara, and Lleck, too. They could at least confirm he was not mad when he told Shou about the reincarnation of his teacher into the form of a bear. Habiba had seen the dragon eat Mara in payment for their passage across the river, however, and he had seemed sure that Llesho would see the healer again.

"We need Habiba."

General Shou winced.

"I thought he was your friend." Habiba had introduced him to the general, and Llesho left the question hanging: *What lie is about to catch up with you now?*

"We are allies." Shou scrunched up his face in a very unmilitary show of mixed feelings. "Habiba often does not agree with my methods."

Llesho set aside that objection with a tart reply. "That makes two of us."

The general laughed. "Don't tell Habiba that when you see him." He led Llesho through the alley rather than back the way they had come, winding around the marketplace rather than through it. They met fewer passersby away from the square, though once a sharp-eyed Harn shoved by them with a sneer for Shou in his disguise as a merchant. The general gave no indication he had noticed the slight, but he uttered a single, sharp word when Llesho's hand wandered to his throat. Killing a single Harn trader wouldn't gain the prince anything but a moment's satisfaction, but it could cost him everything.

A wide boulevard emptied into the market square above the slave block. Crossing, Llesho did not let his gaze linger on the source of his nightmares, except as a reminder of his purpose here. He had a general at his side and tomorrow he would find his most beloved brother, Prince Adar. All he had to do was stand by and let it happen when General Shou bought Adar as a slave. He hoped he wasn't making the biggest mistake of his life. Habiba, and even Mara, could wait.

Chapter Thirty-three

SHOU'S winding path returned them to a secluded spot where a cluster of low bushes obscured the bottom half of the palace wall. Pulling away some branches, the general revealed a wayside shrine, carved in relief into the pink stone wall.

"Turn around," the general instructed Llesho absently, while he studied the carvings intently. "I haven't used this passageway for years; it may take a few minutes to remember the sequence."

Llesho did as he was told, but after a moment Shou gave a thoughtful grunt. With the grinding of stone shifting upon stone, the shrine swung inward to reveal a dark tunnel. The palace walls seemed so riddled with the things that Llesho wondered why they hadn't fallen in on themselves already, but he followed General Shou inside, took up a torch when it was handed to him, and helped to push the massive door back into place. When they were in pitch darkness, Llesho heard the snap of a match firing, saw the tiny flame, and watched it take hold on the fuel-soaked end of Shou's torch. The general waited until his torch burned steadily, then fired the one Llesho carried.

They walked some hundred paces down the straight

passage, until they came to a dead end at a blank wall. Shou found a latch in what seemed to Llesho to be a flaw in the pointing of the rough stone, and another hidden door swung open.

"I used to sneak out of the palace by this route when I was about your age." Shou laughed softly as he led the way up a narrow stairway of age-worn stone. "Good to see it hasn't been discovered since then."

"You lived in the palace?" Llesho asked sharply. Of course, only a high-ranking nobleman could aspire to become a general of the Imperial Guard, but the idea suddenly made him nervous. Shou was also a spy, and when the general had come upon him in the park, Llesho had been too free with his opinions about the emperor. And he'd shown the man Lleck's pearl. Being a spy didn't make him a thief, but he'd clearly known more about the nacreous gem than he was telling.

However, General Shou was nodding. "I was raised here. Had anyone asked what title I wanted attached to my life, I would have told them explorer. Of course, that was not an option even then."

Llesho thought that the general had too much excitement in his life as it was. "All I ever wanted was Thebin," he answered. Not quite a reprimand, or a complaint about the unfairness of the world, it nevertheless made him uncomfortable to have said it out loud.

Fortunately, General Shou did not take the comment as a slight. "Then we will have to win Thebin back for you, won't we?" he promised, and led the prince down another turning.

They came out of the tunnel into a chamber shrouded in richly decorated banners hanging from ceiling to floor. Low couches had been pushed to the edges of the room, and a meeting table and chairs sat in the center. Lling lay in a restless sleep on one of the couches, her color flushed and sweat beading her temples. Hmishi sat next to her, occasionally stroking the hair from her forehead. They both still wore their Thebin uniforms, now stained with the dust and grime of the road—only the bandage on Lling's arm was clean and fresh. In the chairs, an equally travel-worn Bixei and Kaydu had draped themselves in poses of exhaustion and disappointment. Little Brother, Kaydu's monkey companion, sat in the middle of the table, peeling a banana, while Habiba paced nervously back and forth by the door.

Little Brother was the first to notice that Llesho and General Shou had entered through the secret passage. He dropped his banana and began to hop up and down and screech the alarm. Suddenly, the companions were on their feet, reaching for weapons they did not have. Even Lling roused from her sleep and half rose from her couch.

"Lord General!" Habiba bowed low when Shou stepped from behind a long, floating banner. "Or should I say, Lord Merchant?"

When Llesho followed, his guards shouted his name—"Llesho!"—together. All but Lling ran to greet him, and she grinned smugly from her couch.

"So you found him," Habiba remarked. "Did retrieving him cost you much?"

"Not yet, but I expect it will cost me a tael or two before we are done," the general confirmed with a sigh. He took a chair and waited while the companions reassured themselves that Llesho was indeed safe and sound.

"Where were you?" Kaydu demanded, and Bixei exclaimed angrily, "We have been looking for you since noonday! We thought you'd been kidnapped."

Hmishi just shook his head. "He wandered off. I told you he wandered off."

"And I told you he would turn up in his own time," Lling reminded them.

Hmishi pressed her to lie down again, but she resisted. "Habiba says you need rest," he scolded.

"What's the matter with Lling?" Llesho interrupted the welcome with his own question, directed at Habiba. He sat down in the chair between Bixei and Kaydu and tugged on Kaydu's tunic, urging her to sit back down as well.

Lling answered the question tartly for herself. "Lling's wound became infected. It is now well on its way to healing and no cause for alarm."

The look that passed between Hmishi and the witch told a different tale. Habiba shrugged. "She needs to keep the wound clean and the arm still, or she risks losing it."

"Have you alerted the emperor's physician?" Shou asked.

"I don't want a fuss made over a stupid cut on my arm!" Lling snapped. The skin above and below the bandage was pink. Llesho guessed it was hot to the touch, but it was not unduly swollen. He looked for the telltale red streaks that would indicate the infection had invaded her blood, and was relieved to find none.

Habiba graced her with a sour grimace. "That won't be necessary, Lord General. But if you could recommend a good locksmith? I am beginning to fear that nothing short of restraints will ensure the cure is taken."

Llesho smothered his laughter. Lling glared at him, but she did permit Hmishi to help her lie down again on the couch.

"Tell me about your trip," Llesho asked his companions when the greetings were over. "Did you run into any trouble on the road?"

"Since Markko traveled with you," Kaydu pointed out, "we didn't expect much trouble for ourselves."

"We tried to catch up with you." Lling spoke up from her couch. "But you were traveling too fast for the horses to follow, and we didn't want to leave them behind."

Llesho winced. It was his fault she was in danger from her wound, because she had neglected her own care to protect him.

Kaydu nodded, glaring at him. Well he should wince, she seemed to say

"Our troubles began when we arrived at the palace," Bixei said, "and found that the emperor was away, our charge had disappeared, Master Markko had likewise vanished, and no one could find General Shou. Oh, and Master Den had gone out to see if he could find any one of the missing people."

"We thought that Markko must have taken you," Kaydu added. "We were trying to figure out where he might have gone when the general materialized through a solid wall with you in tow. He has our thanks, but I'd still like to know where you were."

"I'd like to know that myself." Master Den, with his usual good timing, chose that moment to open their door. He glowered at them all with a sweeping flash of his eyes. Once he made sure the door was securely closed behind him, he settled the disfavor of his frown on Llesho.

"Markko takes his ease in an unpleasant eating establishment in the city," he said. "The place has a bad reputation for serving the Harnish slavers who frequent the market, and Markko does not dine alone. The traders who attend him have a Harnish look about them, and they seem to be on familiar terms.

"I expect he will be returning soon, and some of us should be in our rooms on the other side of the palace when he does. Before we go our separate ways, however, we'd all like to know what Llesho has been up to."

Llesho stared down at the table, as if the grain of the wood had mesmerized him. Now that it came to telling them, he hesitated, as if speaking about it aloud could somehow put him back in the slave pens. But it had to be done.

"We went to the slave market."

Three of his companions went very still. Kaydu, who had been born free in Thousand Lakes Province, had never seen the slave block or the pens, but she had seen the products of them and she respected the silence of her friends. Little Brother, with the sensitivity of his monkey kind, edged closer to Llesho. The monkey chittered softly, and reached to touch Llesho's hair in a gesture of comfort. Llesho took the monkey's hand and smiled at the distraction.

"I think we have found Adar, my brother," he said.

"You 'think'?" Habiba pressed him. "You do not know him?"

Llesho stared at the witch, trembling suddenly; the afternoon became confused in his mind with his experience as a child on the slave block, and he could not speak.

General Shou watched him with concern while offering an explanation in his place. "Llesho posed as a slave, and I as a merchant with a taste for Thebins and a wish for a Thebin healer to tend my small collection." His smile was thin and dangerous. "They have such a one on their books, and have agreed to broker a sale with the current owner for me."

Kaydu looked from Llesho to her father, balancing the need for secrecy with Llesho's need for reassurance, but her father gave her no signal on which to base a judgment. Finally, she decided that Llesho ought to know. "We brought five hundred soldiers with us in case we had to fight to get you out of here, but we left them outside the city wall until we had scouted out the situation."

"And how long have you told them to wait until they are to attack the palace and rescue you?" General

Shou asked. His voice was harder than Llesho had ever heard it, and the man's piercing gaze made him quail.

"Until midnight, tonight," Kaydu answered. She sounded sure of herself, but her eyes grew dark and calculating. She didn't breathe while she waited to hear the general's response.

"Then perhaps you should send them a message." General Shou spoke very softly, but the steel of a blade rang in his voice.

Kaydu nodded. "Of course. The question is, what message to send. Will we need them tomorrow to secure Llesho's brother?"

"I think a few bits of gold will work better than a foreign army," General Shou answered her. "As an officer in the Imperial Guard, I can tell you that if your soldiers enter the city, the emperor will have no choice but to consider it an invasion by a hostile force. Why set friend against friend when I have gold enough to spare and a willing broker for the bargaining?"

"You have a plan, I see." Master Den took a couch by the wall nearest where General Shou and Llesho had entered. Llesho figured that was no coincidence; he wondered how much Den knew about the palace. Did his teacher know the emperor himself?

"Part of one," Shou admitted. "I should be able to buy Adar with little trouble, and there are officials enough in the palace to prepare the manumission papers. But there is the problem of Master Markko."

"He may be working with the emperor against us," Bixei suggested.

General Shou shook his head. "The emperor is not so easily fooled or frightened as Master Markko may believe."

"But Llesho must still petition the emperor for help to cross the Harn lands and free Thebin," Kaydu insisted.

She hadn't included herself in that goal, and Llesho

wondered if, beyond Shan, he would be traveling alone. Well, not alone if they succeeded tomorrow. Adar would be with him.

"I believe the emperor may sympathize with Llesho's petition," the general confirmed, only to dash their hopes again: "It may not be in the best interest of the Shan Empire—or Thebin—to announce an alliance, however."

"Then what was the point of our mad dash to the capital?" Llesho demanded, frustrated.

General Shou looked at him as if he'd gone quite mad, and even Habiba had the grace to look embarrassed for him.

"A hypothetical problem in strategy, Llesho," the general explained as if to a particularly dim child. "In the name of the governor of Thousand Lakes Province, for the honor of his daughter, the widow of the murdered governor of Farshore Province, a witch marches at the head of his master's troops. In his train he bears a boy whom all know to be the exiled son of the murdered King Khorgan of Thebin.

"In pursuit come the armies of Farshore Province, led by the magician who has murdered that province's governor in the name of Lord Yueh, the usurper. This murderer proclaims himself regent of a child who may or may not be born to the usurper's widow. If the child exists at all, it may be the usurper's own child, born out of the union of husband and wife and blessed by the goddess, or it may be the murderer's child, forced upon the grieving widow. Or it may be the product of a secret union plotted by the widow and her magician lover, to replace her husband with his murderer.

"Regardless, the magician who has murdered three lords of the empire finds himself within the city of Shan, as does the witch who serves the widow of a fourth lord, also dead."

"Her ladyship fled Farshore in defense of her honor,

to escape Master Markko," Llesho pointed out. "When you lay out all these murders in a row, keep in mind that she is sinned upon and injured no one."

General Shou nodded in agreement. "Which may be a ruse, but is likely not to be, or she would not have entrusted her father's troops to her dead husband's chief steward and witch. Unless—" he gave Habiba a thin smile,"—that witch is himself the widow's lover."

Habiba bowed in acknowledgment of the point, but his eyes held a dangerous glint. "I would not have the lady's honor doubted, even in the name of a lesson," he answered mildly.

"To do so, one must assume that all the ladies in the East have fallen under the sway of the overseers to their respective husbands' properties, since Lady Yueh and Lady Chin-shi likewise find themselves widowed." Master Den harrumphed, as if he found the game they played too tedious for words. "And, like her ladyship, they now find their husbands' lands and possessions in the hands of Master Markko."

"Why, then, does Master Habiba march on Shan?" General Shou asked. "And why carrying the heir to a vanquished kingship in his train? And why fight a bloody battle in the shadow of the emperor's throne and bring his troops to the very walls of the empire's chief city? An emperor must suspect that such a one wishes, perhaps, to seize the throne for himself, or for the foreign princeling he dangles on a string."

"Perhaps," Llesho said, taking his time to formulate his answer.

His companions waited, watching him intently. They were all familiar with lessons, and realized that more hung in the balance with this examination than a cuff on the ear for inattention.

"Perhaps," Llesho began again, "her ladyship's father, the appointed governor of Thousand Lakes Province, wished his emperor to know of the terrible destruction that has overtaken his neighbors and threatens his own province, and the very empire itself. With such danger all around him, he could not risk a simple messenger, but must send a delegation of sufficient stature to persuade Shan of the threat all the provinces of the empire now face."

Habiba gave Llesho a bow, and an ironic smile. "Perhaps," the witch began, matching the diffidence of Llesho's own answer, "her ladyship concluded that she could not protect a young prince, beset as she was by the enemies of her husband, enemies who wished to acquire the boy for their own mysterious ends. She might then choose to deliver the boy to the emperor, who might, in his wisdom, have a better idea of what to do with a young and propertyless king."

"None of it makes any sense." Llesho threw himself back into his chair. "Even if Markko could somehow put me on the throne of Thebin, he must know I would never act as his figurehead. He can kill me, but he cannot make me obey."

"He wants your power," Habiba insisted, "the divine power that is your gift from the goddess—"

"I have no such power!" Llesho insisted, and blushed that he had raised his voice. "Excuse me, I did not mean disrespect. But if that's what Markko wanted, he should have waited until after I had completed the vigil of my sixteenth summer."

"Your power as a symbol of kingship will do if that is all he can reach," Habiba conceded, "though her ladyship has conveyed to me her certainty that your vigil did, in fact, succeed in wooing the goddess."

"Then she is more in the confidence of the goddess than the professed bridegroom. But what does *any* of this have to do with the emperor's decision not to grant us an audience or accept our petition?"

"If the emperor had any doubts about you at all, Llesho, you would be quartered here with your friends and enemies alike, and not in the private quarters where you pose a threat to the emperor himself," General Shou pointed out practically. "But if he acknowledges the validity of your claim, he must at the same time reject Master Markko's opposing petition that you belong to him by right of property in Farshore."

"And?" Llesho bristled. He'd thought that, at least, he could gain from his mad dash across Shan Province.

"Markko doesn't work alone, boy," Master Den said. "That was clear at his dinner table, if we did not know it before. His connections to Harn likely run much deeper than a chance encounter at an inn."

Llesho closed his eyes and let his head drop against the straight back of his chair. Hundreds had fallen in battle. Stipes had lost an eye and would never march at Bixei's side again. Master Jaks lay buried in a soldiers' field with no mark upon his grave to proclaim his bravery or his honor.

"I have thrown away the lives of those who trusted me to placate a hallucination," he said. "I should have drowned in the bay before I ever set out on this fool's mission."

"Don't let self-pity spoil your judgment," General Shou chided him. "You have performed a great service for the empire: Shan is forwarned of the danger within its own borders, from whichever direction it may come." He glared at Habiba to show that he hadn't let the witch off his hook yet. "And you have already achieved the first part of your quest. Tomorrow, you will have Prince Adar at your side. And you are in the imperial city, which is more than the capital of the empire."

"The head of the trade route to the West," Kaydu muttered, and the general smiled.

"The trade caravans must pass through Kungol, regardless of which power rules there," Hmishi supplied, with an answering grin.

General Shou gave a little shrug, his smile only half-hidden. "If a future general could travel the length of the trade route by caravan, and explore the city of Kungol unnoticed, so, too, can a future king."

"It will be dangerous," Habiba warned.

Llesho looked at him as if he'd lost his mind. "Ask Lord Chin-shi how safe it is to do nothing."

Habiba bowed in acknowledgment. "It had to be said, though I had no doubt about your answer."

"Speaking of danger," Bixei reminded them, "what is to be done with Markko? We can't very well hire ourselves onto a caravan crossing Harn lands with him following, especially if he is working with the Harn."

Markko's power was subtle and strong, and evil to its very center. Llesho had lost so much to the deadly master already that he could not be certain he had the strength to overcome the magician, even if he were willing to die in the attempt. But he had not lost all, yet.

"I saw Mara in the square today," he whispered.

"I thought you saw her die," Hmishi said, while the rest of the companions held their breath.

"The Golden Dragon swallowed her," Llesho confirmed. "Nevertheless, I saw her today, in the square. A vendor said she has a bear with her, and that the creature dances for coins."

"Do you think the bear is Lleck?" Lling asked.

"What else can it be?" Llesho asked.

"It may be a trap, set to snare a prince," Habiba warned him.

Kaydu picked up Little Brother from the table, cradling him in her arms with a sly smile. "But tame bears are not the only performing animals in Shan. While Llesho and the general are buying the freedom of Prince Adar, Little Brother and I will find a likely spot on the square and see what we can find out."

Master Den nodded his agreement. "If Habiba and

I take up the charge of keeping Master Markko away from the various subterfuges of our young soldiers, our plan is set."

Habiba signaled the end of their meeting with a bow to the general. "I will see to standing down the alert among our guard."

When he had gone, Llesho followed General Shou toward the banner behind which they had entered. Kaydu caught him, however, and laid a hand upon his sleeve before he could make good his escape. "You are not going anywhere without your guards, Llesho. It's not that I don't trust your security, General Shou," she bowed politely to the waiting general, "but Prince Llesho is our responsibility."

Hmishi tried to pull himself away, but he could not seem to let go of Lling's hand. "I can carry her."

General Shou shook his head. "No one is coming with us. I'm taking risk enough bringing Llesho through the tunnels. I won't hazard the palace or its secrets any further."

"Then Llesho can stay here," Lling insisted.

"And Master Markko?" Shou asked. Markko had rooms in the guest quarters just as they did.

Master Den had lied, or not known about the tunnels, when he said there was no access to the private sleeping rooms of the palace. But what Master Den had figured out, Master Markko might also.

"Rest easy," Master Den assured the companions. "Between us, the general and I can keep even Llesho alive."

With a last reassuring smile, Master Den nudged Llesho toward the secret door behind the wall hanging. General Shou led the way, and the three were back in the tunnels, following a twisting course that Llesho could not recall from one turn to the next. Master Den, he noticed, did not hesitate or require confirming directions.

Finally, they stopped at another blank wall which

opened to the general's cautious probing, and Llesho tumbled out into the locked room that adjoined his own, a study lined with books and strange artifacts from many distant lands.

Master Den followed him with more dignity. "Sleep well, my prince." He gave Llesho a deep bow, and left the general alone with Llesho in the study.

"You played a difficult part, and did it well today." The general pulled back the bolts and opened the door for Llesho to pass into his own room. "Ring for the servants to fetch you a meal, so that you can be officially accounted for. No need for explanations; the servants are discreet, and none will ever know save Master Den and your confederates that you were absent for much of the day. As for the trinket you would trade for your brother's freedom, the fewer who know that you have it, the safer will be both the bauble and its bearer.

"Now get some rest. I'll leave word for you in the morning."

With that he closed the door. The walls were thick, so Llesho could not hear the general's departing footsteps, but when he tried the door, he found it unlocked, and when he opened it, the room beyond was empty.

Chapter Thirty-four

IN the morning, Llesho found a folded note sitting on a suit of clothes laid out for him to wear. The note said only, "The garden. One hour."

He had a good idea who had put it there, and the garden must mean the altar of ChiChu at the Imperial Water Garden. But he didn't know how long the note had been waiting for him to wake up. With a groan, he decided he didn't have time for breakfast. Instead, he hurriedly pulled on the white quilted breeches and embroidered red silk jacket that General Shou meant him to wear. The black pearl he had received from Lleck was still where he had hidden it; he put it in the inside pocket of the jacket. Then, slipping his feet into a pair of woven sandals, he headed for the secret tunnels that would lead him to the palace square and the garden beyond.

As they had the day before, the guards he passed showed no interest in where he was going. The sun was well up when he slipped into the square, but few people were yet about their business or worship, and he made his way with few eyes to notice his departure. He soon found himself standing alone in front of the waterfall at the center of the Imperial Water Garden that represented Thousand Lakes Province in the city of Shan. General Shou was not there as Llesho had expected, nor was anyone else about who might have left him the note. For a moment he felt the prickle of danger raise the hair on his neck. Then he heard Bixei, talking to someone as he drew closer to Llesho's position.

"Are you sure this is a good idea?" Bixei said, and Llesho heard a soft murmur in reply. Then the two came into sight. General Shou was dressed in robes of even more outrageous richness than the day before, and Bixei wore a suit of clothes almost identical to Llesho's, except that his embroidered jacket was of blue silk rather than red.

"Is what a good idea?" Llesho asked. He didn't have to stand up because he hadn't bothered to sit while he waited; didn't want to cover the seat of his white pants with dust before they'd even got started.

"Kaydu went to the market square this morning to find out about the dancing bear," Bixei answered. "Hmishi is tending Lling, who is well enough this morning to insist upon rising, but not sufficiently improved to actually get out of bed. Habiba and Master Den have both gone out of the city to check on the troops waiting there, which has left no one watching Master Markko."

"That is not entirely correct." General Shou did not explain what he meant by that. He studied Llesho carefully, and instructed, "Tuck in your chin. You must at least try to look like you are afraid of me, Llesho, or I will never be able to hold my head up in the slave markets again."

"How can you carry yourself with pride while buying and selling human beings?" Llesho snapped at the general, but raised his right hand in a gesture of surrender. "Uncalled for, I know. I owe you this chance to find Adar. It is not my place to speak as your conscience."

"No, it isn't," Shou replied, and his tone was so distant, and so regal that Llesho had to look at him twice to find the general he knew inside the noble stranger who had briefly taken his place. Truly a disciple of the trickster god, with so many layers to him, Llesho wondered if he'd met the real man at their center even yet.

Without another word, Shou began walking. Llesho fell in step behind him, with Bixei at his side. They headed in the direction opposite from the one they had taken the day before, and Llesho realized they were going to enter the market square across from the slave block, nearer to the temple of The Seven. As they moved into the open, he saw Kaydu, clad in an extravagantly shiny set of clashing clothes, capering about while Little Brother, in the garb of the Imperial Guard, begged for coins with his tasseled cap in his paw. The crowd laughed as Kaydu performed some skit in which the "Imperial Guardsman" chittered at her in monkey language and danced on her head.

General Shou, Llesho noticed, was trying to suppress a smile, but his good humor vanished as they approached the Labor Exchange. The pens were full this morning; Llesho tried not to look at them, but still he felt the blood leave his face. The auction had already begun. People from more races than he had known existed, and dressed more strangely than he could have imagined, crowded the Shan market.

"Here's a fine specimen, trained in the crafts of cabinetmaker and coffiner," the auctioneer wheedled while with one hand he gestured at the auction block. A naked man with his hands chained behind his back shivered there in all his desolation. "Presentable enough for household use, strong enough for heavy labor."

The crowd of potential buyers surged forward to inspect the bitter captive displayed for their examination.

Bixei looked about the market square, his eyes wide as teacups. He had been born into slavery and had come to Pearl Island by private purchase, so he had no memories of the market or the slave block to haunt him. Still, he turned his head so that he did not have to look at the man on the block. "They sound like cattle, moaning in their pens," he observed softly.

"Oh, Goddess." Llesho shivered, his teeth chattering, as he repeated, again, "Oh, Goddess, I can't do this, Oh, Goddess. I can't."

Bixei stopped. He reached out to grab Llesho's arm, but Llesho pulled away, screaming, "Don't touch me!" as he retreated further into the agony of his past. Bixei stared at the ongoing auction and then at his companion, but he refused to imagine what it had been like to stand on the slave block.

"I think he is sick!" he informed General Shou between clenched teeth.

"Llesho!" General Shou wrapped a hand around his arm and shook him, hard, when he tried to pull away, until his eyes focused on the general's face.

A woman came next to the block, trying with no success to hold her torn dress together over her breasts. Her weeping drew his gaze, but General Shou took Llesho's chin in his fingers and held him so that he could not look to the block.

"That's right," Shou insisted. "No one is going to hurt you today. Just keep your eyes on me. A little pale is attractive, but we don't want the trader to think you are diseased."

Llesho nodded that he understood, and managed to walk between the slave pens at the general's side, though he flinched. Each groan of misery struck him like a blow. Almost, he envied his sister, who had died in Kungol and had been spared the terror and the misery of the slave auction.

The countinghouse looked very different on trading day. The sliding panels that had separated the trading offices from the entry hall had been pushed aside to make one large room. Now the offices acted as privacy alcoves for conducting business. The room was crowded with Harnish traders and brokers shouting sums at one another and waving slips of paper and purses of coins. Llesho could not figure how they sorted out who had bought and who had sold and what the money changing hands had purchased.

Gradually, however, he realized that the desk on the right served a line of buyers awaited the completion of their transactions. At the desk on the left, sellers received their payment, calculated their commissions and taxes, and departed. The shouters seemed to be trying to strike private bargains with buyers and sellers both. The line of sellers seemed to be mostly Harnish, and Llesho backed away, ducking behind General Shou as if the traders would recognize him and kill him as the raiders had murdered his parents and his sister.

No one noticed them at all, however, until the general raised his voice. "Where is my lady trader?" he insisted with a nasal twang so high and petulant that Llesho did not recognize him. "She promises me a set of fine, plump boys, and a healer to doctor them!"

A few of the traders looked up from their record books and their accounts to give the general's party a scornful examination before returning to their work, but no one seemed to care about the dandy prancing about with his mismatched boys.

Their trader of the day before, however, heard the demand for her attention, and scuttled over. "My lord!" she tucked her hands into her sleeves and bowed deeply before General Shou, a grin pasted on her painted lips. She narrowed her eyes when she caught sight of Bixei, and grabbed his jaw in her hand to count his teeth. "Hmmm," she said, taking his measure with one cold glance.

"Pretty. He's a bit too tall, and shows some wear—"

The latter she said with a well-chosen combination of sly admiration and motherly rebuke. "Some like sweeter flesh, but I can get you a good price. This one, too," she pointed to Llesho and explained, "Thebin stock. He will look like an untried youth well past twenty summers."

"I told you yesterday, old woman. I want to buy, not sell. If you don't have what I want, I will find it elsewhere."

Llesho gave the general a sharp glance, but the woman assured him with much hand-waving that he would have what he wanted. "This way," she said, stopping in her tracks to look at Bixei again. "I can sell you a close match," she bargained. "Female, if you like that sort. The height and skin tones are close enough. Brown hair; a bit of bleach would make a perfect match, but perhaps you'd rather color the girl."

Bixei sniffed indignantly at her, but Shou petted him and gave the trader a simpering smile. "Perhaps next time; I'm looking for Thebins today,"

The trader's shoulders sagged a bit as the prospect of a second sale to the rich but foolish customer faded. Llesho wondered if she would try again, but the trader opened a door at the very back of the countinghouse, and led them into a room empty but for two men standing at a small table. The taller, slimmer man with the tanned, chiseled features in the simply cut jacket and breeches of a gentleman farmer came forward to greet them. His shorter, darker companion in the robe of a healer remained out of the light, a little behind his master.

Llesho had schooled his expression to remain neutral when he saw his brother. He said nothing when the tall man approached General Shou and bowed formally, but Llesho noted the flare around the nostrils, the sudden whitening around his lips. Adar recognized him, and was keeping his own counsel as well.

"I understand you wish to purchase a Thebin healer," Adar said, and Llesho stared at him in confusion.

"I am in need of such a one in my household, yes," Shou answered, a proprietary hand on Llesho's shoulder.

The tall man's eyes narrowed, but he shrugged in a show of indifference. "I am not selling," he said.

"You said you were interested in the offer," the trader huffed, and Adar, masquerading as a farmer, quieted her with a gesture. "I am interested," he said. "I have a mind to purchase the boy."

"Then perhaps it is time to show our bids." Shou pulled a coin purse from his belt and took out three gold coins, which he set on the table between the bidders.

Adar held out a hand to his attendant. When the second man moved out of his shadow to put a stack of coins on Adar's outstretched palm, Llesho gasped.

"Shokar," he said, and the tears he had been holding back spilled down his face. "Shokar."

Llesho pushed his way passed the general. Bixei reached to stop him, but he slipped by him, and lunged for the short, stocky stranger, burying his face in the man's shoulder.

"Llesho?" the man whispered, and the other, Adar, stepped in front of the two so that he could hide their embrace at almost the same moment that Llesho realized the danger they were in.

"Sell!" he whispered to his older brother, and released Shokar with a blush and an apology.

"It has been so long since I have seen someone new from my own lands," he explained, bowing as deeply as he could to the general. "I did not mean to distress your lordship."

"The exuberance of youth!" The general waved a hand. "Show such enthusiasm when we return home, and it will not go ill for you." Shou placed the gold coins in the hand of the trader with a smile. "For your trouble," he told her. "We will continue this negotiation over wine, I think."

Adar said nothing for a moment, and Llesho urged him silently to agree. Finally, the healer nodded.

"I have rooms nearby." The general bowed as he offered his hospitality. "And the wine is excellent. If we can come to no permanent agreement, perhaps you will do me the favor of having your man look at my boy."

Adar who wore the clothing of the master rather than the slave, seemed little inclined to trust the offer. Taking advantage of the cover Adar gave him, Llesho reached out and pressed his fingers against his brother's hand, signaling reassurance, he hoped. Adar finally bowed his agreement.

The trader narrowed her eyes, but General Shou, in his disguise as a merchant, returned her suspicion with a guileless smile. He took another coin out of the purse and handed it over. "For your efforts on my behalf, and so that you will remember me if you see something to my taste cross your block," he said.

Llesho was amazed at how stupid the general looked at that moment, but it seemed to disarm the trader, who bit into the coin with her cracked teeth and pronounced herself happy to be of service to his lordship. With much bowing, they made their way back through the press of commerce at the front of the countinghouse, and found themselves once again in the market square.

"The boys must be hungry," Shou announced, still in the guise of the foolish merchant. He made his way across the square toward Darit's booth, and waved four fingers in the air to order four of her wonderful breads. When they drew close enough to reach their food, she gave General Shou a crinkling smile. "You've collected another one, I see." She handed Bixei and Llesho two each of the delicacies, and then held out a fifth, wrapped in paper, to Shou himself. "I have a new filling I thought you might like to try."

She gave a loud laugh which did not startle her customers at all, who were used to her manner, but her eyes were serious. Llesho thought he read a warning in their depths. General Shou's smile likewise did not move beyond the mechanical flexing of his mouth, which caused Llesho to wonder what Darit was to the general, besides a source of delicious food.

Shou did not say anything, however, but tucked the packet into his coat. "Do you still want to see the dancing bear?" he asked. Shokar tensed, and Adar placed a comforting hand on Llesho's shoulder. Both men were surprised when Llesho answered around a mouthful of food: "Yes! I hope we are able to see the monkey as well!"

"Your master seems very kind," Adar ventured in low tones as their party skirted the shops of the cloth merchants, which were again blocked by the laughing crowds.

"He's an unusual man," Llesho agreed. He had picked up on the general's guarded study of the crowds in the marketplace, and it had heightened his own alertness. He wondered what the general saw that he did not know enough to recognize.

Shou led them around the crowd, and up the steps of the impoverished Temple of The Seven Gods on the far side of the crowd.

Adar gave him a strange look, but held his tongue when Llesho frowned, darting quick glances over the heads of the crowds.

"Soldiers," Llesho muttered, and Shokar communicated his surprise and his question with a raised eyebrow. Llesho shrugged, trying to put "later" in the gesture. The troops were not wearing the uniforms of guard or militia, but soldiers going into battle carried themselves as no one else in Llesho's experience. And if that were true, there were too many of them in the market square. And far too many wore the garb of Harnish traders.

At the center of the laughing crowd, a monkey in the uniform of an Imperial Guard did backflips on the shoulders of a brown bear. Kaydu carried a basket which she stuck under the noses of the audience, many of whom had a coarse word or joke about the uniform the monkey wore. A slim young woman in a long, flowing gown sat on the steps, smiling at the antics of the bear, but watching the crowd with careful, attentive eyes. She looked like Mara, except that she was too young, too straight and slim to be the old healer woman. But she had Mara's face and Mara's eyes. She caught Llesho's glance and rose from her perch, skipping down the steps with light dance moves.

"Come back later!" she called to the crowd as she took the bear's paw in her hand and danced him once around the little open circle. Kaydu finished her collection with a flourishing bow, and gathered Little Brother to her as the bear and its leader danced their way around the corner of the temple.

General Shou waited only until the market performers were out of sight before ducking into the temple. Bixei followed, and Llesho came after with Adar and Shokar.

"That didn't go quite as I'd planned it," Shou remarked. "What exactly were you doing, Llesho?"

The two newcomers stepped between Llesho and the man they took to be a merchant, but Llesho responded to the familiar commanding tone with a quick snap to attention.

"May I present my brothers," he said, stepping between them and bowing to the general. "Adar, the healer of whom I have often spoken—" he smiled and gestured at the taller man, "—and Shokar, whom I had thought lost to us."

Shou made a bow to the brothers, and would have spoken, except that a priest of the temple approached, a frown creasing his forehead. "As always, you come to us with trouble close behind," the priest said.

"Master Markko's people?" Shou skinned out of his merchant's robe. Under it he wore his uniform and had a sword strapped to his side.

"He does seem to be in the thick of it." The priest took the merchant's robe and handed Shou his helmet. "And he seems to command not just the remnant of the force he brought from Farshore Province, but Harnish raiders as well, scattered among the honest tradesmen in the marketplace."

"A man would have to be mad to trust the Harn as allies," Adar swore heatedly.

"Mad he may be," Llesho agreed, "but no less dangerous for it."

His brothers stared at him, surprised at the force and confidence of his words. Their surprise turned to astonishment when Kaydu skidded into the temple. She had shed her fool's costume, and wore the uniform of Thousand Lakes Province. Little Brother sat on her shoulder, his paws clinging around her neck, and the bear from the marketplace scampered at her heels. The bear's companion from the marketplace followed at a more sedate pace.

"Mara?" Llesho asked Kaydu.

The stranger answered, with a smile. "I'm Carina, Mara's daughter. But my companion is an old friend of yours."

"Lleck?" Llesho whispered. The cub nuzzled his hand and moaned, "Lleeee-shooooo!"

"Lleck?" Shokar choked on the name. "You have named a dancing bear after our father's chief adviser?"

Llesho shrugged with a rueful smile. "Not exactly."

"Shoooooo-karrrrrr?" the bear sniffed at his hand. "Shoookarrrrr!"

Shokar gasped. "That bear said my name!"

"It *is* Lleck," Llesho explained, "our father's adviser. He has taken the form of a bear as protector until Thebin is regained."

Adar looked shaken and seemed about to speak, but General Shou was addressing Kaydu, and Llesho turned to listen.

"Are the emperor's troops holding?" Shou asked her.

"They are outnumbered," she gasped. "My father is bringing his reinforcements from outside the city."

"We need time," the general muttered. "We have to hold Markko to the square."

A second priest joined them, and Llesho grinned when he saw the bundles he carried. "Is that my sword?" he asked. The bundle was wrapped in his Thebin coat and he unbound the pack and put on his coat first. His sword belt and sheath followed; Llesho drew the sword and loosened his wrist by twirling the weapon in small circles pointed at the floor.

Shokar was still confused, but one thing seemed clear. "I take it you are not the pampered pleasure slave of a stupid Shannish merchant, then?" he asked dryly.

"No, brother." Llesho flashed a predatory grin that was new to him since the battle with Master Markko on the border of Shan Province. He drew his Thebin knife and tossed it in the air, catching it again by the hilt and casting about with it to measure the balance of it in his hand. Bixei was testing the heft of his spear, and Kaydu had drawn her sword and taken up a trident with it.

"Are you certain of what you are doing?" Shokar asked his brother. "You're just a boy. This temple would surely protect you if there is to be fighting."

"I'm a soldier," Llesho answered with a shrug. "And it is *my* battle as much as Shan Province's. Master Markko followed *me* here. If he now conspires with the Harn, all of Shan may soon fall under the same yoke as Thebin."

Shokar pulled off his healer's robe and handed it to Adar. Beneath the robe, he wore his own sword belted to his waist, and he loosened it in its scabbard. "Would you mind if I joined you, then?" he asked, with a bow to General Shou.

"Be my guest," the general invited him with a tight smile.

They had begun to move, following the priest to the back of the temple, when the first priest returned bearing a slim burden in his hands.

"This was delivered for you, young master." The priest bowed and unwrapped the oiled cloths that protected the short spear contained within.

Llesho shuddered.

"Is that what I think it is?" Adar asked, his voice grown husky with awe.

"I don't know what it is, except that her ladyship has bid me carry it, and that I feel my own death clinging to it like a cobra waiting to strike." He thrust the weapon into his brother's hands.

Pain crossed Adar's face, but he did not let the spear fall, even when it blistered his palm.

"Why is it doing that?" Horrified, Llesho snatched it back, too late to save his brother from the hurt that bubbled on his hand.

"Because it belongs to you." Adar smiled, though his hand must still hurt.

Llesho didn't want to understand, but they had run out of time, and Carina was leading his brother away with words soothing as the burble of a dove: "My mother has taught me much of her herb lore, and the tending of wounds."

Torn between protecting his brother and his own duty to the battle's wounded soon to come, Adar hesitated.

"Go," Llesho said. "If we win, there will be time to talk later. If we lose, we already know what we needed to say."

"Go with the goddess," Adar whispered his farewell like a prayer.

Still as stone, General Shou waited until Carina had taken the wounded healer away.

"It's time," he said, and led their small force out of the temple.

Chapter Thirty-five

IN the market square Harnish raiders had drawn their short, thick swords. The soldiers who had marched from Farshore with Master Markko brandished the more familiar weapons they had kept hidden under their disguises until the signal ordered them into action. Llesho figured they had expected only the weak opposition of shopkeepers and their customers in the square.

But General Shou had laid his plans carefully, and the invaders found themselves confronting grim-faced Imperial Guardsmen who threw off their own disguises and fought to defend their homes and their families. The very auction block at the center of the marketplace served as a reminder of Harn's treatment of its conquests, and civilians fought alongside the emperor's guards with any implement they could find.

Stalls overturned in the fray spilled food and trinkets and pots and pans onto the square. Wares scattered underfoot as raiders hacked at the proprietors with their swords. Llesho saw the food vendor Darit hit a Harnish raider over the head with a heavy copper platter and then swing her makeshift weapon in the face of another soldier.

Finally she whirled it like a discus at a Harnishman

who directed the action of his raiders from the auction block. He went down, spilling blood from a deep gash in his brow and Darit was over her counter, with a chopping knife in one hand and a bone cleaver in the other. He lost sight of her when Markko's troops rushed his own position on the steps of the temple.

"Can you fight?" he asked Shokar, who stood at his shoulder.

"For you, I can fight," Shokar answered, and drew his own Thebin knife. He took the two-handed defensive stance of the Thebin fighter, sword raised, knife extended, and soon proved his worth. A band of soldiers in the uniform of Lord Yueh's guards rushed their position, laying about them with bloodied swords. From the determined savagery of their attack, Llesho knew they had but one objective: to bring down Master Markko's chosen prey at all costs.

Llesho slashed with his knife, jumped out of range of a swinging sword, and jabbed with his own long blade. He heard his brother grunt with the exertion of wielding his weapons. Shokar did not move with Llesho's practiced ease, but he had not forgotten all he had learned as a young man in Thebin.

Bixei fought at his right side, his battle cry a low growl in his throat. Kaydu screeched like the spirits of the thirsty dead as she cleared the steps on his right. Llesho whipped around to take on the next assault, and discovered that for the moment they had driven back their attackers.

Trying to catch his breath and his senses at the same time, Llesho looked about him in dismay. General Shou had placed cadres of Imperial Guardsmen in disguise throughout the square, but they were seriously outnumbered. Though the emperor's men strove valiantly to contain the attack, the Harnish raiders pressed outward, unstoppable in their attempt to escape the square and join up with reinforcements flooding into the square from the streets of the city.

Already two of the Harnish bands had drawn off from the fighting, making for the eastern corner of the square, from which a tangle of paths and roads led to the palace. In the chaos of the fighting, he had no intelligence about how many Harnish reinforcements lurked in the city, or if they waged their battle against the palace as well as in the market square. It must have been like this on the streets of Kungol, he thought, except that the Thebin palace had no high walls to protect it, nor a standing army to defend it.

Even in Shan, however, too much lay vulnerable to attack. The thought of the Imperial Water Garden trampled in battle burned in his chest. His own imagination would have paralyzed him then, but General Shou shook him out of his thoughts. "Hold fast, if you can," Shou directed Llesho's little band. "Don't let the Harn join their forces in the city." Then he disappeared into the fray.

Llesho took a quick survey of their position. The temple stood at one corner of the market square. They had themselves come out a side door and down a small alley, which the priests had cluttered after them with baskets and old cooking pots to delay the enemy. A wide avenue on the far side of the building would be much harder to secure, however. With the point of his sword, he directed Bixei and Kaydu to the more open position. He would have sent Shokar with them, but his brother read his mind and gave him a baleful glare.

"Harry them and fall back," he told his two guards. "We cannot hope to hold for long, but we can make them pay in blood for every step they win."

General Shou had gathered to himself a small troop of Imperial Guards, still dressed as peasant farmers come to sell their wares. These farmers, however, wielded swords instead of plowshares, and they followed the general, defending the roads that led to the palace. If the city fell, Llesho knew, all of the Shan

Empire fell with it, and all hope that they might free Thebin as well. Though his arm had grown heavy, he raised his sword in fighting position again, his Thebin knife held poised for the next attack. He would stop Master Markko and his allies or die in the attempt.

Although the Thebin princes were badly outnumbered, no enemy could touch them. Pressed on all sides, Llesho moved without thought, one with his blades and the rhythm of his deadly dance. Blood slicked the paving stones and he slipped, righted himself before he fell, and plunged his knife to the hilt into the throat of a soldier. The man opened his mouth to scream, but only blood spewed forth, and a death rattle as he strove to draw breath while drowning in his own blood.

The knife had caught on bone, and Llesho could not pull it free. For an almost fatal second he held on, while the falling man dragged Llesho's arm down with it, leaving the heart in his breast an open target. A spear came toward him out of the melee, was knocked away by his brother's sword but not before the tip had drawn blood. Shocked at how close he had come to losing his life, Llesho abandoned the knife along with the body of the Harnish raider and turned to the next attacker, then the next, until he and Shokar were surrounded by a ring of wary soldiers held at bay by the swords of their prey.

For a moment the battle seemed to pause, as if the world held its breath, and Llesho became aware of the bodies, and the gore, and his own hands, slick with blood up to the elbow, gripping the hilt of his sword between them. On one knee, his brother gasped for breath, and Llesho felt his own blood trickle down his cheek, though he did not remember the strike that had cut him. Stealing a glance toward his companions who struggled to hold the wide boulevard, he raised his head, a triumphant grimace turning his blood-smeared face into a death mask. Habiba's troops had arrived, orderly columns of them passing into the square from the main road at each of the four corners.

"Surrender!" Llesho demanded. His attackers followed Llesho's gloating stare, and struck again with a fervor fueled by their desperation. It was now or never, he realized. Of the two choices that confronted them, most of the enemy soldiers would rather face death at Llesho's hand than the slow, lingering torment they would suffer from Master Markko if they failed.

Shokar struggled to his feet, but his sword dragged heavily at an arm leaden with fatigue. Llesho shifted closer to his brother. He didn't have to win, he told himself, he needed only to hold off the attack until Habiba's men had secured the road. He would have reinforcements, if he could just keep his brother alive for a few minutes more. A sword slipped past his guard and cut him under the arm, but he rallied and knocked it away before it could do more than scratch the skin. He heard Kaydu's voice urging him to hold, but her words were cut off by the sudden cry of a great bird.

The creature swooped from the sky with talons stretched; Master Markko's own men dropped to their faces in terror as the beast flew at his prey. Llesho raised his sword over his head to stop the beast, which opened its beak to cry its scorn and defiance. With one powerful foot it swept aside Llesho's sword, and with the other it tore past his shoulder, talons gouging deep gashes from Llesho's throat to his hip.

Llesho grunted and fell, at the mercy of the bird, his sight blurring as the curved beak drew closer.

I will tear out your heart, and eat it in the market square.

Though the bird could not speak, Llesho heard the words in his mind. *So this is dying,* he answered, and heard again Master Markko's answer in his mind: *Among cowards and weaklings, yes; this is dying.*

He felt the piercing pain as the beak cut into the

flesh over his heart, and then he heard a growl behind him.

"Lleeee-shhhoooo!"

Lleck! The bear raised up on his hind legs and howled over his fallen charge, the spittle flying from his long, sharp fangs. With his claws extended like curved knives, he swatted at the bird, raking long streaks of blood across its feathered breast. It seemed then that he was cradling the bird, for both huge arms wrapped about its wings, pressing it down, until the full weight of bird and bear crashed to the paving stones at Llesho's feet.

The bird redirected its attack, raking Lleck's thick pelt with claw and beak. Lleck cried out and lowered his head over the neck of the magician, who changed himself into smoke as the bear's teeth clamped together. Taking solid form again, the invincible bird of prey that Master Markko had become transformed again, growing the head of a lion and the long, spiked tail of a serpent held aloft by the feathered wings of the bird. The creature fell upon the bear and locked its teeth into the back of his head.

The lion jaws tightened. Bone crunched. Lleck bellowed one last anguished cry and the light went out of his eyes.

"No!" Llesho cried, while Markko's insane laughter filled his head.

He had lost his sword and a good deal of blood. Llesho stood and faced the creature of his nightmares with no hope of victory, only a determination to take the evil creature before him into hell. As his bloody end drew near, however, Llesho saw a woman standing just above him on the temple steps. Carina, the young healer, defied the monster with calm, sure eyes. Unarmed, she raised both hands above her head, chanting some prayer of supplication. Although he knew she must follow him quickly into death, he was unaccountably comforted by the sight of her.

In that moment of peace, the short spear from her ladyship pressed a reminder against his side. He drew it. "Die!" He screamed, "Die! You twisted demon out of hell. Die!"

He plunged the spear into the side of the monster, and it screamed, dripping gouts of blood that steamed and blackened the paving stones where it fell. Enraged, the creature writhed away from the weapon and rose into the sky, still shrieking in pain and fury.

Suddenly an answering roar filled the sky and made the very temple shake. A horde of dragons filled the sky, the Golden River Dragon in the lead, a smaller silver queen following with three younger dragons behind her. The dragons separated at the market square, the younger ones fanning out into city, while the silver queen descended upon the battle being waged before the palace.

The Golden River Dragon, vastly larger and more terrible than the magical apparition that Master Markko had created, fell in a steep dive aimed right at the magician. The dragon's roar spat fire into the marketplace, and Shannish citizens as well as Harnish raiders fell to the ground, cowering with their hands over their heads. Markko's beast roared an answering challenge.

The two unearthly creatures met, the long and sinuous body of the dragon tangling with the lashing tail of the beast in the air above the market square. As they tore at each other, the patched-together beast of Master Markko's creation struggled frantically for the advantage. The larger and more powerful Golden Dragon thrashed its tail in anger. Up, up, they flew, until they were just glittering specks in a sharp blue sky. Then a path of flame reached out, and the fiercely struggling monsters were falling, growing larger and larger. A scream rose to shatter the sky, and the beast that was Master Markko vanished.

With a last trumpeting bellow of victory, the Golden

Dragon circled lightly on a thermal created by his own fiery breath. Lazily he floated to a soft landing in the square, and lowered his head at the feet of Carina, the young healer, on the temple steps.

"Father." She kissed him between his smoking nostrils, and tapped him sharply where she had placed the kiss. "Time to let Mother go."

The dragon's eyes sparkled in the sun, a deeper glint than his golden scales. He opened his huge mouth as wide as the temple doors, and belched. From his throat a querulous voice drifted.

"Wretched beast. I don't know what I ever saw in you. Put me down." Mara, but as they had never seen her before, walked out of the dragon's gorge and stood on his tongue, arms folded over her singed and smoking garments, while he gently put her down. She looked taller than she had in the forest, her back straight and her hair black instead of gray. She did not look young, but neither did she look old. In fact, traveling in the belly of a dragon seemed to agree with her.

"Thank you, Father." Carina hugged her mother and patted the giant head of the Golden River Dragon.

"Where is your sister dragon, old husband?" Mara asked the dragon.

Llesho did not find out if the dragon could in fact answer the question, because at that moment the silver queen descended lightly at the foot of the temple steps. His vision blurred, and Llesho wiped his eyes, leaving a bloody streak across his forehead. "Am I hallucinating?" he wondered. No silver dragon stood beside the golden monster, but Kwan-ti, the healer he had thought lost at Pearl Island.

"Llesho. You look awful." She brushed his hair out of his eyes and pursed her lips in displeasure. "Three healers standing about while the young prince bleeds unattended."

"You were dead—" He resisted her urging toward the door. "This is some kind of trick!"

"Never dead," she answered with an enigmatic smile. "A trick, yes, but the same trick it was when you knew me as Kwan-ti."

"You saved my life." Llesho remembered the sea dragon that had come to him when he had tried to die in the bay. It was not a moment he wished to relive, and Kwan-ti acknowledged it with a bow of her head, but did not intrude the memory upon him further.

"The children have returned to Golden River, brother," she addressed the Golden Dragon with a sad droop to her shoulders. "The sea around Pearl Island still reeks of death. You will take care of them until it is safe for them to come home?"

The dragon nodded his head in an affirmative. With an affectionate snort of curling smoke, he hauled his body into the open square, picking his way carefully among the fallen, too many dead for Llesho to count in his dazed condition. Survivors helped their more severely wounded brethren out of the dragon's path, more frightened of their terrible ally than they had been of the battle.

When the Golden River Dragon lifted on his powerful wings, the wind he created in his passing nearly knocked Llesho to his knees. Falling down seemed like a good idea, but while he could stand, he needed to find his companions. Shokar sat at the head of the bear who had saved Llesho's life, stroking the fur between Lleck's ears. The prince did not seem to have any physical wounds on him. Shokar was no soldier, however; the horrors of battle had almost broken him.

Slowly, the living converged on the temple. Stupid with the shock, Llesho watched them ascend the wide steps and enter the sanctuary. Though weary and bleak, Kaydu and Bixei seemed unhurt as well.

"You must come inside," Mara reminded him. "Those wounds need tending."

"Soon."

Carina and Kwan-ti had already entered the temple, following the wounded who would need their care, but Mara waited at Llesho's side as Kaydu drew up before them to report.

"Did the general make it?"

"I don't know." Kaydu shrugged, not indifferent, but helpless to offer greater assurances. "Maybe he's already inside."

Bixei took Shokar by the arm and drew him away from their dead companion. Together the four entered the temple, where the wounded were laid out in rows on the floor. Llesho scanned the rows, seeking Adar as he had with scrapes and minor hurts when he was a child.

"Llesho, you've been hurt." Adar came to them, and touched his arm.

"The brother. Good." Mara nodded with satisfaction and left them to offer aid among the injured groaning on their mats.

The tension in the pit of Llesho's stomach relaxed. "When you have time." He waved a careless hand and dropped it to his side again, suddenly realizing that he was brandishing the short spear in his bloody fist. "I just need to sleep."

Adar used his hold on Llesho's arm to guide him deeper into the temple. "Now," Adar said. "Before you bleed out on the priest's nice floor."

Llesho hadn't realized he was still bleeding, but he accepted Adar's word, and followed him to the bandaging station. "I'm glad you're alive," Adar told him, and Llesho let his head drop on the curve of his brother's shoulder.

"I'm so glad I found you," Llesho agreed. And then he fainted.

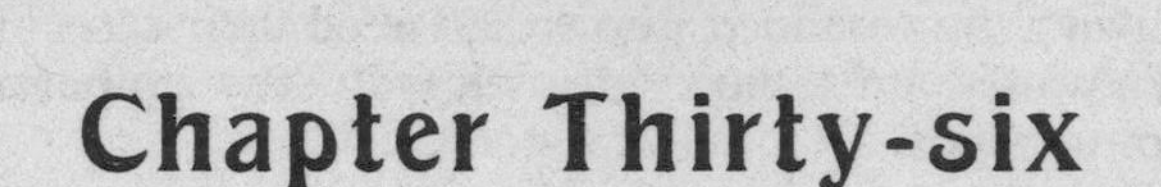

Chapter Thirty-six

SHADOWS moved through the darkness, broken only by the dim glow of scattered lamps and the weak moans of the wounded. At Llesho's head, a heavier darkness sat, solid and reassuring. Shokar snored lightly. Tomorrow, the healers said, Llesho could leave the makeshift infirmary set up in the Temple of The Seven Mortal Gods. He would be taking with him his brother, who refused to leave his side, and his guards, who refused to accept any defense of his sleep but their own. Bixei had assumed guard duty at the front entrance to the temple and Kaydu had watched over the secret entrance into the side alley. Torn between his duty and Lling who had joined them after the battle at the palace, Hmishi had spent days pacing the length of the long hall from her bedside to the entrance onto the square and back again.

When the companions paused in their vigilance to meet the new princes and tell their stories, Shokar had listened with avid horror. Alternately, he'd berated Llesho for the chances he had taken and scolded Adar to check Llesho's wounds for proper healing and signs of lingering damage. Llesho forgave the healers their unseemly relief at his recovery; his protectors were starting to get on his nerves as well. And, much as he loved his brother, Shokar's worry was driving him mad. These few moments of contemplative silence while his brother slept nearby were precious. Not as dear as the opportunity to speak with Adar, however. The healer sank to the floor beside him with a wry smile mellowed by the lamplight.

"He just wants you to be safe." Adar gave the sleeping prince an indulgent smile.

"I love him, too." Llesho sighed. "But there is no safety anywhere for us. And I am not a child he can protect from the truth."

Adar laughed softly. "Convincing Shokar that you are no longer a seedling of seven summers will take stronger magic than either of us possess.

"As for the danger," the healer shook his head, sorrow creasing his features, "Shokar has always blamed himself that he was not in Kungol when the Harn attacked."

"The raiders would have killed him." Shokar could have rallied the Thebin people to his cause; the Harn would never have let him live.

"He's not a coward," Adar said, as if that needed explaining, "but he is a man of peace. A farmer. And when he saw you in the countinghouse, he truly believed the goddess had given him a second chance at redemption. If you died, it would surely destroy him."

"I do understand." Llesho closed his eyes, weary and achy, and unwilling to think about it anymore. "But I can't stay."

Adar patted his shoulder. "Sleep," he said.

Llesho decided it was just too much work to open his eyes. In the distance he heard the soft voices of the priests, and a name—ChiChu, god of laughter and tears—called. And it seemed that the god answered in Master Den's voice. But that must be a dream, and then it was a dream.

And then it was morning, and Master Den was standing at the foot of Llesho's pallet, roaring for him to get up, no time to waste on sleeping. He dropped a stack of linen beside him, and Llesho noted that the clothes were day wear of her ladyship's household, neither the uniform he had fought in nor the house pet disguise he had worn on the day of the battle. And he did not know where Lleck's pearl had gone. Llesho moved stiffly, and the sharp pain when he lifted his arms to slip into his shirt was explanation enough of his pallor. General Shou had advised him to confide in Master Den, but he could hardly do so while surrounded by his well-meaning companions. But if he could discover the whereabouts of his other possessions, perhaps he would find the pearl there as well.

"My weapons?" he asked. "And the gifts her ladyship returned to me?"

Den had not been there when her ladyship had given Llesho the short spear and the jadeite cup, but he knew of them nevertheless. "In your room at the palace," he said, "with whatever other valuables you may have acquired on your journey."

That sounded like Master Den knew more than he was telling, but he couldn't ask about it here.

"General Shou?" he said, one thought turning on another, "Was he hurt? Has anyone seen him since the battle?"

Kaydu shifted Little Brother in her arms and shook her head. "The last time I saw him, he was exhorting us to hold the square."

"I saw him in the palace before I joined you here," Lling added. "He seemed unhurt, and was directing the Imperial Guard in a street-by-street search to rout out the last of the Harnish spies."

Llesho had known the fighting wasn't over with the first battle, and he felt foolish for feeling let down that the man hadn't come to see him.

"And Mara is well?" He still had trouble believing that the healer had lived through what had seemed like certain death on the Golden Dragon River.

"Mara will say nothing about her travels in the belly of the Golden Dragon," Lling offered, "but she smiles rather more than seems appropriate for someone who has met a horrible fate at the hands of a monster."

Llesho laughed, whether at Lling's indignation or Mara's satisfaction with her travel arrangements he wasn't sure. He'd thought laughing would hurt his chest more than it did, but apparently he really was getting better. If he could erase the memory of the terrible beak digging at his chest to tear his heart out, he would consider himself well served.

As it was, he wished with all the heart that remained to him that he could talk to Master Den. The washerman sensed something that Llesho was thinking. "Let's get you back home," he said, and dropped a hand on Llesho's shoulder. Llesho wondered what home he meant, but decided he would settle for his room at the palace.

The market square was bright with morning sunshine and the sound of clashing cymbals and ringing bells. A crowd had gathered, and Llesho craned his neck from his place on the temple steps to see what was passing. Carina stood on the step just below his, a shawl held tightly at her throat. She looked a lot like her mother, cloaked in the same strength and dignity, but it was softer in the younger woman. Everything about Carina was softer, even her hair, which she wore in a long braid wrapped around her head. Llesho realized he wanted to touch the shining braid, but he restrained himself with some horror at how improper such longing must be in a young prince.

"The emperor is passing," she told him with a bright smile that did funny things to his insides that Lling's voice had never done, even when he considered being to her what Hmishi had become.

It took an effort of will, but he turned his eyes away from her face, and looked out into the square, where troops of Imperial Guards were passing in review. At their head, in a gold-encrusted chariot, rode the emperor, his robes so richly decorated that Llesho wondered if the man inside of them could move at all, or whether he just stood like the center support of some elaborate statue. The royal headdress of the Shan Empire was no simple crown, but an ancient helmet that covered the sides of the face and the chin, and flared at the shoulders and over the forehead to protect the wearer's face. The helmet was black, with gold and jewels worked into it. So dazzling was the display of wealth and power that Llesho almost didn't recognize the man under it.

"General Shou?" Llesho muttered.

Kaydu had followed him out of the temple, and she'd come to her own conclusions: "He looks like General Shou. They could be brothers." She gave Llesho a measuring frown. "They look more like brothers than you and Adar, at any rate."

"He said once that he was a member of the nobility," Llesho offered her the weak explanation, but inside, he knew. General Shou *was* the Emperor of Shan and for some reason, he had kept that knowledge from Llesho and his party while he roamed the city with them. He'd even fought in Habiba's war under a false identity. Llesho wanted an explanation. First, however, he wanted his pearl back, and the few other possessions that were supposed to be waiting for him in the palace.

He did not immediately get his wish. After the emperor's procession had passed, his own party made their way to the palace and, for a change, presented themselves at the Ministry of Government for entrance. The clerk who guarded the gate assured them that they were expected within. Unfortunately, he determined that, as they represented no recognized government, neither Llesho nor his brothers carried any standing sufficient to gain entrance to the palace. Master Den, as a former general and adviser to the emperor's army had had the necessary rank at one time, but unless he carried a present rank in that army, he could not be admitted either.

As the daughter of the representative of Thousand Lakes Province and Farshore Province, Kaydu, however, had the necessary position for admittance. With a sweep of her hand, Kaydu declared the rest of their party, princes and general and soldiers alike, her personal servants. They had no sooner entered the palace as a group than they were separated again, Llesho's guard to a wide hallway with gilt panels, and Llesho down a darker, more forbidding passage, into a room that the prince knew from his first explorations of the palace. He had thought the room a private one for the questioning of Shou's spies. It had a few chairs and a small table, but nothing more to see or hold the attention. Shokar trembled with fine tremors of terror but refused to be separated from his brother.

Llesho knew the way to his room in the palace from here. He tried the panel to the outer hall, but the two guards that waited there with swords drawn would not let him pass this time. The recent battle had left them all, on both sides of the door, too ready to fight. Llesho shook his head and withdrew.

He didn't have to wait long, however. A panel opened in the opposite wall, and Shou walked through, wearing comfortable robes that suited neither the general nor the emperor, but ably fit the man. Shokar bowed deeply to the emperor, but Llesho didn't move. "Why didn't you tell me?"

"I thought Lleck taught you better than that," the emperor chided him. He sat in one of the stiff wooden armchairs, threw one booted leg over the arm, and tossed a peach into the air, absently catching it with no thought to regal dignity, but exuding a lethal menace without even trying.

In spite of his apparent informality, this face of the man scared Llesho more than any of the others he had seen, because he had a sick feeling that this was the real thing. He blushed, feeling foolish for having asked the question. He knew the answer, really. "I suppose you wanted to see for yourself if I was who Habiba said I was, or if it was some sort of plot. But you could not trust to official appearances."

"Part of it, yes." The emperor waited.

"You wanted to know if I was worth taking a stand for."

"Not that." The emperor was laughing softly, but with no humor. "Shan could not afford to acknowledge your claim under any circumstances, however true and worthy that claim might be."

"It didn't matter, then? That my claims for Thebin are true." The reminder of that truth was carved over Llesho's heart, and he laid a protective hand over the bandages that covered his chest.

"Oh, yes, it did matter." Shou wasn't laughing now. His face was hard and his eyes looked past Llesho, into some time or place that was closed to his questioner. "We have won a small skirmish, but the war remains to be fought. And while the Harn press at our borders, we cannot give the Prince of Thebin what he wants."

"And what is that?"

"Thebin, of course." Shou—it was hard not to think of him that way—let go of an exasperated sigh and swung his leg off the chair. "But privately, as a man who speaks to a man, and not as an emperor who speaks to a deposed prince, we can acknowledge mutual interest in the downfall of our shared enemy."

"How does that help either of us?"

"It has already helped Shan." General Shou—the emperor—stood with a predatory grin that showed all his teeth and led them to the panel that had been denied them earlier. "Master Markko has failed in his attempt to throw down the empire. The Harn have failed to garner the spoils of their puppet's campaign, and must return to their plotting. Thebin isn't the problem of Shan's emperor."

"Then how am I to go home?"

"The way you had planned to do it originally, but with a bit more help than I should be giving you," Shou admitted. He frowned at Llesho and sighed. When he slid the panel open, the guard entered with sword drawn. Llesho swallowed around the dry lump in his throat, but the emperor dismissed the man with a careless wave.

"I had planned to offer my services to the guard detail of a trade caravan leaving for the West," Llesho explained as he followed the emperor down a hall that looked far too shabby and unused to be a part of the formal palace. It looked more like they were wandering through more of those hidden passageways that riddled the place like an abandoned beehive.

"And so you will." Shou stopped in front of a sturdy looking door and pressed the release. "Actually, the Harn raiders fell right into our hands with their little raid. The traders who organize the caravans have already approached the palace for protection along the route."

Inside the room behind the door, three women waited at a table on which were spread all of Llesho's missing belongings: his knife and sword and his bow and arrows, the jadeite cup and the short spear from her ladyship, and inside the cup, Lleck's black pearl. Llesho first took inventory of his possessions, not because he cared about their material value, but because he knew they were somehow vital to his quest. But he did not touch them, looking instead to the women who waited for his acknowledgment.

"Your ladyship." He bowed to the woman who had tested him on Pearl Island, and who had taught him archery. She wore clothes of white and green and blue, diaphanous layers that blended into the murky water colors of the Imperial Water Garden.

"SienMa." She received his bow with a tilt of her head, and set another pearl, the match to the one he had received from Lleck's ghost in Pearl Bay, into the cup.

SienMa. One of the Seven Mortal Gods, the goddess of war. Llesho shivered.

"Kwan-ti." Trembling, he bowed again, this time to the middle woman, dressed in silver, and with sparks of liquid silver in her hair. Kwan-ti had already shown herself as a dragon queen; but was she a goddess as well?

"Pearl Bay Dragon," she revealed her true name with a nod, and a rueful smile. "You already have my gift, I am afraid. Your wily ghost stole it while my attention was elsewhere."

Lleck's pearl. Llesho blushed. The third woman, dressed in gold, he had lately seen walking from the mouth of the Golden River Dragon. Was no one who they seemed? "Mara."

"And Mara I am," she said, "a seeker. Aspiring to be the eighth." She, too, set a black pearl, the match of the others, into the jadeite cup. "Since the coming of the Harn to Thebin, the gates of heaven are sealed to us. We cannot return to serve the goddess as is our duty, and the goddess can reach us only in dreams."

SeinMa, her ladyship, stretched out a hand to the pearls. "This is all that we could rescue of the goddess' most treasured adornment, the necklace called "string of midnights." The goddess weeps for her necklace day and day, for night has fled from heaven."

"The seas weep," Pearl Bay Dragon said. "The goddess does not come. Open the gates. Return the balance to heaven and earth."

The gates of heaven, high above Kungol in the mountains of Thebin. "You have my oath," Llesho vowed, and Mara smiled at him like a mother.

"And you have my daughter. Carina will travel with you."

Llesho wondered if they could see the heat rising in his face, but he didn't say anything. The emperor rescued him with more mundane details.

"You and your companions will be fitted with uniforms as soon as you are ready to travel. Now get some sleep. The guards will take you back to your old room, and orders have been given to billet your companions nearby."

Llesho still had one question, however, and the presence of Master Den in their party told him more than anything how vital it was that he have an answer before they traveled any farther. He did not have to ask it, however. Den found in his hand a slip of paper that Llesho recognized from his first meeting with General Shou in the Imperial Water Garden.

"An unusual request to make of a trickster god." He handed the offering back to the emperor.

"The gates of heaven are closed to all of us, Master ChiChu," he said, "and not just to us mortals."

"You were always a clever boy," the god of the laundry, he of tears and laughter, smiled benignly on the emperor. "I will do what I can to keep this one safe. But even a god cannot know the future."

The emperor bowed to the trickster god and then to the ladies, who preceded him from the room.

"Well, Llesho, what do you think?" the trickster god asked him.

Llesho answered as he always had, as student to teacher, with a bow and a smile. "The journey is begun. We are going home."

Shokar, at his back, said nothing.

Read on for a preview of
the sequel to *The Prince of Shadow,*

The Prince of Dreams,

new in hardcover
this month from DAW.

"So this is dying."

Llesho strained against his bonds, tormented by the fire burning in his gut and the icy sweat dripping from his shivering body. In his brief moments of lucidity, he wondered how he could burn and tremble with cold at the same time and where he was and how he had come to be a prisoner again. In his delirium, Master Markko came to him as a winged beast with the claws of a lion and the tail of a snake, or sometimes as a great bird with talons sharp as swords tearing the entrails from his belly. Always Llesho heard the magician's voice echoing inside his head:

"Among the weak, yes; this is dying."

No escape. He knew, vaguely, that he cried out in his sleep, just as he knew that help wouldn't come. . . .

"Are you waiting for someone?" Master Den rounded the rough wooden bench and sat next to Llesho, quiet until the confusion had cleared from his face. "Your eyes were open, but you didn't answer when I called."

"I was dreaming," Llesho answered, his voice still fogged with distant horror. "Remembering a dream, actually."

A low waterfall chuckled in front of him, reminding him of where he was. The Imperial City of Shan had many gardens, but the Imperial Water Garden in honor of Thousand Lakes Province had become Llesho's special place, where he came to sort out his thoughts. Like him, the Water Garden had taken some damage in the recent fighting. A delicate wooden bridge had burned to ash, and Harnish raiders had trampled a section of marsh grasses beside a stream that had flowed red with the blood of the fallen for many days. At the heart of the Imperial Water Garden, however, the waterfall still poured its clean bounty into a stone basin that fed the numerous streams winding among the river reeds. Water lilies still floated in the many protected pools and the lotus still rose out of the mud on defiant stalks. The little stone altar to ChiChu, the trickster god of laughter and tears, still lay hidden under a ledge beneath the chuckling water.

Like the garden, Llesho had survived and healed. He sat on the split log bench just beyond the reach of the fine spray the waterfall kicked up, contemplating the altar to the trickster god—a favored deity of an emperor fond of disguises and mentor to a young prince still learning how to be a king—as if it would give up the secrets of the heavens. In his hand he held a quarter tael of silver and a slip of paper, much wrinkled and dampened from the tight grip he held on it. With a sideways look at Master Den, who was the trickster god ChiChu in disguise, he placed the petition on the tiny altar with the coin inside it for an anchor. Then he sat back down on his bench and prepared to wait.

Master Den said nothing, nor did he reach for the offering on his altar. If it came to a contest, the trickster god had eternity to outsit him. Llesho gave a little sigh and surrendered.

"He comes to me in my dreams. Master Markko.

He tells me I'm dying, and I believe him. Then I wake up, and he's gone, and I'm still here." Still alive. But the dreams sometimes felt more real than the waking world.

"And you want to know—?"

"Is it real? Or am I going mad?"

"Ah."

Llesho waited for Master Den to go on, fretfully at first, but as the silence stretched between them, he found that his fears, all his conscious thought, for that matter, drifted away. He heard the merry chime of water dashing on stone, and saw the bright flick of the light bouncing off the droplets in myriad rainbows. He felt the sun on his back, and the breeze on his face, and the rough split logs of the bench under his backside. The sun moved, and he turned his head to feel its heat on his closed eyes, on his smile. Without realizing it was happening, the moment stole through him, sunlight filling all the chinks and crannies of his fractured existence. He was aware only of a profound peace settling in his heart and his gut, pinning him to his bench in a perfect eternity of now.

"As long as you hold the world in your heart, he can't touch you." Master Den gave a little shrug. "But if you ever tire of the world, have something else to grab onto."

His mind went to Carina, the healer with hair the color of the Golden River Dragon, and eyes like Mara's, who aspired to be the eighth mortal god. But he knew instinctively that wasn't what his teacher meant. He already had a purpose to hold him: to free his country and open the gates of heaven. Now he needed a dream more powerful than the ones Master Markko sent to trouble his sleep. His questions, about the brothers still lost to him that he had pledged his quest to free and the necklace of the Great Goddess that the mortal goddess SeinMa had charged him to find, would keep for another day. This lesson, to store up the sights and sounds and smell and touch of peace against the struggle to come, he finally understood.

They sat in comfortable silence together until the sun had reached the zenith, and then Master Den swept up the petition Llesho had placed on his altar.

"You are wanted at the palace." He flipped Llesho's silver coin in the air, and when it had landed in the palm of his hand, he tucked it into his own purse with a wink and a lopsided grin. He was, after all, a trickster god. "It's time to go."

The round, full light of Great Moon Lun hung low in the sky—Lun chasing her smaller brothers Han and Chen, already touching the zenith. Habiba moved about his workshop with precise, studied motions. The magician once had told him that Lun was no moon at all but a dying sun smoldering in the dark, and somehow Llesho knew that he was waiting for Lun's faint light to shine more fully through the window that overlooked the workbench.

He took a shallow bowl of polished silver from a shelf and carefully wiped it clean with a soft cloth. From an earthen pitcher he poured pure, cold water, filling the bowl to the brim.

"What's that for?"

The magician bent over so that his nose almost touched the water in the bowl but gave no answer.

"Habiba?"

Llesho wondered briefly how he'd come to be here, and why Habiba didn't seem to hear him or even notice his presence, but the youth couldn't seem to muster much worry about it. He stretched on tiptoe to peer over the magician's shoulder. As Great Moon Lun rose, its glow filled the sky in the silver bowl with pearly light. It overpowered the lesser shine of little Han Moon, which floated like a black pearl in the reflection. The pattern from the silver bowl drifted on the waster, so that the pearl of Han seemed to hang suspended from a silver chain.

"Ah! But where are you?" Habiba asked the image in the water. The magician was looking for the String of Midnights, the pearls of the Great Goddess lost in the attack on the gates of heaven. Llesho had three of them; it seemed that Habiba had found another.

As if some spell had taken control of his body, Llesho's hand reached out for the dark moon-pearl floating in the bowl. Part of him expected to close his fingers around the pearl while another part braced for a cold wet hand.

Instead, he fell headfirst through the water, which parted like a mist around him.

"Help!"

"Grab hold!" a voice answered.

Llesho reached out and grabbed onto the wide silver chain he was passing as he fell. The chain pulled him up short and he swung for a moment over an abyss before he managed to wrap his legs around the broad flat links and pull himself up on them.

"Who's there?" he asked. It wasn't Habiba's voice, or Kaydu's. He might have expected ChiChu to show up at a moment like this, but it wasn't the voice of the trickster god either.

"It's me." The moon swimming in Habiba's silver bowl began to jump like a fish on a hook, nearly dislodging Llesho from his perch. He peered more closely: the moon was no pearl at all, but almost manlike. Round in the body and naked, his skin was black as pitch and gleamed like the pearls Llesho carried in the velvet pouch at his breast. The pearl-man sprouted tiny arms and legs that he flailed in his effort to escape the chain that ran through a hook set in his back. The creature snuffled through a round, upturned nose that was pink around its flaring nostrils. His mouth, lined with pearly white teeth, shouted, "Get me down from here!" in a voice far too large for its pearly head.

"Stop that!" Llesho shouted as the chain that held them both swayed dangerously. "How can I get you down anyway? I'm stuck here myself, and about to fall if you don't stop rocking the chain."

"I beg your pardon," the creature apologized politely. "I let my anxiety overcome my good sense."

"Pardon given," Llesho returned with equal grace and added, when curiosity would allow silence no longer, "What magical creature are you? And," he thought to ask, "why are you hanging around like this, naked like a pearl from the goddess' jewel chest?"

The creature sniffed indignantly. "My name is Pig. I'm a Jinn in the service of the Great Goddess, chief gardener in her heavenly orchards." The pearl-man, who called himself a Jinn, stopped struggling and allowed his body to swing slowly on its chain. The whole situation should have disturbed him more, Llesho thought in passing. But the Jinn was waiting patiently to tell his tale, so he tucked his left foot into the open loop of one of the links and grabbed hold of another with his right hand. Securely anchored against a fall, he settled in to listen.

"Ever since the demon invader laid siege to the gates of heaven, I have searched for a way to escape and seek help for my lady, the Great Goddess. Finally I devised a plan; I would make myself small as a pearl from her lost necklace and slip through the cracks, so to speak. I thought to fall to earth far from the gates where our enemies lie in wait, and then I hoped to raise an army and march to the rescue."

"Doesn't seem to have worked out that way." Llesho felt it needed to be said.

The Jinn puffed out his cheeks and gave Llesho a sour glare. "I didn't need you to tell me that. Now, if you will just release the pin in my back, I can go about my business. Heaven can't wait forever, you know. There's planting to be done."

"You should have thought of that before you turned

yourself into a pearl. What if you're lying to me?" The question added an unwelcome note of reality to the situation. Jinn were a notoriously untrustworthy caste, which even Pig had to recognize.

"You can make me promise to give you wishes," Pig suggested with a trustworthy smile. "You can use your wishes to make me tell the truth." His efforts to look dependable were thwarted by the way he swayed hypnotically, like a pendulum, which made Llesho very dizzy.

Pig's present state suggested that ideas were not, perhaps, his strongest game. This one seemed fairly simple, though. Foolproof even.

"I'll do it." Llesho stretched over the abyss to grasp the pin in the Jinn's back, but Pig wriggled out of reach.

"I have to promise first."

"You just did."

"No, I said I *would* promise. You haven't asked me to do it yet."

Llesho was growing more annoyed with the strange pearly creature by the minute. When he stopped to consider this strange situation, none of it made sense, least of all his own patience in dealing with the captive Jinn. He was in it now, however, and could see no way out except through to the end.

"Promise me three wishes," he insisted, and started pulling himself closer on the chain even before the words "I promise" left Pig's mouth.

Suddenly, a hand big enough to hold Llesho and the Jinn together in its palm swept him off the silver chain and held him up to the face he most dreaded in the world. "Welcome home, Llesho."

"Master Markko!" he shouted. . . .